VENDETTA

TONY PARK

Ingwe
PUBLISHING

ABOUT THE AUTHOR

TonyPark was born in 1964 and grew up in the western suburbs of Sydney. He has worked as a newspaper reporter, a press secretary, a PR consultant and a freelance writer. He also served 34 years in the Australian Army Reserve, including six months as a public affairs officer in Afghanistan in 2002. He and his wife, Nicola, divide their time equally between Australia and southern Africa. He is the author of twenty other African novels and several biographies.

www.tonypark.net

First published 2023 in Macmillan by Pan Macmillan Australia Pty Ltd

This edition published by Ingwe Publishing 2023

Copyright © Tony Park 2023

All rights reserved

www.ingwepublishing.com

Vendetta

EPUB: 978-1-922825-10-0

POD: 978-1-922825-11-7

Cover design by Leandra Wicks

Cover image of walking soldiers © Al J. Venter

ALSO BY TONY PARK

Far Horizon

Zambezi

African Sky

Safari

Silent Predator

Ivory

The Delta

African Dawn

Dark Heart

The Prey

The Hunter

An Empty Coast

Red Earth

The Cull

Captive

Scent of Fear

Ghosts of the Past

Last Survivor

Blood Trail

The Pride

Part of the Pride, with Kevin Richardson

War Dogs, with Shane Bryant

The Grey Man, with John Curtis

Courage Under Fire, with Daniel Keighran VC

No One Left Behind, with Keith Payne VC

Bwana, There's a Body in the Bath! with Peter Whitehead

Rhino War, with Major General (Ret) Johan Jooste

For Nicola

PROLOGUE
HAZYVIEW, MPUMALANGA, 2012

The book of the dead. That's what Frank Greenaway called the old photograph album he was hunting for in the mildew-smelling reaches of the top cupboard of his second-hand wardrobe.

Frank's fingers found it, and as he dragged it out from under a mouldy suitcase he felt the clear plastic dust cover start to crackle and disintegrate under his touch. The catalogue of memories, good and bad, had lain there, undisturbed, for more years than some of the men in it had been alive; longer still since the dates of their deaths.

He swayed on the small stepladder. Frank felt dizzy, weak. He was babalaas, but when was he not hungover? This, though, was a bad one. Perhaps it was the DTs, delirium tremens, from having been in the Hazyview police cells for the best part of the previous two days. He didn't know the symptoms – he couldn't remember how long it had been since he'd gone thirty-six hours without a drink.

Slowly, he navigated his way down and retraced his tracks, sticky spots of blood on the floor tiles, from the bedroom to The lounge. He usually went barefoot around town, in the same uniform of rugby shorts and T-shirt that he wore this warm September day. He told anyone in the pub who would listen how he could walk the length of the Kruger without shoes, but he was human. Just. He was bleeding from whatever piece of rubbish he'd trodden on in his unkempt front yard.

Frank sat at the cane and glass dining table – someone's castoff, though he couldn't remember whose. Mia smiled down at him from the school portrait on the wall. She had her mother's eyes. Frank sniffed. He opened the album, then reached for the half-jack of Klip-drift brandy and poured himself a tot.

'Frik.' He raised his glass to the first of the fallen, the twenty-year-old grinning under the weight of the radio on his back and flashing a peace sign. Frank drank.

The edges of the album pages were stained brown with the same nicotine that had dyed his fingers and coated the grimy ceiling fan above him. Outside, Mrs Baloyi's Africanus dog barked incessantly and a cape dove mocked him with its call. Work harder, work harder. He hadn't had a proper job since the bloody parks board had fired him.

Frank took his eyes off the photos to fossick in the ashtray for a stompie with a little life left in it. He found one, lit the cigarette butt and coughed through the burned, stubbed-out end.

Mia would have loved to have got her hands on this album. She asked him about the army often, and he could hear the amateur psych in her questions, wanting to know how he felt, did he have flashbacks, did he want to talk about the war? He was a Parabat, and 'Bats didn't get PTS-bloody-D. The war hadn't fucked him up, bloody people had.

He didn't talk; he drank. Smoke curled upwards as Frank turned the pages, tracking his time through basics, infantry training, learning to jump out of aeroplanes, then perfecting the business of killing, in Angola. He found the photo he was looking for. Ondangwa, 1987 was written in faded pencil on the back. He stared at Evan, Ferri, Adam, himself and the trackers. The others were smiling.

After all these years of hardening himself, medicating with the booze, trying and failing to get on with life, the memories broke free. They pushed out from his brain and his soul, through his skin, oozing out of his pores and into the judgmental daylight. He started to cry.

How many times had he sat at this table, planning how to take his own life? It was usually moments like this one, when he knew Mia was away on some school camp or visiting a friend, so that she would not be the first to find his body.

That had been his answer, his one certain way to escape the memories, the shame, the failures of his life. Frank turned another page. There he was in his dress uniform, sergeant's stripes freshly sewn on, ramrod-straight. Dead eyes. Lost a war, lost a wife, lost a job.

Frank blinked. He felt nauseous, weak, like a bad flu was coming on. He coughed again; looked at his watch. Midday on a perfect Lowveld day. As good a time as any to put an end to twenty-five years of hurt.

NOKUTHULA MATHEBULA alighted from the minibus taxi at the fourway stop, where the Zimbabwean man sold his metal warthogs and the tiny tin San hunters, who crouched with their bows and arrows. She tutted at the tourist trinkets and shook her head. Nokuthula hadn't seen a Bushman, as the San used to be called, in her entire life.

She checked her phone. It was two o'clock, but Frank was not a stickler for punctuality. She walked slowly, not wanting to perspire into her new blouse. Sometimes Frank didn't know what day it was. Her heart was heavy for him, but it would be good to see Mia again.

Nokuthula had known Mia since the day she was born, and had carried her on her back, wrapped up like a Shangaan baby, and taught her the language and the ways of her people. When Mia's mother had died, the little girl had become like one of her own.

They had all cried when Frank had told them, some years earlier, that he had lost his job in the Kruger Park, and that he could no longer afford to employ Nokuthula fulltime. Now Mia was nearing the end of her schooling, a beautiful, smart, independent young woman, but Nokuthula still secretly thought of her as her baby.

Nokuthula looked forward to seeing Mia on the infrequent occasions when Frank had enough money from whatever casual job he had found to pay for her to clean the house.

As Nokuthula walked up the street, with its face brick and tile single-storey homes set behind walls topped with razor wire, she saw Mrs Eva Baloyi, Frank's neighbour, standing outside his security gate.

'Inhlikanhi, Eva,' Nokuthula said.

'Ayeh minjani.'

'Phukile,' Nokuthula replied. She was 'awake' and well this afternoon, happy at the thought of seeing her daughter when Mia returned from the school camp tomorrow. The plan was for Nokuthula to stay the night in her old room, the domestic's quarters.

Mrs Baloyi was wide-eyed. 'Ndzi swi twile gunshot.'

'What?' Nokuthula recoiled a pace. 'You heard a gun firing? In Frank's place?'

'Yes.'

Nokuthula scrabbled in her big handbag for the gate remote. She pressed it hard and Mrs Baloyi followed her in and across the overgrown lawn. She fumbled with the keys until she found the one for the front door, then burst inside.

Nokuthula screamed.

1

KWAZULU-NATAL, THE PRESENT

H e must be the town drunk,' the teenage girl said, her voice low but audible from the open window of the Porsche Cayenne.

Adam Kruger pretended not to have heard her. Stereotypes – his country was still fixated with them. He saw himself through her eyes – why else would a middle-aged white man be working in a car park? The boy behind the wheel was not much older than the girl, maybe first year varsity, here on the coast south of Durban for the holidays. The number plate was GP – Gauteng Province, Gangster's Paradise; vaalies, tourists. Stereotypes. As he reversed from the low-rise open-air Scottburgh Mall parking spot the driver reached a gym-fit, tattooed arm out the window and handed Adam a two-rand coin.

'Baie dankie,' Adam said, touching the tip of his faded Toyota baseball cap. He started to direct the young man out of the car space, but the youngster floored the accelerator. The girl screeched with joy; an older Indian couple stepped back to avoid being hit. Adam remembered himself at that age, showing off to girls, wearing a tank top to display his Parabat ink, his paratrooper's wings. Stupid. The girl's words cut him, partly because there was a grain of truth in them. He was not an alcoholic – even though he might have been one at some points in his adult life – but it was true that the money he made as a car guard at Scottburgh Mall went on the meagre booze ration he allowed himself these days.

Sweat trickled down his body under the second-hand long sleeve shirt and reflective vest that read 'Car Guard'. The shirt was fraying at the collar, but the creases in the sleeves were ironed to a knife's edge. The jeans were hot in this weather, but like the shirt they kept the sun off him. Rassie Erasmus, the medic who Adam had fought along-side in the war, had survived Angola, two marriages and a proper battle with the bottle, then passed from melanoma five years ago.

Adam heard a horn hoot and turned, narrowing his eyes as he slipped the single coin into his zippered imitation leather bum bag. Porsche boy had not got far; he was stopped behind a white Fortuner. There was a young man behind the wheel of the Toyota, which was parked in the middle of the road, blocking the exit. The youths in the Cayenne yelled abuse.

The Fortuner driver was alert, checking the rear-view mirror, not checking his phone. Why had he stopped? Adam felt the hairs come to attention on the back of his neck. He looked to the mall entrance. A security guard in body armour had his back against a wall, an LM5 assault rifle held at the ready; he'd chosen a good position but his attention, like most of the people in the car park, had been diverted by the road-rage incident currently unfolding fifty metres away from where Adam was standing. A cash-in-transit van was parked in the disabled spot near the entrance to the mall; two guards were walking out with boxes full of money.

Adam looked around. He saw four young men striding between the cars. Like him, their clothes were wrong for the beach and the weather. One opened his jacket and Adam saw the glint of sun on steel, a short-barrelled AK-47.

'Gun!'

Adam had the attention of the security guard; he pointed at the advancing men. All of them had now drawn weapons: two had rifles, two pistols.

The guard raised his weapon but was too slow. The first round from the AK thudded into his body armour. The man was slammed back into the wall, winded, his eyes wide with surprise – maybe that he was still alive. Gasping and clearly in pain, he tried to raise his rifle again, but the second round hit him in the neck.

Adam bent low and ran between the parked cars as shoppers screamed and fled. The Porsche was reversing. One of the armed bandits fired at it. The others opened up on the cash-in-transit guards, who dropped their cashboxes and were fumbling for side-arms.

Adam was unarmed, but he moved towards the robbers anyway. There was a thud and the screech of metal on metal as one car backed into another. The Fortuner was still blocking the way out, and the line of holiday shoppers that had been circling the car park looking for convenient spaces near the mall was gridlocked as panicked people tried and failed to get away from the shootout. The two guards who'd been inside the mall were firing back. By calling out a warning, Adam had forced the hijackers to show their hands much earlier than they would have liked. One was advancing; the way he walked tall, rifle up and firing, made Adam wonder if he was jacked up on drugs. Maybe he'd purchased umuthi from a sangoma to make him bulletproof. A slug from one of the guards' guns punched him backwards.

'Adam!' a voice hissed.

Adam, still ducking and moving, glanced over the bonnet of a Ford Ranger and saw Wilfred, a Zimbabwean parking attendant, keeping pace with him.

'Go back, take cover,' Adam said.

Wilfred shook his head. 'No. This is our duty.'

Madness, more like it, thought Adam, but he felt the adrenaline, all but absent in this second half of his time on earth. It powered him up, making him forget this life, taking him back to another.

He smelled the cordite, heard the percolator pop of an AK on full auto. Another windscreen shattered; people were screaming.

Adam heard his own pulse, then the report of a pistol being fired from further away in the car park. A bullet punched a hole in the door of a Polo right in front of him. The shot had come from the flank. Adam raised his head and saw a shopper, a man going grey, like himself, aiming a nine-mil. The robber with the AK swung and fired a burst on full automatic and the vigilante dropped to his belly.

Adam looked around for a weapon and saw a broken paver on the edge of a garden bed. He picked it up. The thieves' momentum had slowed and Adam heard a siren. The man with the AK turned his attention back to the guards and emptied his magazine at them. One of the security men cried out in pain and this prompted the remaining two criminals to resume their advance.

The rifleman fumbled while replacing his magazine and Adam closed in on him from behind.

One of the man's comrades called a warning as Adam rose fully upright; he knew he only had a second or two in which to act. The gunman spun around and raised his AK-47. Adam noted that while the fresh magazine was now fitted, he hadn't seen the man pull back the rifle's cocking handle. The robber pulled the trigger; nothing happened. Adam drove into him, knocking the rifle barrel to one side, and smashed the broken paver into his face. The man's head snapped back. Adam was on him, unleashing his rage; he dropped the broken piece of cement and punched the man in the face. Wilfred joined him and Adam took the rifle from the dazed and wounded man's hands. Wilfred held the man down while Adam cocked the AK with practised ease.

The feel of the wooden handgrip and stock; the weight of the rifle; the heat from the barrel; the smell of oil – all threatened to over-whelm his senses. The muscle memory brought the weapon up into his shoulder and he almost craved the kick of the recoil as he searched for a target.

The thief who had called the warning turned, moving between an Amarok and a Land Cruiser Prado, and his gun hand tracked towards Adam.

'Drop it!' Adam leaned over the bonnet of the Polo, lowering his profile, making himself a smaller target as he took a sight picture. The young man grinned and pulled the trigger. Adam saw the boy's hand buck, heard the crack-thump of the nine-millimetre projectile cleave the air next to him, then squeezed the trigger himself. Adam's bullet hit the target in the shoulder, knocking him backwards.

Adam ran to the downed man. He had dropped his pistol when he was hit, and was now trying to roll over to get to it. Adam bent down, picked up the pistol and stuffed it in the waistband of his jeans.

The last of the thieves sprinted for the Fortuner that had been blocking the car park exit in the instant the attack went down. As Adam had suspected, this was the getaway vehicle.

Adam tracked the fleeing man through the AK's sights, but he was not about to shoot him in the back. As the robber opened the rear door of the Fortuner the driver put his foot down, forcing the bandit to run faster, holding on to the handle. He managed to hop, skip and drag himself into the back as the Toyota reached the mall entry. A battered South African Police Service bakkie rolled into the car park, heading the wrong way up the one-way access road, and the two vehicles collided, head-on.

Steam hissed from the two punctured radiators and the driver of the Fortuner was struggling to get out from behind his airbag as the police exited their vehicle, guns drawn. The two men in the getaway car surrendered.

Two other car guards emerged from where they had taken cover behind vehicles and ran to Adam, who was now on his feet. 'Watch this one with the bullet hole in his shoulder. Find something to stop the bleeding,' Adam said to them.

Adam ran to the wounded security guard. He was being treated by one of the cash-in-transit guards, but Adam immediately saw that the man holding his hand to the other's neck was also wounded. His face was grey and as Adam arrived, the first responder slumped back against the wall.

Blood spurted from the other man's neck in a straight jet, staining the white-painted concrete. Adam ripped off his shirt, popping the buttons, and balled up it and his vest, pressing the makeshift dressing against the man's neck. A stream of blood hit him in the face and chest as he fought to find purchase and stem the bleeding. The third guard was on his phone.

'Ambulance on the way. Do you know what you're doing?' he said to Adam.

'His carotid's severed.' Adam pressed down harder on the wound, shifting his fingers so that he could push the severed artery against the bones of the man's spine, slowing the flow. Rassie had taught them that move. The spurting stopped.

The guard who was questioning him was now tending to his other comrade, who had been shot in the shoulder. Adam saw that the other casualty had gone into shock, but the wound looked like a through-and-through. He would live. The driver of the cash-in-transit van emerged from the armoured vehicle with a first aid kit, then stood over all of them, pump-action shotgun in hand.

The man in Adam's arms came to. 'I . . . I am alive,' he croaked.

'Yes, bru,' Adam said. 'What's your name?'

'Themba.'

Adam held him, keeping his hand on the man's neck. 'You're going to be fine, Themba. Hang in there, man.' Adam was not at all sure of his words but he said them as confidently as he could. 'Help is coming for you; you'll be in hospital just now.'

People were drifting back to the mall and the scene of the shootings, curious now that the gunfire had stopped. Adam glanced up and saw that the girl from the Porsche was videoing him.

'Check out this guy's abs,' she said to the tattooed boy next to her, 'the old dude's ripped.'

Adam shook his head, concentrating on the man in his arms. He closed his eyes, tight, but not enough to force away the image of Frik Rossouw, who had died in the dust in Angola from a gunshot wound to the head.

He heard the thwap of rotor blades. Now I really am crazy.

The noise grew louder, but Adam couldn't turn to face it because if he moved, he might relax the pressure on the wounded guard's artery. A hail of grit sandblasted his bare torso as a real-life helicopter touched down in the now half-empty car park.

'It's one of our car-tracker choppers, from our company,' the van driver yelled over the whine of the engine.

The other guard performing first aid finished tying a dressing around the man with the shoulder wound, then came to Adam. 'Come, let's get Themba to the chopper. He needs to get to a hospital as soon as possible. He's lost too much blood already.'

Adam felt light-headed. Maybe it was the heat, or the sounds of the gunfire and the chopper. He felt like he was floating, hovering in the air, watching himself and the other man half walk, half carry Themba to the little Robinson helicopter.

'You need to go with him, to Ondangwa,' Adam said. 'Hold your hand against his neck like I'm doing.'

'Huh? Isn't Ondangwa in Namibia?' the man asked. Adam shook his head. 'I mean Durban, to the hospital.'

The pilot was out of the chopper and had the rear door open. The three of them managed to slide Themba onto the seat. Adam took the guard's hand and placed it over his, holding his shirt, then slid his hand out. Blood spurted as the man relaxed the pressure when climbing into the chopper. Adam showed him again and they managed to staunch the flow once more.

'Go!' Adam said.

The pilot needed no further encouragement. Within seconds she was strapped in and the helicopter lifted off. The guard in the back, still holding his hand pressed firmly against Themba's neck, caught Adam's eye and gave him a nod.

Adam turned away from the rotor downwash and when the chopper was gone, he walked to the planter where he'd stashed his backpack and a bottle of water that Pinkie, one of the checkout ladies from Food Lovers' Market, kept in the deep freeze for him. It had all but melted in the heat. He sat down heavily and tipped cold water over his head, running a hand through his bristly salt and pepper crewcut. The guard's blood, mixed with Adam's sweat, ran in rivulets over his skin.

An ambulance arrived and the paramedics on board began triaging the wounded robbers and security guard. Wilfred was keeping watch on the man Adam had smashed with the broken paver. He was sitting up, holding a hand to his head.

A shadow fell over Adam and he looked up. It was the boy with the tattooed arm and the loudmouth girl from the Porsche.

'That was hectic, man,' the boy said. 'You were like Chuck Norris on steroids, dude.'

Adam blinked and stood. He clenched his fists to stop them trembling. He was returning to earth from his out-of-body experience, but now that the adrenaline and rage were leaving his body he felt the crippling tiredness taking hold of him.

'We thought you were, like, just a car guard,' the girl said. She looked him up and down, appraising him anew, and twirled her hair in the fingers of one hand.

At nearly two metres in height and broad across the shoulders, Adam towered over them. The boy took an involuntary pace backwards. His eyes were drawn to the parachute wings tattooed on Adam's bicep.

'Were you, like, a Parabat, in the parachute battalion or something?' the boy asked; he held his phone towards Adam.

Adam raised a hand to try to obscure the tiny lens. He glanced around the car park. The area was now swarming with police, armed response security officers and emergency services personnel. If they needed him, they would find him.

'I'm just a car guard.' He turned and walked away.

2

Captain Susan van Rensburg, known to most as Sannie, had been in the Galleria shopping mall in Amanzimtoti, looking at bikinis in the Rip Curl shop when her phone had rung with a message about the robbery and shootings at Scottburgh. She had left the store immediately and driven 35 kilometres south on the N2 to Scottburgh Mall.

Although senior to her in rank, Gita was younger than Sannie by a few years and, as on every one of the few occasions Sannie had met her, looked as if she had just stepped out of a day spa. Not a strand of her straight black hair was out of place and her makeup accentuated her eyes, which Sannie thought were one of her best features.

'Sannie, howzit, sorry to disturb you on your day off,' Gita said before excusing herself with a smile from her media interview.

In contrast to Gita, who wore a crisp white linen suit and a silk blouse, Sannie was dressed in denim shorts, a white V-neck T-shirt and imitation Birkenstocks. Her Z88 service pistol was clipped to her belt in a holster and her South African Police Service ID hung on a chain around her neck.

'No problem.' Sannie took her sunglasses from the top of her head and put them on; she was still getting used to how bright the light seemed in KwaZulu-Natal, as well as the coastal climate. The Kruger National Park, in Mpumalanga, where she had last been based as head of the Stock Theft and Endangered Species Unit, had been very hot in summer, but KZN elevated heat, and humidity, to a whole new level. Not for the first time she wondered if she had made the right decision, applying for a transfer and uprooting her life. Sannie looked around the car park. 'Well, this is a mess.'

'Sannie, I know you're still settling in, and house-hunting, but I already know from my own sources that you're an exceptional detective.' Gita nodded to the television crew, a cameraman and a young woman with an elaborate hairdo, who were packing up their gear. 'My gut tells me this is going to be a big media story, so I want someone clever interviewing the guy who neutralised two of the robbers. Half a dozen witnesses have already been talking about this "superman" who saved the day.'

'Was he one of the cash-in-transit guards?' Police crime scene investigators were photographing the van, whose thick armoured glass windows were starred from gunshots; another technician was taking pictures of a bloodstained wall. Small flags with numbers were placed in several locations, indicating spent bullet casings. 'This looks like a moer of a shootout.'

'Not exactly. A parking attendant, would you believe it?' Sannie raised her eyebrows. 'Some poor Nigerian or Zimbabwean earned their five rands' worth today.'

'He's a white guy, Sannie. One of the eyewitnesses said the man had a military tattoo, parachute wings. He took out one of the robbers by klapping him with a broken paver, grabbed the guy's AK and shot and wounded one of the others. He also saved the life of one of the security guards, who was shot in the neck; the man made it to hospital in a chopper and he's listed as serious but stable.'

'Impressive, but this could get political,' Sannie said.

Gita nodded. 'That's why I was right to call you in today. The story's already breaking on social media and it will be on TV tonight and in the newspapers tomorrow. Even for South Africa it's incredible

– car guard saves the day. Check out the I'm going nowhere Facebook group.'

Sannie took out her phone and opened the Facebook app. The page was popular, with a couple of hundred thousand followers – proud South Africans who were bucking the trend of the many who had emigrated from South Africa to countries such as Australia, New Zealand and the United States. The site would never normally post a video of an armed robbery, but this was a criminal event with a twist – a citizen had saved the day.

Sannie heard the distinctive sound of an AK-47 firing on full auto through the phone's speaker. There was no vision of a robber being shot, but an excited young man was giving a running commentary.

'Hectic; this car guard dude picks up the guy's AK and foils the robbery, then the cops ram the getaway car.'

The video of the car guard was grainy and jerky. Sannie paused it a couple of times. She saw the man, maybe early fifties, with short grey hair. A later snippet showed him shirtless, giving first aid to a fallen security guard. The next clip showed the man's face, briefly, but then he put his hand up, as if covering his identity.

'I'm just a car guard,' he said, in response to a question about whether he had been in one of the army's parachute battalions.

'Modest,' Sannie said to Gita as she closed the app. 'Have we got a name for him?'

'Adam Kruger. Mall management has the names of all the car guards, but there's no address listed for Kruger – not unusual, as some of the guards are homeless. The uniforms found a till operator from Food Lovers' who said she thinks he stays somewhere south of Scottburgh. I need you to find him, quickly, Sannie. The girl says Kruger does not have a car, and he left straight after the attempted robbery. He dropped off the pistol he took from one of the tsotsis with a security guard before he fled the scene. I've got a couple of bakkies out looking for him, but no one's found him yet.'

'I'll need to talk to the supermarket worker,' Sannie said.

Gita looked around. A female officer was talking to a younger woman by the entrance to the mall. 'That's her.'

'Thanks.' Sannie strode over and thanked the uniformed officer. 'I'll take it from here,' she said, turning to the other young woman. 'Hello, how are you? I'm Captain Susan van Rensburg. I'd like to talk to you about Adam Kruger. What's your name?' Sannie took her notebook and pen from the back pocket of her shorts.

'I'm Pinkie Ndlovu, but I've already told the other police everything I know about Adam.'

'Yes, I understand, but I may have just a few more questions for you.'

The young woman looked at her watch. 'I need to get back on shift, but all right.'

'Does he wear a wedding ring?'

Pinkie looked taken aback. She hadn't been asked that question. 'Um, no. I told the other officer that he doesn't talk about himself.'

'You're friends with him, though?'

She shrugged. 'He is quiet, but he is a good man.'

'Why do you say that?' Sannie made a note.

'He helped me, once. There were some guys, not local, in the car park one day when I was coming off shift in the evening. They were drinking beer and brandy, whistling at me, saying some suggestive things. One of them touched me, and I screamed. Adam came and sorted them out.'

'"Sorted them out"? How many of them were there?'

'Four.'

'What did he do to them?'

Pinkie looked around, not wanting to make eye contact. 'I don't want to make trouble for him. Those guys never came back.'

Four to one. 'Is he a violent man?'

Pinkie shook her head. 'No, another time, some different guys were taunting him, calling him trash and names like that. People think . . . Well, some people say that as well as the poor people and those without jobs, that sometimes people work as car guards to get money for drugs or beers. Adam is never drunk. Even when those guys insulted him, he just stood there, saying nothing.'

'You told the other officer that Adam does not have a car. Does he come by taxi? Does he walk?'

'He runs.'

It was Sannie's turn to be surprised. 'In this heat?'

'Every day that he works here.'

Sannie made a note. 'He doesn't come here every day?'

Pinkie shook her head. 'No. Maybe three or four days a week, then I might not see him for another week, then he comes again. But I see him in the afternoon or evening, when he finishes. He goes to the bathroom in the mall and he comes out in his running gear, with his day clothes in a small backpack.'

'Does he run to work?'

'He runs to Scottburgh Beach.' Pinkie pointed towards the coast. The beach was only a couple of kilometres from the mall, which was on the R102, the coastal road, set back from the town. 'I saw him on my day off once, by the caravan park; he showered there and got changed, then walked to the mall. When he finishes work, he runs to wherever he lives.'

'Do you know where that is?'

She shook her head again. 'I asked him once and he said, "south", that was all. One time I wanted to know how far he ran and he said, "about twelve kilometres".'

Sannie made a note and pictured where that would be. 'Pennington?'

Pinkie just shrugged.

'Did you talk to him, the day you saw him at Scottburgh, after he had changed?'

'Yes, I did,' Pinkie said. 'I asked him if he had been swimming. He said no, not there, but that he liked to swim at Rocky Bay. Will he get in trouble, for shooting that man?'

'I don't know,' Sannie said. 'But it's important I talk to him.'

'People are saying that he told the robber to put down his gun, and that the man fired at Adam. It was self-defence,' Pinkie said.

'We'll see.' Sannie put her notebook away.

Gita was busy talking to a man with a notebook and pen – probably another reporter. Sannie went to her Fortuner, got in and started the engine. The air conditioner provided some much-needed relief.

She turned on her sat nav and used her fingers to examine a map of the coast. She was getting to know this part of South Africa, mostly through her house-hunting. The Hawks' regional office was in Port Shepstone, about sixty-five kilometres to the south of Scottburgh. Sannie was staying in a flatlet above the garage of her brother-in-law Johan's house in Pennington, twelve kilometres in the same direction; Rocky Bay, where Kruger liked to swim, was between where she was now and her temporary home.

It was hellishly hot and he had just shot a man. If he wanted to get away, for whatever reason, he might head for the sea. Sannie checked her watch; by her reckoning it had been forty-five minutes since the brief but bloody firefight had gone down.

This Adam Kruger was a man with no car, who was fit and ran to work. Sannie would find him.

NORTHERN CAPE, South Africa

THE BLACK-MANED LION, beautifully silhouetted against the red sands of the Kalahari Desert, gave a low, rumbling call. The big cat was so close to head guide Mia Greenaway and her guests that it felt like the aluminium body panels of the Land Rover were vibrating from the noise.

Digital cameras clicked and beeped, but the lion wasn't bothered.

'He's sending a warning to another male,' Mia said softly, 'to let him know that this is his territory, and not to enter.'

Here in this vast inland ocean of sand Mia still felt, sometimes, like an outsider, as though she was on someone else's turf. She had grown up in South Africa's Lowveld, on the edge of the Kruger National Park. Her natural habitat was the thickly vegetated banks of the Sabie River, where one was more likely to encounter a prowling leopard than one of the resident lion prides. It wasn't only the landscape that was different, it was also the culture. Mia was fluent in Xitsonga, thanks to Nokuthula Mathebula, the Shangaan carer who had raised her after her own mother passed, and she had left her best friend, tracker and mentor Bongani Ngobeni behind in order to further her career. Occasionally she wondered if she'd made the right choice. Also back 'home' in Khaya Ngala Lodge in the Sabi Sand Game Reserve was her on-again, off-again, now former boyfriend, Graham Foster. Handsome and too alpha for his own good, Graham could drive her mad for different reasons. She had told herself, when the opportunity came up to transfer to Dune Lodge, that she needed a change of scenery for many reasons, and the Kalahari had certainly delivered that.

'What would happen if the other guy came onto this one's turf?' Joe, one of her four American clients asked. They were two couples: a pair of dentists – Bill and Judy – and a pair of doctors – Joe and Melanie – from Michigan.

'There'd be a big fight,' Mia said, 'probably to the death.'

'Say, if Luiz isn't well I could always take a look at him,' Melanie said.

'Thanks, Melanie,' Mia said. 'That's really kind of you, especially as you're on holiday, but I'm sure the lodge manager will get him to the local doctor in Askham if he's quite ill.'

Luiz Siboa was Mia's San tracker and Mia had made up a story about him not feeling well to cover the fact that he had not reported for work prior to the early-morning game drive at Dune Lodge. Mia was worried but was trying not to show it. In all the time she'd been at the lodge, Luiz had never missed a scheduled drive. There had been no sign of him in his room in the staff quarters, either, when Mia had checked in the pre-dawn darkness as she readied for the morning safari.

They watched the lion for a few minutes more, listening to him call. After the big cat had padded across the sand to sit down in the shade of a lone thorn tree, the Canons and the Nikons ceased fire.

'Are we all good?' Mia asked, running a hand through her short dark hair.

'Sure thing.' Bill had a habit of speaking for the group. Mia did a quick scan of faces and they all nodded. They'd stayed out a little later than normal; it was nearly eleven am and Mia knew that as keen as the Americans would be, they would be getting hungry and starting to cook themselves in the open-topped vehicle.

She started her engine and radioed camp to let them know that they were fifteen minutes out. The manager, Shirley Hennessy, would make sure there was a staff member waiting with cold towels and an icy mocktail, or chilled champagne, to welcome the guests back to the lodge.

The guests were buoyed after the lion sighting, which had been the highlight of their morning. It was as though the unspoken pressure on Mia to deliver amazing game sightings had been lifted and the group could relax.

'So,' Joe said, leaning forward in his seat so Mia could hear him over the engine noise as she drove through a patch of thick sand, 'how long have you been at Dune Lodge?'

'Three months.' Mia changed gear. 'I was working as head guide at Julianne Clyde-Smith's other lodge, Khaya Ngala, for the last couple of years.'

'That's where we're headed next,' Melanie chimed in.

'You'll love it,' Mia said. 'The Sabi Sand Game Reserve, where Khaya Ngala's located, is very different from the Kalahari. Lots of thick bush and big trees – good leopard country, but you won't see big black-maned lions the size of the guy we just had.'

'But no pangolins or aardvarks, right?' said Judy, with a note of triumphalism.

'Let's just say that in my five years at Khaya Ngala I saw pangolin five times and aardvark maybe nine or ten – here in the desert, we drive past the aardvarks to get to the pangolin.' It was true – Mia had found the sightings of these two safari bucket list creatures amazingly plentiful on the equally surprisingly chilly nights at her new lodge.

'Why did you move here, Mia?' Joe asked as they bounced along the undulating road.

'Julianne encourages movement between her lodges for professional development, not just here in South Africa, but also part-time exchanges with staff from properties in Zimbabwe and Tanzania. I've got a master tracker's qualification, but the San people, like Luiz, take tracking to a whole new level and I wanted to improve my knowledge and skills. I've learned so much here.' There was also another reason Julianne had wanted Mia to move to Dune Lodge, but that was commercial-in-confidence and her guests didn't need to know.

'Are the San, like, the Bushmen of the Kalahari?' Judy asked.

They passed a magnificent male gemsbok, better known to the tourists as oryx, but whereas the striking grey antelope with its black-and-white face and long, pointed horns had been a fascinating photographic subject for the tourists on their first day, now Mia knew better than to stop. 'That's their old name, which isn't used anymore,' Mia said. 'It's considered disrespectful.'

'What kind of a name is Luiz, for a San man?' Melanie asked. Where to start? Mia glanced over her shoulder. 'It's Portuguese.' Bill raised his eyebrows. 'He's from Portugal?'

'No, Angola, originally. That was once a Portuguese colony. Luiz was born there – sometime in the mid-to late 1950s – he told me once he's not a hundred per cent sure of his age, but he thinks he's sixty-six. In his younger years he lived a totally traditional life as a San hunter-gatherer in the bush. When he was about seventeen, he joined the Portuguese army to fight against the forces trying to liberate Angola during the 1960s and early seventies.'

'Against his own people?' Judy said.

Mia knew she'd opened a can of worms, but the guests were asking questions, which meant they were engaged, and that meant they were happy. 'Not really. The San have been marginalised throughout their history. They were the original inhabitants of much of southern Africa, but migration by more numerous African tribes started to displace them from their hunting grounds, and the arrival of colonial armies and settlers just made things worse. They were enemies of some of the other tribes.'

'So they fought on the side of the whites, the Portuguese?' Joe said.

Mia nodded. 'Yes. Luiz's family were pro-Portuguese. I'm not exactly sure of his family's history – he's a very reserved guy – but I do know he had a stepsister who was half-Portuguese. She was the mother of Shirley, our lodge manager, who is Luiz's niece.'

'OK,' said Melanie. 'I was wondering about Shirley's surname, Hennessy. I've got distant cousins with the same name, and they're Irish Americans. Is she married?'

'No,' Mia said. 'I don't know the ins and outs of her family, but Shirley did tell me once that her late father actually was an Irishman living in South Africa. Anyway, when Portugal pulled out of all its African and other colonies after a coup in Lisbon in the 1970s, the white South African army took on Luiz and hundreds of other San soldiers and employed them in their fight against the new Angolan government, and against other nationalists, fighting for independence in Namibia.'

'Boy, Africa is complicated, with all these different tribes and so forth,' Bill said.

Mia held her tongue. So too was the American Civil War, she wanted to say.

'What was this war over?' Judy asked.

Mia took a deep breath. 'In South Africa we called it the Border War. In the seventies and eighties the apartheid-era government was under threat from within, with the rise of Nelson Mandela's ANC – the African National Congress. Angola provided a safe haven for the ANC, and for an organisation called SWAPO, the South West Africa People's Organisation.'

'South West Africa was the old name for Namibia, right?' Bill interjected.

'Exactly, Bill,' Mia said. 'And their military wing, PLAN, the People's Liberation Army of Namibia, was launching raids across the border into what we know as Namibia, which back then was considered almost part of South Africa. The South African government was fiercely anti-communist and they were concerned about the election of a left-wing government in Angola, which was backed by Cuba and Russia. The South African Defence Force waged war in

Angola, propping up a guy called Jonas Savimbi and his party, UNITA.'

'And Uncle Sam played a role,' Bill said. 'The CIA was backing Savimbi and I read a novel that said Savimbi financed his war effort with elephant ivory, rhino horn and blood diamonds that the US and South Africa helped him sell abroad.'

'Correct again, Bill, on all counts. White South African men, including my father, were conscripted to fight and sent to the border with Angola. There were some big battles inside Angola, and fighting in South West Africa. It all ended in a kind of draw in 1990 when Namibia was proclaimed as an independent country.'

'How did someone like Luiz end up here,' Melanie asked, 'so far from home and his traditional life?'

Mia liked Melanie. She was compassionate and caring, which Mia guessed made her a good doctor. 'At the end of the war in Angola, Luiz and hundreds of San soldiers and their families were moved to South Africa, to a military base near the diamond mining town of Kimberley; they would have been persecuted if they'd tried to return to Angola. Nelson Mandela granted them land and a permanent home close by, in a township called Platfontein, when he took power in South Africa.'

'That was good of him,' Melanie said.

Mia didn't want to disagree, but she'd learned, through Luiz and Shirley that life was hard for the San refugees from the war.

'Sure,' Mia said. 'But they ended up in basic housing in an arid area far from their homelands, with nowhere to hunt and very few prospects for jobs. After the democratic elections here in South Africa, many people still saw them as enemies.'

Melanie nodded. 'I see. I'd love to talk to Luiz, when he's feeling better; or, like I say, if there's anything I can do . . .'

'Thank you, Melanie,' Mia said, meaning it.

Mia returned her eyes to the road, but caught sight of a dark speck in the sky in her peripheral vision. She slowed and looked up.

'Vultures,' she said, seeing that there was more than one, coming in to land.

'Where?' Bill asked.

'Ten o'clock high, buddy,' Joe said. 'You need some new glasses.'

Mia drove to the crest of the next dune to get a better look at what the vultures were interested in. She stopped and took out her Swarovski binoculars, a tip from some other clients from the United States; Americans could be incredibly generous and appreciative guests. She knew this spot well; the big camel thorn tree standing stark and picturesque against the sparse desert view was a favourite shady spot for Mia and the other guides to break their game drives for morning coffee or afternoon sundowners. She focused, then bit her lower lip.

'Um, everyone, just sit still in the vehicle here for me. I'm going to take a look.'

'Will you be safe?' Judy asked.

'For sure, just stay in the Land Rover.' Mia took the long, green canvas bag from the racks on the Land Rover's dashboard and unzipped it. She pulled out her .375 Brno rifle, got out of the vehicle, opened the bolt and loaded her weapon with five fat slugs from the hand-tooled leather cartridge belt around her waist. 'Back in a minute, please sit tight.'

'OK. You be careful, now,' Melanie said.

Mia nodded and walked away from the game viewer. The red sand was loose, and she felt each step in her calves, but the thudding in her chest worried her more. She looked around. For kilometre after kilometre the desert stretched away like an empty sea of red waves. It was the nothingness she'd found hard to get used to, at first. She had longed to see the towering leadwood and jackalberry trees that lined even the dry watercourses of her homeland, let alone the flowing Sabie River, but in time she had come to appreciate the desolation. It made the impressive camel thorn she was heading towards an even more special landmark. Here, in the middle of nowhere where the reserve was situated, nearly one hundred kilometres from the nearest town, Askham, she felt a peace she hadn't known since before the death of her father. What she hadn't told her guests was that her dad, Frank, had killed himself, and that she was sure the war she'd spoken of, like a history teacher, had been part of the reason why he'd done it. The silence, at first eerie, almost scary, now calmed her.

A vulture took flight as she came closer and others hopped away from the carcass they were feasting on, close to the base of the tree. She could hear the thwap-thwap of massive wings cleaving the air as others hauled themselves skyward.

The sun overhead stung the back of her neck; perspiration beaded her upper lip. She gripped the rifle tighter, her palms slick. The lion the big male had been challenging could be close, in the lee of the next sandhill, resting in between eating. She did not think, however, that a lion, cheetah, or one of the secretive Kalahari leopards had made this kill.

Mia looked at the sand. Tracking in this place was maddeningly difficult; she tried to remember everything that Luiz had told and shown her in the last three months. Mia glanced over her shoulder. Her tourists were sitting still, at least, the two men watching her through binoculars.

She brought the butt of the Brno into her shoulder, ready, just in case. A movement to her right startled her, and she swung the barrel around. It was just another vulture, a late departure.

Her Rogue boots squeaked beneath her and she felt grains of sand being kicked up onto the backs of her legs. The kill was no more than twenty metres away now and she could confirm that her first instinct had been right.

Again, she scanned around her, 360 degrees, searching for danger. When she looked back to the place where the vultures had been, she saw the blood, and on the hot desert breeze, she smelled the first telltale odours of death. Mia closed her eyes, but a tear forced its way out and rolled down her cheek.

'No,' she whispered.

She stopped and saw what the vultures had begun feasting on. She didn't need to go closer to confirm it was a human, a man dressed in the khaki shirt and green shorts of Dune Lodge.

Luiz.

3

From Scottburgh, Sannie took the R102 and headed south. The old main road meandered along the country's eastern coastline, all the way to Cape Town on the southern tip of the continent. The Indian Ocean sparkled on her left.

She kept her eyes peeled for men jogging along the road but saw no one. Running in this heat would be murder; never had she been so grateful for the Fortuner's air conditioning.

After Park Rynie she took the turnoff on the left to Rocky Bay and crossed the railway line. Passenger services had been discontinued on the line some years earlier, she had learned, and freight trains ran infrequently – and not at all since the huge floods that had ravaged the province. At Pennington she'd seen people walking and running along the line, hopping from sleeper to sleeper – maybe Adam Kruger had taken this route.

She could be wrong about her theory that Kruger had walked or run here, but as a detective she'd learned long ago to follow her instincts. As always, she was keeping an open mind about this case, but she was hoping she would be able to wrap it up quickly.

She'd only been in her new job for three weeks and now she was due to go on leave the following week. She was looking forward to the break to visit her good friend Mia Greenaway, though the Kalahari Desert and the Kgalagadi Transfrontier Park would be just as hot as the south coast, if not more so.

Sannie nosed the Fortuner into a spot in the municipal car park overlooking the ocean. To her right was the rocky promontory that gave the bay its name, topped with a short concrete walkway with safety railings, perfect for fishermen. Two anglers had lines in the water. In front of her an older couple, maybe from the caravan park on the other side of the parking area, lay in the shade of a beach umbrella, reading. A family was sitting down to a picnic meal under a fold-out gazebo; three teenage boys laughed in the surf as waves broke over them.

Sannie got out and pulled her sunglasses down. To her left was the ski boat club, a rather small, two-storey brick building with a kitchen downstairs and a bar with a wooden deck above. She could see a couple sitting at wooden picnic tables upstairs.

She crossed the car park and went to the club. Inside, she took the stairs.

'Morning, can I help?' asked the blonde bartender who was wiping the counter. A heavy-set grey-haired man with a red face, a quart bottle of Castle Lite in a cooler in front of him, nodded hello.

'Just looking for a friend,' Sannie said.

'Who?' the bartender asked. 'Chances are I'll know him or her.'

'Adam Kruger.'

The older man at the bar burped. 'Sharky.'

'Sorry?' Sannie said.

The bartender set down her cloth and put her hands on her hips. Her eyes went to the pistol on Sannie's hip – her shirt had ridden up, exposing the handgrip. 'What do you want with Adam?'

Sannie took out her police ID, held it outstretched for the bartender to see, then hung the lanyard around her neck.

'Here.' Sannie turned at the sound of a male voice and the blonde woman looked over Sannie's shoulder. A man's head and shoulders appeared through an open window; he was shirtless and had been sitting at one of the outside picnic tables, though she hadn't seen him from the car park. The face disappeared.

As Sannie walked onto the wooden deck, which was just wide enough to accommodate the table-and-bench combos, the couple who had been outside passed her and headed downstairs.

'Adam Kruger?'

He looked her way and gave a small nod. He had short hair, dark speckled with grey, and was deeply tanned. His torso was virtually hairless, and his abdominal muscles were clearly etched, though she doubted he was the kind to wax or pay for a gym membership. Like the old guy propping up the bar inside, Kruger was also drinking from a quart – Black Label, this time. The cheapest beer in the bar.

As she walked to him, she noticed his eyes. They were the most striking shade of green, and even though he was looking at her it felt like she was invisible to him, like he was looking through her to some far horizon. Maybe he was drunk already, but in his body language she detected no sign of relaxation or inebriation; if anything, he seemed hypervigilant. He sat in the far corner, which is why she hadn't seen him; his back was to the wall, the ocean to his left.

'I'm Captain Susan van Rensburg, from the Hawks. I need to talk to you about the events at Scottburgh Mall this morning.'

He took a swig of beer out of the bottle. 'How did you find me?'

'It's my job.'

He nodded, twice, slowly. 'You're good at it.'

She stood there, her right hand resting on the pistol grip of the Z88. 'Why did you flee the scene of the robbery and shooting?'

'I didn't flee. My shift was over.' He glanced away, back to the Indian Ocean. 'And I don't like crowds.'

'Yet you work in a shopping mall car park. Month-end must be a bitch.'

He glanced back at her. 'I need the money.'

Sannie nodded to the half-full bottle he'd just set down. 'For that?'

Adam shrugged. 'As it happens, yes.'

He was being flippant, or insolent, or maybe both. 'I need to take a statement from you and decide whether or not to charge you. We can do it here, or I'll put the cuffs on you and take you to Port Shepstone.'

'Can I buy you a drink?' he asked.

'No.' Sannie sat down on the picnic table seat opposite him and took out her notebook. She asked him his full name and date of birth. He was fifty-five, twelve years older than her. She would have put him at mid-forties. If he was a drunk, working in a car park to buy cheap beers, he kept himself in good shape. 'Occupation?'

'Parking attendant.'

'No other job?' she asked.

He shrugged. 'I do some odd jobs here and there. In the peak tourist season I get work on the dive boats if someone else calls in ill.'

'Address?'

He gave the number of a house in Botha Place, in Pennington. It was immediately recognisable to her, although she still did not know the village well. 'Is it for sale?'

'Not anymore.'

'Ah.' She nodded.

'You in the market?' He finished his beer and set it down on the table.

'I'm asking the questions.' She remembered the place. It was old, the garden overgrown, the house in terrible shape, but she'd noted the plastic sheeting over a broken window, the rusted guttering and an old roof that would have once covered the stoep lying in the front yard as though it had recently been pulled down. 'That one was for sale,' Pam, the real estate agent showing her around had told her. It was the worst house in one of the best streets, and Sannie had said that because of her budget she would consider a place that needed work. 'The old woman who owned it passed away,' Pam had told her. 'Shame, but her son came back from Australia and wants to do it up before they try to sell again.'

What Sannie did not tell Pam was that she could have had her pick of most of the houses she had seen so far, because her late husband, Tom, had died in Iraq, leaving her a significant life insurance payout. As a military contractor working as a bodyguard in a dangerous place, the premiums for his life insurance had been astronomical. At one point, Sannie had tried to persuade him to stop paying – in hindsight she now realised she was trying to convince herself that he would never be harmed. She felt guilty now for even thinking that she might benefit in some way from her husband's death, but he had insisted. He wanted a policy payout to cover the children's education and for Sannie to live her life wherever she wanted. Even allowing for little Tommy to finish university, Sannie had calculated that she still had more than enough to buy a very nice house and to live comfortably for thirty years or more, without even taking into consideration her police pension, should she retire. However, that did not mean she would waste money. Also, the thought of a fixer-upper appealed to her as it would keep her busy outside of work hours.

'Why did you come back from Australia?' she asked him.

His demeanour changed. He looked at her with different eyes, which focused on her rather than the view beyond.

'How did you know that?'

'It's my job.' She saw the smallest hint of a smile. He was clean-shaven, she noticed; again, it didn't fit with the image of the dronkie working as a car guard to fuel his addiction.

He nodded. 'Now I know where I've seen you before – walking on the beach in Pennington. Everyone knows everyone there, so a new face always stands out.'

It was her turn to be surprised. Sannie cleared her throat. 'Let's get this over with, Mr Kruger.'

He waved a hand in the air. 'There must have been a dozen people with their phones out when the shooting started. Only in South Africa . . .'

'Tell me what happened, from the start.'

She took notes as Kruger relayed the events of the morning. He spoke slowly and concisely, giving her time to write. Twice, when she looked up from her notebook, she saw he had his eyes closed, as if reliving the events in his mind.

'I struck the one tsotsi with a piece of broken paver. Your forensic people will probably find it, with blood on it.'

'Were you behind him?'

He nodded. 'I was, but one of his tjommies alerted him. He turned and pointed his rifle – an AK-47 – at me.'

'And you attacked him with a broken paver?' She couldn't hide her incredulity.

'I'd just seen him load a fresh magazine, but he hadn't yet cocked the rifle – he couldn't have shot me.'

'You know weapons?'

He shrugged. 'I was in the army; conscripted, like everyone my age.'

Like nearly every white South African male around his age during the apartheid era, he meant. Her first husband, Christo, had served in the army, in Namibia as a conscript. Her friend Mia's father had suffered from PTSD as a result of his service in Angola, and had ended his own life. South Africa's Border War had a lasting legacy.

'Where did you serve?'

'Angola.'

'1 Parachute Battalion?'

Again, the micro-smile. 'That video went viral, did it?'

'You were conscripted, but you would have had to volunteer to join the Parabats.'

He shrugged. 'After basics I was sent to 7 SAI, 7 South African Infantry Battalion, at Phalaborwa. The 'Bats came in their maroon berets and gave us a talk, told us how proud we'd be if we were like them, how we could defend our country. I fell for it. I was young.'

Sannie checked her notebook, then his eyes, again. He talked down his service, but he would have joined the Parabats in search of action. 'You took the AK-47 from the man you assaulted with the broken paver?'

'Assaulted? There was a security guard bleeding out and a gun battle going on.'

'Watch your tone of voice, Mr Kruger. I'm just getting the facts.' He took a deep breath and settled himself.

'You shot a man.' She took notes as he told her how it unfolded; how he had said 'drop it' to the man with the pistol; the robber had then fired a shot at Adam, he said, and then Adam fired back, hitting him in the shoulder.

'Why did you wait until he fired first?' Sannie asked.

'I didn't want to kill him, nor be accused of murder. I hoped he would lose his nerve.'

'Yes, but in a case like that – you say he was pointing the pistol at you – you could have fired first.'

'He's young – he still has his life ahead of him, even if he spends some of it in jail.'

'And you? What about your life?' Sannie asked. He shrugged.

'I'll get this statement typed up, and then you need to sign it. We have several videos of the entire incident to go through.' She closed her notebook and slid it into the rear pocket of her shorts. 'We don't condone bystanders getting in the middle of gunfights, but that security officer who was shot in the neck probably owes you his life.'

'He lived?'

'Yes,' Sannie said. 'Last I heard, his condition was listed as serious but stable.'

He exhaled. 'Good.'

She could see he meant it.

'It was brave, what you did,' she said to him. 'Stupid, but brave.'

'Are we done, Captain?' he asked.

'You didn't tell me why you came back from Australia. I know it happens, sometimes, but once most people leave, they never return to Africa, except maybe on holidays. People say it's the rules, in Australia...'

'Why are you still in South Africa, Captain?'

She regretted lapsing into conversation with him. She should have kept it by the book, but he was not what she'd expected. In the Kruger Park, as head of the Stock Theft and Endangered Species Unit, she'd overseen crime scene investigations and preparation of dockets for prosecuting poachers; it had been a long time since she'd interviewed a suspect or a witness to a crime, especially a handsome one. And despite her joke, he had been brave.

'My kids are here. They're all studying and hopefully they'll find jobs locally. Some of my friends left for their kids to get a better education and have more opportunities. I don't begrudge them that.'

He nodded, lips pursed. His chest swelled as he drew a deep breath. He was holding something in.

He had deflected her question about why he had returned to South Africa, so she tried a different tack. 'Was that why you left South Africa? For your children?'

'Are you finished interviewing me, Captain?' he asked.

The blonde bartender came out. 'Do you want a Coke, Sharky? How about for madam?'

'I'm fine,' they both said in unison and the woman loitered in the doorway to the deck, either keeping a motherly eye on Adam, or eavesdropping.

'A Coke, not another beer?' Sannie asked.

'I limit myself these days.'

She wondered if that was because he didn't make much money guarding cars, or if he'd had a problem with alcohol in the past. And there was the nickname again. 'Sharky?'

The bartender spoke up. 'Hasn't Adam told you about his research?'

'No,' Sannie said. 'He's being the strong, silent type.'

The older woman came back to their table and picked up the empty quart. 'He's quite the expert on anything to do with sharks. He's studying for his doctor thingy, aren't you, Adam? You sure you won't have a drink, dear?'

Sannie smiled. 'OK. A Coke Zero, please.' She was intrigued – Mr Adam Kruger was more than a car park attendant and part-time dive-boat hand.

'Coming right up. Adam, I'll get you a sparkling water on the house, OK? I've just been watching the Facebook. Seems like you're quite the hero today.'

Adam rolled his eyes and the woman went back inside. 'Doctor thingy?' Sannie said.

'Doctorate.'

'As in PHD?'

He nodded. 'Unlikely, but yes.'

The bartender returned with their drinks. Sannie noticed that Adam's hands were shaking as he picked up his plastic bottle of water.

'Are you OK?' she asked.

He took a long drink. 'Fine.'

The breeze coming off the ocean brought some relief from the humidity and the sky was a beautiful, clear blue. It was lovely here, she thought, but it was impossible to escape the world beyond the edge of the beach, for either of them.

'You should maybe see a counsellor,' she said.

'Been there, done that,' he said.

So had she. Sannie had even enlisted the help of a traditional healer who lived near the Kruger Park and had gone through a cleansing ceremony to help her deal with her grief over the loss of Tom, her second husband. This taciturn man was a witness to and participant in a shooting incident. She should just take his statement and leave, but there was something vulnerable about him that made her linger, made her want to help him. She looked inside and saw that the bartender was keeping an eye on them as she wiped a glass. This Adam Kruger was a man of contrasts – the handsome middle-aged car park attendant living one step above a beggar; the 'town drunk' drinking cheap beer who was also a phd candidate; the shark researcher who was also a former paratrooper and trained soldier.

Sannie had not been with a man for two years. She had downloaded a dating app and signed up to Liefie, the Afrikaans online dating website, mostly at the urging of her daughter, Ilana. She had been out with four men: one didn't stop talking about himself; another barely said a word; a third, she strongly suspected, was married, and the last one had grabbed her breast and planted a kiss on her lips after dinner on their first and only date.

She didn't know if it was the bare torso or those oddly appealing eyes, but Adam Kruger was unsettling her.

Sannie stood up from the picnic table and picked up her unopened drink. It was unprofessional to continue to sit on the deck of a bar, socialising with a man she was interviewing in relation to a shooting incident – no matter how handsome or how troubled he was. She wondered if part of this strange attraction was due to him suffering; she was only just coming out of a period of grief herself.

Sannie paused a moment, but Kruger said nothing and nor did he give any indication that would have encouraged her to stay. Maybe he had been expecting to be treated like a hero for what he had done. If that was the case, he was wrong.

'Thank you for your time. I'll be in touch if we need anything else,' Sannie said.

Both of them turned their heads at the sound of a helicopter. A BK 117 in camouflage livery flew fast and low over the water, from the north, tracking the coastline.

Kruger watched the chopper fly past them but said nothing more. Sannie turned and walked into the bar and down the stairs, wondering what was going on in his mind.

4

SOUTH WEST AFRICA (MODERN-DAY NAMIBIA), 1987

Adam sweated in the shade of the hangar's tin roof at Ondangwa Air Force base. He lay on the concrete floor, which radiated heat from below, his head resting on a Rolled belt of 7.62-millimetre rounds for his machine gun.

Through half-open eyes he looked down across his chest to where an Alouette helicopter was swallowed by shimmering heat haze as the pilot touched down. He heard the rumble of a diesel engine and the grinding of gears and glanced to his right. A Land Rover had passed through the checkpoint and was heading their way. Bon Jovi's 'Livin' on a Prayer' was screeching out of Rossouw's radio cassette player.

Hennie and Rassie were sitting at a fold-out table playing cards, and Sergeant Greenaway looked up from the Wilbur Smith novel he was reading.

The Land Rover pulled up outside the open hangar door. Odd. Normally the calls for their Reaksie Mag – the proper name for what the Parabats called a fire force – to stand up came in via the radio, in the ops room attached to the hangar. It was unusual for them to receive a visitor. The Reaksie Mag was off limits; the reaction force needed to be ready to lift off at a moment's notice.

A tall, thin man got out of the front passenger seat. His sideburns beneath his beret were grey, his uniform was starched and his boots gleamed. He strode into the cavernous building, stopped and put his hands on his hips. 'Lieutenant Ferri!'

Tony Ferri scurried out of the operations room at the sound of his name, running his hands down the front of his uniform and smoothing his black hair out of his eyes. The young officer was an outsider, an REMF from 44 Parachute Brigade headquarters, who'd been dropped on them like bird shit when their regular platoon commander, Lieutenant Jooste, had taken ill with malaria. Jooste had been one of them, a troepie who'd been promoted from the ranks. Ferri, by contrast, was a rear echelon mother-fucker looking to squeeze some combat into his three-month tour in between shuffling papers at brigade headquarters. Frik Rossouw, the signaller from Benoni sitting behind Adam, said Ferri was a lawyer before his military service. Ferri had only been on one other mission with them so far, and nothing had happened. Ferri, Adam, Evan Litis, Luiz Siboa – one of the San trackers – and a reluctant Frank had posed for a photo afterwards at Ferri's insistence. He was excited to be on operations, but still untested in combat.

'Sir.' Ferri weaved his way between the sitting and lying Parabats.

Frank Greenaway put down his book, stood and went to intercept the two officers.

'Stay with your men, Sergeant,' the older officer said. 'Ferri, with me.'

Adam noted how Ferri quickened his step, like a puppy excited by a new game, and followed the older man, a colonel, outside. Sergeant Frank Greenaway stood where he'd been told to stop and watched the other two.

The colonel waved to the driver of the Land Rover and called some command the men in the hangar couldn't hear. Two soldiers climbed out of the back of the truck. They wore nutria-brown uniforms and South African webbing and carried older R1 rifles. Adam recognised them, as did the others. The San trackers, from the

31 Bushman Battalion, were sometimes attached to the Parabats when their particular skills were needed.

'The Siboa brothers,' Rossouw said. 'You know we going to find the shit with those two tracking for us.'

Evan Litis emerged from the latrine and came to Adam. 'What's going on, boet?'

'Not sure,' Adam said, but he started to stand and shrugged on his webbing.

On the tarmac outside the hangar Lieutenant Ferri saluted the colonel, who got back in his Land Rover. The driver started the engine and drove off.

Ferri strode in, his chest leading the way. 'A Bosbok's been shot down inside Angola, in FAPLA territory. Our mission is to find and rescue the two-man crew, and bring them back. The Puma will drop us two klicks from the crash site and we must patrol in and back out to a safe LZ. Let's move it!'

'A Bosbok?' Evan asked as they grabbed their weapons.

'Single-engine aircraft, used for spotting and forward air control. Not a bushbuck antelope, you idiot,' Frank Greenaway said as they ran across the tarmac towards a waiting Puma helicopter. 'And Busboys only carry a crew of one, a pilot.'

Frank had just contradicted their officer and Adam sensed the sergeant's annoyance – maybe at being excluded from the tarmac briefing. Adam's eyes briefly met Frank's once they had settled themselves in their assigned positions in the Puma. The sergeant was one of the ou manne, an old man with a beard and an emptiness in those eyes to prove it. He'd been on many operations before, and on this tour for nine months, as compared to Evan and Adam's two.

Frank gave Adam a thumbs up, but no smile. Adam nodded; everything was not lekker. Adam felt his stomach drop as the Puma lifted off. He smelled sweat and oil and the tang of something far more stringent, maybe disinfectant, as the metal skin of the cocoon vibrated around them. Adam sat in the open doorway of the chopper, his legs dangling outside, his LMG at the ready.

Evan leaned close to Adam and yelled into his ear, over the noise of the engine and rush of air. 'Who was that fucking leg officer who came to see the loot?'

The Parabat slang was already second nature to them; a 'leg' was anyone who walked, rather than jumped into battle: someone outside the parachute battalion.

'I think it was the sector commander, Colonel de Villiers,' Adam said. Another jam stealer who got the best rations and a soft bed.

'Weird how he drove all the way out to tell us an aircraft had just been shot down,' Evan said.

Adam nodded. Why hadn't such an urgent call come via radio? They crossed Oom Willie se Pad, Uncle Willie's Road, clearly visible below as the big Puma helicopter's shadow passed over it. The cutline through the parched bush that marked the border between South West Africa and Angola was as stark as a fresh scar on smooth young skin.

The LMG was heavy across Adam's knees. As the man carrying the stick's light machine gun he was ready to lay down covering fire if needed. Ferri had said the Bosbok had gone down behind the FAPLA lines, which meant the Angolan army would be in the area if they weren't already at the crash site. Adam looked around him. He saw eyes and teeth; the white Parabats' faces and the exposed skin of their hands and arms were covered in black-is-beautiful camouflage. Luiz, one of the two San trackers, grinned back at him. Luiz's brother Roberto sat next to him, unsmiling, staring out of the helicopter.

Ferri was up front, on a headset, crouching between and behind the two pilots, pointing through the windscreen.

Adam looked out over the endless mopane. He could barely remember the Indian Ocean. They came from different parts of South Africa, their military service their only common denominator. Adam's father was of Afrikaans heritage, but his family spoke English at their home in Natal because of his British-born mother. Evan, with his black curly hair, was from a family of Greek fishermen from Port Elizabeth. Frank had been studying nature conservation and wanted to be a game ranger in the Eastern Transvaal, in Kruger, after the war, but he said the army had suited him and he had transferred to the permanent force. Maybe it was the war that suited Frank, Adam wasn't sure. Rassie Erasmus, the ops medic from Potchefstroom, wanted to study medicine and be a doctor one day. Hennie Steyn, the corporal, a farmer's son from the Free State, was another of the ou manne. He had his brown army-issue scarf wrapped around his head as a sweat band.

The chopper tech, the crewman, pressed the talk switch on his radio intercom and nodded. He held up one finger, a signal they passed on to each other. One minute.

Adam felt the jolt of adrenaline, his body tense from his sphincter to his chest as the pilot took the Puma down. He held the wooden pistol grip on the Belgian-designed machine gun tighter, and scanned the bush.

'Go!' the crewman screamed.

Heart thumping in his chest, Adam jumped from the helicopter the moment the wheels touched down. He ran a few metres through brittle, dry grass, then dropped to one knee. He scanned the bush around him, ready to kill or die for the men clambering out of the Puma.

5

DUNE LODGE, KALAHARI DESERT, THE
PRESENT

Mia stood on a timber deck, under the shade of a Bedouin-style awning made of khaki-coloured ripstop canvas, outside the Dune Lodge dining area. The building was steel-framed but clad in canvas, to give guests the illusion of being in a large, tastefully appointed tent.

The deck wrapped around the main communal structure and a swimming pool glittered invitingly in front of Mia. Beyond that, the dunes stretched away to the horizon.

Her phone rang; she knew it was Julianne Clyde-Smith, her boss. Julianne's ever-efficient PA, Audrey Uren, had called earlier to arrange a time.

'Mia, how are you?' Julianne asked in her plummy British accent.

'Fine, and you?'

'Could be better. Have the police gone?'

As usual, Julianne was straight down to business, with minimal small talk. 'Yes.'

'Did the guests see what was going on?'

'No, fortunately it was just the four Americans in camp and they were off having their midday snooze when the detectives and forensic people got here. They're saying it's suicide.' Mia shuddered, remembering her father.

'How did he . . . ?'

Mia swallowed. 'Shot himself in the head, the one detective said. I didn't even know Luiz had a gun.'

'He didn't use one of our rifles?' Julianne asked.

'No.' The lodge had five .375 large-calibre rifles which the guides carried if guests went on walks, to protect them against dangerous game, as well as a Winchester 300 hunting rifle with a scope for animal control, and LM5 assault rifles and pistols for the antipoaching unit. 'A pistol – not one of ours.'

'How was he lately? Did he have any personal problems that you knew of? Was he depressed?'

The police had asked her all the same questions. 'Fine, and no, and no – but he wasn't the kind to share his feelings. His English wasn't great, but we were getting on very well. He taught me so much, Julianne . . .'

'I'm so sorry, Mia. I know how hard this must be for you. Especially for you. Sorry, I hope you know what I mean.'

Mia sniffed, but managed to keep her tears in check. 'It's OK, yes, thank you.'

Mia's father had killed himself in the same way, which Julianne knew. There had been no need for Mia to see Luiz's remains up close – his niece, Shirley, had identified the body – but just the thought of the way he had taken his life had shaken Mia and brought back terrible memories. In her mind she saw the streaks of red on the tiled floor of her home. Nokuthula had been too distraught to clean the house properly after her father's body had been taken away.

'Mia?'

'I'm here. I'm OK – well, as OK as can be expected.'

'Do you need some time?'

'My friend Sannie's coming to stay. I'm planning on using some bed nights for her and me.' All of Julianne's key staff had an allocation of 'bed nights', free accommodation they could use for themselves, family and friends as a perk of working for a lodge.

'Ah yes, of course, the irrepressible Captain van Rensburg. Give her my best. I hope you both have a lovely time and enjoy life on the other side of the lodge. I don't envy whoever your guide is, though.'

Mia forced a little laugh, for her employer's sake. 'I won't correct them; at least not until I'm back on duty.'

'Very good. I'm sorry, Mia. I've scheduled a call with Shirley so I've got to go. Please contact me if there's anything you need.'

'Thank you.'

Julianne was businesslike, even when being compassionate. Mia didn't doubt Julianne's sincerity, but communicating with staff in a time of crisis, like this, and making sure guests were shielded from the worst of it were as much about money and Tripadvisor ratings as they were about doing the right thing.

Mia sat down on a sun bed. She was very shaken, not just by the news, but by the way in which Luiz had taken his own life. She started to cry. Miriam, one of the hospitality staff, came over to her. 'I've brought you something to eat, Mia. Some fresh sushi, your favourite.'

Mia wiped her eyes and smiled, touched by the small gesture. She had not even asked. 'Thank you, Miriam. How are you?'

Miriam frowned. 'We're all sad. Everyone loved Luiz and he'd been here since the lodge opened, many years ago.'

'It's so terrible.' Mia took a bite of a sushi roll, for Miriam's sake, but found she wasn't hungry. 'Do you think he was having troubles?'

Miriam shook her head. 'No. You know, he was always laughing, playing little jokes on people, like the time he put boot polish in Mathias's socks. Mathias screamed so loud everyone in the staff quarters heard him.'

That was Luiz, from the little Mia knew of him after three months. He was much older than all the other guides and trackers, but still had the sparkle of a mischievous teenager in his eyes.

Mia guessed, however, that Luiz kept many secrets in his heart. She had tried to broach the subject of his military service with him, but he'd pretended not to understand. What she had learned had come from Shirley. Mia's father had served with San soldiers in

Angola and Mia had been keen to learn more about what Luiz had done.

Miriam went back to the kitchen, and Shirley walked slowly out onto the deck. 'Hi.'

Mia looked up. Shirley's hazel eyes were red-rimmed. She was beautiful, in her early thirties, her skin the colour of honey, her red-brown hair lustrously curled. She'd told Mia that her mother, Luiz's sister, had married a defrocked Irish priest. Mia had left that little detail out when briefing her guests. Both of Shirley's parents had passed away. Normally brimming with confidence and energy, Shirley now looked to Mia like her grief over Luiz had taken a physical toll on her.

'I just spoke to Julianne.' Shirley winced.

'Me as well. How are you feeling?' Mia thought Shirley had just reapplied her makeup, perhaps to cover the tracks of her tears.

'I cried, but mostly I feel numb. Tired. I just can't believe it, Mia.'

Mia stood up, went to Shirley and hugged her. 'Thanks,' Shirley said after a few moments.

'You want some food?' Mia gestured to her unfinished sushi. 'No, I'm fine. He didn't say anything to you, did he, Mia?'

'No, nothing about being sad. He just seemed the same as always.'

'Actually, I wasn't crying for Luiz.' Shirley ran her hands down the front of her uniform pants. 'At least, not yet. One of the cleaning staff went to his room this morning and found something terrible, which you're bound to hear about from someone.'

'What?'

Shirley looked around, then lowered her voice. 'I need you to come with me. I feel sick to my stomach. Also, you'll know what to do.'

'What is it?'

'I can't say.'

Shirley led and Mia followed, back through the dining and lounge area with its sofas, rugs and library of wildlife books, through the office and out into the sand. They took the path that meandered through the vehicle park, where the game viewers stood under carports made of poles and shade cloth, to the simple yet tasteful rooms that made up the staff quarters.

Shirley looked around again, making sure no one was in sight, then let herself into Luiz's room. 'He let me have his spare key – he was a genius in the desert, but he locked himself out a couple of times. He told me he never even knew what a lock was until he joined the army, and never got used to them.'

It was dark inside, a place of respite from the Kalahari and the sun. Luiz slept by choice on a thin mattress on the floor, no bed. His uniforms hung from a wooden rack, pressed and ready, his spare pair of boots polished.

Shirley went to the wardrobe in the corner. 'Open it.' She stood back.

Mia, her pulse quickening, brushed past Shirley in the confines of the small room and opened the door. She heard a scratching sound and saw that the wardrobe was empty apart from a wooden box. She shifted a jacket from the top and lifted the lid.

'Oh my word.' Mia put a hand over her mouth as she looked in and saw the scaly creature inside. 'A pangolin!'

'Shush,' Shirley said, and went back to the door, again casting her eyes left and right before closing it.

'What the hell do we do, Mia?'

Mia was speechless. This had happened to her once before, when she had first met Sannie van Rensburg, who had been investigating the disappearance of some teenaged girls from a village near the Kruger Park. A young man who Mia knew had been caught with a pangolin in his room, so this discovery felt eerily familiar. However, given that pangolins were probably the most trafficked animal in Africa, it probably wasn't all that surprising. She turned back to the cupboard, reached down into the box and lifted the pangolin out. The creature curled itself into a ball.

'Mia?'

'I'm thinking.' She nursed it. Mia knew that pangolins did not fare well in captivity; many died of dehydration when first taken by poachers. Was that what Luiz had been? A poacher?

'You knew nothing about this?' Shirley asked.

'No, of course not,' Mia said. 'This is totally illegal. I can't believe Luiz was involved in poaching.'

'My uncle was not a poacher.' Shirley put her hands on her hips. 'He loved wildlife and the desert. He played the clown, the practical joker sometimes, but he'd also been through trauma in his life; this was as close as he'd been to being happy the whole time I knew him. He loved it here, Mia. He wouldn't have done anything to mess up this job.'

Finding the pangolin in Luiz's room did not fit with anything Mia knew about the tracker, but she also knew there were good men and women in the Kruger Park and the neighbouring reserves, where she had worked as a guide, who had been corrupted by the large sums of money poaching gangs offered. There, in the Lowveld, the big money was in rhino poaching, but pangolins were also a very lucrative commodity in the illegal wildlife trade.

Mia inspected the pangolin, as fascinated with it as she was horrified by the prospect that Luiz may have been a poacher. 'Could he have wanted it for umuthi or something like that?'

'I doubt it,' Shirley said. 'There's nothing in our culture that says that pangolins have any magical powers, or that they're used for traditional medicines. It beats me why people want these things anyway.'

'People in Asia believe the scales help women who are breast-feeding to produce milk, and that they cure cancer and psoriasis. It's all unfounded nonsense.' Mia was not one to knock people's beliefs, but if they resulted in the decline or demise of a species or plant and there was no scientific basis to the claims, then it just made her mad. 'Pangolin meat is also an expensive delicacy in restaurants.'

'What do we do, Mia?'

'First off, we have to get this little guy back into the wild and eating as soon as possible, then we really need to get him to some experts I know in Askham.'

'What about my uncle? Do we need to tell the police?'

Mia had no idea. If Luiz had been involved in a crime, then the police really did need to know about it, but it would cast a pall over the lodge and ruin his reputation forever. Luiz, although a man of few words, had been the star of a number of online videos and advertisements commissioned by Julianne. She did not think her boss would be part of covering up a crime, but this would hurt her and the business, which was really only just coming back after COVID-19. 'I just don't know, Shirley. If he was trafficking this pangolin, I wonder who his contact was?'

'No idea,' Shirley said. 'Uncle Luiz rarely went back to Platfontein, because it's so far away, and as far as I knew he kept pretty much to himself.'

'What about family?'

'He had a wife and a child in Angola, when he was very young, but they were killed during the war. It was some kind of reprisal attack, which sometimes happened to the San because they supported the Portuguese.'

'That's terrible,' Mia said.

'Yes.' Shirley ran a hand through her hair. 'Even for those families who moved with their men to Namibia and then on to South Africa, life has been hard. Our community at Platfontein has plenty of problems – unemployment, violence, men disrespecting women and girls, and unwanted sex and pregnancies. We're working on it, but it's hard.'

'I see.'

Shirley looked at her for a few seconds and Mia couldn't help but wonder if Shirley was thinking to herself: Do you really?

'I grew up without a mom and my dad drank too much,' Mia said. 'I know what alcoholism can do to people, to communities.'

'I'm sorry, Mia,' Shirley said, 'I didn't mean to insinuate that you couldn't understand us. I guess every community has its problems.'

Mia gently set the pangolin back down in its box. 'What are you going to do with it?' Shirley asked.

'Sheesh, I really don't know, Shirley. I suppose we can just let it go into the wild, but if it's not well then maybe it needs some care first. I'll call a pangolin researcher I know and just make some general inquiries; I won't say Luiz was involved.'

'We don't know that Luiz was involved,' Shirley shot back.

'Sorry,' Mia said, but privately she felt the evidence did not look good. 'Maybe we can check his things, see if maybe there was some reason he had the pangolin. Maybe he left a note?'

Even though she had seen his body briefly, the reality that Luiz was gone suddenly hit her. She knew what Shirley would be going through now, asking herself why Luiz had done what he did. Her father had left no note.

'You're right, Mia.' Shirley started to look through Luiz's clothes, checking the pockets of the shirts and a couple of fleeces – it could be bitingly cold in the Kalahari at night, and on early-morning and evening drives – but finding nothing. She checked a small bedside table with three drawers and Mia looked over her shoulder, still uncomfortable about going through the dead man's possessions.

Mia saw a bible on Luiz's bedside table. Shirley picked it up and leafed through it; the text was in Portuguese. Then a picture fell out. Shirley retrieved it from the ground.

'Who's that?' Mia asked, looking at the woman in the small black-and-white photo.

'His wife, my late aunt, Maria. I think he loved her very much.' It was so sad, Mia thought. Shirley opened the three bedside drawers. She checked through Luiz's shorts, again finding nothing in the pockets. In the second drawer were some traditional clothes, including a jackal-skin kaross, which was worn around the waist. Mia felt her cheeks turn red at this intrusion not only into Luiz's privacy, but also his core beliefs.

Shirley bent and looked under the bed, then got down on all fours and reached underneath. She slid out a black metal trunk, then sat on the bed and opened the tin box's lid. 'Army stuff, by the look of it.'

Mia shifted the trunk across the floor so she could get a better look, then sat down on the bed next to Shirley. This was actually of interest to her. She'd asked Luiz about his time in the old South African Defence Force, because she remembered her father talking about the 'Bushmen' soldiers and telling her what amazing trackers they were. It was the stories of some of their feats, which she'd over-heard as a child during some of her father's drinking sessions with old army friends, that had partly kindled her own fascination with tracking.

She sighed. She'd hoped to learn so much from Luiz and while he had shown her a trick or two, such as tracking snakes and lizards in the sand by looking for the disturbances caused by their under-ground burrowing, he had been reluctant to engage in long conversa-tions with her. She had hoped that asking him about his military service, in the light of her father's own time in the army, would help break the ice, but she now thought that it was at precisely that point that Luiz had really clammed up.

Mia caught a whiff of mouldy canvas as Shirley reached into the trunk and took out two old ammunition pouches, a belt and a bonnet hat.

'I've never seen any of this stuff.' Shirley lifted out a handful of photos, mostly faded colour images with white borders. There were a few monochrome prints and these, like the picture of Luiz's wife, were smaller. 'This is amazing.'

Shirley handed the pictures to Mia one at a time as she finished studying them.

'This must be him when he first joined the Portuguese army, in Angola,' Shirley said.

Mia looked at the image.

She could see it was Luiz, but he looked so young. He was in a camouflage uniform and though the picture was black and white, she could see that the bonnet he wore, at a jaunty angle, was of the same pattern as the hat from the trunk. There was another young San man with him.

'He's just a boy,' Shirley said. 'And that's my mother's other brother, Roberto, with him. He died in the war.'

Luiz looked no more than sixteen or seventeen and he carried a G3 rifle, which Mia knew had been used by the Portuguese. Roberto could have been a couple of years older, but it was hard to tell. Mia turned over the picture; written on the back was 'Flechas 1972'. Mia didn't want to say anything, but she had read quite a bit online and bought a book about the South African Defence Force's Bushman Battalions. The book pointed out that when the San had fought for the Portuguese in Angola, they had been devastatingly effective – the word 'ruthless' was also used.

The next picture Shirley handed Mia was in colour and showed Luiz and another San man in a plain brown uniform – Mia recognised it as typical of the old South African Defence Force, which had changed its name to 'national' defence force after the end of the apartheid era. In this image, Luiz wore a different hat, a type of bonnet similar to those Mia had seen worn by pipers in bagpipe bands.

Luiz had swapped his G3 for a South African R1, the same rifle her father had carried in the Bush War. Mia thought the men in this picture, Luiz and Roberto, had been staged. They were in the bush, walking along, half looking at the ground as though they were tracking, though their uniforms looked starched and clean, as if the men had just come off a parade ground. She doubted they would have worn the impractical bonnets in the field.

South Africa had made much of the use of Bushmen at the time; her father had told her that politicians and journalists would often visit the Bushmen Battalions on guided tours, to reinforce a message that the SADF was not fighting a war based on race, but one of good versus evil, democracy against communism. She had read that the San had been mistreated and enslaved by some of the other African tribes in Angola, which had made them easy converts to the Portuguese cause. Likewise, they did not like the Ovambo, who made up the majority of the Namibian independence fighters in SWAPO, the South West Africa People's Organisation, and its military wing, PLAN.

Men such as Luiz had been at war for a decade or more in the seventies and eighties, uprooted from their traditional lands and unable to return, given the shifts in world politics.

'Oh, my word,' said Shirley, who never took the Lord's name in vain, even when she was shocked.

She handed Mia a picture but showed her the reverse of the photo instead of the image. On the back was written: Luiz, Lt Ferri, Litis, Kruger, Sgt Greenaway.

Mia felt an invisible hand grip her heart. When she turned the picture over, she saw her father.

6

Adam stared out over the Indian Ocean. The boat bobbed in the vast emptiness, above the Aliwal Shoal, five kilometres off the KwaZulu-Natal Coast. The only sound, for now was the gentle slap of the water against the hull.

Somewhere across the ocean were the wife and children he had left behind.

'You can almost see Australia on a day like today,' Bruce said. Bruce Kirkwood was a cane farmer from Mtubatuba, who also had a big house in Pennington with panoramic ocean views. When he was at the coast, which was as often as possible, Bruce was happy to supply his boat and fuel to help Adam's research, or take him along when he took his friends fishing. Today it was just the two of them.

Adam wondered if Bruce could read his mind, or had just picked up on the way he'd been gazing out to sea.

'How are your kids doing?' Bruce asked.

Bruce liked to talk when he fished, whereas Adam preferred peace and quiet. This was the price, however, of having a magnanimous friend and unofficial patron who supported Adam's research. 'Ja, OK. Phillip's nearly ready to graduate law and Jolene's studying to be a teacher.'

'Ah, yes, I remember you saying your kids were studying.'

Adam had two rods sitting in holders, baited and ready. On the horizon, where he'd been staring, he saw a dark speck. He went into the wheelhouse and fetched Bruce's binoculars. When he returned to his position he checked the tension on the lines – still nothing – and focused on where he'd seen the object.

'Another fisherman?' Bruce asked.

Adam nodded as he held the focus. 'Looks like.' He adjusted and saw that the other vessel was coming towards them. The superstructure was distinctive.

'Renshaw,' Adam said. He gripped the binoculars tighter as he stared.

'We're not the Sea Shepherd, Adam.' Bruce tried a laugh. 'I'm not going to ram him, at least not with my boat, boet.'

Adam said nothing, but felt his blood boil as he saw someone at the back of the boat slopping out bloodied fish guts and offal. 'He's chumming,' Adam said eventually. 'Looking for sharks. Bastard.'

Adam saw a glint of sun on glass and shifted his gaze slightly. Someone else, standing behind the wheel of the other boat, was now looking at him.

In his peripheral vision Adam saw one of his fishing rods jerk. He put down the binoculars just as he registered the other boat changing course, then darted to the rod and hauled it out of its holder. From the immediate pull he knew it was a big fish. Adam adjusted the drag and started to reel in the line.

Thirty metres out, Adam saw an overly long fin break the surface. His heart pounded. 'Yes! It's a guitarfish, Bruce! Get the sling and gaffer ready.'

Bruce picked up the gaffer hook and came to Adam's side. 'Sure, he's a big one. Looks like a big bladdy stingray with a shark's fin.'

'That's pretty much what he is.' Adam hauled on the rod and reeled in the slack. This was why he was here, his purpose; he could not lose this shark. Adam could see the big fish clearly now, maybe two and a half metres long, its sandy-brown skin peppered with white dots.

Bruce hooked the hefty shark under its gill and managed to hold it more or less steady against the side of the boat as Adam stowed the rod again, leaned over and slid the nylon sling under the fish's sleek body. He secured the sling.

'Got you!' Adam set to work quickly but methodically. He went to his stash of research gear and took up his popper, a small spear gun with a GPS tracking device already loaded. He leaned over the gunwale again and held the device against the shark's thick, fleshy fin then pulled the trigger.

'Bloody amazing,' Bruce said. 'That will allow you to, what, monitor it on your computer?'

'Exactly,' Adam said. Next he took up a pair of clippers and cut a small piece of skin out of the fin. 'This biopsy will go into our gene bank,' he said to Bruce as he put the sample into a ziplock bag.

'What the fok . . . Hey!'

Adam looked up to see Bruce waving. Beyond him, looming in size and bulk was the boat that had been heading towards them, the name Sea Predator and a sea star logo painted on the side. It was, as he'd suspected, Renshaw's boat.

'What the hell's he doing?' Bruce said. 'Back off, man!'

Adam reached over again to start the process of releasing the guitarfish. He would have loved to just sit there for a moment and take in the simple wonder of this sleek, perfect creature, but he also knew that every second the shark was held captive was a risk to its wellbeing.

Adam assumed Renshaw was just coming to see what they were doing, or to hurl some abuse at him. He worked on the knot securing the sling.

'Fokof!' Bruce yelled this time.

Adam glanced up again to see the bow of Renshaw's boat coming towards them. The other skipper was grinning, and Adam could see the can of Windhoek Lager raised in Renshaw's hand in a mock salute. Renshaw spun the wheel of his vessel hard to starboard and his big cruiser turned.

Adam knew what was about to happen, and braced himself for

the bow wave that hit them broadside, but Bruce chose that moment to stand and give Renshaw the finger. Bruce lost his footing as spray washed over them, soaking them, and he slammed into Adam and sent him over the railing into the water. Renshaw's crewman, a scarred-faced man named Jaapie, laughed as he tipped a bucket of offal over the back of the departing cruiser. The water around Adam was dyed red and smelled of rotten fish. 'Adam!'

'I'm fine, Bruce.' Adam trod water next to the guitarfish, careful to keep his hand away from the shark's mouth. The big creature didn't have the wickedly angled teeth of a great white, but its crushing plates were made to pulverise crayfish or crabs and could do some damage. Gingerly, Adam reached for the big hook that had landed the fish.

'No, behind you!' Bruce called. 'Shark!'

Adam shot his head around and saw the dark grey-coloured fin of a bull shark knifing through the water. Unlike the guitarfish, this was a killer of humans, no doubt attracted by the combination of the swirling chum and the thrashing creature tied to the boat.

Adam reached down to his right calf and unsheathed his diving knife. He slashed the fishing line attached to the hook and then the cord securing the sling to the boat. The guitarfish rewarded his kindness with a slap in his face from its tailfin as it dived for the cover of the deep.

Bruce was reaching down for him, but the bull shark changed its course from the disappearing guitarfish to Adam with a minute correction. Adam knew that if he took Bruce's offered hand there was no way the other man could pull him out of the water in time. He turned in the water, knife hand up and braced for impact. The bull shark slammed into him with the force of a motor scooter hitting a pedestrian and he felt pain in his chest. Adam was ready for the blow, however, and slammed his fist down on the shark's nose.

Adam glimpsed teeth as the shark turned, mouth open, then seemed to spin in the water as it readied for another attack. Adam reversed the big stainless-steel knife in his hand and drove the point down into the shark's nose this time. The shark dived, not mortally wounded but deterred. Adam reached for Bruce, who hauled him up and back on board.

'That was crazy, even for a man who spends too much time in the water with those things.'

Adam sat on the deck, his back against the railing, chest heaving. He said nothing but his heart was thumping.

'Hell, Adam, that thing nearly killed you. How did you know to punch it? I've heard of surfers doing that, but I didn't think it would actually work.'

Adam shook his head. 'I wasn't sure either. A shark . . .' he gasped for air, '. . . Has a complex network of neuromast cells all linked together in its nose – they're called the ampullae of Lorenzini. They help the shark sense what's in the water and make the nose incredibly sensitive. It was . . . It was worth a shot.' He wiped seawater from his face and coughed.

'Check, Adam! You're bleeding, man.'

'I'm fine, Bruce.' Adam looked at the gash in his wetsuit and inspected it. There was blood, but the wound wasn't serious; he felt no pain at all, though he knew that would come later. For now, he just felt good that he'd managed to tag a rare specimen and do his job.

Adam felt light-headed.

'You OK?' Bruce asked. 'I'll get you some water.' He fished a bottle from the cooler box, unscrewed the cap and handed it to Adam.

Adam drank greedily, looking up as he downed the contents of the bottle. The sky, he noticed, was the most vivid blue he could recall seeing in a long time. He smelled the salt in the air.

'You're grinning like a madman, Adam.' Bruce shook his head.

What the fuck, Adam said to himself. I'm alive.

As Adam sat there, Bruce climbed upstairs to the bridge and started the boat's engines. Adam felt the vibration through his body; it reminded him of riding in a chopper, where his whole being seemed to throb in time to his heartbeat as they flew towards another contact, another battle in Angola or South West, where any of them might be killed or wounded.

He'd thought he would never feel as alive as he had during the war. It was crazy, a paradox, that one could feel so fulfilled, so in touch with life, when death was all around. He had gone into battle with men to whom he had entrusted his life, knowing they felt the same about him. It had been like that, just now; Adam had known Bruce was there, that he would pull him from the water if he was mauled.

Bruce reeled in their lines and set the boat on its course, heading back to Rocky Bay. Then he came downstairs to where Adam was still sitting on the deck, recovering.

Bruce went to the cooler box again and opened it. 'You need a beer after what you went through just now.'

Adam shook his head. 'I'll take a Coke or a Stoney if you've got one.'

Bruce opened his eyes and mouth wide in a theatrical double take. 'You, saying no to a beer?'

'I'm working this afternoon.'

'At the car park?'

'Yes,' Adam said.

'Why?' Bruce handed Adam a can of ginger beer and opened a Long Tom of Castle Lite for himself.

Just the sound of the pfft of the gas escaping the silver can made Adam's mouth water. He licked his lips, wondering if he could tell Bruce the truth.

'Are you all right, China? Do you need a loan?' Bruce asked.

Adam shook his head. 'I work at the mall to earn a few rand, for food and a couple of beers. It keeps me honest, Bruce. I get money, from the university in Australia I'm doing my phd through, but I've been sending nearly all of that back to Oz to support the kids. If I didn't work, I wouldn't send all the money, and I'd just sit in the boat club and drink.'

Bruce raised his can and took a sip. 'I'm not sure I understand you, Adam, but you're a good man. I like what you're doing for the sharks. Is that why, when I offered you some money to help with your research, you said no?'

'Yes.' Adam opened the cool drink and took a long sip. 'I would have just pissed your money away. This way, I have to be accountable. If I want a drink, I need to earn it.'

Bruce nodded. 'I heard about the shootout in the car park yesterday. That was hectic, even for South Africa. Are you OK?'

'Yes,' Adam said.

'I never saw action, in the army. I spent most of my time in the townships. You've nearly been killed twice in two days.'

'That must have been hard,' Adam said, 'having to deal with our own people, other South Africans.'

Bruce shrugged. He went back upstairs to the helm. Adam looked out over the water again. Sometimes he wished he could live at sea, and never go back to shore. With the coastline in sight, Adam's phone beeped from his dive bag.

He found it and checked the screen. It was a message from Evan Litis. He hadn't heard from Evan in maybe five or six years, when Evan had come looking for him, before he moved to Australia. Adam had ignored Evan's last approach, and was not even sure how he'd found his number, but this was different.

Luiz is dead. Killed himself.

Bruce came downstairs again. 'Forgot my beer.' Adam looked at his friend.

'Sheesh, Adam, you look like you're going to be seasick for the first time since I met you.'

SANNIE WALKED along Pennington Beach late that afternoon. She was between the raised timber viewing deck in front of the café and the tidal pool when she saw Adam Kruger emerge from the surf further south.

As she came closer, she saw that his daypack, running shirt and shoes were on the beach.

He ran a hand through his wet hair as she approached him. 'Captain van Rensburg. Is this an official interview again?'

'No, I was just out for a walk.' He really was in very good shape. She needed to start running again. 'Good news. I spoke to my boss today, and she says there's no need for any further action in regards to you shooting that suspect, though we will need to call you as a witness for the prosecution if he pleads not guilty.'

'Of course.' He picked up his T-shirt and shrugged it on. 'How goes the house-hunting?'

'Who says I'm looking for a house?' she said.

He smiled. 'When I first told you the address of my place you asked if it was for sale. Who asks that? I'm guessing you've been talking to Pam, and that she probably told you about me coming back from Australia and taking my folks' house off the market.'

'Guilty.' He was clever, observant. 'I'm taking my time. And I'm off on leave soon.'

'Going away?'

'Yes, the Kgalagadi.'

'Really?'

Sannie noticed how Kruger looked instantly alert and engaged. When she had interviewed him at the boat club, he'd seemed distant much of the time, as if his mind was in another place, or another time.

'You know it – the Kgalagadi?' she said, of the Transfrontier Park that spanned the Kalahari Desert on both sides of the South Africa–Botswana border.

'Um, no, not really . . . It's just that I have – had – a friend who worked near there.'

'Me as well,' Sannie said. 'Mine's a guide. You said "had"?' He picked up his running shoes and cast his eyes away from her. 'I should get home. Thank you for letting me know, about the case.'

'I'm heading in the same direction,' Sannie said. As he started to walk, she stayed in step with him.

'My friend . . .' He glanced over at her, briefly, 'he was a San tracker, working for a larney place, called Dune something.'

'Dune Lodge?' Sannie said.

'Yes, that's the one,' he said. 'Do you know it?'

'My friend works at the same place. Maybe she knows your friend.'

Adam looked at her again. 'He killed himself.'

'Oh. Shame, I'm so sorry to hear that. Did you know he was troubled?'

He looked straight ahead and Sannie worked harder to keep up with him in the soft sand. 'We're all troubled, sometimes, but, no, I didn't know that Luiz was particularly worried. Of all of us, he always seemed the most resilient, the least concerned about the things we saw.'

'In Angola?' she asked.

The tide was going out and, mercifully, Adam steered back to the firm, wet sand on the edge of the waterline. His stride was long, and though she was not short, she still had to step out.

'Yes. My friend, Luiz, was a member of 31 Battalion.'

'One of the San who fought for the old South African army?'

'Yes,' he said.

The setting, the light from the sunset, the temperature were all beautiful, but as happened so often in her world, the talk was of death and loss. 'I remember reading somewhere, in a newspaper, that life is tough for the San communities, away from their traditional lands and ways.'

'Luiz had a job, and unlike the rest of us he didn't drink.'

'The rest of you, Mr Kruger?'

'Call me Adam, if you like. A lot of veterans have struggled with alcoholism. Not me – at least not lately.'

The same was true of police officers. 'My first husband used to talk about you guys, the Parabats – I think with some admiration, maybe even longing.'

'First husband?'

'Long story,' Sannie said. 'But I want to hear yours first. You were saying, about Luiz? Sorry for interrupting.'

'We were used in a fire force role, responding to contacts with the enemy in South West and Angola. We mostly flew in choppers, or drove out in Buffels.'

'The troop carriers?'

He nodded. 'Anyway, we worked with the 31 Battalion guys, the

San, from time to time, and we had our favourites. We went on several patrols with Luiz, and his brother, Roberto. We got to know them – that is, the guys from my section and me.' He started to trail off again, and looked out to sea.

'And you stayed in touch . . . ?'

He nodded. 'We try – a few of us, at least. Or should I say, we tried. We put the word out to help as many of the San as possible find jobs. There's a colonel who keeps in contact with the community and helps with some upliftment programs. All of us moved on, though.'

'You went to Australia,' she said.

He looked at her again, although this time she saw the hint of a smile. 'Yes, but you ask a lot of questions, even for a cop . . .'

'Oh. Susan,' she said. 'Sannie.' He put out his hand.

It still felt funny, after COVID-19, shaking hands with a stranger, but she took his. It was cool, from the sea, but not cold. 'Nice to meet you. I hope you find a house here, and find some peace,' he said.

'Who says I'm looking for peace?'

'People come to the south coast to retire, mostly, or maybe to get away. You're not old enough to go on pension yet. For sure you didn't come here to bust hijackers or murderers.'

Sannie laughed. 'You're taking care of that, at the mall.'

'That was a one-off, trust me. The local newspaper's still fishing around for follow-up stories.'

Sannie watched the waves breaking on the rocks further south on Umdoni Point, the spray flying high into the air. 'But, yes, I'm looking for a change. I remarried . . .'

They walked on, and he said nothing. Sannie cursed herself, silently, for opening up so soon. She hardly knew this strange, handsome man.

'Where's your husband?'

There was the cleverness again, asking an open-ended question that she couldn't blunt with a yes or no answer.

'He died, in Iraq. He was also a policeman, in England, but he moved to South Africa to be with me, then he felt like he needed to do more, to earn more money to provide for us. He got a job as a contract bodyguard for diplomats and vips. He was killed in a rocket strike in Baghdad.'

Adam said nothing as they walked on. There was just the background noise of waves breaking and their feet squeaking in the sand. 'Was he happy, do you think, doing that work?' Adam asked.

Most people just said 'sorry for your loss' at that point, but he had asked a good question. 'I think that it was more than the money. "Happy" may not be the right word, but he felt like what he was doing was worth it, protecting people.'

Adam looked at his feet. 'He sounds like a good man, Sannie.' She'd invited him to use her first name, but it was weird, hearing it, from a man walking next to her. He sounded like he meant what he said. 'He was. We had a son, the two of us. And I have two other children from my first marriage, a boy and a girl.'

'My son and daughter are in Australia.'

'You must miss them,' Sannie said. All of her children lived away from her now, and while Sannie would not want to do anything to limit their horizons or opportunities, she did not want to think of them moving overseas.

'I do,' he said. 'Every day, but they were supportive of me coming back to South Africa.'

'I felt bad,' Sannie said, 'not trying to stop Tom from going to Iraq. We could have survived on the money I made, and Tom was also working part-time as a safari guide in the Kruger Park. The money wasn't great, but he loved the work. When he was killed, I felt guilty for a long time that I didn't force him to stay.'

He looked at her again, that penetrating gaze from those striking eyes. 'It's not love if you have to force someone to do something.'

She thought he was speaking from experience, but she let it rest. 'Your friend, Luiz,' she asked, 'will you go to his funeral?'

Adam sighed. 'It's a long way, and I don't have a car.'

'But you'd like to go?'

'Yes. Although I think that if I take a taxi to Durban and get a bus from there across the country to the Northern Cape, I won't make it in time.'

'You can't fly?'

'The money I make as a car guard isn't that good.'

'I'm sorry.' She looked at him and saw the grin spreading across his face. Sannie laughed.

They reached a rocky part of the beach where the waves broke further out against a sandbank or submerged reef. There were tidal pools among the fissured granite formations. A fisherman, a hundred metres further on, cast out into the surf.

Adam pointed to a gap in the lush green vegetation on the fringe of the rocks. 'I live through there.'

Sannie stopped, hands on hips, pleasantly tired. 'I usually turn around here.'

They looked at each other for a few moments. She was reluctant to head back to her flat so soon, and she wanted to know more about him.

'Would you like to come up for a cup of coffee?' he asked. 'I'm afraid it's Ricoffy.'

She gave herself a brief moment to change her mind. 'I'd love a cup. It'll remind me of my oupa. It's all he used to drink.'

They walked through the band of jungle-like greenery, a tangle of palms and vines and wild bananas that fringed the coastline behind the beach. He asked her where she had come from and she told him a little of her story, and about her last job, in the Kruger Park. Walking behind him, Sannie's eyes were drawn to the muscles in Adam's back, where his thin wet T-shirt clung to his skin.

She felt a pang of guilt; she'd been talking about Tom and here she was inspecting another man's body. She blushed, and was glad the path through the dense vegetation was too narrow for Adam to be alongside her, where he might see her face. Maybe she should make an excuse to turn back.

They emerged at the single-track railway line and crossed it, to Botha Place. These were nice houses, a mix of newer, two-storey places, and older cottages that had been renovated. Off to the left was a modern, fenced estate called Umdoni Point. There the land rose steeply; new houses and two-storey maisonettes of near-identical designs looked out over the ocean. A troop of a dozen curious vervet monkeys stopped their afternoon foraging patrol to watch the two humans.

'Won't you miss the Kruger Park?' Adam said, glancing over his shoulder as she caught up to him.

'I don't know,' Sannie said. 'I saw so many terrible things there. I worked serious and violent crimes for a while, in Nelspruit, but there's something especially tragic about seeing the carcasses of dead rhinos. Such magnificent animals, killed purely for greed, for nothing.' She wanted to add that it was like seeing a dead child, but filtered herself.

'I hear you. I'm sickened by what some people will do to satisfy their vanity. It's the same with many marine species, which are being wiped out so some rich guy can show off to his friends,' Adam said.

They came to the house she had seen on one of her first tours with Pam, the real estate agent. Sannie walked up a garden path of cracked concrete pavers, wondering just what it was she was doing.

7

Outside, the place was a wreck, just as she remembered it. The plastered facade was cracked and had fallen away in places, and the remains of the tin roof over the stoep sat in the front garden like the twisted wreckage of a crashed aircraft. The gutters were sprouting grass and the garden was nearly as wild as the strip of jungle they had just passed through across the road.

Adam led Sannie up the stairs and pushed and kicked a door, swollen with damp, until it screeched open.

Inside was different. She smelled fresh sawdust and her eye was drawn to the pale floorboards, stripped of carpet and sanded back to their natural finish. The timber glowed golden in the slanting rays of the late-afternoon sun, streaming in through the curtainless kitchen window. The walls of what would probably be the living room had been painted a pale grey and the windowsills were in a contrasting dark blue.

Adam walked through a dividing wall of plastic sheeting which he held open for Sannie. The kitchen was clearly original, perhaps from the 1970s. Sannie shuddered. The chipboard cupboards were swollen, with doors hanging askew or missing, and the old linoleum floor covering was stained and torn. Adam used a match to light a

camping gas hob and put a battered saucepan of water on the flame
to boil. He blew dust out of a chipped mug and set it next to another.
Sannie saw a bag of pap, mealie meal, sitting on the worn benchtop.
A rusting fridge rattled in a corner.

'Come through, while the water boils,' he said.

Adam held open another piece of sheeting and Sannie once again
found herself in a different house.

'This was one of the bedrooms, originally,' he said, 'but I've made
it my library and office.'

Through a picture window, beyond a gnarled umdoni – a water-
berry tree – she could see the ocean, dappled with golden sunlight.
Across the hallway she could see into a bathroom, with an old,
cracked basin and a grubby shower with a mouldy plastic curtain.
Sannie returned her attention to Adam's office. She ran her finger
along a row of books sitting in built-in shelving that filled two entire
walls and looked new. 'Did you make all these shelves yourself?'

He nodded. 'I can barely afford the timber, so I only use labour if
it's something I absolutely can't do on my own.'

She looked at the spines of the books. 'Marine biology, sharks,
whales, seahorses . . .'

'I had boxes of books from my varsity days. Fortunately, my mom
kept them all. I thought she might have given them away to the
hospice shop or sold them.'

Sannie's eyes kept roving. There was fiction, including some Deon
Meyer, which she loved, and a shelf of books devoted to the Border
War, in Angola and South West Africa. There were also cookbooks
and others on gardening and home design.

'You're making me feel self-conscious now,' he said. 'You can tell a
lot about a person from their bookshelf.'

He left, to check on the water. Sannie looked around some more.
The furniture was old, but she could tell that Adam had been renovating and re-purposing it, and the paint colours were just like the
other work-in-progress room, blues, greys and whites. In the library-
cum-office, the bare floorboards shone with coats of varnish. The
Apple laptop sat on a roll-top desk, which had also been lovingly

restored. The computer was probably the most expensive thing in the house.

On the desktop were more books, mostly on sharks, and print-outs. She picked up a piece of paper and saw that it was a draft of a thesis. Adam walked in.

'Sorry,' she said.

'No problem.' He set down a cup of coffee for her on the desk and she replaced the paper. 'You might be the only person other than my supervisor who will ever read that.'

What was interesting was that he had spent much of his time and energy, and presumably his limited savings and income, setting up his study space, before tackling rooms that other people might have considered a priority, such as the kitchen or bathroom.

'Take a seat.' He gestured to a leather armchair, well worn but perfectly at home among the books.

'Guitarfish?' she said, remembering the cover page of the thesis. She blew on her coffee.

'It's actually a type of ray, but looks like a flat shark. They're facing extinction.'

'Am I allowed to ask what the thesis is about?' She sipped the coffee. It wasn't what she drank these days, but the smell and taste did remind her of her childhood, and made her smile.

'I'm looking at new ways to track shark fin. Finning's a huge crime, but it doesn't get nearly the same amount of publicity as rhino poaching.' He paused. 'Oh, sorry.'

'Why?' She realised he was referring to her last job. 'Oh, no need to apologise. Even when it comes to rhinos we didn't get enough money, although the Kruger and other people involved in anti-poaching and conservation do get a lot of funding from overseas donors. But, yes, I know what you mean. There are so many priorities in this country for tackling crime that it feels like there's never enough money. You should see the state of our police stations.'

He nodded. 'I have.'

Her guard went up. 'You've had dealings with the police?'

He looked up from his cup. 'It's embarrassing.'

She wished neither of them had said anything. Sannie sighed inwardly. She'd ended up in the home of a criminal.

'No, no.' He'd read her face and held up a hand like a stop signal. 'I was the victim of a crime, but it's so stupid I almost don't want to tell you.'

She smiled, relieved. 'I've seen and heard it all.'

He nodded. 'After the divorce, which was amicable, we sold our house in Australia and split the proceeds. We got a good price for it. I still needed to keep aside money for the kids, especially as I was going back to university so I wouldn't be earning much. I came back to South Africa because I missed it, but also because property's much more affordable than in Australia. I had enough to buy a nice house here, on the coast, and still have money left over.' He drew a breath.

'What happened?' She sipped her coffee.

'You think that fraud and that sort of thing only happens to idiots, or elderly people who are maybe getting a little confused.'

'Oh, no,' Sannie said.

'Oh, yes. Somehow, someone's email was hacked – either mine, the estate agent's, the seller or the attorney the owner of the house was using. The con artists were intercepting all our messages and had set up a fake Gmail account that looked almost the same as mine. They set up false versions of the conveyancer's emails and were passing on all the documentation to me, and reading all of our messages to each other.'

'And let me guess,' Sannie said, because she already knew the answer, 'they sent their bank account details on the lawyer's office's letterhead, even with a so-called proof of account from the bank.'

'Yes.'

'Adam, you can at least rest assured that you're not the only person in South Africa this has happened to. It's becoming more and more common.'

He set down his cup. 'Ja, thanks. I googled it soon after it happened. It wasn't much comfort, but at least it wasn't just me. I lost everything, the whole purchase price. The problem, it seems, is that we're all so used to doing everything via email that people don't pick up the phone and talk to each other anymore, to check things like bank account numbers.'

Her heart went out to him. She could not imagine losing that much money, but she knew it happened. 'They didn't get any of it back?'

Adam shook his head. 'I felt like such a fool.'

'These people are very clever; experts, you could say,' she said. It was true. 'It's a whole profession. In Nigeria they call the hackers the Yahoo Boys.'

He shrugged. 'So, now I'm living on a university stipend, guarding cars, trying to finish my thesis and renovating my folks' old home. What money I had left over from the divorce settlement in Australia is now paying for the kids' university studies in Australia. I'm meeting my commitments, and I have a leaky roof over my head, but I feel like such a failure sometimes.'

'Don't,' Sannie said. 'If you had a friend who'd been in the same situation, had the same thing happen to them, what would you say to them?'

He laughed. 'You sound like my shrink, when I could still afford one.'

Sannie felt her cheeks colour. It was something her own therapist had said to her, when Sannie told her that she felt responsible for Tom's death, because she hadn't tried harder to discourage him from working in Iraq. Sannie's answer was that Tom enjoyed the work, and was doing it for the family, and that he was an adult, capable of making his own decisions.

'Sorry,' he said.

She shrugged. 'I had some therapy. You said "when you could still afford one". Was that before the real estate scam?'

'Yes. In Australia. I was having a rough time, before the marriage breakup. It was probably all part of it. Nothing to worry about now, I'm all fixed.'

She doubted that, by the way he looked away from her, out towards the ocean again, but she didn't push it. They had covered an awful lot of ground over just half a cup of coffee, she thought. 'I'm sure this house will be beautiful when you finish,' she said. 'You've done a lovely job in here.'

He looked at her. 'Thanks.'

She glanced at her watch. She should probably leave, but she didn't want to go back to her flat and watch TV, or wait for a Zoom call from Ilana or the boys, who all probably had more important things to do. 'You were going to tell me about your thesis?'

He sat up a little straighter. 'Yes, the guitarfish. I'm not sure how much you know about finning?'

'I know it's a lucrative trade; that shark fins, legally and illegally harvested, are worth a lot of money and that people in Asia make a soup out of them.'

'That's right, but finning's also the name for the practice of cutting off a shark's fin while it's still alive.'

'What? That sounds barbaric,' Sannie said.

'It is, but it's all about money. The trade in shark fin, which is prized as a delicacy for soup in parts of Asia, is huge.'

'How big?' she asked. Sannie was no stranger to high-stakes wildlife crime.

'About one hundred million sharks are killed every year,' Adam said, 'many of them illegally. Finning happens when an artisanal fisherman – a small-time guy – or a trawler pulls in a shark and then slices the fin off and throws the shark, still alive, back into the water to die.'

'Why would they do that?'

'A fin doesn't take up much space, certainly not as much as a whole shark. A fisherman can kill dozens and not have his boat full of shark meat, which isn't worth nearly as much as the fins.'

'That's terrible,' Sannie said, though the lengths and depths people would go to in order to satisfy their greed was not new to her.

'A fin can be worth up to three hundred US dollars. That makes it an industry worth billions of rand per year.'

'I never knew,' Sannie said. 'I mean, I'd heard of it, but had no idea of the scale.'

'That's the problem. We don't get the coverage or the airtime that other endangered species do, but this is happening on our watch, in our region. South Africa's banned finning, but it's rife in Mozambique. Chinese exporters buy newer boats and outboards for small-time fishermen and send them out just to fin.'

'You're very passionate about this.'

He nodded. 'When I was young, before I went into the army, I used to dive off the Aliwal Shoal, not far from here, and there would be whale sharks, same time every year. There hasn't been a sighting of one for years now – they're the gentlest creatures, totally harmless to humans, and they're being wiped out.'

She could tell him stories, of rhinos she had seen, their spines severed after being wounded so they couldn't run. More than once she'd come across them, their faces scalped to the bone to remove the entire horn, but still alive. It was heartbreaking. She couldn't bear to tell him.

'Would you like a proper drink?' Adam asked. 'This is depressing.'

Sannie looked at her watch again. 'It's getting late.'

'You're right,' he said. 'And I shouldn't break my one-beer-per-day rule. Sometimes I have one at Rocky Bay, sometimes here if I've been studying late or working on the house.'

She felt sorry for him, for all the work still to do on the house, for the losses he'd suffered, of his family and his finances. 'You must be really committed, to take on all this and to keep on with your studies.'

'Instead of getting a proper job, you mean?'

'I didn't say that.' She had thought it, though.

He shrugged. 'Call it a midlife crisis, maybe. Probably more productive than an affair. I just felt . . . I had plans for my life when I was younger, to be a marine biologist and to make a difference to the environment, and then the army got in the way and, well, life took over. I got married, probably to the wrong girl, and we had the kids, who we both love, and then there was the whole moving from South Africa thing.'

Sannie thought she understood. She had been asking similar questions of herself, lately. What had she contributed to the world, other than her kids and putting a few criminals behind bars? Was that enough?

'My supervisor, the professor overseeing my PHD back in Australia, says he loves older students.' Adam gave a small laugh. 'He says we're more serious, more committed than the youngsters.'

'I'm sure he's right. You seem to be sacrificing quite a bit to carry on with your research,' Sannie said.

He got up, went to the kitchen and opened the rattling old fridge.

'I've got some wine here, if you'd like a glass. It's cask.'

Sannie stood up. 'No thanks, I'm fine. I think I'd better get home before dark.'

He straightened. 'Ja, fine. Thanks for stopping by.' Adam walked her to the front door.

Sannie hesitated on the stoep. She wondered if she should have said yes to the drink, but then her mind started racing ahead. He was a good-looking guy, troubled but principled.

'It was nice meeting you,' he said, then smiled, 'outside of work.'

'Yes, yes it was.' She could feel her heart rate increase.

He looked at her, saying nothing. She tucked a strand of hair behind her ear.

'Can I maybe see you again, some time?' he blurted. 'I mean, I'll probably see you on the beach, walking.'

'I should run, like you,' she said, trying to think of something to say, but knowing she should just leave.

'We could . . .'

She looked up at him. He was very tall.

'Yes,' Sannie said. 'Yes, we can see each other again. Goodnight.' Sannie turned and walked down the stairs and along the broken garden path, through the tangle of overgrown shrubbery. Her cheeks were burning and her heart was still racing. She turned and saw him still standing there, looking at her. Or maybe he was looking out over the sea again. She walked briskly down the potholed road.

. . .

MIA SAT on her bed in her single-room unit in the staff quarters at Dune Lodge, looking at the old picture of her father with Luiz and the others in Angola.

In some ways her life was like a soldier's. She wore a uniform to work every day, kept ridiculous hours, and lived in accommodation that was probably only a couple of steps up from a barracks block. Her existence was governed by routine and if she'd had any family anymore – she didn't – she would be away from them for weeks, maybe months, at a time.

All the same, she loved what she did, spending time in the bush or the desert, tracking animals and sharing her love of nature with guests. She'd inherited her passion for nature and the environment from her troubled father. He'd drunk too much, become angry easily, and had trouble advancing in the workplace, particularly after the ANC came to power, but the one thing that could calm him and bring out his gentler, true side, was spending time in the wild.

Mia had read enough about PTSD to be able to now fully realise that despite his protestations that he was fine, her father had been suffering for a long time before he took his own life. She knew that sometimes the condition came later in life, many years after a person had experienced trauma such as war. She guessed that losing his job in South African National Parks – he was made redundant and his job given to an African employee – had made things worse. Certainly, she remembered his drinking going off the charts after he became unemployed.

Looking back, she could see her father had gone downhill over a number of years, but Luiz had seemed fine, outwardly, since she'd known him. Then one day he had killed himself.

The boys in the picture, with their wild hair, grimy faces and dirty uniforms grinned at her, though she thought her father's smile looked forced, even back then. She knew that look. He could smile, and he was quite handsome, but there had long been a blankness in his eyes that she could also see in the creased, time-faded photograph.

Her dad was a sergeant when the picture was taken – Luiz had printed the abbreviation 'SGT' next to his name. Knowing what she did of his wartime service, she guessed that meant the picture was taken in the late eighties, maybe around 1987. She knew he'd been in Angola that year, and his hair was long in the picture and he sported a beard, which probably meant he was nearing the end of his tour. Mia had read a great deal about the war after her father's death. Too late. And why hadn't Luiz told her that he knew her father?

Frank would have seen more action than the rest of the men in the picture. By then her father was a 'Bos Oupa', a bush grandfather, who had already completed one tour of duty on the border, and into Angola, and was on his second.

The lieutenant, or LT, Ferri, looked very young, like the other two, Kruger and Litis. She recalled her father speaking disparagingly of officers in general, but didn't remember him saying anything about a 'Ferri' in particular.

Kruger was the tallest of them. She stared at his face; he looked like he should have been in high school, still, which he probably had been not long before this picture was taken. There was something familiar about him. There were no first names on the back of the picture and Shirley said she didn't recognise any of them.

Unlike Kruger, Ferri was not a common South African surname, but the lieutenant also looked like someone she had seen somewhere else before.

Mia took her laptop from the drawer of her small bedside table and opened it. She was connected to the lodge's wi-fi and opened her internet browser. She typed in 'Ferri Angola South African army' and clicked on 'Images'.

One of the pictures was a portrait shot of a man in a suit, smiling. His hair was black flecked with grey and neatly cut. The caption read: Tony Ferri: 'You can be proud of your service and those you served with, even if you believe war is wrong'.

Mia double-clicked on the picture and was taken to a Daily Maverick article about Tony Ferri, a member of parliament from the Western Cape, who was being touted as the next leader of the Democratic Alliance. The DA, one of the main opposition parties, had recently gained ground against the ruling African National Congress in provincial elections and was busy forging coalitions with other opposition groups.

Mia scrolled through the article.

Like most white South African men of his age, Ferri was called up for compulsory national service, and served as a paratroop officer in Angola.

Her father had been a Parabat. Mia opened a new window and went to Facebook. She followed a Parabat veterans' group, but had not looked at the page for a long time. When she opened it she saw a post that showed the same head shot of Ferri.

We wish our comrade Tony Ferri all the best for the upcoming DA leadership vote. Mia saw there were more pictures to view, so she clicked on the plus icon. There was a picture of Ferri with a pretty blonde woman and a boy and a girl in their late teens, by the look of it. The next showed him with an African baby in his arms – typical politician.

'Yes!' she said. The next picture was of Ferri in Angola, as a young lieutenant. She held Luiz's photograph next to her screen. It was the same man.

Mia now realised that the reason she thought she had seen Ferri before was that she had, in the newspapers and on television a couple of times thanks to his political career.

When her dad had died there had been many posts on the Parabat Facebook page, praising him and expressing condolences. A dozen or so men in matching blazers, ties and maroon berets had come to the funeral and saluted as her father's coffin had been lowered into the ground. One of them, the tallest, she now recognised from Luiz's picture when she took another look. Kruger. She remembered his first name, and meeting him – Adam. That was it.

She was young at the time, and Mia remembered a few of the men hugging her, brandy on their breath, nicotine in their moustaches, but only Adam Kruger's name. He'd been to their house before, she was sure of it now. She stared some more at one of the recent pictures of Tony Ferri again. Unlike some of the old soldiers she recalled, who sported large beer boeps and ruddy faces from too much drinking, Ferri still looked fit and handsome. He might have also made an impression on her when she was younger, but she couldn't recall seeing him at the service.

Mia got off the bed and went to her small bar fridge. She took out a can of iced tea. There were a couple of beers in the fridge and a pre-mixed gin and tonic, but it was getting late and she had an early start, as usual, the next day. She popped the can, and as she lay back on the bed her phone rang. Mia looked at the screen.

'Sannie, howzit?'

'Fine, and you, Mia?' Sannie van Rensburg said.

'Great. Getting excited about your trip? I'm really looking forward to seeing you.'

'Ja, me as well. I'm sorry to call so late. I know you're usually up at four-thirty.'

'It's fine. I'm not really tired. Just, um, looking at some stuff online.'

'Mia, I have a question for you – did you have a guide or a tracker pass away recently? Someone who took his own life?'

Mia sat up straight. 'Yes, Luiz. I worked with him. He was a tracker.'

'A San guy?'

'Yes. How did you know?'

Sannie told Mia about meeting a man through his involvement in foiling an armed robbery, and how his friend, the tracker, had killed himself.

'How did he know Luiz?' Mia asked.

'He served with him in the army, in Angola. He was in one of the parachute battalions. Wasn't your dad a Parabat, Mia?'

'Yes, he was.' A chill went down Mia's spine.

'This guy, Adam, he seems to have been really close with your friend Luiz, and would like to attend the funeral, but he's got no money. He doesn't even own a car.'

'Adam?' Mia said. 'What's his surname?'

'Kruger,' Sannie said. 'Why?'

'Just let me put you on speaker, Sannie.' She did so, then picked up the photograph she'd been looking at, snapped a picture of it, and messaged it to Sannie.

There was a pause on the end of the line, presumably as Sannie looked at the image. Mia held her breath.

'That's him, the guy I was talking about. Adam Kruger, fourth from the left.'

8

ANGOLA, 1987

When the Puma lifted off and turned back towards the cutline, the bush fell silent. Evan Litis held his rifle so tightly his hands hurt. He blinked sweat from his eyes.

On the ground, amid the mopane trees, it was stifling. There was no breeze and heat radiated up from the sandy soil under his boots and beat down on him from the sun above.

Tiny flies zeroed in on the moisture in Evan's eyes and invaded his nose as the Parabats shook out into their patrol formation.

The two San trackers, Luiz and Roberto, were up front, followed by Hennie, the corporal. Hennie's eyes went wherever the tip of the barrel of his R4 assault rifle was pointing.

Next was Lance Corporal Erasmus, the medic, then Lieutenant Ferri, followed by the signaller, Rossouw, who needed to be by the loot's side at all times. Sergeant Greenaway followed Ferri, then Adam with the machine gun and Evan as his number two, carrying extra ammunition and watching their rear.

Evan watched where he was putting his feet, to make sure he didn't step on a dead branch and make a noise, and forced himself to remember to turn 180 degrees every few steps, to make sure no one was following them. His heart was pounding. Evan was terrified, not of being shot or killed, but of doing the wrong thing.

Sergeant Greenaway dropped back until he was beside Evan. 'You OK?'

'Ja, Sergeant,' Evan whispered back.

Greenaway gave a little smile. 'Out here, in the bush, Frank will do, and you can talk English. Remember, eyes open, keep watching our six.'

'Yes . . . Frank.'

Evan's chest swelled. In basic training he'd been singled out because of his Greek surname. In the Parabats, however, he'd learned that a man's background meant nothing. The 'Bats fought not for a flag, or a country, or apartheid, but for each other. They despised anyone not in the parachute battalion equally, regardless of race, creed or rank.

They had rehearsed the formation they were in now in training. Evan knew he must be by Adam's side at all times, to feed his hungry machine gun more ammunition and to be ready to take over the gun if Adam was hit. He was weighed down with eight hundred rounds, six magazines for his own R4, two grenades, a spare battery for Rossouw's radio, six one-litre water bottles and a twenty-four-hour rat pack. The ration pack could, if eaten sparingly, be eked out to last three days.

They moved off. Evan figured that at the pace they were going – slow enough to be cautious, but with an urgency that acknowledged that the crew of the Bosbok might still be alive – they should reach the downed aircraft in about half an hour.

Evan had loved visiting the African bush, especially the Kruger National Park, since he was a little boy. But if the wilds of Africa were paradise from the back seat of his family's Ford, then on foot they were a hot, dusty hell, with the prospect of death looming at every step. Evan thought of his mother, in the kitchen at home baking moussaka, and of his father, who had built a successful mini empire after starting with one fishing boat. Evan had lived in his pop's shadow, and everyone assumed he would take over the family business one day. But he wanted to prove himself, to make his mark as a man in his own right. Maybe the army would give him that chance, if it didn't kill him first.

Adam looked back at him, swinging the long barrel of the LMG as he turned. Evan smiled at him and Adam nodded in return.

The crack-thump of a gunshot sounded from somewhere up ahead.

'Contact!' Greenaway yelled.

Evan remembered his training and his job on this patrol. He ran a few metres to what looked like a stout tree, dropped to his belly and faced rearward. Adam pushed forward and unfolded the bipod of his machine gun as he lay down.

There were two more gunshots. Someone screamed.

'MR LITIS? MR LITIS.'

Evan looked up from his computer screen, though he hadn't really been concentrating on the financial news site in front of him. His personal assistant, Phumzile Msani, stood in the door of his office.

'Sorry, Phum, my mind was elsewhere.'

'Is there anything else I can do, or must I go now?'

It was getting dark outside. Johannesburg's lights glowed hazily through a smog of car exhaust and cooking fires. 'No, it's fine, Phum, but I need you to clear my diary for the coming week.'

'Another business trip?' She smiled sympathetically. He travelled a good deal, checking on his existing businesses acquiring new ones.

Evan pushed his glasses up his nose. 'No, a funeral.'

'Haibo! I'm so sorry. Not family?'

He shook his head. 'No, but someone I was close to, a long time ago. I'll still go to the conference tomorrow, but after that I have to fly to Upington and I'll need a charter flight from there to Dune Lodge for three people. I've emailed you the rough timings.'

'All right, Mr Litis. I will do all that in the morning, and I will pray for your friend.'

Evan smiled. 'Thanks, Phum.'

Phum left. Evan got up and opened the built-in fridge in the book-case lining one wall of his office on the tenth floor of the office block in Melrose Arch. The city was spread out below him. A red Ferrari with tinted windows roared out of the underground car park; a man dressed in layers of second-hand clothing who was pushing a shop-ping trolley full of aluminium cans and plastic bags had to run to get out of the way.

The Ferrari belonged to his friend, Bongi. They played golf together every second weekend and Bongi was one of his major investors. So much had changed in South Africa, yet, still, the inequities remained.

Evan took out some ice cubes, put them in a tumbler and poured himself a double measure of Johnny Walker Blue Label. He sipped the Scotch and thought about Luiz.

Before Phum had come in he'd been remembering that day in Angola, and how keen he had been to see action. Evan went back to his desk and sat down. He clicked on the 'My pictures' icon on his computer and opened the 'Army' folder. He'd scanned all of his old photos years ago and now clicked on the one of Luiz, Ferri, Adam, Greenaway and him.

Evan had given a hard copy of that photo, with their names written on the back, to Luiz. He wondered where it was now; if the old tracker had kept it.

He sipped his Scotch, rocked back in his leather office chair and closed his eyes. Evan's phone vibrated in his shirt pocket. He took it out. It was Tony Ferri.

'Howzit, boet?' Evan said.

'Ja, so-so, and you?'

'Still reeling,' Evan said. 'This is kak news, man.'

'Luiz . . . He always seemed so . . . together, you know what I mean? Almost zen-like, and he'd been fighting the war for about ten years before we came on the scene. To have lasted all this time . . .'

'Where are you?' Evan asked.

'In an Uber, in Cape Town, on the way to a fundraising dinner. Lisa's here with me.'

Ferri was the consummate politician, Evan thought, but all the same, there was a realness to him.

'Say hi to Lisa from me. I'm just pleased we were able to see him again,' Evan said.

'Ja, me as well. I'd hoped to find out what happened to him, when I went to Platfontein, but it was lekker to actually find him and meet him again.'

'For sure,' Evan said. As part of his political campaigning in the Northern Cape and as a member of the DA's housing committee, Tony had gone to Platfontein, at Evan's urging, to highlight the poor living conditions of the San people residing there. It was a high-risk issue to tackle. White, male voters who had served in the war would feel sympathy for the Platfontein San, who were only living in the settlement northwest of Kimberley because of their service in the old South African Defence Force, but African voters might not have much sympathy for San people from Angola who'd fought against their fathers.

Evan was no stranger to the San community at Platfontein. He had been a regular visitor for the past thirty years or more, and Tony had visited the community centre and youth outreach and vocational training programs that Evan's company sponsored.

'Are you going to the funeral?' Tony asked.

'Yes, I've just asked Phum to clear the coming week.'

'Cool,' Tony said. 'I'll also be there. I spoke to Shirley, the lodge manager; she says it's definitely Thursday.'

'Good,' Evan said. 'Are you going to stay at Dune Lodge again?'

'It's a bit out of my budget, boet, and I can't ask the party to pay for accommodation for a private visit. I might find a B&B at Askham or somewhere.'

'Don't be silly,' Evan said. 'It's my treat. And I've booked a charter flight from Upington to the lodge and made sure there's enough room for you and Lisa.'

'Sheesh, that's kind. But you covered me last time,' Tony said. 'I feel bad. At least let me chip in. A member of parliament's wage isn't great, but I can help.'

'I told you, Tony, it's fine,' Evan said. 'At least it proves you're an honest politician.'

'Are you doing OK, boet?' Tony asked. 'I know that this kind of thing, losing an old comrade, can bring things back to the surface. I've been thinking a lot about the war, lately, and this just brought back even more stuff.'

'I hear you,' Evan said. 'Same for me.'

Evan stared out over the city, but instead of the streetlights and cars he was seeing the spot fires in the Angolan bush at night, the side effects of the mortar bombs and tracer. He remembered the cacophony, and the smells of cordite, cooked blood, and the sulphurous chemical odour of explosives. Hell.

'Lisa told me about your latest donation, Evan. Thanks.'

Tony was trying to change the subject, which was good. 'No problem,' Evan said. 'You know I'm happy to help, and that I'm invested in the party, and you. I think we can really make a difference in the next election.'

'I'm glad you said "we", boet, it's like you're part of the team.'

'Thanks,' Evan said. He wanted so much to believe that Tony could make a difference. Tony could have wangled himself a freebie at Dune Lodge just by picking up the phone to Julianne Clyde-Smith – Evan had seen the billionaire at a couple of DA fundraisers in the past. But he wouldn't. Tony was principled. 'I'll have Phum send Lisa the details of my flight to Upington and the charter, so we can coordinate.'

'Thanks, Evan.'

Evan's phone started vibrating again. 'I've got another call coming through, Tony.' He checked the screen. 'It's Annelle. I'd better take it.'

'Sure, boet. Don't want to get in trouble with the boss.'

'Exactly. I'll see you next week.'

'Thanks, Evan, I really appreciate all this.' Tony ended the call.

'Hi, babes,' Evan said as he answered the incoming call.

'When are you coming home, Evan?'

'Soon, babe.' He sipped his Scotch.

'Are you drinking?'

'No.'

The pause hung between them. He was drinking a little more than usual, and Annelle had noticed. She hit the gym every day and watched what she ate and drank religiously. Evan told himself that he'd ease off once he got on top of a few things, but the list just seemed to get longer every day and the need to blow off steam never went away.

'Well, hurry up and get back here. My mom will be here by seven for dinner. Don't be late.'

'OK.'

'Evan? Are you all right?'

He sighed. 'Yes, I'm fine.'

'You sure? I can tell that the news about that guy from the Kalahari you served with shook you up. It's OK, you know. Maybe you should make another appointment to see Dr van Tonder.'

Van Tonder was a psychiatrist. Evan had been to see him once. He was a friend of Annelle's family and he'd served in the army during the Border War. He'd told Evan how the South African military had been ahead of the curve in diagnosing and treating mental health issues, before the Americans, before all the Vietnam veterans started presenting with PTSD. Evan believed him, but he didn't think he was suffering from post-traumatic stress disorder.

'I'm sure. I'll see you soon, babes.'

Evan ended the call and stared at the screen. His phone beeped again.

'Fuck,' he said. He looked at the screen. It was Tony.

Don't suppose you've heard from Adam?

Evan tapped out a reply. *No, still AWOL as always.*

Evan drained the glass and put the bottle away. He picked up his suit jacket and turned off the lights. No, he wasn't suffering from PTSD, he was simply carrying a burden on behalf of all of them.

In the lift, he took out his phone and opened the internet browser. For the hell of it, for maybe the thousandth time, he googled: Adam Kruger Parabat.

'Shit,' Evan said out loud.

9

ANGOLA, 1987

There was a bang and a whoosh, and Tony saw a streak of dirty grey smoke coming from the front left. It seemed to happen in slow motion. He glimpsed a man on the other end of the smoke trail and another figure darted through the mopane trees directly ahead of him.

The man up front, Hennie, was still screaming. 'RPG!' Greenaway yelled.

Tony dived to the ground as the rocket-propelled grenade slammed into a tree to his right and exploded. He had his face in the dirt, but Greenaway was on one knee, giving orders.

'Kruger, target, one hundred metres half-left, fire!'

The machine gunner opened up, firing a long burst into the bush in the direction the rocket had come from. The noise was deafening. Greenaway grabbed Tony by his webbing strap and hauled him up. 'Come with me, Loot.'

Every instinct in Tony's mind and body told him to stay where he was, flattened into the sandy earth, but he knew that he had to get up, to move, and to lead.

'Rossouw,' Greenaway said to the signaller lying beside Tony, 'take the loot and push right. Get around these guys.'

'Ja, Sarge,' Rossouw said. 'Come on, sir.'

Tony just nodded and dumbly followed the radioman. He scanned the bush around them as they moved and saw a man in green emerge from behind a tree, an AK-47 in his hands. The man brought the rifle up to his shoulder. Clumsily, Tony raised his own rifle, aimed and pulled the trigger. Nothing happened.

'Fuck.' Tony realised he still had his safety catch on. He flicked it to fire, took aim again and felt the rifle kick into his shoulder. His round missed and the man ducked, taking cover behind a tree. Other weapons were opening up around him.

The man Tony had aimed at popped up again and started to run. Rossouw lifted his rifle, fired two rounds, and dropped the man before Tony could even get a sight picture. Tony knew that he should be at the centre of all this, calling out the orders and leading from the front, but it was all so confusing. Greenaway had ordered him and Rossouw to flank the enemy as if Tony was just another soldier. The resentment rose inside Tony, but he didn't know whether to go back and confront the sergeant or do as he was told. Kruger was still laying down fire from his machine gun. They came abreast of Greenaway, who had also moved forward and was now kneeling beside Rassie. The medic had cut away Hennie's shirt and managed to wrap a field dressing around Hennie's chest. The bulky cotton pad was already soaked with blood and Hennie sobbed as Rassie ran an IV line into his arm.

'Bly by my, man,' Rassie said to his patient, telling him to say with him.

Greenaway looked over at them. 'Rossouw, call in a casevac. Get that fucking Puma back here.'

'The mission –' Tony began.

'Just do as I fucking say.' Greenaway's nostrils flared. His eyes stared out from his blackened face at Tony as if Tony, the officer, were somehow responsible for Hennie's wound. Greenaway pushed forward. He ran a few metres, dropped to one knee and fired two shots. 'Forward! Push right.' The sergeant was on his feet again, moving, giving orders as if all of this was second nature.

Tony paused and looked down at the wounded soldier. His vision started to blur at the edges and he felt his stomach turn. The bile rose up and burned the back of his throat; he threw up. There were more shots from in front of them, then silence.

Tony didn't know if the enemy had retreated or Frank had killed them all. Tony spat and wiped his mouth. Rossouw called their base at Ondangwa. 'This is Romeo-Mike-Zero-Nine.'

Greenaway came walking back through the bush. He said nothing to Tony but addressed Rossouw. 'Tell Ondangwa we've got two enemy KIA, one WIA, plus Hennie. Get that casevac for Hennie. I've told Rassie to check the wounded enemy once Hennie's stable.'

'Ja, Sarge,' Rossouw said.

Two killed in action, and one enemy and one friendly wounded. And Tony had done nothing. He needed to show some leadership, so he said, 'Where are the Bushmen, Sergeant, are they OK?'

Greenaway nodded. 'Fine. We hold the position here until the casevac comes in.' Greenaway fell back to where Kruger and Litis were waiting.

Tony felt like he should be doing something more; he still needed to complete his mission. 'Come with me,' he said to Rossouw.

'But Sergeant Greenaway said –'

'Sergeant Greenaway's not in command here, Troep, I am.'

Rossouw cast a glance over his shoulder to Greenaway and the others, but then shrugged and followed Tony, who pushed forward in search of the San scouts. Colonel de Villiers had been very clear to him about the importance of this mission. They had to press on to the crash site soon.

Ahead of him, through thick bush, Tony heard a single gunshot. He pushed forward, but gripped his rifle tight in his hands and had it at the ready. He saw movement through the trees and slowed.

In front of him was Luiz, one of the Bushman trackers. He held his R1 rifle loosely by his side as he looked down at a body. The other San tracker, Roberto, squatted in the grass nearby.

Luiz turned his face and saw Tony, as he came close, then nodded to Rossouw.

Tony looked at the dead man. He could see no rifle or pistol. Tony went to the body, knelt and rolled it over. The man had been shot through the back of the head, and had another wound in his shoulder. Much of his face was missing. Tony's stomach turned again, but he managed to stop himself from being sick.

Tony looked at Luiz. 'This man – he has no weapon. Had he surrendered?' he said in Afrikaans. 'Was he the wounded man?'

Luiz blinked but said nothing, and nor did Roberto. 'Answer me,' he tried in English.

'He doesn't speak much English, either, Loot,' Rossouw volunteered. 'They mostly talk in Portuguese, or their own language, with the clicks.'

Luiz turned his back on the two men and walked about ten metres away from them. He bent and picked up an RPG launcher. He carried it back to where Tony stood.

'Was that man armed, when you shot him?' Tony asked.

Luiz came and dropped the launcher at his feet, next to the dead Angolan.

'He is the one who wounded Hennie,' Luiz said. Roberto looked on silently, his face impassive.

That was not what Tony had asked the tracker. He heard a hiss of static from the radio and Rossouw speaking softly into the radio handset.

'Sir,' Rossouw said. 'It's Ondangs. They're looking for a sitrep.'

All this madness, and now the bloody headquarters at Ondangwa wanted a situation report from him. Tony ran a hand through his hair. He had been confused, then sick to his stomach seeing the injured South African, Hennie. Now he was dealing with the shock of what looked like a summary execution of a wounded man who was nowhere near his weapon. No one seemed to care.

'Sir?' Rossouw said.

Tony went to him and snatched the proffered handset. 'This is Romeo-Mike-Zero-Nine. Confirm three, not two, enemy Kilo-India-Alpha, one friendly WIA. Where's our casevac, over?'

'Roger, Romeo-Mike-Zero-Nine, your casualty evacuation is on its way,' the operations room replied.

Tony passed the handset back to Rossouw. He glared at Luiz and pointed a finger while he waited for the reply from base. 'You . . .'

Luiz stared back at him, unmoving, unemotional.

'Sir,' Rossouw said softly. 'These guys, they were Flechas, Portuguese special forces. For them killing is second nature.'

Tony turned on the signaller. 'Shut your mouth. We'll investigate this.'

Rossouw shrugged, then began picking his nose.

'TONY? ARE YOU AWAKE?' his election campaign manager, Lisa Ingram, asked.

He'd had his head resting against the cool glass window of the Uber Black, where he was sitting in the back seat with Lisa. He hadn't been sleeping, just remembering that encounter with Luiz. It was hard to imagine him being dead, let alone him killing himself. Luiz had always seemed so devoid of emotion.

'I'm here. Just lost in thought.' He looked into her eyes and wanted to touch her long red hair.

Lisa reached out and put a hand on his thigh. 'You OK? The schedule's been gruelling.'

Tony's phone vibrated. It was Sanette, his wife. *Love you, good luck tonight,* her message read.

Love you as well x, he replied.

Lisa squeezed his leg, then glanced up, as though checking to see if the Uber driver was looking in her rear-view mirror, then ran her fingers lightly along his suit pants, higher up his inner thigh.

He smiled but put his hand on hers, stopping her progress. He wanted to kiss her, but his profile was now high enough that he could not risk the driver seeing and recognising him. Lisa was being dangerous, but he had learned that she liked risk. It made her unpredictable and sensational in bed, but she, as his campaign manager, knew even better than he that a whiff of scandal could ruin his position as leader and their chances, already slim at best, at winning government.

'Later,' he whispered.

'Yes, sir,' she said.

He was stirring, and at least her attentions took his mind off Luiz and the others, if only for a moment. 'I need to read over my speaking notes.'

He took them from the inside pocket of his suit jacket and tried to focus, but the dirty, unshaven faces of the men – his men – and the sounds and smells of Angola began invading his brain again, like a creeping Cuban artillery barrage. The Uber hit a pothole and he flinched.

'You OK?' Lisa asked.

He swallowed hard. 'Fine.'

'Are you sure?' Lisa asked.

The Uber driver was indicating right, waiting to turn into the car park of the hotel where the fundraising dinner was being held.

'Yes, just thinking about my speech.'

'You never worry about your speaking notes and you weren't even looking at the pages. Do you want to tell me what's going on? Is it about us?'

'No.'

He didn't need this, not the memories of the war and Luiz, not Luiz's funeral, not Lisa – not now.

'I know you're under a lot of pressure, and it's only going to get worse,' Lisa said. 'You can open up to me.'

He looked at her. She was clever and funny and sexy and she desired him – at least, he thought she did. The Uber pulled up under the covered portico of the hotel and they thanked the driver and got out. The local party chairman, a balding businessman in a suit, and his pretty, younger wife were waiting to greet Tony and Lisa. A photographer, maybe from the local newspaper, snapped some pictures of Tony and the chairman.

'Tony just needs to freshen up before the function and we need to go over his speech,' Lisa said.

'No problem,' the chairman said. 'Your rooms are ready and people are still arriving. We're not due to start for half an hour.' He handed them key cards to their rooms, which were on the eighth floor.

'Plenty of time,' Lisa said.

'Plenty of time for what?' Tony said, lowering his voice as they went to the elevators.

In the lift, they kissed, pressing themselves against each other. She grabbed his arse and he raised the hem of her dress, which was the same colour as her eyes. The fabric was silky smooth, like her. She ground against him.

As the lift doors separated, they broke their embrace and straightened their clothes, then walked quickly down the corridor. Checking both ways, Tony let Lisa into his room and slammed the door closed.

'There's barely time,' he said, in between kissing her.

'I need your head in the game.' She reached between them and unbuckled his belt.

His mind had been elsewhere, in the car, but Lisa had a way of bringing him back to the present, and to her. She was like an addiction – wrong, dangerous, perhaps a means of avoiding some other problem or issue, but he could not get enough of her. Tony freed one of her breasts from her dress and bra and lowered his mouth to her nipple. Lisa threw back her head and moaned, then took his face in her hands and kissed him on the lips. She stepped back, smiled, and lowered herself to her knees.

He ran his fingers through her long red hair as she unzipped and consumed him. Tony closed his eyes, trying to surrender to the incredible softness of her mouth, to the illicit thrill of the moment. There was a full-length mirror on the other side of the room. He looked at their reflections.

It should have been enough to totally distract him, to take his thoughts away from the pressures of the campaign trail and the ghosts of Angola and his other life. He tried, emptying his mind and focusing on the sight and feel of her.

The guilt, however, swirled around his brain like a poisoned pill fizzing in water, turning clarity to a cloudy, deadly brew. It infected his soul and paralysed his body. Lisa stopped. Tony looked down.

She raised her eyes to his.

'Tony?' She had replaced her mouth with her palm and fingers, moving rhythmically, but it was no use.

He pinched the bridge of his nose with two fingers.

Lisa looked up, and gave him a sympathetic frown. 'It's OK. It happens to guys sometimes. It's the stress, that's all.'

He lowered his hand.

'Tony?' Lisa got to her feet. 'Are you crying?'

10

Sannie walked along the beach, from Nkomba towards Pennington, sticking to the intertidal zone where the sand was wet and firm. Her GPS watch, a gift from the kids, buzzed and told her she had reached her daily step goal already. It felt good to be walking. When she had lived in the Hippo Rock Private Nature Reserve, on the edge of the Kruger Park, her opportunities to exercise had been limited. There were wild animals about, and while one could walk on the reserve during daylight hours, there never seemed to be enough time. At any moment she could get a call-out about another rhino being killed and have to respond.

Here on the coast, her hours were more regulated. Sure, there was crime to deal with, but it was not as hectic as somewhere like Johannesburg. She nodded and said good morning to an elderly couple, out walking with their Jack Russell.

This stretch of beach was more than two kilometres long and was populated with just a handful of early risers. None of the houses in the area was more than two storeys high, and the narrow but thick belt of green coastal vegetation screened all but the odd roofline from view.

The Indian Ocean was calm, the morning sun dappling the blue-grey waters. A lone paddler on a wave ski cut his way towards the beach. At the far end, waves crashed on the red rocks of Umdoni Point. Sannie took a deep breath of clean air. This place was what she needed.

She thought again about the conversation she'd had with Mia. As a detective she did not believe in coincidences, but sometimes they happened. Sannie was looking at another house today, in Botha Place, so she would pass by Adam Kruger's house.

She debated what she would say to him. By the time she reached the tidal pool, the man on the wave ski was riding a wave in to shore, expertly steering himself so that he made the high-speed manoeuvre look effortless. Sannie raised a hand to her eyes and looked at the tall, muscular figure emerging from the water.

'Adam!'

He looked her way as he lifted his wave ski under one arm. She was still some way off, but she could see his smile of recognition. Sannie walked to him.

'Good morning,' she said.

'Hi.'

'That looked like fun,' Sannie said.

'Have you not tried it?'

'No. But I'd like to.'

'I'm just heading home,' Adam said.

'Mind if I walk with you?'

He smiled. 'Not at all.'

Water beaded on his smooth, tanned skin and even though he was carrying the wave ski, which looked quite heavy, Sannie still had to walk quickly to match his long, even stride. He noticed, and slowed for her, which was nice.

'I was on the phone last night with my friend at Dune Lodge. She actually worked very closely with your old army comrade, Luiz. He was her tracker. She wants to meet you, Adam.'

He stopped in the sand and looked at her. 'Me? Why?'

'She says you knew her father, during the war in Angola, and that you were maybe in the same unit. Her name's Mia Greenaway.'

Adam closed his eyes and stood there a moment. Sannie wondered what memories the name had conjured up.

'Mia's dad also killed himself. Did you know that?'

He nodded and took a deep breath, as if to still himself. 'I went to the funeral. I remember Mia.'

'Do you still want to go to Luiz's funeral?'

Adam chewed his lower lip. Again, Sannie wondered what was going through his mind. She had expected him to say 'yes' immediately, as he had already indicated that he wanted to go but couldn't afford it. She wondered if money was still playing on his mind.

'Did Mia say if she knew that Luiz had served with Frank, her dad?'

'No,' Sannie said. 'From what I gathered it was a surprise to her.'

Adam started to walk again and Sannie kept up with him. It looked like he was turning the information over in his mind. 'Do you believe in coincidences?' he asked.

'In my job, no, though I suppose things happen that defy logic.'

'Like your friend ending up working at the same lodge as a San tracker who served with her father?'

Sannie shrugged. 'Maybe. My first husband was always running into people he had served with in the army and not seen for years, or friends of friends. It sometimes seemed like everyone knew everyone who served in the army. Were you close to Frank Greenaway?'

'That's a good question,' he said as they turned off the main beach and the narrow sand pathway through the green belt that led, Sannie now knew, straight to Adam's house. 'I knew him for six months in Angola, more than thirty-five years ago. It might be the same with the police, I don't know, but what we went through back then was enough to tie us together for life. I only saw Frank a few times over the years, but every time it was as if we'd been lifelong friends, living next door to each other.'

'When he killed himself, was it a shock to you?'

Adam stopped at the single-track railway line. He wasn't watching for a train, just pondering her question in the methodical way he seemed to analyse everything. Sannie wondered if it was to do with his scientific, research-minded brain.

'Yes and no. I'd seen him maybe six months earlier, and he wasn't too bad. I don't know what your friend Mia told you, but Frank was an alcoholic. Plenty of us who went through the war drank too much – I've had my ups and downs; I'm just lucky I can't really afford it these days. But Frank was in a different league. The booze was his escape – the only way he could get to sleep, he told me.'

'Nightmares?'

Adam nodded. 'And "day-mares". What the Americans call flash-backs. Frank had a lot to run from. When I first met him I was just nineteen – he was a sergeant, only a few years older than me, but he had an old man's eyes, you know what I mean?'

'The Americans also have an expression for that in my line of work – "cop eyes". Seen it all.'

'Ja, well I think Frank had seen it all and then some. He was on his second tour. We were tough, you know? And the Bushmen, the San with us, had been at war when the rest of us were still laaities.'

'My first husband saw some action in South West,' Sannie said, meaning modern-day Namibia, 'but probably nothing like you guys.'

Adam carried on towards his house. 'Frank had his demons, and I knew he was not well – post-traumatic stress, for sure. But he loved that daughter of his, and I think they became even closer after Frank's wife passed.'

'Mia told me she was more or less raised by her Shangaan nanny. She's very close to the local people who live on the border of the Kruger.'

Adam nodded. 'Yes, I remember Frank talking about Nokuthula, the woman who brought Mia up. But Frank wanted the best for Mia, so that's what surprised me, when he shot himself.'

Sannie thought back to the time just after her second husband, Tom, was killed, when she had been at her lowest ebb. 'Did you ever . . . I mean, think of taking your own life?'

He stopped again and stared at her. 'Yes. Have you thought about it?'

She looked down, almost ashamed. 'Yes.'

'But you didn't, clearly,' he said.

She gave a little laugh. 'No.'

'What stopped you?'

'Thinking about my children. I was in despair after Tom was killed, and I felt like I couldn't go on, that there was no point. I was sitting in my car, overlooking the Skukuza golf course, in the Kruger Park – such a beautiful place – but all I could see was misery. My youngest son called me. I had my gun in my hand, and I knew I couldn't do it to them, the kids.'

Adam nodded. 'That's what I thought, about Frank. As screwed up as he was, he had his daughter.'

They came to Adam's house. 'Ricoffy?'

'Sure,' she said.

They walked up the stairs and when he opened the door there was the now familiar smell of sawdust and paint. He went into the makeshift kitchen and put some water on. Sannie stood in the doorway.

'Adam?'

'Yes?'

He spooned the instant coffee into mugs. 'Would you like to go to the Kalahari, to the funeral?'

This time he responded. 'If money were no object, I would go. But I just don't think I can afford to.'

'I could take you.'

He looked into her eyes. 'You hardly know me.'

'Trust me, that thought crossed my mind. Especially since we only met because Gyou shot someone.'

'I'd seen you on the beach already,' he said.

'And? Were you planning on saying hello?'

He looked around, gesturing to the house. 'I'm not exactly a man of means, so I thought I couldn't very well just say hi, or ask you out to dinner.'

But the thought had crossed his mind. Sannie felt her cheeks burn. 'Anyway, what do you think? I've got leave and I'm driving to the Kalahari. Mia's using some of her bed nights – free stays they give staff – to put me up in Dune Lodge, and she says she can get you a room as well.'

The water boiled and Adam busied himself pouring. Sannie walked through the library-cum-office onto the stoep. It was a beautiful, calm morning and the glare off the ocean was almost blinding.

Adam brought the coffee and they sat down on cheap plastic chairs by a battered old table with rusting metal legs.

'It's very kind of you to offer,' Adam said.

'So, you'll come?'

He sipped his coffee. 'I'm not sure.'

'What? Hey, I'm offering you a free trip across the country and a couple of nights at one of the most expensive luxury game lodges in South Africa.'

'I'm grateful,' Adam said. 'Believe me, I am. It's just that . . . I wonder who else will be there, and why.'

Sannie felt foolish. She had offered a virtual stranger, a man who had a violent past, the chance to spend two days in her car with her. What had she been thinking? He'd said he wanted to go to his friend's funeral and now he was acting weird. Her coffee was half drunk, but she stood.

'I should get going.'

Adam looked up at her, but made no move to stop her, and said nothing to make her change her mind.

ADAM WATCHED Sannie walk down the stairs onto Botha Place, and probably out of his life.

It was for the best. He had felt stupid, telling her that he had noticed her on the beach, and that he'd thought about asking her out. She was beautiful, and he'd learned from Pam – half real estate agent, half village matchmaker – that she was single. He hadn't told Sannie that he had asked about her, because he didn't want to appear like a stalker.

What the fuck were you thinking?

Sannie disappeared from view. He turned his thoughts to the others – Ferri and Litis. Who would be at the funeral? Maybe he was just being paranoid, but the last thing he wanted to do was to put Sannie van Rensburg in a position of danger.

Adam knew that Tony and Evan had been looking for him. They'd given up calling years earlier, but every now and then he would hear from an old army friend or acquaintance that one or the other of them had been asking about him. Even in Sydney, they'd reached out through the South African Military Veterans of Australia organisation, via their Facebook page, asking if anyone knew where he was.

He was not hiding. Nor, however, did he want to see either of them. It might come to that, if he did go to the funeral, but if that happened, Adam didn't want to be in a position where he would have to introduce Sannie to them.

Adam thought about Mia as he sipped his coffee and looked out over the water. He remembered her as a baby, when Frank's wife had still been around, and Mia's tears as a teenager at Frank's funeral. Ferri and Litis would find her, at Dune Lodge. Would they tell her the truth?

The war had scarred them all, though they had dealt with their wounds in different ways and their fortunes had varied. Evan was rich; Ferri had the potential to be the most powerful man in South Africa one day; Frank and Luiz were dead; Rassie had been the only other survivor and he had died of skin cancer.

Hennie Steyn had survived his wounds but had later been killed at the battle of Cuito Cuanavale. Adam knew that his own service had changed his life. It was not the only reason he was divorced and penniless, but it was a factor.

Adam took a cold shower; he husbanded his electricity to charge his laptop and phone and did not run an electric geyser because of the cost. He dressed in a T-shirt and running shorts, ate a breakfast of fresh mangoes, and spent the morning trying to work on his thesis. He found it hard to concentrate.

Sannie van Rensburg kept intruding into his thoughts – the way she smiled, her figure, her honesty in relaying her own thoughts of self-harm, the scent of lavender soap. He'd felt a jolt of something, maybe adrenaline, when she'd suggested driving him to the Kalahari. He loved the idea and he really did want to be at Luiz's send-off, even if it meant tearing the scab off old wounds and putting others at risk.

At midday he laced on his running shoes, packed his clothes and car guard's reflective vest in his backpack, and set off for the punishing run along the sand and road under the full force of the sun. As he sweated and pounded his way from Pennington to Rocky Bay he imagined the pain in his calves and glutes as a kind of punishment for his own wrongdoings in Angola.

'What would you say to a friend if he was in the same situation?' the shrink had repeatedly said to him.

He said it to himself, his mantra, again as he ran.

You served your country.

You should be proud of yourself.

You did not let your comrades down.

The war may not have been a just one in the minds of many, but you did your duty, honourably.

You killed to protect your comrades, and only when necessary.

No one could go through war, see what you have seen, and not be affected.

You are a good man, Adam Kruger.

'Bullshit,' he said out loud. He shook his head as he ran, trying to rid himself of the memories.

HIS SHIFT in the car park dragged, and the tips were small.

He jogged slowly home along the beach, scanning the late-afternoon walkers from a distance, hoping and dreading that one of them might be Sannie.

It was almost dark by the time he turned off the sand onto the path leading to his house. Inside, he lit a couple of paraffin lanterns and started boiling water on the gas hob to make pap. While he waited, he took out his frustration on the old carpet in the master bedroom, ripping it up off the floor and cutting and rolling it into sections that he would be able to carry.

He ate dinner and treated himself to his third-last bottle of Black Label as he sat on the stoep.

Adam blew his lanterns out at nine pm and went to bed. He lay there, listening to the rush of the surf. Normally comforting, tonight it was like white noise, played on a loop to torment him and prevent him from sleeping.

At midnight, he got out of bed, walked through to his office and opened his laptop. The battery was low so he plugged the computer in, but there was no power. There was no load shedding, the South African power company Eskom's euphemism for rolling blackouts due to a lack of maintenance, planned for this time of night, and the weather was good, so it was unlikely a storm had disrupted supply. There was nothing he could do – this was Africa. He still had enough battery life to do some work so he tried to make up for his wasted time during the day.

After half an hour more of fruitless reading and tapping a few words, Adam leaned back in his chair, stretched and yawned. Perhaps he could go back to bed and hope for sleep this time.

He went through to his bedroom and lay on his back, one arm crooked behind his head. He thought about Sannie again.

Outside, his wooden deck creaked.

He sat up. Early mornings, after daybreak, he often heard one of Pennington's resident troops of vervet monkeys scampering about on the deck or roof. They were especially active on garbage collection days. Monkeys, however, were not active at night-time. Adam got out of bed and went to the window. He pulled aside the stained bedsheet he'd nailed to the wooden frame as a makeshift curtain. He thought he saw movement, but at this hour it could have been his eyes playing tricks on him. Maybe it had been a stray cat. He picked up his phone off the upturned plastic beer crate that served as a bedside table.

Adam heard a crack, like splintering timber, from the rear of the house.

He left his bedroom and went through to the next room, where he'd been pulling up the carpet. He picked up a claw hammer and padded softly through to the kitchen. He could feel the sawdust sticking to his bare feet and his pulse throbbing in his neck. He had no alarm or panic button, but nor did he have many possessions of real value. He slept with his phone beside him and his laptop under his bed – it was essential for his studies and, apart from his tools, which had been his late grandfather's, there was nothing else worth stealing.

His phone vibrated in his hand. He looked at the screen and was surprised to see a whatsapp message, at this late hour, from Sannie van Rensburg.

Spoke to Mia G this evening. She says room is still free at the lodge if you change your mind.

She could have sent that message in the morning, or earlier in the evening, Adam thought. Had the detective been mulling over whether or not to contact him, and now, like him, found herself tossing and turning?

Adam selected the torch app on his phone and shone it out the kitchen window, casting the light around the backyard. There was nothing. He took hold of the back door's handle and jiggled it. It was locked and the frame was intact.

He went into the hallway and could see that the front door was also still locked. At the opposite end of the house to his bedroom he had removed a door and window that had previously led onto a small timber deck, its planks and steps long since rotted. He'd covered the openings with plastic sheeting, sealing them off when he'd realised halfway through the project that it was beyond his current budget. The plastic was intact. Relieved, he headed down the corridor towards his room, reading the message on his phone again and turning his mind back to Sannie's thought processes.

Maybe their discussion about suicide and grief had awakened her own demons? He felt concerned for her. He could, he supposed, just ask her why she'd sent a message at three in the morning.

As he walked, he started tapping out a message. *Howzit? You're up lat–*

The blow from behind knocked Adam straight to the floor and his face smashed into the bare wooden boards of the hallway.

SANNIE'S PHONE beeped and she sat up, quickly, and grabbed it off the nightstand.

The ceiling fan squeaked above her, providing some relief from the lingering heat. Instead of pyjamas she was dressed only in a T-shirt and underpants. For all its faults, Adam's place, set just across the road from the beach, seemed to have a continual breeze. By contrast, Johan's house, just a few hundred metres back from the beach, was sheltered and therefore much hotter.

She read Adam's message, a fragment of a sentence. Sannie switched on the bedside light, propped herself up against two pillows, and waited for him to finish. But after a minute, there was still nothing more.

Sannie was surprised how quickly Adam had replied. She'd agonised over sending the message to him, after speaking to Mia that evening at about nine, when she knew Mia would be back from her evening game drive. Mia had repeated her offer and told Sannie that she was very keen to meet Adam. She had some memories of him from her childhood and her father's funeral and wanted to reconnect. Mia had messaged her to say she would not be able to take time off when Sannie visited, as had been her plan, because of the arrival of some unexpected guests at the lodge. However, they would still be able to spend time together.

Sannie had told Mia she would try again, but she was worried about being seen to be desperate, or somehow stalking this hand-some, troubled man. She tried to tell herself she was just doing the right thing, the Christian thing, by offering a poor man a lift to a funeral, but she could not deny she felt a physical attraction to him as well.

For a moment, she wondered if Adam might be drunk – she'd gone to bed after just one glass of wine with Johan and Annelien. Then she remembered Adam's paltry stash of three bottles of warm

Carling Black Label. That was hardly enough to get a man his size so drunk that he couldn't finish a sentence.

Up late yourself, she typed into her phone, and hit send. Again, she waited. Her phone buzzed with a message.

Mmmmmmmmmmmmmmmmmm.

'What the hell?' she said out loud. Was that some kind of vulgar expression of pleasure? She doubted it. Something felt very odd about the weird reply. Sannie called Adam's phone, waiting impatiently while it rang. He answered.

'Adam?'

He said nothing, but she heard a noise like heavy breathing. 'What are you doing?'

She was about to end the call when she heard what sounded like a gasp of pain. The call ended. When she tried to redial she got a message saying the phone was out of range.

'Shit.' She got out of bed, pulled on a pair of swimming shorts and put on her slops. She grabbed her keys, and her Z88 pistol out of its holster. Sannie also picked up the high-powered LED torch she kept by her bed because of load shedding. She opened the door, then the Xpanda security gate, slammed it shut, and ran down the external stairs leading to the flat. She pressed the remote control to deactivate the main house's external alarm beams, then fumbled for the other remote to open the electric gate. 'Bloody South Africa.'

She dialled as she drove, talking into the Bluetooth microphone. 'This is Captain Susan van Rensburg, South African Police Service,' she said as soon as the emergency operator answered. She gave Adam's address and ordered them to send an ambulance.

Sannie accelerated down Pennington Drive. Her Fortuner bounced over the speed humps and her tyres squealed as she turned hard right just past the OK supermarket into Botha Place. She floored the pedal again, the car now smacking in and out of potholes until she braked hard outside Adam's house.

She racked the Z88 and held it in her right hand, then got out of the car.

'Adam!'

She turned on the torch and used it to light her way as she ran up the overgrown garden path. Out of habit she held the torch away from her body.

'Adam, are you all right?'

When she came to the front door, she saw that it was partially open. She kicked it so that it swung wide, but stood just to one side.

Sannie heard a noise from inside the house, to the left. She tried to remember the layout; Adam's bedroom was to the right. She drew a breath then stepped in, pivoting at the waist and bringing her pistol and torch up at the sound of feet thumping down the hall on bare floorboards.

It was dark, and she saw no one.

She was about to run down the hall in the direction she'd heard the footsteps, but when she looked to her right she saw Adam, lying on the floor on his back, his left arm outstretched. Sannie pulled out her phone, called the emergency number again, and reported a home invasion at Adam's address. Then she went to Adam, knelt and put a hand to his neck, feeling for his carotid artery. He was still alive, but out cold. She rolled him onto his side but could see no sign of a gunshot wound. She got to her feet again, ran down the hallway and brought her pistol up as she came to the end room.

'Stop, police!' She kicked in the door and entered, ducking as she did so, to give herself a tiny advantage. The end of the building was open. Adam, in the course of his renovations, had taken out a door and a window leading to the outside, and covered them with plastic sheeting. Now, however, there was a man-sized rip in the plastic, which fluttered in the ocean breeze.

Sannie moved cautiously to the torn wall and stuck her head out. The remains of a clearly rotten wooden deck and stairs had been partly demolished and she found herself looking out over a precipice at a drop of a couple of metres. The man must have exited in a rush, then dropped and run. There was no sign of the intruder.

She turned and hurried back to Adam.

When she reached him, he was conscious and groaning. 'Adam, talk to me. Are you OK?'

'Ja, fine. I think I passed out.'

'The guy is gone. What happened?'

Adam sat up and put a hand to his throat. His Adam's apple bobbed as he swallowed. 'He came up behind me, hit me, and I think he choked me.'

'Unusual for a robbery,' Sannie said, as much to herself as to Adam.

He coughed. 'I can't remember what happened after that.'

Sannie exhaled, relieved that Adam was not hurt badly. She glanced around. 'Is that your gun?'

Adam followed her gaze. On the floor next to where Adam's outstretched hand had been was a pistol. It looked like a CZ, a Czech-made small-calibre handgun.

'I've never seen it before in my life. I don't own a gun.' Apart from his role in foiling the robbery at Scottburgh Mall, the last time Adam had fired a gun was in the army.

11

ANGOLA, 1987

'We have to complete the mission, Sergeant,' Ferri said to Greenaway.

Adam watched the bush, scanning the area Frank had allocated him, but he cocked his head to better hear the increasingly heated argument between the two senior members of the fire force.

'I'll take the trackers and a couple of the men,' Ferri continued. 'We need to get to the aircraft.'

Frank shook his head. 'We stay here until the chopper comes for Hennie, then we re-assess. Sir, we can't split the patrol. The enemy knows we're here now and they'll be waiting for us.'

'You're not in command here,' Ferri said.

Frank spat in the dirt. Rassie the medic knelt beside Hennie who lay, bandaged, in the blood-soaked dirt, gasping for breath. Rassie held Hennie's hand and squeezed it.

'Rossouw, Litis, come with me,' Ferri ordered.

Adam glanced at Evan, who was lying a few metres to his left. Evan looked back at Adam, gave a small shrug of his shoulders, and dragged himself to his feet.

'Fuck.' Frank shook his head, 'Rossouw stays with me. I need him to guide the Puma in, and to call in air support if we need it to cover the evacuation. Sir . . . I strongly advise that we all stick together; we don't know how many enemy are waiting for us, and our priority right now is our man, Corporal Steyn. We can go look for the downed aircraft just now, or, better still, get the air force to do a photo recce, an aerial reconnaissance to look for survivors.'

'All right, Rossouw can stay with you, but stop telling me what to do.' Ferri pointed to Luiz and Roberto. 'You two – come, Litis as well.'

The San soldiers exchanged a few words in their language with each other then stood and moved to Ferri's side.

Evan stood and adjusted his webbing before joining Ferri and the San. Part of Adam wanted to go with them, in search of action, but he felt safer, more assured, sticking with Sergeant Greenaway.

'Sheesh.' Frank sighed. 'The gunfire will have alerted every fucking Cuban and Angolan within five klicks of here, sir. Just go for a recce, all right?'

Ferri nodded.

'Then come back, and we all go together,' Frank continued.

'I will take your suggestion on board, Sergeant,' Ferri said.

'Take care, bru,' Adam whispered to Evan, who nodded. The two trackers led the way into the bush, and the officer and Evan followed them.

'That doos is going to get himself and the others killed,' Rossouw said.

'Shut the fuck up,' Frank said. 'Find out where the Puma is.'

'All right, Sarge,' Rossouw said, then spoke into his handset.

Adam thought that Frank probably agreed with Rossouw; Ferri was a cunt. His retort to Rossouw had been more matter-of-fact than admonishing. Adam felt the hairs on the back of his neck rise; there was definitely something not right about this mission, and not just in the way the sergeant and the officer were at each other's throats. He'd noted the way Frank had been excluded from the briefing between the lieutenant and the colonel back at Ondangwa.

'Sarge,' Adam said.

'What?'

'We got dropped two klicks from the crash site and we already bumped the enemy. Surely they're all over that crash site, and if the air force guys survived they'll be prisoners by now.'

Frank just nodded.

They waited; Adam blinked away the sting as the sweat ran through the camouflage cream on his forehead and washed it into his eyes.

The thwap of rotor blades cleaving hot air interrupted Frank, and Rossouw announced that the bird was inbound.

'Keep watch, Adam,' Frank said. 'If the enemy have closed in on us, they'll likely open fire with everything they've got when the chopper comes in.'

Adam licked his lips and squeezed the pistol grip of his LMG tighter. He was ready. The noise of the helicopter grew louder and Adam, lying on his belly, felt a wave of grit, twigs and leaves sandblast his back as the pilot brought the Puma down.

Frank, Rassie and Rossouw each grabbed the poncho Hennie was lying on and lifted him. Rassie carried the IV bag as well and the chopper tech climbed out and helped them slide Hennie onto the floor of the helicopter amid the swirling dust storm. Adam blinked away grit and scanned the trees, ready to open up at the first sign of movement. Just as he'd wanted to go with Evan and the lieutenant in search of action, now he felt an almost uncontrollable urge to get up, run to the Puma and throw himself on board. However, he held his ground, and his nerve.

Silence and the oppressive heat returned to the bush as soon as the helicopter lifted off. Frank and Rassie came to Adam, who stood. Rassie took a cigarette from a packet in his shirt pocket and lit it with bloodstained hands.

'Do you think Hennie will be all right, Rassie?' Frank said.

Rassie inhaled deeply, then closed his eyes as he let the smoke exit his nostrils. He shook his head. 'I don't know. It's bad.'

Frank gave Rassie a minute to compose himself. 'All right, put that cigarette out now. We must move to find the others.'

Adam hefted the machine gun and adjusted the belts of ammunition around his body. Frank set off, leading the way in the direction Ferri and the others had gone. They had only been patrolling a few minutes when Frank raised his hand and dropped to one knee. Adam and Rassie did the same and watched as Frank brought his R1 up into his shoulder. While the rest of the white South African soldiers in the stick carried the newer, lighter R4, Frank was old school, preferring his heavy-barrelled version of the R1, which packed a harder punch with bigger rounds.

'It's me,' Lieutenant Ferri called softly as he emerged from the dense mopane bush. He came to Frank and Adam and moved in closer while still watching out, so he could hear what was happening. Evan arrived soon after Ferri, and nodded to Adam. Ferri pointed in the direction they had just come from. 'The wreck of the Bosbok is just over there, five hundred metres. There's five terrs there; three are searching the plane, picking through it, and the other two are keeping watch, one with an RPD. I left the Bushmen there to keep an eye on the enemy.'

Frank nodded. 'They would have heard the chopper and the gunfight. They know we're here.'

Ferri ignored the words of caution. 'Luiz also picked up the fresh tracks of a man walking, across our path, right to left. East German boots; Luiz says he's limping and bleeding.'

'Somebody who got separated from his unit, maybe?' Adam volunteered, wanting to be useful.

Frank shrugged. 'Just watch out, Kruger. They're out here, all around us.' He looked to Ferri again. 'Any sign of the pilot?'

Ferri nodded. 'There was the body of one man near the wreckage of the cockpit. It looked like they'd pulled him out. He had a pilot's helmet on. There was no sign of the other one. Colonel de Villiers told me there were two people on board.'

'Like I've been saying, a Bosbok has a crew of one, the pilot.

Who's the passenger?' Frank asked.

Ferri looked away from him, out at the bush. 'I don't know, but there was no sign of him.'

'If he lived, he's a prisoner,' Frank said. 'The Angolans would have taken him straight away. The others are probably just looking for intel or souvenirs.'

'All right, listen up,' Ferri said, motioning with his hand for all of them to gather around him. 'We're going to take out the guys at the crash site and check the aircraft wreckage. Frank, when we get there, I want you to push out to the right, with Kruger and Rassie, to provide fire support with the LMG. Rossouw, Litis and I will be the assault group.'

Frank stared at him for a few moments. 'That's your plan ... Sir?'

Ferri glared at him. 'You got a problem with that, Sergeant Greenaway?'

'Sir, you said one of those guys has an RPD, a machine gun.'

'I know what an RPD is, Sergeant. Are you scared? We've got a machine gun as well.'

Frank sneered. Adam did not like the way this was playing out. 'Sir,' Frank continued, 'I'm not any more scared than you should be, but usually we'd want odds of three to one to attack the enemy. Those soldiers at the crash site won't be the only ones in the area. I suggest we call in a sitrep to Ondangs, and ask for aerial photo–'

'No, Sergeant, we go. Now.'

Adam was torn. He hadn't been in serious action yet and the thought of hitting the five enemy soldiers, with the element of surprise on their side, was exciting. However, Frank had been in more contacts than all of them put together, except for Luiz and Roberto, and he knew what he was doing. Frank was tired, for sure, but he was no coward.

'Sir –' Frank began again.

'I have orders to get to that aircraft and to clear it,' Ferri said.

'What do you mean, "clear it"?' Frank said. 'I thought we were just looking for the crew?'

'We are,' Ferri said.

'Is there something you're not telling us?' Frank said.

Ferri looked away again, in the direction he had just come from. 'There are five enemy over there. We have the element of surprise and we will launch an immediate action, and clear the ... Target.'

Frank shook his head but said nothing more. Adam felt his heart rate increase.

'ADAM?' Sannie said.

He was sitting in his home office-cum-library. The paramedics and the local police had left. Neighbours had reported hearing noises when Sannie had arrived, and a couple of volunteers from Pennington Community Watch had also responded. One of them tidied Adam's ramshackle kitchen after making coffee and rooibos tea for everyone.

Sannie had sat with Adam, drinking her tea. He had gone into one of his lapses of staring out at the sea. It was too dark to see the waves, with no moon above, but the roar of the surf helped calm her.

He turned and smiled at her. 'Thank you, again, for saving my life.'

She shrugged. 'All part of the job. You couldn't sleep either?'

He shook his head. 'I got up and did some work on my thesis, then went back to bed and was trying to go to sleep when I heard a noise. I thought I was imagining it, but then he jumped me from behind. He must have used some kind of choke hold on me, because I passed out, like, straight away.'

'You didn't see anything of him?'

'No. Like I told the local guys, it was pitch dark and I saw nothing. I do remember, though, that he was wearing gloves.'

Sannie had told the Scottburgh police that she had heard a person in the house when she first arrived, but could not provide a description.

'Do you have any enemies, Adam? Anyone who would want to hurt you, someone who might think you've wronged them?'

He seemed to give the question some thought, then answered with a question.

'Why would the intruder have left a pistol behind?'

'I've been thinking about that as well,' Sannie said. 'Of course, he could have just dropped it.'

Adam nodded. 'Maybe, but we didn't have much of a struggle. The guy came up behind me and before I knew it, I was out cold. He sure knew what he was doing.'

'I told the Scottburgh police that I want to see the results of the fingerprints on the pistol.' The local police had bagged the weapon and taken it with them.

'You know I said the attacker had gloves on,' Adam said.

'Yes.'

He was looking into her eyes now, present in the moment, not delving back into his memories. They were both thinking the same thing. 'You think they might find my prints on the gun, that the guy put it in my hand?'

'I don't want to get ahead of myself, or to interfere with the local detectives' investigation, but yes, I did wonder if that person was going to put the gun in your hand when you were unconscious and use it to make it look like you had shot yourself.'

He simply nodded.

'If someone was going to murder you and make it look like you'd committed suicide then there must be a reason, Adam, and you must know that reason.'

Adam drew a deep breath, then exhaled. 'There's a local fisherman. He threatened to kill me.'

Sannie raised her eyebrows. 'Why?'

'He's guilty of shark finning. He wiggled his way out of a charge, but I've seen him; I had a video of him doing it and supplied it to the police on a USB stick. It went missing from the evidence locker at Port Shepstone.'

'Hmm,' said Sannie. 'Would someone kill you over shark fins?'

'George Renshaw, the fisherman, is making millions of rands per year in fin smuggling. He's not just active here; he runs fishing operations in Mozambique, too. He's like the Chinese, supplying boats and outboards to the little guys across the border. They're the ones doing the most damage to the shark populations.'

'And he sees you as a threat, because of what? Bad PR?'

'Well, when my attempt to have him prosecuted failed I may have also accidentally damaged one of his boats.'

'Adam . . .'

He held up his hands. 'I had an old Land Rover that came with this house. I mistakenly reversed into his boat,' he couldn't hide his smile, 'in the parking lot of the ski boat club at Rocky Bay.'

Sannie folded her arms. 'I have no time for vigilantes, Adam.'

'I got my comeuppance. The Land Rover was stolen and torched. Can you think of anyone who would steal a clapped-out old Defender?'

'I drive a Toyota, so, no. You think it was this Renshaw?' Adam nodded. 'I'm as certain as I can be. I went to the police, but they seemed content just to open a case and give me a docket number so I could claim on my insurance. Of course, I didn't have insurance as I couldn't afford it.'

'Do you really think Renshaw would kill you and set it up to make it look like you killed yourself?'

'Maybe. He did his best to get me eaten by a shark the other day. He was chumming the water, probably to catch sharks and fin them, and came too close to the boat I was on while I was GPS-tagging a guitarfish. I fell in the water and a bull shark came for me – Renshaw just motored away without even stopping to help.'

'Adam!'

Adam shrugged. 'Renshaw has good reason to hate me. I pretended to be his friend. He says he was a recce during the war and I buddied up to him for a while, spinning him some stories about my time in Angola and telling him I needed work; this was before he knew I was a phd student researching sharks.'

Sannie held up a hand. 'Wait a minute. You went undercover?'

'Yes,' he said. 'I wanted to see finning for myself. It was awful to watch, but I was able to get some video on my phone without him noticing. He knows the South African authorities are trying to crack down on finning and that it's illegal here, but I think he likes to show off how he can flout the law. It was almost as if he enjoyed it, as well, cutting the fin off a live animal. In the video he was laughing as he tossed a shark back into the water.'

'Sickening,' she said. As with what she'd seen with the rhinos, Sannie found the thought of someone being so cruel to an animal hard to stomach. 'You say he "says" he was a recce-commando?'

'He's a loudmouth with too many war stories. Recces aren't like that, so I thought he might be lying. Anyway, he soon found out who I was – I went to the fisheries authorities and the police with the video. What really set him off, though, was when I went online to a couple of military imposter sites that out guys who make up stuff about their army service. Renshaw saw me posting some questions about him and his service and he went ballistic.'

'Which either means he really did serve in the recces, or he was embarrassed about being outed,' Sannie said.

'The latter, I think. I received a few private messages from guys who said they had served in the recces around the same time Renshaw claims to have, and they'd never heard of him. He called me up after he saw I'd been on Facebook and told me that he was going to kill me, some time when I least expected it.'

'Those were his words?'

'Yes,' Adam said.

'How long ago did all this happen?' she asked.

'Two months ago. In the meantime the case was dropped because the copy of the video I gave to the police went missing, and there was the business with me backing into his boat, him stealing my Land Rover, and then him trying to get a shark to eat me.'

Sannie shook her head. Men. 'I can talk to my boss at the Hawks. They also had a problem with a load of drugs being stolen from the evidence locker at Port Shepstone, so I'm ashamed to say your video disappearing is something that does happen from time to time.'

'Yes, I read about the drugs in the *Witness*.'

'Didn't you have a backup of the video?'

'I did,' Adam said, 'on my old desktop computer. I had to erase it from my phone as I needed the memory. My desktop was stolen one day while I was out at sea. Luckily I had my laptop with me. It's my turn to say I'm ashamed that I hadn't got around to loading the video on my laptop.'

'Sheesh, I think you personally have accounted for most of Pennington's crime stats for the whole year.'

He smiled. 'Seems like it.'

She looked around at the dark, quiet house. 'Do you want to stay the night somewhere else?'

'Are you offering?'

She hoped she wasn't blushing again. 'That's not what I meant.'

'I know, sorry, I didn't mean that either. No, I think I'll be fine. If it was Renshaw then he'll know he's lost the element of surprise.'

Sannie thought about what had brought her here, to Adam's aid, and the fact that they'd both been up late, messaging each other. 'Why didn't you accept my offer of a lift to the Kalahari, Adam?'

He looked out into the darkness again. 'I think there'll be other guys going to the funeral, men I served with in the war. I didn't want to risk dragging you or Mia into some bad stuff that went on between us.'

'You don't need to worry about me. Mia and I will keep to ourselves, though she's naturally going to have questions for men who served with her father. Maybe you should be there, for her. And trust me, Mia has grown into quite a fearless, tough young woman.'

'I'm not surprised,' he said. 'You know, I think I will take you up on your offer, if you're still willing to drive me all the way to Dune Lodge.'

'I am,' Sannie said, 'but you seem to have some issues about your time in the army. Trust me, I know that trauma can have lasting effects on people, but I just need you to tell me one thing, honestly, about this "bad stuff" you mentioned.'

'Anything.'

'Did you do anything illegal when you were in the war? Is there anything I need to know about?'

'No.'

She looked into his eyes. Sannie had met hundreds of liars in her job. This man was telling the truth. 'OK. Consider the offer still valid.

If I think you're a responsible driver you can share the time behind the wheel.'

'I've got some money put away so I can contribute towards the fuel.'

'Thanks,' she said. Fuel was expensive these days, and while she was mindful of his financial state, she also told herself that if he had wanted to get to Luiz's funeral under his own steam he would have had to pay the bus fare. She stood.

'I'll talk to the Scottburgh guys tomorrow and see what they turn up with Mr Renshaw.' She raised a finger, admonishing him. 'But you stay away from him.'

He put his right hand over his heart. 'I promise.'

Adam stood as well and when Sannie turned to look back at him she saw that half of his face was glowing warm from the light of the paraffin lamp; the other was in darkness. She waved goodbye, not lingering or putting herself in a situation where the thought of a farewell peck on the cheek might put one or both of them in an awkward situation. As she walked out the door onto the stoep, pausing to check the garden, she glanced back over her shoulder.

He smiled at her and put his hand over his heart again. It was a simple gesture, but it gave her a flutter. Despite her tiredness and the rollercoaster evening she'd just been through, her step felt lighter as she walked through Adam's jungled front yard to her car.

12

Mia walked through the sand in the cool of the early morning towards the place where Luiz's body had been found. She carried her .375-calibre rifle loosely in her right hand. The pangolin waddled ahead of her, seeming content to head in the same direction.

She had spoken to the pangolin researcher she knew, and he had told her that the animal needed to build up its strength before they could release it into the wild again. This involved someone accompanying the little fellow – it was a male – on daily foraging trips of an hour or two. The researcher was away doing some field work in the Kgalagadi Transfrontier Park, but Mia made a plan to take the pangolin to him as soon as possible, so he could examine it and continue with its rehabilitation.

'Why did Luiz take you?' she said out loud to the pangolin.

Mia had to admit that while she'd thought Luiz was a nice guy, there was a whole lifetime's worth of experience she did not know about him. Perhaps he had been a poacher in his younger years, in Angola? No doubt he had hunted to feed himself, but was that illegal or legal? He'd made his living in recent years finding game for delighted tourists, but did he empathise with their love of nature or just see wildlife as a means of making money? She didn't relish asking Shirley these questions.

The pangolin busied itself snuffling in the sand, digging for ants. Mia scanned the ground around her. The place where Luiz had gone to die was just off the game-viewing road she had been on with her guests, but it was a well-trodden area. At least one of the game-viewing vehicles stopped each day under the big camel thorn tree for sundowner drinks or the coffee break on the morning drive.

Mia felt a chill, even though the sun was climbing. Something had moved her; perhaps it was Luiz's spirit.

Fortunately, in the way of luxury safari lodges, guests usually only stayed two or three nights – four or five at most – and the people on her vehicle had left before news of Luiz's suicide had reached them. Mia checked her watch; there were three new clients arriving at Dune Lodge's airstrip off an afternoon charter flight at two o'clock. Another guide would pick them up, but Mia would meet them for afternoon tea and a game drive at four.

Out of respect for Luiz, and because the site had been treated as a crime scene when his body was first discovered, the big tree had not been used as a drinks stop since she had found his body there three days earlier. Again, Mia felt the downy hairs on the back of her neck stand up as she approached the tree.

There was little sign of his death and the wind had airbrushed away the tracks around where his body had been. The dunes in the distance were a vivid red, their rolling, wave-like crests silhouetted crisply against the deep blue sky. She loved it here; it was like being on a different planet compared to the bushveld of Mpumalanga and the thickly vegetated fringes of the Sabie River where she had daily hunted leopards for tourists armed with cameras and smartphones.

Out here there was a feeling of true isolation and wilderness. The settlements around the Kalahari were few and sparsely populated; what most overseas visitors to Kruger and its adjoining game reserves rarely glimpsed was that about two million people lived along the edge of those wildlife-rich reserves.

Mia had enjoyed learning about different species – gemsbok, or oryx, with their long-pointed horns; bat-eared foxes; desert mongooses; and brown hyena, something she'd never seen prior to arriving at Dune Lodge.

The different cultures, especially the San, also fascinated her and she had looked forward to learning much more from Luiz. She had fully expected the quiet older man to share his knowledge only at his own pace, but now he was gone.

Mia was looking forward to seeing Sannie again, and it was good news that Adam Kruger had agreed, at last, to come with her. Mia wondered why Adam had taken his time. Perhaps he had thought it too much of an imposition on Sannie, a woman he had met through the course of a police investigation, to take him on a two-day drive across South Africa.

'He's nice,' Sannie had said of Adam when Mia asked her what he was like. She had dim childhood memories of him. She recalled his height – even among adults, she remembered, he was tall. 'Fit. But troubled,' Sannie had said.

There was something else Mia had picked up in Sannie's voice. Sannie liked him.

Mia's thoughts turned to the days ahead. These were no normal, run-of-the-mill guests that she was picking up this afternoon. Shirley had told her that the two men were Evan Litis and Tony Ferri, two of the men who were in the photo with her father. Evan, Shirley said, had visited Luiz a few times over the years that Luiz had been working at Dune Lodge. And Tony Ferri was well on the way to becoming a household name in South Africa, if he wasn't one already. Apparently, he was bringing his campaign manager, Lisa Ingram, with him. Lisa had been liaising with Shirley.

'Absolutely no selfies, pictures or mention of his visit to the media,' Shirley had warned Mia and the other staff at the lodge. Mia had guided for several celebrities in the past, including famous Hollywood actors and music stars from around the world. Julianne Clyde-Smith's lodges were expensive and the staff were all used to being given special instructions, from bizarre dietary requirements to rules about privacy.

Tony Ferri's request for privacy was not unusual, and Mia respected it.

'He wants to fly under the radar,' Shirley had said, 'so as not to be seen as using Luiz's funeral as a PR stunt for his election campaign.'

Mia had messaged Sannie an apology – the arrival of the surprise guests and the need to help organise a service for Luiz meant that Mia would not be able to take leave while Sannie was visiting. She would, however, be able to see Sannie between game drives.

Mia sat down in the shade under the thorn tree, a discreet few metres away from where she had found Luiz. She kept an eye on the pangolin, which continued huffing and snuffling about. She would have to turn him around and take him home to camp before the sun climbed much higher.

Mia was about to get up when she glimpsed movement in her peripheral vision. When she swivelled her head to the right, she saw nothing. For a moment, she wondered if she had imagined it, but then reminded herself to trust her instincts. She lived by her wits and experience in the bush. There was no water here in this arid landscape, so it was unlikely to have been a bird. The Kalahari was a wonderful place to view raptors, such as snake eagles and goshawks, but she had seen something on the ground, not in the air.

She stared at a nearby dune. Again, she saw a flicker. Something white. Mia held her breath, watched, and listened. She heard nothing.

The pangolin was off to her left, walking away from the dune where Mia had seen the movement. White? She pondered.

Mia felt her heart skip as a bewhiskered spotted face and golden eyes slowly, cautiously, appeared over the crest of the dune. If there was one thing that gave away a leopard it was the snowy white tip of its perennially curled tail. She loved seeing leopards – they were her favourite cat – but normally she was perched safely behind the wheel of a game viewer.

Mia watched as the feline, a female, she thought, judging by its slender body, moved fluidly over the top of the dune on crouching legs, its body hugging the sand. Mia realised that sitting where she was, perfectly still, the leopard had not seen her. It was focused on the pangolin.

Very slowly, a centimetre at a time, Mia reached for her rifle, which was propped up against the tree beside her. She was torn. In the wild, she would never dare to do anything to come between a predator and its prey.

'Can't you do something to save that baby impala?' she had been asked more than once by a tourist client as she and her guests had sat quietly and watched a leopard stalk an antelope.

'Leopards have babies as well, you know,' was her usual reply. 'And they need to eat.'

This, however, was different. The pangolin was in a weakened state, undernourished because of his time in captivity. Mia had taken him out walking, in search of ants to eat, at a time convenient to her, not the pangolin. Ordinarily it would have been foraging at night. It would also have been fair game for a leopard at night, if the cat had chanced upon it, but now, by being here in broad daylight, albeit in the cool early hours, Mia had tipped the balance of power in favour of the leopard.

Mia did not fear for her own safety. She knew cats – lions, leopards and cheetahs – and other dangerous game, and how to act around them and approach them. This was a little unusual, however. She had successfully tracked and followed a leopard on foot a couple of times without the cat knowing she was there, but she had never been in a position where a leopard was approaching her without being aware of her.

As much as she wanted to protect the pangolin, she was not prepared to hurt or kill the leopard for following its natural instincts. She let go of her rifle and looked down at the ground around her. She found a thick stick, about thirty centimetres long, part of a branch that had fallen from the camel thorn tree above her, and wrapped her hand around it.

The leopard seemed to lower itself so much that it became part of the sand as it crept forward. Mia saw it give a little shake of its behind as it tensed, ready to sprint the remaining distance between itself and the pangolin and then pounce on the hapless little creature. It was now or never.

Mia drew back her arm and hurled the stick at the leopard. The cat got a fright, stopped its stalking and pivoted towards Mia, looking for the source of the distraction. Mia scrambled to her feet, grabbing her rifle as she did so and holding it above her head, one-handed to make herself look big and threatening.

'Hah!'

The leopard sized her up and for an instant Mia thought she had just made the last, and worst, decision of her life. The predator glared at her, but then turned and ran off, back over the dune.

Mia exhaled. She looked at the pangolin, which was still blithely rummaging in the sand. 'You'll be the death of me.'

Mia walked around the pangolin and began shepherding it back towards her vehicle, parked on the game-viewing road. But as they passed the spot where Luiz had died, the pangolin stopped and started digging in the sand.

'Hey . . .' she objected.

Mia walked up beside the pangolin, which was now quite relaxed around her. The morning sun glinted on something in the pile of sand the pangolin had just disturbed. Thinking it was a scrap of rubbish, perhaps the foil wrapping cap from a sundowner bottle of sparkling wine, she bent to retrieve it.

Mia ran her fingers through the sand and found the object. She took the stretchy wrap from around her neck and used it to pick up a copper-coloured bullet casing.

She held the casing up to the light and inspected the markings at the base, around the primer. Mia was an accomplished markswoman, by virtue of her job, and while she did not own a pistol, she could tell immediately that this was from a pistol, and the same calibre as the weapon Luiz had used to shoot himself.

'Hell.'

. . .

TONY AND LISA were signed into the SABC studios in the Johannesburg suburb of Auckland Park by a young producer from the morning Expresso show.

Tony stifled a yawn. They'd been on tour all over South Africa and were up at four to get an early flight to Johannesburg to get to his morning television interview appointment. There had been no chance for a nap on the flight, as he'd spent the time reading the morning newspapers and preparing for his TV appearance. As soon as the interview was done, they'd be heading back to the airport to catch a flight to Upington, then the charter to Dune Lodge, organised by Evan's personal assistant.

'I'll show you to the green room, Lisa,' the producer said, 'and Mr Ferri, you'll please go straight into hair and makeup.'

They parted and Tony took a seat in front of a mirror surrounded by lights.

'Hi, Mr Ferri,' the pretty young stylist said to him in his reflection. 'I'm –'

'Zandile, how are you?'

'You remembered?' She beamed.

He smiled. 'How could I not? You told me about your mom's dialysis problems last time.'

'Yes!' She set to work powdering his face. 'She was thrilled when she got a call from that doctor who agreed to help her. I sent an email to your office, thanking you, and a lady replied.'

'Lisa, my campaign manager.'

'Wow.' Zandile went to work on his hair. 'I still can't believe you were able to help us like that.'

'There's no point being in public office, whether in government or not, if you can't help people.'

Zandile stepped back half a pace to admire her expert handiwork, then leaned in close to him. Tony could smell her perfume, bubblegum sweet, as she whispered in his ear.

'My mom's only ever voted ANC, but she said she might vote for you guys next time. She says you're the only person who can fix Eskom and stop the load shedding!'

Tony held a finger to his lips. 'It'll be our secret.'

Zandile stepped back again and Tony stood up. She took the cape from around his neck. 'Knock 'em dead, Mr Ferri.'

'Please, it's Tony.'

Zandile grinned. 'Good luck . . . Tony.'

'Thank you, and give your mom my best.'

Tony just had time for a cup of coffee in the green room before the producer came for him and led him onto the set of the breakfast TV show. He stepped over snaking cables, and a technician fitted a lapel microphone to his sports jacket, with the power unit clipped to his belt.

The hosts, a man and a woman, indicated where he should sit and face.

'We're live in four, three, two, one,' a producer said.

The hostess looked at an autocue. 'Well, he's on track to gain the leadership of the Democratic Alliance at the party's next conference, and if the opinion polls are anything to go by – and some complex behind-the-scenes alliances work out – he might just have a shot at unseating the long-ruling ANC from their decades of power in South Africa. Welcome to the couch, Tony Ferri.'

'Great to be here again,' Tony said, smiling. He was a seasoned media performer and knew that one of the tricks to a good interview was to get some of his key messages out and on the record right from the start. 'And thank you for that very flattering intro, but the important thing to remember is that this is not about deals and party politics, it's about a better future for all South Africans, starting with accountability and a drive to end corruption.'

'For sure,' the host said, 'and as we can see on the monitor now, you've been busy campaigning across South Africa, almost as if you're running for President already, and not just the leadership of the DA.'

'I'm just doing my job. If more of our elected representatives – on all sides – spent more time out among the people instead of cloistered in parliament or off on taxpayer-funded trips or sitting in committee rooms, they'd be better able to gauge the mood of the people. We've got service delivery failures, unemployment, load shedding and crime. People are not happy and I don't blame them. As well as looking internally, it's also time for South Africa to play a bigger role in helping our neighbours in –'

'Disturbing news, though, in The Star this morning,' the hostess interrupted, dropping her smile, 'in which a government MEC has claimed you were part of an army unit that committed atrocities during the so-called Border War in Angola in the 1980s. What's your reaction to that?'

He'd read the news report. 'Like many men my age I was ordered to serve in the military – conscripted. The MEC has been vague in his mud-flinging. I served my country and if it were the law of the land for me to be called up to defend this great country of ours, I would do so again. The important thing to note here is that the ANC government, whose armed members were sheltered by Angola during the war, has done little, if anything, to repay that support, or to help the country. By contrast, I was part of a veterans' charitable organisation which raised money to build schoolhouses and dig wells in Angola, and we have started a program to support disabled Angolan veterans – the people we fought against – to live a better, fairer life.'

'So you deny claims of atrocities?'

'Categorically,' Tony said. 'One can be proud of one's service even if one wishes the war had never happened. I think just about any veteran of any conflict anywhere in the world would say the same thing.'

'Well said,' the male host said.

'And speaking of people with disabilities,' Tony jumped in, unprompted, determined to steer this interview back to where it should have been going in the first place, 'let me tell you about the DA's policy on this subject that we'll be taking to the next election.'

AFTER THE INTERVIEW, Lisa, who had been allowed to watch from behind the cameras, came to him. 'You snatched victory from the jaws of defeat there.'

'Just a minute while I take off my microphone.' With the sound technician's help, Tony unclipped the devices from his lapel and belt and thanked the man. He'd seen too many politicians caught out by carrying on a conversation after forgetting they were wearing a mic.

Tony waved and smiled to members of the crew as they left the studio. The producer who had met them signed them out.

Their Uber arrived to take them to OR Tambo Airport. Tony slumped in the back seat of the Mercedes. 'I knew that question was coming, given this morning's headlines, but it still shook me up.'

Lisa put a hand on his knee. 'You did fine, boss.'

He put his hand on hers and gently removed it. 'Thanks. The ANC's just fishing, I'm sure. However, if they trawl the online communities and a couple of sensationalist memoirs they'll probably find enough mud to throw at me again. Reminding people about the war is a sign of desperation.'

'As long as the EFF doesn't get on the bandwagon,' Lisa said. 'Our learned colleagues, the Economic Freedom Fighters, are too busy trying to start their own glorious wars to worry about one that happened before most of them were born.'

Lisa chuckled, but Tony was not smiling.

'You're doing that "gazing out the window" thing again,' she said. She was right. Any mention of military service or the Border War seemed to set him off these days. Today he realised it was the business with Luiz.

'International or domestic?' the driver asked.

'Domestic, please,' Tony said.

'Holiday? Business?'

Tony could see that the man kept glancing in the rear-view mirror, like he was trying to work out where he'd seen him before. 'A funeral.'

'Oh, sorry, my condolences.'

'Thank you.' That seemed to shut the driver up. Normally, Tony would have struck up a conversation, but this time he did not feel like making small talk or trying to secure one more of the tens of millions of votes he and his party would need if they were ever to have a chance of winning government.

Sometimes it just all seemed so hard. He knew that thinking about the army and the war could bring him down. Also, it seemed there was no future for him and Lisa – after his failure to respond to her advances before the speech, he hadn't wanted to try again with her later in the night. Sex, for Tony, had been a way to forget his past, but now even that had been taken away from him.

The comments by the ANC member of parliament had worried him far more than he let on. When he'd seen the headline in The Star, he'd felt a jolt of adrenaline so pure and rich that he thought it might give him a heart attack over breakfast.

The story had been baseless, with no specifics other than accusing his 'unit' – which could refer to his platoon, company, battalion or even 44 Parachute Brigade – of atrocities. Bad stuff had happened during the war, as it did in any conflict. The one thing he feared being made public about his time in Angola was, it seemed, still under wraps. He was sure that if the ANC had any concrete information about that then they would have given it to the media in the article, or before now. He remembered Luiz standing in the clearing, next to the body of the Angolan soldier who had been shot in the back of the head, the one who had wounded Hennie.

There was a risk the government was perhaps muddying the waters now, to plant the idea of atrocities in the minds of the media and the public, and to get him on record as denying the allegations, as he just had, only to then land some killer blow closer to the election.

Tony sighed. He had to live with that possibility; there was nothing he could do about it if the truth did come out. The fact was, though, that very few people had shared his secret of what happened on that day in Angola when they had gone looking for the missing aircraft. Three of them – Greenaway, Luiz and Colonel de Villiers – were now dead.

Tony had carried the burden of this secret and its attendant risks since agreeing to run for the DA, and he had always known the information could be made public at any time. If it was, it would make it almost impossible for him to ascend to higher office, even if he stayed in the party and parliament.

There was a chance, though, that he would get through this, and perhaps, one day, be able to put the war and Angola behind him. He longed for that day.

'What are you thinking about?' Lisa asked him.

'Nothing.' They were approaching the airport terminal. Tony looked up and saw that the driver was staring at him in the mirror again.

'You look familiar,' Tony said, deciding to be proactive.

'I'm Sipho, I drove you once before, sir.'

'Ah yes, I remember now, to the event at the Coca Cola Dome.'

He smiled. 'Yes, sir.'

'You must call me Tony, Sipho, now that we are old friends.'

Sipho laughed. 'OK . . . Tony. I was trying to think where I have seen you again, and I now realised, it was in the newspaper.'

'Possibly,' Tony said.

'You are the politician, the leader of the DA.'

Tony shook his head. 'No, not the leader.'

'Not yet,' Lisa chimed in. 'But we're hoping he will be.'

'I think you will be better than the current leader,' Sipho said. Lisa laughed.

'I am loyal to the leader, but the decision will not be mine, it will be for the party.'

'Sir?'

'Tony.'

'Yes, Tony . . . I have a question, if you don't mind.'

'Fire away.' They drove up the ramp to Departures and Sipho navigated through the throng of arriving and departing cars to the domestic terminal. Tony had reneged on his no-small-talk idea, so now he had to see it through, or else the driver would remember him as being rude.

'They said on the radio that you committed crimes in the war, but you said you categorically did not. Did you believe in the war for apartheid?'

He could correct Sipho, and tell him the war was not about protecting apartheid but rather about stopping the spread of influence of communist countries in Africa. But like most wars, it had probably been more about resources – diamonds and Angola's oil – than ideology.

'In hindsight, no, Sipho. War should always be a last resort. But I was proud to serve my country. I was ready to die for my country when I was twenty-two, even though the thought scared me, and I would die to defend South Africa today, as well.'

Sipho pulled into a car spot and turned around to look at Tony. 'We need more leaders like you. God bless you, Tony.'

13

S annie picked Adam up from his house at five am, the day
after the early-morning invasion of Adam's home. They
wanted to beat the N2 commuter traffic heading into Durban,
to the north, and then take the N3, through Pietermaritzburg to
Harrismith before it got too busy.

From there the journey would take them roughly westward,
skirting south of Johannesburg. It was a shade over a thousand kilometres to their first stop, at Kuruman, but the route they were taking
would break the back of the long trip on their first day, so they would
arrive at Dune Lodge, on the edge of the great Kalahari Desert, at a
reasonable time the next day.

'I know a good B&B in Kuruman and they've got two rooms available,' Sannie said as they set off. She wanted to clear the air about
sleeping arrangements as early on as possible. 'It's not too
expensive.'

'Thanks,' Adam said. 'I do have a little money put away for rainy
days, and this is one of them.'

It was, in fact, raining, and Sannie took it easy on the N2. As a
young uniformed police officer she had attended many fatal road
accidents. Lush green cane fields to the left and the Indian Ocean off

to their right gave way to Durban's port and urban sprawl as they headed left, inland, into the Natal midlands.

'It's pretty up here,' Sannie said, taking in the hedges and farms that had probably reminded so many of the English people who had settled here in the old days of their homeland. Natal had often referred to itself as Britain's last colony, and she could see why.

'It is,' Adam said. 'Though I don't think I could live far away from a beach for too long.'

'Whereabouts in Australia did you live?'

'South of Sydney, on the New South Wales south coast; it reminded me a lot of Pennington and Scottburgh, without the sugar cane – and the humidity, and the monkeys.'

She laughed.

'I think I was always homesick for South Africa,' he added.

Sannie nodded. 'I understand. I don't think I could leave, and there would be no point now; I'm too old.'

'You're not.'

She glanced at him and rewarded him with a smile.

'Oh, I got a call from Scottburgh Police,' she said, indicating to overtake a truck. 'They followed up on your friend Renshaw. He claims he was in Durban the night you were attacked. They're checking his alibi.'

'It's only an hour from Durban to Pennington,' Adam said. 'He could have ducked out of wherever he was staying and driven back.'

'True,' Sannie said. 'He says he was at a fishing industry conference.'

Adam scoffed. 'Probably all sitting around telling each other how environmentally sustainable they are, or complaining about people like me trying to ruin their livelihoods. The truth is, I love seafood, and fishing. It's just that people are so damned greedy; that's what I hate.'

'Yes, well, he was staying at the Suncoast Casino complex. We can check CCTV from the hotel to see if he left during the night, and we can also track his cell phone, maybe, though if he left it in his room then it would show he was there all night.'

'I think it's good I'm getting away from Pennington for a few days. I don't know how I'd react if I saw Renshaw on the street.'

She tried to keep her voice calm, casual. 'Do you have a problem with anger?'

'I did, for a while, until I got some help. But I was never violent with my wife or the kids, trust me on that.'

'OK, good to know,' she said, breathing an internal sigh of relief.

'It was just like I could be fine, and relaxed, and then my anxiety levels, my temper, would go from zero to red-lining in a couple of minutes. Sometimes we'd be at a party, in Australia, and people would be complaining about the politics or the prices of stuff while ignoring the fact they were all on good wages and had nothing to worry about. I felt like saying: "If you want to talk about politics, talk about Africa, where you can be killed for supporting the wrong party, or sent off to war when you're a kid." Then I'd have to leave, and my wife kind of understood, but she didn't really. That sort of kak was hard on her.'

'I understand. I'm sometimes the same around my friends when they complain about a split nail, and all I can think of is some murder victim with a panga in their head.'

He looked at her.

'Sorry.'

'No, don't be. You understand.'

On the Highveld it was a like a different country, sprawling farms and wide-open grasslands. When they stopped every two hundred kilometres to change drivers or refuel, or grab a snack, the air was cooler, crisp. She wondered how she would take to the south coast with its high humidity and almost tropical heat. She had lived in Johannesburg, in Kempton Park, the only place she and Christo could afford after they got married, and had grown up in the Lowveld, but the towns they passed through were also very Afrikaans. She felt a kinship with these farmers in their two-tone shirts and Toyotas. Everyone was so English in KwaZulu-Natal.

'I hope you find a house,' he said.

It was as if he was reading her mind, which was weird, but nice. 'Thanks. I was just wondering if I could fit into the south coast scene.'

'I'll teach you to surf.' She laughed.

'Serious. You'd love it.'

'I can't even stay on a boogie board.'

'I taught my kids to surf . . .'

Sannie waited for him to finish the sentence, but he didn't. 'You miss them?'

He nodded. 'I do.'

'If it's any consolation,' Sannie said, 'my daughter, Ilana, is in the Cape and she may as well be in Australia given the amount of time I get to spend with her.'

'You said she's studying to be a doctor?'

Sannie squared her shoulders. 'Yes; she's an intern already.'

'My daughter has no connection to Africa. I think that's what worried me most, that she can't see what I see.'

Sannie was sitting on 120 kilometres per hour, the speed limit, but a car in the oncoming lane pulled out to overtake a truck. There was no way the driver would make it if Sannie didn't slow down. She touched the brake and flashed her lights as the man finally passed the truck. 'What I see is bad driving.'

'Yeah,' Adam said.

'Sorry, what did you mean, by "what I see"?'

'The humanity,' Adam said. 'Everything in Australia is so orderly, so safe, so predictable, that people rarely get exposed to situations where they have to step up, to really help. Sure, there are bushfires and floods and they bring out the best in people, but most Australians just go through their lives with very few cares.'

'That's probably a little unfair, Adam. We all have trouble in our lives, no matter where we live.'

'Yes, I agree,' he said, 'but think of the everyday kindness that people show here, the way they help each other, because they have nothing, because they experience the worst of life, but they have the will to carry on.'

They drove on in silence. Sannie agreed with what Adam said, but in her job she had also seen the very worst of humankind.

'Tell me about the guys you know, who you think are going to be at the funeral,' Sannie asked after a while. 'I'm going to meet them soon enough anyway.'

'You've heard of Tony Ferri, the guy the media is touting to be the next leader of the DA, maybe a future president?'

'Yes, of course. You were in Angola with him?'

Adam nodded. 'He was our loot. Our lieutenant for a very short time while our regular platoon commander was ill.'

'He seems like a good guy.'

Adam shrugged. She cast a glance at him. His jaw was clenched tight and he had folded his arms.

'What is it, Adam?'

He turned his gaze back to her and blinked. 'One of the reasons I moved to Australia was to get away from my past. Frank and I were close, almost like brothers, even though we lived far apart and didn't see each other all the time. It wasn't like that with everyone in our unit. Some of us left Angola with old scores to settle.'

'Do you maybe want to talk about it?'

He forced a smile. 'Maybe some time. I don't know. Would you like me to drive?'

'Sure. I'm feeling a bit tired. Thanks.' Sannie indicated and pulled over. They got out, stretched, and changed sides.

Adam was quiet as he drove and Sannie wondered if, in his mind, he was back in the war.

ANGOLA, 1987

'SIT TIGHT, Adam, and watch our backs,' Frank Greenaway whispered, then left Adam in order to catch up to Ferri, who had already set off back towards the location of the downed aircraft.

Adam crouched behind a fallen tree, his light machine gun

resting on the trunk. He still didn't know who was right – the sergeant or the lieutenant. He wanted to get into the fight and was now slightly disappointed that he had been left out. Adam knew that Frank was no coward and Frank had been able to convince Ferri to make a minor change to his plan.

Frank, now reluctantly committed to the attack on the crashed Bosbok, had said that rather than organising an all-guns-blazing attack on the Angolans guarding the wreck, he would act in an over-watch position, using his R1 and his sniper's training to take out as many of the enemy as he could before the Parabats assaulted. Adam would be left to cover their rear. Frank had clearly worked hard to rein in his anger, and Ferri had accepted Frank's proposal rather than digging his heels in once more, like a petulant child.

Adam scanned the bush behind them. A few minutes later, he started at the sound of gunfire. He heard the heavy, decisive crack of Frank's rifle, three well-aimed shots, then the lighter rattle of R4s. There was the sound of an AK-47 answering, then silence.

A dove cooed somewhere in a tree. Adam felt keyed up, ready, scared and excited. He knew he was supposed to keep watching out, but he craned his head to look behind him, where the action had just taken place. There was no further firing. Adam turned back to where he should have been watching and froze. Coming through the bush was an African soldier with an AK-47. Adam recognised the Cuban lizard pattern camouflage uniform the man was wearing – he was FAPLA, Angolan regular army.

The man saw Adam at that moment and started to raise his rifle. While Adam had initially been looking the wrong way, his LMG was still pointed to the rear, the area he was covering. Adam pulled the trigger. A burst of rounds sprayed from the other man's weapon as he fell backwards. In shock, Adam realised he had hit the man.

'Contact!' Adam remembered to yell. A rifle opened up and Adam was aware of shredded leaves and twigs falling around him.

More gunfire erupted from behind Adam, who pitched himself forward, onto his belly, beside the roots of the fallen tree. His bush hat slipped forward, covering his eyes. Adam scrambled with his hand to move the hat and felt a bullet fly over his head. He realised that if he had not lain down just then, he would have been killed. He saw a man running through the bush, across his front. Adam fired, but the man kept on running. Adam realised that Frank had been right to leave him behind, guessing that additional Angolans in the area would be drawn to the sound of the battle at the crash site, and it was Adam's job to provide cover for the other Parabats when they pulled back from the Bosbok.

He fired another five-round burst at the FAPLA soldier running towards him, using the last of his ammunition belt. The man must not have seen Adam, lying on the ground. At least one of Adam's bullets hit him and knocked him down.

Adam rolled onto his side, flipped open the feed cover of his machine gun, brushed away a stray piece of metal link, and took a new two-hundred-round belt from one of his pouches. Trying to keep his hands steady, he laid the new belt on the breech, closed the feed cover and cocked the gun. He heard movement behind him and craned his neck.

'Halt!' Adam hissed.

Erasmus, the lance corporal, emerged from the trees. 'Kruger, it's me.'

'Sorry, Corporal,' Adam said.

'Ag, don't apologise, man,' Rassie said in Afrikaans. He lay down beside Adam. 'You did the right thing. Now, what the hell is going on here?'

'Three, maybe four of them,' Adam blurted. 'I hit two.'

'Good man,' Rassie said. 'Just as well Frank left you here to cover our arses, instead of sending you with us. We got four of the five at the crash site. The other ran off. The loot, Luiz, Roberto and Litis have gone forward to clear the wreckage. Greenaway's covering them.'

'What should I do?'

'What you're doing now. Keep watch. Protect our arses, boy, and give us a way out of this fokken shit hole.' Rassie clapped him on the shoulder. 'And well done.'

'Thank you.' Adam swelled with pride.

'Don't fokken thank me, just keep watch. We're most likely surrounded. This whole mission is FUBAR.'

Fucked up beyond all recognition seemed to be right, judging by the fight between their officer and sergeant, but Adam's heart was racing with excitement. He heard gunfire, another two shots from behind them, where the others were clearing the crash site. Adam risked another glance over his shoulder and saw Ferri, Evan, Luiz and Roberto running his way through the bush. Rossouw and Frank emerged from their flank. The men all linked up, then fell back to where Adam was.

Evan dropped down beside Adam, while Rassie got up and joined Ferri and Frank in a huddle. 'No survivors at the aircraft,' Evan said.

'What were those last two shots?' Adam asked.

'There was a wounded terr, by the wreckage. He'd been pretending to be dead, but he raised his rifle when we got close.' Evan paused to catch his breath. 'The loot shot him, man, through the head. It was hectic. Ferri saved my life, man.'

'We surrounded now?' Adam asked.

Evan shrugged and looked out at the bush. 'Did you drill that guy over there?' He pointed to a body.

'Jip,' Adam said.

'Serious?'

'And another one.'

'Shit,' Evan said. 'I heard the firing, didn't know what was happening.'

Frank came to them, no-nonsense. 'Stop your tuning, you two. We have to move. We're going to pull back to a pickup LZ. Stay sharp, there's FAPLA all around us.'

'Yes, Sergeant,' Adam said, thinking now was not the time for familiarity.

Frank looked around. 'Rassie told me you protected our arses. Good work, boet.'

Adam felt ten feet tall. 'Come,' Frank said.

There was a burst of machine-gun fire from behind them. Frank turned and fired his heavy-barrelled R1 in that direction. Bullets sailed over their heads.

'Move!' Rassie grabbed Evan by the back of his webbing straps and hauled him up. Adam was already on his feet.

It was all so confusing, Adam thought. These guys were making decisions by the second and he was flat-out trying to remember to put his safety catch on and off. Now he was running while still trying to watch his front and either side for FAPLA soldiers who he thought might emerge from the bush at any instant.

As they moved off, Adam passed the first of the two men he had killed and the full realisation of what he had just done sank in. He saw the man's wide-open eyes, staring at the sky, the blood on his uniform shirt, and the look of surprise or horror frozen on his face forever. The FAPLA soldier was young, maybe Adam's age.

Frank came to Adam, dropped to one knee and quickly, expertly, searched the dead man's pockets and gear.

'We look for intelligence,' he said while his hands roamed over the body, 'maps, diaries, that kind of shit, but this one's too young to be carrying much, and he's not an officer or NCO.' Frank then picked up the man's discarded AK-47, removed the magazine and tossed the rifle in the bush. 'Let's go.'

Adam stood there, looking down at the dead soldier. He felt nauseous, but did not want to throw up in front of the others. Frank grabbed his arm, firm but not rough. 'Come.'

Adam let himself be led away.

'They're all around us, Kruger,' Frank said. 'You need to get your head back in the game.'

'OK,' Adam said, swallowing hard. Frank was right. He could not dwell on killing the man now; that would have to wait.

Luiz and Roberto were in the lead, retracing their path, and Ferri was alongside Luiz, pointing at something on the ground. Luiz turned off to the right, though Adam was sure they had not come that way. Luiz, Roberto and Ferri spoke to Evan, then left him and went off on the new track.

'And now?' Frank asked, rhetorically. 'Where the fuck is he going?'

Evan was ahead of Frank and Adam. He beckoned to them to catch up. 'The loot says we must wait here,' Evan said.

'What the fuck?' Frank said. He looked at the ground, where the others had stopped. 'This is the spoor we cut earlier, of the FAPLA guy.' Frank walked a few metres to the left, still studying the tracks, then came back to them. 'This guy has actually walked in a circle. I think he's come from the crash site as well.'

'So why have the others gone off without us?' Adam asked. 'Ferri won't listen to anything I say,' Frank said. 'Something's up here, Chinas, and I don't like it.'

'Ferri's following some FAPLA guy?' Adam asked.

Frank rubbed his stubbled chin. 'Not necessarily, hey. A lot of guys souvenir Cuban boots and wear them. Ferri confirmed the colonel told him there were two people on board – the pilot and a passenger, but Ferri's not saying who the other person is. He couldn't meet my eye just now when I asked him about it, before we cleared the wreckage. There's something he's not telling us.'

'Really?' Evan sounded incredulous.

Frank scanned the bush around them, wary as always. 'Think about it – Ferri decides to recce the crash himself, and now he and the trackers go off like hunting dogs by themselves. There's something not right here.'

Adam scanned the bush too, imagining another enemy soldier behind every tree.

'What do we do?' Evan asked.

'If we stay here, we might get overrun by FAPLA.'

'Those were our orders from Ferri, to remain here,' Evan said.

They heard gunfire, three quick shots, from the direction the others had just headed.

SANNIE OPENED HER EYES. She was surprised at how easily she had fallen asleep. A thought occurred to her.

'Do you really think that guy Renshaw would break into your house and assault you in the middle of the night?' she asked.

Adam shrugged and indicated to pass a truck. He accelerated firmly and deliberately and, Sannie noted with approval, he also indicated when returning to his lane.

'He's a loudmouth and a bully,' Adam said, 'but a big oke.'

'Yes, but that attack took planning, and he was trying to disguise his identity. Wouldn't it have made more sense for him to maybe pick a fight with you in public?'

'Yes, he's as strong as an ox,' Adam said, 'and I did see him hit a man in a brawl in the car park of the East Coast Brewery, at Umkomaas, once.'

Sannie nodded. 'Which makes sneaking around at night a different thing altogether.'

Adam stared through the windscreen.

'Could it have been someone else? Over something different?' she asked.

'I don't know.' Adam didn't take his eyes off the road.

14

At four pm Mia met her guests in the main dining and lounge area at Dune Lodge.

Her boots squeaked on the polished screed concrete floor of the tasteful, canvas-walled building as she approached the two men. The afternoon-tea buffet had been set up and the guests were standing, drinking coffee. Mia was in a khaki shirt and shorts and a tan-coloured baseball cap with the lodge's gemsbok logo.

She smiled broadly as she extended her hand to the man in jeans and a grey polo shirt. She recognised Tony Ferri immediately. He was even more handsome in person than in his pictures on the internet. 'Good afternoon. I'm Mia.'

'I'm Tony Ferri – nice to meet you Mia, and this is Evan. We both served with your father. I'm so sorry for your loss.'

'Thank you.' She almost said, 'You don't need to introduce yourself', but the policy with high-profile guests at all of Julianne's luxury lodges was to treat them the same as everyone else, and not to fawn over them or, worse, ask them to pose for selfies.

'Hi, Mia.' Evan Litis shook her hand. He was also good-looking, but if Tony had that rugged ageing rugby player and head boy look about him, Evan, in his Cape Union Mart safari gear, was more nerdy professor. He had a lovely smile, though, and put his other hand on hers. 'I'm also sorry about Frank. He was a great guy, and it's so nice to meet you.'

'I don't know where to start,' Mia said. 'Normally game drives are about, well, game . . . I don't want to intrude on your visit by asking a hundred questions.'

'It's not a problem, Mia,' Tony said. 'This is no ordinary safari. We're here to pay our respects to Luiz, primarily, but Evan and I know each other well and we thought that we could also spend some time getting to know the area in which Luiz worked. Meeting you is a bonus, even if the circumstances are sad.'

A 'bonus'? Mia thought. The way he smiled when he said it made her blush. 'It's only us on the game drive, so I'll be guided by you, as the guests, which is the way it should be and always is around here. There's a third member of your group? Lisa Ingram?'

'She's sitting this game drive out,' Tony said. 'Lisa's my campaign manager and something of a workaholic.'

'Tony's the same,' Evan said. 'Mia, you can't imagine how difficult it was for him to take three days out of his schedule, but he did, for Luiz.'

'Shall we go?' Tony said, and to Mia it sounded like an order dressed up as a question. He had a natural confidence about him, which she guessed was needed in a politician, and a leader's ability to make people do things while thinking it was their idea. Her ex-boyfriend Graham could be arrogant, but Tony Ferri was – she searched for the right word – commanding.

'Ready when you are,' Mia said.

Evan gulped his coffee and picked up an expensive Nikon camera off the coffee table next to him. Mia led them outside.

'It's nice and warm now,' she said, as the two men climbed onto the back of her Land Rover Defender game viewer, 'but as soon as the sun sets it will get bitterly cold. There are blankets and fleece-lined ponchos in the boxes between the seats, and you can store your cameras and gear there as well.'

'Thank you.' Tony smiled.

Tony and Evan positioned themselves on the seats immediately behind Mia, which would make it easier for them all to communicate. Mia could have taken one of the trackers with her, but she felt like she wanted some privacy with these guests. She was aching to start firing questions at them about her father, but she had to be respectful of their wishes.

Mia stopped a little way outside of the lodge's perimeter, on a road that crested a dune and afforded them a panoramic view over the desert. She switched off the engine and gave them her standard briefing about not standing up in the back of the vehicle, and not moving about or talking loudly when they were at a sighting.

'Do either of you have any special requests, about animals or birds or anything else you'd particularly like to see?' she asked them.

'I do,' Evan said. 'I'd really like to see one of those famous big black-maned Kalahari lions.'

'We do have a coalition of two males active in our reserve at the moment,' Mia said. 'They're a couple of beautiful boys; they've just come into their prime and their manes are looking good. I'm sure that they'll be challenging the one old male from our resident pride very soon.'

'That would be cool,' Evan said.

'Mia?'

She turned to Tony. 'Yes?'

'Do you think it would be possible to visit the spot where Luiz ...'

'Of course,' Mia said. 'I was there just this morning. It's no longer a crime scene. In fact, ironically, it's a place we often take guests.'

'Thank you.'

They set off. Soon into their drive they saw a herd of springbok and a stately, lone male gemsbok. Mia stopped for Evan to take photos. Tony seemed lost in his own thoughts and Mia couldn't tell if he was enjoying being on safari or not. They were here for a sombre reason, but she hoped that the politician could at least unwind a little.

Evan leaned forward as she drove off, so Mia could better hear him. 'You know, your dad was a good guy. A lot of us more junior soldiers really looked up to him.'

'That's nice to know, thank you, Evan. The army – the war – were such big things in his life, but I only really saw the aftermath, what it did to him. I have some memories of him catching up with some of his friends, usually drinking, and they would laugh about stuff, but he never actually told me very much of what he did, or what might have been funny.'

Evan nodded. 'That's pretty common. I have a wife and two sons, but I would find it hard to tell them about some of the things that happened to me, even if I thought they wanted to hear. I'm not sure they do.'

'You might be surprised,' Mia said. 'My dad was a pretty experienced soldier, right?'

'Yes,' Evan said. 'He'd been in Angola long before I arrived, and had been in plenty of contacts – gunfights. He had a cool head and an amazing ability to make decisions under fire. I used to feel sorry for those above him, sometimes, like Tony.'

Mia glanced back at the politician. 'Is that right?'

Tony gave a little laugh. 'Your father was the consummate professional soldier, Mia. In fact, I think he should have been selected for officer training. Evan's right – he could be a nightmare to lead, mostly because he had way more experience than many of us. A couple of times I gave orders and Frank queried them.'

'That does sound like my dad,' Mia said. 'He never could avoid an argument, if he thought he was in the right.'

'The problem for me,' Tony said, 'was that more often than not Frank was right, and that was a bitter pill for a young officer to swallow, but we would talk things through and get past our differences. I learned from Frank, and men like him who were under me, and in the end we all got on OK.'

'I guess the army's like that, when you put your lives in each other's hands,' Mia said.

'That's right,' said Tony, 'you'd do anything for the person next to you, even put your life on the line for them, because you know they would do the same for you. It forges friendships and links between people that last forever.'

Mia thought about that as she drove. It seemed that Tony and Evan were close, but she could not recall either of them being at her father's funeral, or visiting him any time before then. There were men, old army buddies, who her father sometimes caught up with in Hazyview, at the pub, when they were passing through town.

'Did you ever see my father, after the war?' Mia asked over her shoulder. She had to keep her eyes on the road and scour the desert for game at the same time, so it was hard to make eye contact with either of the men.

'Once,' Evan said, 'after he had left the Kruger Park.'

Mia remembered that time of her father's life. Frank was depressed; he had been made redundant from the South African National Parks and his drinking had increased.

'I could tell Frank was doing it tough then,' Evan said. 'I want to apologise to you, Mia. There might have been more I could have done for him, and maybe I should have stayed in touch more often.'

Mia shook her head, and it was easier to watch for game than look at Evan this time. 'There's no need for you to apologise, Evan. Believe me, I've asked myself too many times what I could have done differently and I keep coming back to the same conclusion – Dad chose to take his own life, and as much as it pains me, I can't hold myself responsible for that, so nor should anyone else.'

'Thank you for saying that,' Evan said.

'Same here, I'm afraid, Mia,' Tony said. 'I only saw your dad once, when I was in Hazyview supporting a DA election campaign. Greg Mahoney, a safari guide friend of your father, was our candidate. It was a brief meeting. Like I said, we had our differences, but it was good to catch up with him, and I got a real feeling that any difficulties we'd had in the army were in the past.'

'I'm sure that was the case,' Mia said. 'Look!' She put on the brakes and snatched up her binoculars.

Evan leaned forward. 'What is it?'

'Cheetah.' She lowered the binoculars and pointed to the top of a dune a hundred metres away.

Tony took up his own binoculars. 'Mia, you're incredible.'

She grinned. It was a great start to their game drive and she felt doubly blessed to be in the company of these men who had known her dad. Tony watched the cat for a few seconds then turned to her; his eyes were smiling and she felt a little thrill.

Evan fumbled for his camera in the stowage box and began snapping pictures. Mia forced herself to look through her binoculars again; it was like she'd just had a moment with Tony that she was reluctant to break. But she was sure she could impress him even more. 'That's a female. I know this one. If we're lucky . . .'

As if on cue, the cheetah stood and started walking down the dune in their direction. In her wake came four fluffy cubs, their backs bristling with white hair.

'Wow,' Tony said.

'Yes!' Evan's digital camera fired in bursts, like a machine gun.

'I was just about to say if we're lucky we'll see this one's cubs. And there they are. Did you know that they have that white marking on their backs so that they look like honey badgers, an animal that even other predators stay away from?'

'That's amazing,' said Evan. He paused his photography to revel in the sighting. The cheetah veered off from them and crossed the road about thirty metres in front of Mia's Land Rover. Mia started the engine and moved forward slowly so that her guests could get a close-up view of the cats.

Two of the cubs paused and turned back towards the vehicle, and Evan opened up with his camera again. Glancing over her shoulder, Mia saw that Tony didn't have a camera, or even his phone out; he seemed content to simply take in the majestic beauty of the mother cheetah and the cute antics of her cubs. The two curious cubs started a mock fight with each other.

'Astonishing,' Tony said. 'Mia, I know your dad loved the bush, through his job as a ranger. I saw it in him, in Angola. Shirley the lodge manager told me when we checked in that you're a master tracker. I'm sure Frank would be so proud of you.'

Mia beamed. 'Thank you, Mr Ferri.'

'Tony.'

'Thank you, Tony.'

The mother cheetah made a high-pitched squeaking noise, almost like a bird call, and her cubs scampered after her as she headed off, over another sand dune. Mia stayed until the last of the cats had disappeared and Evan finally lowered his camera.

'Guys, if you're ready, we can move on?'

'Fine by me,' Tony said.

'Yes, that was awesome, thank you, Mia. What a great start to our drive,' Evan said.

Before she started the engine, Mia was able to turn around and look both of them in the eye properly, one at a time. 'Would you like to go to the spot where I found Luiz now?'

They looked at each other and nodded. 'Yes, please,' Tony said. Both men seemed to have genuinely enjoyed seeing the cheetah and her cubs, and Mia felt like it was a shame to bring the mood back to one of sad reality, but they had asked to go to the sundowner tree and this was, after all, related to the reason they had visited. Mia drove on, stopping briefly to point out a brown snake eagle.

The bird stood atop a thorn tree, as ramrod-straight as a soldier on a parade ground, as it surveyed its domain, looking for prey. The sun was low, turning the bark of the sundowner tree a mellow orange-brown when they arrived. Mia switched off the engine.

The silence descended over them like a blanket and seemed to prevent any of them from speaking or moving in the Land Rover.

At last, Evan said: 'OK, let's do this.'

MIA THOUGHT it was interesting that it was the businessman rather than the former army officer and aspiring leader of the country who made the first move.

'Yes,' said Tony.

The vehicle's springs creaked as they climbed down. Mia scanned the landscape, looking and listening for the telltale presence of predators – the flick of an ear or tail, or the sound of a bird alarm-calling. The morning's encounter with the leopard was still very fresh in her mind. Even Mother Nature, however, seemed to be holding her breath.

Mia opened her door, got out and caught up with the men who were headed towards the big tree. She pointed to a spot about ten metres away, in the open. 'I found him there.'

Evan looked where she was pointing, but Tony was still looking in a different direction, out over the desert. Nonetheless, he started walking in the direction Mia had just indicated.

'It's like I can feel him here, still,' Tony said.

'Can we go there, stand there?' Evan asked.

'Sure,' Mia said.

Tony walked ahead of them, as if he was drawn to the place by Luiz's ghost. He looked around him, on the ground. The wind and sun and the hungry sand had already obliterated all traces of Luiz's grisly death.

'You found him?' Evan said. She nodded and closed her eyes.

Tony nodded. 'I'm afraid we all saw death too often, men killed by guns.'

Mia remembered the vultures and the effect of the hyenas, who had also partially fed on Luiz's body. She said nothing of that to her two guests.

'It must have been very hard on you,' Evan said.

Mia gave a little shudder. 'I called it in, but it was worse for Shirley, his niece, who had to formally identify him.'

'Poor woman,' Evan said, 'having to see something as horrific as that, and to identify a warrior that way.'

'I remember he had a Flechas tattoo,' Tony said. 'That was his Portuguese unit, the "arrows". You know, they had almost crushed the various resistance movements in Angola before Portugal threw away all its colonies, in 1975?'

'They didn't count on the Cold War, or Russia and Cuba getting involved to the extent they did, after they legged it,' Evan said.

Tony nodded. 'There's no point trying to rewrite history, or refight old wars.'

'Luiz was as brave as a lion,' Evan said to Mia.

She stared at the spot where he had died, then out over the endless desert. 'I wish I'd got to know him better; that he had opened up to me.'

'He was always quiet,' Tony said. 'Colonel de Villiers told me that many of Luiz's family had been killed in a massacre in Angola. After the Portuguese withdrew, some of the local African guerrillas sought payback on the San, who had fought against them. By all accounts it was a brutal conflict, with atrocities committed on both sides.'

'Did you . . .' Mia almost wanted to withdraw the question that had spilled from her lips.

Tony turned to her. 'Did I commit any atrocities or war crimes? Is that what you mean, Mia?'

She shook her head. It was not. She had been trying to ask if Tony had witnessed anything illegal.

'No,' he added quickly. 'And nor did your father or any of my men. Frank was tough, and could be a pain in the arse for his superiors, but he was no war criminal. As for what he saw, I can't say.'

She noted how Tony had used the politician's trick of deflecting her question in a direction he was comfortable with rather than necessarily telling the truth. Mia did not feel like she had the right to press the question.

'War is brutal,' Evan said. 'I think all of us saw or heard things we would rather not have. Mostly, for me, combat was confusing and hectic, but then unlike Tony I wasn't in command. I just had to do what I was told.'

Mia thought she might be on safer ground asking about Luiz. She wanted to try and understand why he had killed himself. 'What about Luiz? Tony, you said there were atrocities committed on both sides in the war in Angola?'

'Do you really want to know, Mia?'

'Yes,' she said.

He sighed. 'Some of it may have been boasting, or rumour, but there were stories of the Flechas, in the Portuguese colonial days, cutting the ears off corpses. There was even a tale of a Flecha who cut the heart from a guerrilla while he was still alive, and then took a bite out of it while it was still beating.'

Mia felt sick. But if the San soldiers had mutilated corpses, what effect did that have on a person? Had Luiz been unable to live with the memory of some thing, or things, he had done? 'What about Luiz?' she repeated. 'Did you ever see him do anything wrong?'

Tony stared at her, his face unsmiling. She had done it after all, she realised; she'd pressed him for a straight answer to her earlier half-formed question.

The politician spoke slowly and deliberately. 'I never saw Luiz commit a war crime.'

Unable to hold his gaze, Mia glanced at Evan. The other man was looking sideways at Tony, and Mia wondered what Evan was thinking. Did he know or think the possible future leader of the nation was lying? Mia had read about Tony in the news and she wanted so much to like him. She'd been taken aback by how good-looking he was in the flesh, as well. Was he too good to be true?

'But did Luiz do anything outside of military regulations?' Tony continued. Mia returned her gaze to him. Tony nodded. 'Yes, Mia, I believe there is a good chance that he or maybe his brother did. They came from an era and a culture different from ours, even though we were separated by only a few years. The world remembers the brutality of the apartheid years, but few people know of the iron fist that other countries, such as Portugal, Belgium and Germany, used to rule their African possessions. We all have blood on our hands, in some way, shape or form, and people can be brutalised by war and persecution. As Evan just said, none of us can take back the things we saw or heard. All I can tell you is what I did, and what I saw. I'll share it with you, if you like.'

'I'm sorry,' Mia said. 'I just wanted to learn, perhaps to understand.'

Tony exhaled audibly. 'I came across Luiz, after one contact, and found him standing over the body of a dead Angolan soldier. The man had been wounded in a contact, but then he'd been shot in the head. His weapon, a rocket-propelled grenade launcher, was far away from him, in the bush. At the time, I thought Luiz had shot a prisoner in cold blood. I later reported it to my superior, the sector commander, and was told that because I had not actually witnessed any wrongdoing then I should keep my mouth shut. I haven't told anyone that story since, Mia, just you.'

Mia was stunned. She had thought him a 'typical' politician, with his half-answers and misdirections, but now he had opened up to her, entrusting her with something he had not told the world. 'Thank you.'

'Sheesh,' Tony said. 'I've been carrying that around with me a long time.'

'Did you know that Luiz had a gun?' Evan asked Mia.

Mia shook her head. 'No idea, and nor did Shirley. It was such a shock. He seemed like such a gentle man; it's amazing to hear of his past. But you know, I never thought my father would kill himself, either.'

'Frank always seemed so . . . strong,' Evan said. 'He was like the glue that held the platoon together. He was tough, but you could go to him if you had a personal problem and he always stood by us.'

'Losing his job really hurt him,' Mia said, 'but I hoped he would get work in one of the safari lodges. I don't think he was the kind to be a guide, but with what I know about the industry these days he would have been a great maintenance or operations manager. He had all the skills, and the bush was his true home.'

'Sometimes it creeps up on you later in life,' Tony said. 'You tell yourself you're doing fine, that it's all behind you, but when you get older, when you mature and start thinking about the things you've done in your life, those very things that you tried to push aside with work, or booze, or whatever, come back to haunt you.'

'Do you think that's what happened to my father, and to Luiz?' Mia asked.

Tony just stared out over the desert, where the sun was heading for the dunes, in silence. Mia wondered if it was happening to him.

15

Adam enjoyed the feeling of being back behind the wheel of a car: the speed, the barely audible hum of the engine and the sensation of moving forward, not backwards.

Sannie had fallen asleep again. Her mouth was half open and while the look was not flattering, he smiled. It was a memory from another time, a road trip with a beautiful woman who felt safe enough to be able to let herself sleep while he drove.

He remembered family holidays in a different life. It had been, to some extent, an illusion of happiness. The poison that killed his relationship had been present in him even before he met his wife. He hadn't been aware of it, when he went back to university and told himself he could put the army, Angola and the war behind him.

Sannie woke. 'Where are we?'

'Only about an hour out of Kuruman.' The sun was setting, the sky turning pink.

'I can't remember the last long road trip I did. It feels like holidays, almost.'

'You're reading my mind, now,' he said, glancing over at her and smiling to hide the hurt. 'I was just thinking how happy I seemed to be.'

'Seemed?'

'You're perceptive,' he said. 'I think I was playing at happy families, playing at life. I married a girl I'd gone out with before the army, since I was seventeen, because it seemed like the right thing to do, and we had kids for the same reason. We were very different people, and the army had changed me.'

'You went to university after the army?'

'Yes. And even while we were making plans to marry and our families were getting excited, I knew that I couldn't support a family on a marine biologist's wages. I let my studies fall away, and I was drinking too much.'

'I'm sorry to hear that.'

He shook his head. 'No, I look back and I can see that I had a wild time, that I enjoyed it, but I think I was running away, or hiding, or both. Funnily enough I ran towards stability, a wife, kids and a job. OK, it was a good, fun job, running a dive business and being out on the water all the time, but it wasn't what I had wanted to do, before the army.'

'I've heard of people with PTSD who are fully functioning,' Sannie said. 'Instead of drinking or taking drugs, or withdrawing or whatever, they channel all their energy, all their anxiety into becoming consummate professionals. They use their work to escape from their problems.'

'It feels good, though, to be going somewhere,' he said, changing the subject.

She looked at him and smiled and it warmed his heart. 'Yes. It does.'

Adam had the almost uncontrollable urge to reach out and touch her, not sexually, but just to have his hand on her, to feel some sort of connection between them. In the next instant, however, he knew that such a move would not only be inappropriate, but also a waste of time.

Here he was, hitching a lift with a widow across South Africa to go to a funeral. He barely had enough money to meet his promise of paying half her fuel, let alone enough to take her out to dinner or woo her, or provide for her. If it was another century then his prospects would have been described as non-existent. If, however, he could finish renovating the house and sell it, then he might have enough capital to start up another small business.

If.

He was kidding himself. If he hadn't been so stupid and in such a rush to close the deal on the house he'd wanted to buy, he wouldn't have lost all his money to the Nigerian fraudsters and he could have been funding himself through his studies with money to spare. If he'd taken the time to call the attorney, rather than just transferring the money, he'd be living in a grand place, and his parents' house would have been fully renovated and sold to provide him with money to live on and cover the kids' airfares when they wanted to visit. If he wasn't such a failure.

They arrived in Kuruman and Sannie's sat nav directed them to the B&B she had mentioned. They checked in. 'Two rooms, please,' Sannie said.

'Yes,' said the elderly proprietor. 'My wife said you had specified that. Breakfast is from seven to nine in the morning.'

'Thank you,' Sannie said. They took their bags from the car to their respective rooms. 'They don't do dinner here, so I was thinking the Spur?'

'Um, yes, fine by me,' Adam said, wondering what he would be able to afford on his budget, without looking like a cheapskate or a pauper. 'Half an hour?'

'Sounds good to me,' she said, 'I'll just have a quick shower.'

When they met again, Sannie had not only washed, but also changed. She wore jeans and a light long-sleeved pink top. She had tied back her hair. She smelled clean and he detected a hint of perfume.

They drove the short distance to the open-air mall and went into the Del Rio Spur. The restaurant, with its Wild West–themed decor, was as familiar as any of the more than three hundred other steakhouses in the chain across South Africa. A waitress showed them to a table and asked if she could take their drinks order.

'Please can I see the wine list?' Sannie asked.

When the waitress went to fetch it, Sannie put her hands on the table and leaned towards Adam. 'I have a business proposition for you.'

He felt nervous. He was still wondering what he would do about dinner. 'I'm all ears.'

'Whatever house I buy is sure to need some work. I can see by all the painting and renovating that you're doing at your folks' place that you must be good with your hands.'

'I like the work, always have.'

'Well,' Sannie said, 'I'll make you a deal. I'll pay for dinner, and for fuel for this trip, if you agree to give me, say, three days' worth of your time doing home handyman jobs around my new place. Or mowing the lawn or what-what-what.'

He clasped his hands together. 'No.'

'Oh.' She looked crestfallen, then frowned. 'If this is some male ego thing, I –'

Adam grinned. 'Let's make it seven days and it will be a pleasure.'

Sannie looked relieved. 'I could bargain you down, but I'll be working full-time and even a police captain's pay is not great, so, I reluctantly accept.'

Adam put out his hand and she took it. They shook. He did not want to let go.

Sannie didn't pull her hand away but sat there, just holding his, smiling.

The waitress returned and Adam cleared his throat. 'Well, since I'm going to be paying for this with the sweat of my brow, I'll have a Castle Lite, draught, please.'

Sannie quickly scanned the list. 'Will you share a bottle of red with me?'

'With pleasure,' Adam said.

Sannie ordered a bottle of Beyerskloof Pinotage and Adam told her it was one of his favourites.

At Sannie's urging they ordered starters as well as a main course. The food at the Spur was not high cuisine, but Adam closed his eyes in raptures as he devoured the fried calamari and a medium rare fillet steak.

'You look like you enjoyed that.'

'I can't remember the last time I had fillet.' The thought could have brought him down, but he reminded himself of his shrink's advice, to try and stay in the moment and not dwell on the past. 'Thank you.'

'Thank you for all the work you're going to be doing for me.' Sannie nodded to the bottle of wine. 'I don't want to drink the rest of that here. It wouldn't do for a police captain to get caught for drunk driving. You can finish it if you like.'

'Let's take it with us,' Adam suggested.

'Good idea.'

Sannie paid, and while Adam felt a little uncomfortable, he admired the way she had given him a way to save face through her offer of work. She was kind and thoughtful, and as he followed her out, he thought she looked great in her skinny jeans.

They drove back to their bed and breakfast and went to their rooms, then reunited at the small table and chairs outside Sannie's room. They each brought a glass and Adam poured for them. The sky above was clear, the stars coming out, and the air was cool.

'Thank you again,' Adam said.

She waved off his gratitude. 'My pleasure. It's been a more enjoyable trip for me than travelling across the country solo.'

'And much better than a bus ride for me.'

She raised her glass. 'Cheers to that.'

Adam looked into her eyes as they clinked glasses. He worked every day of the week, on his thesis, out on the water doing research, watching cars at the mall, or hammering, sanding, painting and sawing at the house. He knew that on some level, as Sannie had mentioned, he was drowning his demons with hard work, but it also left him little time to think about women, or love. Now, he was not only well fed, he had time on his hands.

He wondered what her lips would feel like against his. They drank their wine in a companionable silence, broken only by a brief discussion of how beautiful the moon looked. He wondered what she was thinking.

Sannie finished her drink and stood. 'It's been a long day.' Adam got to his feet, too, but she made no move to leave.

He wanted to kiss her, but at the same time he didn't want to do anything to spoil things. He put out his hand. 'Goodnight, co-driver.'

'Goodnight, nutsman.'

He laughed at the Afrikaans word for handyman. They shook hands and, as before, lingered just a few seconds longer than was necessary.

'Goodnight, Adam,' she said, this time.

'Goodnight, Sannie.'

They let go of each other and she went to her door. He waited while she opened it, and when she stepped inside, she turned and looked over her shoulder at him. Just before she closed the door, she smiled.

JUST AFTER NINE, in contravention of Dune Lodge's rules, Tony left his suite.

Normally after dark guests could not leave their accommodation without being escorted by their guide or one of the lodge's security staff. The lodge was unfenced and lion and leopard were active in the area.

Tony paused in the dark and looked up. The stars were sometimes the only thing that had grounded him when he was in the bush in Angola. He could picture himself back home, in South Africa, lying on his back with a girl by his side, or as a child, gazing up at the night sky in awe. The stars reminded him of innocence. Now he felt guilty as he made his way through the chilly night to Lisa's room. She was waiting for him and opened her door before he was even on the stairs leading to her permanent safari tent.

'Hurry,' she hissed. 'It's freezing out.'

He bounded up the stairs and into her room and arms. They kissed. She began to undress him.

'Can we just talk?'

'Just?' she chided.

'For now.' He broke apart from her and sat in a chair in the corner of her tent. Lisa flopped down on her bed. Her hair was tousled, her top few buttons already undone. She was barefoot, sexy, ready.

He took a deep breath. 'I went to the place where Luiz died today.'

'I'm sorry, babe,' she said. 'It must be hard for you.'

He ran a hand through his hair. 'I said some stuff, to the guide, and later I regretted it. The words just spilled out, like I'd been stabbed and they were bleeding from me.'

She leaned forward, elbows on knees, eyes searching. 'What did you say to her? Tell me, Tony. No surprises.'

He held up a hand. 'That's why I'm talking to you, not making love to you right now. As my campaign manager you need to know.'

'And as your friend, Tony, your lover.'

'OK, yes, thanks. I told her about how one day I came across Luiz in the bush with a dead Angolan guy. I'm pretty sure he had executed him in cold blood.'

'It was war, Tony. However, this is the first I've heard of this.'

'I've never told anyone this stuff. At the time, I was told to forget it, and that as I didn't actually see Luiz pull the trigger, it was not worth pursuing. Bad stuff happened, but this happened at a time when other things were going on.'

'What sort of other things?'

He waved his hand. 'Nothing too bad. But it's all coming back to me now. It's unsettling me. If I didn't commit a war crime, is it just as bad that I turned my back on one, Lisa? What would the media make of the story I told Mia today? What if she leaks it?'

She stood and came to him. Her hair framed his face as she bent forward and kissed him. He smelled her shampoo; normally it was enough to stir him.

Lisa sat in his lap and stroked his cheek with a finger. 'She won't. I could see how excited she was to meet you, a man who served with her father. She probably worships you.'

'Her father was a disrespectful insolent little shit. He was always questioning my orders and thought that no one could tell him how to fight or what to do. He was experienced, but also arrogant.'

She leaned back. 'I don't think I've ever heard you talk about someone other than the President with such vitriol. This guy really got to you, huh?'

He took a deep breath to try and calm himself. 'I'm a politician, I can't bad-mouth anyone, except the government, of course. Frank Greenaway had it in for me from the moment I took over the platoon. Everyone thinks the army is one big happy family, all pulling together, but when you get a bunch of alpha males in close proximity in a stressful environment it's like lighting a match in an explosives factory. One time –'

Tony realised he had said enough about the past for one day. And why had he felt the need to unburden himself to Frank's daughter, of all people?

'One time, what?' Lisa said. 'What happened between you and this guy, Greenaway?'

ANGOLA, 1987

TONY HEARD footsteps coming up behind him. He and the two Bushmen were still following the tracks of the man who had left the crash site alone. Tony turned and saw Frank Greenaway. Tony cocked his head at the sound of the crump, crump, crump of mortars leaving their tubes.

'What the hell are you doing?' Greenaway demanded. 'Do you think the guy wearing the FAPLA boots is one of ours? What aren't you telling me?'

Tony winced at the sound of the three mortar bombs detonating. It sounded like they were landing near or on the wrecked Bosbok aircraft they had just left.

'We've got our orders,' Tony said to the sergeant. 'You know them as well as I do. I told Litis to tell you to stay put. You've disobeyed an order.'

Greenaway glared at Tony for a second but said nothing. Rossouw, with his radio, was hovering just behind Greenaway. The rest of the stick caught up with them.

'Don't shoot, it's us.' Evan emerged from the bush, followed by Kruger.

Tony was livid. He glared at Greenaway and then at Evan. 'I Told you to wait for the Bushmen and me to return.'

Frank stuck his chin out. 'It's stupid to split a small patrol like this.'

'Stu– I'm going to charge you when we get back.'

'I'd rather be in the cells than out here with people who don't know what they're doing.'

Tony felt his body trembling. He wanted to lash out and hit the sergeant, but he knew that would be an admission that he had completely lost control. Also, if it came to a fight, Greenaway would probably kill him with his bare hands. The others watched like dirty, sweaty schoolboys waiting for a playground bout.

'Listen . . .' Greenaway took a breath. 'Sir, with respect, I felt it was unsafe for us to be left waiting for you and the others. Someone's started an eighty-two-millimetre mortar barrage close by. They're looking for us.'

'I heard,' Tony said coldly, regaining control. 'All right, you can stay with us for now.'

'Who are we looking for?' Greenaway said.

'The other member of the Bosbok's crew.'

'Like I told the guys, it's a one-man crew on that thing. It's a passenger you're looking for, not a crewman.'

'Sergeant Greenaway, you've been told what you need to know. Now, to tell you the truth, I don't give a fok if you come with us, walk back to South West Africa, or sit in the bush and get yourself killed, but we are tracking this man, and I am in command of this patrol. If I hear anything else from you other than "Yes sir", I'll have you charged. Do I make myself clear?'

'Yes . . . Sir.'

Tony turned on his heel and strode away to catch up to the San trackers. He didn't bother to look over his shoulder, but he heard Greenaway marshalling the others behind him. He did not have to justify himself to a sergeant.

Luiz had stopped up ahead and Roberto was kneeling next to him. Tony moved forward to join them. Lance Corporal Erasmus, the medic, was beside them.

'What is it?' Tony asked.

'Luiz says we're close,' Erasmus said, 'and he's picking up a blood trail.'

'Some blood, earlier,' Luiz said. He spoke rarely and very little and Tony thought it was because his English was not good. 'Now, worse.'

Tony looked where the tracker was pointing and could see where the dirt was darkened with blood. 'We need to get to him, quickly.'

There was a whistling sound, followed by an explosion off to their left that rocked the ground.

'Mortars are getting closer,' Greenaway said. 'Someone really wants us dead.'

'Shit,' Rossouw said. Luiz was on his feet, moving, with Roberto in tow.

'This way,' Tony yelled, pointing after the Bushmen.

'No arguments from me,' Greenaway said. 'It's away from where that shell just landed.'

As if to propel them along faster, a second bomb detonated somewhere near the first.

'Come on, let's move it,' Tony said, finally feeling like he was in control. 'We follow Luiz and Roberto.' Part of him wanted to do what Greenaway had suggested, to bug out, but he had his orders, direct from the colonel.

Luiz moved in a crouch, as though he was stalking game. He would be the first to catch sight of the man they were following, and he probably wanted to present as small a target as possible.

The tracker held up a hand. Rassie raised his rifle as he closed the gap between himself and Roberto. Tony held up his hand too, to make Greenaway and the others stop. Thankfully the sergeant obeyed, and quietly told Kruger and Litis to face outwards, protecting their flanks and rear.

Tony went to Rassie, Luiz and Roberto.

'Hey!' a voice called out from ahead.

Tony saw the man, who raised a pistol, and realised that it must have been his own movement, lifting his hand in a stop signal, that alerted their quarry. A gunshot rang out, and the bullet smacked into a tree a metre from Tony.

'Put down your gun, we're bloody South Africans!' Erasmus stood and waved his R4 over his head.

The man they were following staggered out of the bush, fully into view. He wore a South African nutria-brown uniform and was holding his nine-millimetre pistol by his side in his right hand and a brown leather satchel in his left.

'What the fuck is he carrying?' Greenaway asked. 'His luggage?'

Tony looked over his shoulder and saw the sergeant looking his way. 'Do your job and watch our rear, Greenaway.'

Tony leapfrogged Erasmus, Luiz and Roberto and rushed to the wounded man, taking him by the arm. 'Come. This way.' He led the man through a stand of trees, away from the rest of the patrol. 'Sit down.'

Erasmus unslung his medic's bag and followed in Tony's footsteps.

The man was young, probably another conscript, and he wore air force insignia. As well as wearing enemy boots he had a holster on his belt; his pistol looked like a Russian Tokarev pistol. In his brief time in South West Africa and Angola Tony had already learned that personnel working away from the front line still liked to dress the part, with unauthorised and captured gear that had most likely been souvenired by frontline fighting men.

'Airman Duarte?' Tony asked.

The man looked up at him. 'Yes . . . Sir. You know my name?' Duarte seemed dazed, most likely in shock. His face, which, judging by his colouring and name Tony thought might normally have been an olive colour, was deathly pale. Blood from the wound in his left shoulder had soaked his uniform. He had black hair with non-regulation sideburns and dark eyes bright with fear.

'What happened to you?' Tony asked. Erasmus knelt beside them and opened his first aid kit.

'We were shot down soon after take-off, and crashed. The pilot was killed. I managed to get out, but the FAPLA came. I ran. They shot me, but they seemed more interested in searching the Bosbok than coming after me.'

Tony took out a field dressing, unwrapped it and placed the bulky cotton pad against the wound in Duarte's side. He needed to keep him talking.

'Sir,' Erasmus said. 'Let me do that.'

Ferri ignored the medic for now. It was important he speak to Duarte first. 'Your name, what is that? Portuguese?'

'Yes, sir.' He winced as Erasmus, who had knelt down and set to work anyway, cut away part of his shirt to better access the wound in his torso. The medic took over from Tony, removing the remains of Duarte's shirt and the hastily applied dressing. He replaced the pad then set to work wrapping a bandage around Duarte's body.

Luiz came over and crouched next to Erasmus as he worked, watching him. Roberto squatted nearby.

'Luiz, go to the others, to Sergeant Greenaway.' Tony did not want a full-house audience while he questioned the airman.

Luiz blinked and stared at Tony.

'Duarte, can you tell this oke to go to Sergeant Greenaway, in Portuguese.'

The airman shook his head. 'Sorry, sir, I don't actually speak Portuguese. When I finished my basic training, an officer asked me if Duarte was a Portuguese name. I said that yes, my dad was Portuguese. They assigned me to air force intelligence as an interpreter.'

'An interpreter who can't speak Portuguese? So, what, they gave you some kind of courier job?' No doubt the airman had thought intelligence would be a cushy job.

Duarte looked around him furtively. 'I'm not supposed to talk about what I do, sir. Not to anyone.'

'I was briefed on what you're carrying, Duarte, so don't fuck about.'

'Yes, sir.'

Tony noted that when he had sat down, Duarte had placed the leather satchel he had been carrying under his butt; he was sitting on it now, with his left hand by his side.

'Lift your left arm up high so I can tie off this bandage,' Erasmus said to Duarte.

'I can't do that.'

Duarte shifted his left hand and both Tony and Erasmus could see that the satchel was handcuffed to his wrist.

'What the fok is that?' Erasmus asked.

16

Mia was up before dawn, as usual. She made her way to the lodge's main building, where she sat down in Shirley's office to call Tony, Lisa and Evan's suites at five-thirty, to give them a wake-up call for the early-morning game drive.

'Sorry, Mia, I'm man-down. I feel terrible; I'm going to have to miss the drive,' Evan said. 'It must have been something I ate. I had a chicken mayo sandwich at the airport before we left; I think it might be that.'

'Shame, I'm so sorry to hear that, Evan. I hope you feel better later. I'll let Shirley, our manager, know, in case we need to call a doctor.'

'I'm sure it will pass . . . A lot has, already.'

'Take care, Evan.' Mia rang off. 'Shit,' she said to herself. If Evan had contracted food poisoning at the lodge there would be hell to pay once Julianne Clyde-Smith found out. Also, if one guest was ill then another could be too.

'Hi, Lisa, this is your wake-up call,' Mia said when she dialled the next number. 'How are you?'

'I'm fine. Sorry, I won't be coming on the drive. Bye.'

Tony's campaign manager hung up and Mia was left wondering

what was wrong with her. It didn't sound like she was ill, but nor was she happy.

'Morning, Tony,' Mia began as she made her final call. 'Morning, Mia. I'm on my way.'

'You've still got half an hour. This was just supposed to be your wake-up call.'

'I'm a habitual early riser. I'll see you in five.'

The politician was true to his word and looked, Mia thought, as ruggedly handsome and polished as if he were setting out for a meet-and-greet media event. He wore a navy polo shirt and matching spray jacket, chinos and practical but stylish low-profile hiking shoes.

He smiled at her. 'Morning.'

'Good morning, again. Would you like tea or coffee before we go? We have rusks, croissants and some small pastries.'

'You've got something for morning tea in the Land Rover, right?'

'Sure do,' Mia said. He clearly knew the safari routine.

'Then let's head out and get an early start on the big game.'

'Fine by me. The others aren't coming. Shame, Evan isn't well.'

Tony nodded as they walked together out of the lodge to the game-viewing vehicle. 'Yes, he called me and let me know. Lisa is . . . well, snowed under with work as usual.'

'Is she OK? She sounded a little – I don't know – stressed?'

'She's a workaholic, Mia. I worry about her, but I'd be lost without her.'

They climbed into the Land Rover. Mia got on the radio and told Shirley, who was now in her office, that they were setting off early and would be exploring the western side of the reserve.

Tony stretched his arms wide and leaned back as Mia set off. 'I can't tell you how good it feels to be out in the wild and, as much as I hate to say it, alone. Or, rather, just with you.'

'Well, I'm glad you can enjoy a break,' Mia said, 'even though you're here for a sad occasion.'

'Yes, you put that well, Mia. Luiz was a good man, and we were all close to him. I think it's terrible that he decided the only way he could cope was by killing himself, but I want to remember the good things about him. While I told you that stuff about my suspicions about him, I have to say that he saved many of our guys, by finding the enemy before they found us.'

'About that,' Mia glanced over her shoulder as she drove, 'I want you to know that you have my word that I won't repeat anything you told me to anyone.'

'Thank you.' He gave a little laugh. 'I have to tell you that Lisa was worried that you might go off and sell your story to the news media after I confided in you, but I told her I didn't think you were that sort of person.'

'Thank you. I have a question, though – a personal one, if you don't mind?'

'Fire away,' he said as they came across a herd of springbok making for a nearby waterhole.

Mia stopped and turned off the engine. 'Why did you tell me that stuff about Luiz? You said you'd never told anyone else.'

'That's true.'

'Not even your wife?' she pressed.

'No. We're not really close, emotionally or – well, generally.'

'Oh. I'm so sorry I pried. We're not supposed to ask such personal questions, as guides, unless guests volunteer stuff about their families. Forgive me.'

'It's fine, don't worry at all. I guess Evan and I fall into a slightly different category than your normal run-of-the-mill guest, in that we have a personal connection to you and we're not actually here for a holiday. Although, I have to say it almost feels like one because I'm enjoying this so much – especially being on safari with a knowledgeable, wonderful person.'

Mia blushed. 'Thank you.' Tony was old enough to be her father, but he was handsome and charming and honest – even about not getting on with her dad. She did not think he was trying to give her a pickup line; it was probably just that in his line of work he was used to complimenting strangers to win them over. And, even then, he'd done it without it feeling contrived.

'You can ask me anything, Mia. Trust me, I've probably heard it before.'

She laughed. She was dying to ask about his wife, but didn't dare cross that line again. 'What would you do differently, if, say, the DA was actually able to win government?'

'That's a very good question,' he said.

Mia set off again and drove at a steady pace, listening intently – to him and the desert – but still scanning for game.

'As leader,' he went on, 'the first thing I would do is give myself a pay cut.'

'Really?'

'Yes. It wouldn't be a big one.' Mia laughed again.

'But I'd cut out perks and excessive government spending. It's true that some politicians in South Africa, and probably some of the people we'd like to see recruited to parliament, are not wealthy individuals, so we need to make sure that our politicians get a decent wage, but they, and the people, must be totally disavowed of the idea that power brings wealth.'

'I agree with that,' Mia said. 'I've seen political conferences hosted at hotels, and even at Julianne's other lodges, and the spending and consumption is almost obscene. It's lobster and Johnny Walker Blue Label all the way.'

'Exactly. That and the Blue Light brigades – minor politicians travelling in a convoy of expensive cars, forcing citizens off the road. I'd also stop politicians using the annual opening of parliament as a fashion parade to show off their new designer clothes and bling. This stuff belongs in corrupt banana republics of the past. Politicians must be what they call "servant leaders" these days. They should have a mindset that they exist to better the lot of the average person, not make money off them or flaunt their new-found wealth. There will be people on all sides of politics who won't like this, and who will disagree with me.'

'But the people would love it,' Mia said.

'I'd increase the minimum wage, which would not be popular with big business, but I'd seek a trade-off from the trade union movements, with a promise of no unnecessary strikes, and I'd make it easier for overseas companies that offered more jobs to invest in South Africa. I'd also set up a truly independent anticorruption body.'

'Sounds like you might make as many enemies as you make friends.' She looked back at him.

Tony smiled and nodded. 'I'll let you in on another secret.'

'You sure you want to trust me?'

He laughed. 'I've already done that. I figure I'd have one term in office, at best. It's likely some in my own party, who already see me as too moderate and too progressive, would vote me out. But if I can achieve real change, Mia – if I can make it harder for politicians to be corrupt or abuse their positions of power, and create more jobs – then we'll never look back.'

'Wow,' she said. 'You'd fight your way to the top, knowing that you'd only have a few years?'

He nodded. 'Yes, but it would be worth it. My life has been good, but I'm unfulfilled in so many ways. I'd like to retire before I get voted out, and to start a new life, with someone else, doing something really worthwhile. I'd really like to get involved with wildlife conservation.'

'You really are baring all, aren't you?'

Mia saw a pair of ostriches and, as she slowed, noticed more at their feet. She stopped. 'Look at the chicks.' Running around between the two adults were a dozen or more tiny birds.

'Beautiful,' Tony said. 'And yes, I have told you a lot. I feel like you're a trustworthy person, Mia, and even though your dad and I didn't always see eye to eye, he was honest. He told it like it was and he cared for the men under his command. As a soldier, you couldn't ask for more.'

Mia felt a lump rise in her throat. 'Thank you. It's lovely of you to say that and, as I said before, your secrets are safe with me. Can I ask you something else personal?'

'I said you could. I'd like you to, in fact.'

She wondered why. Now that they were stopped, she turned in

her seat so she could see him properly. 'You said just then that you wanted to start another life with another person. Are things bad with your wife?'

'No, not bad, just not workable long-term.'

Mia's sleazy-old-man radar fired up. 'Khaki Fever', where women fell for their attractive young male safari guides, was a well-known malaise in her industry and, while it was less common, it was not unheard of for female guides to attract uninvited attention and advances, too. She'd been hit on by a couple of married male guests in the past. Usually their pickup routine started with a line about how their wives did not understand them.

'How so?' she said, ready to drop this conversation and return to strictly guide–client rules in a heartbeat. But, at the same time, her heart was pounding.

'She's gay.'

'Oh.'

Tony laughed. 'Don't look so shocked.'

'I'm not . . . I mean, I am, but . . .' Why the hell was he telling her all this?

'My wife had a good friend – they went to varsity together – and Elize, her friend, later came out and left her husband. She and my wife, Sanette, have always been close and, well, it turned out they'd both had feelings for each other when they were younger, but neither had felt it right or proper to act on them. They both came from strict, Christian Afrikaans families. They ended up having an affair. I found out by accident. I had the flu and pulled out of a party meeting I had to attend in Cape Town and, well, found them.'

'Oh my gosh. I'm sorry.'

Tony nodded. 'It was quite a shock, I'm telling you. Not only did I question what we had together, but it made me question myself, as a man. At the time, quite selfishly, I was trying to work out what was wrong with me, but it turned out that living that way, in love with another woman, was actually right for Sanette.'

'What did you do? I've seen in the newspapers and online – even just the other day when I googled you, there was a story about you and your wife and kids and how happy you all were, or seemed.'

'We are happy, Mia, just not in a conventional way. Sanette said and still says she loves me and she wants me to have my shot at leadership of the party, and to go to an election in a strong position, not just for my own benefit, but for the good of the party. Elize feels the same way – she's actually a very active member of my own local DA branch, ironically.' He gave a little laugh, but Mia could tell this must have been terribly difficult for him, and for all of them.

'So what happened?'

'The three of us, and our kids now that they're old enough to understand these things, have accepted that Sanette and Elize will be a couple someday soon, and that Sanette will carry on as if nothing's changed for the moment, at least until the next general election. In most ways things are still the same. She and I still love each other, although in a different way now, and we live together as a family. The deal is that after the election Sanette and I will separate, publicly. If the DA loses, which is the most likely outcome, we'll do it once the dust settles. If I've been elected leader prior to the election, then I'll most likely be replaced by the party when we lose. If the almost unimaginable happens and we win, then Sanette has agreed to keep up our arrangement for a year, and then we'll split.'

'Wow. Again.'

'Sanette and Elize see each other, often, and with me away on the campaign trail they have time together. We brought up our children to be respectful to all people, regardless of race, religion or how they identify sexually, so they're all on board with the plan.'

'And you?'

Tony smiled. 'I'm very busy, Mia. The deal is that if I meet someone then I'm free to do what I want, discreetly. If I told you how many politicians I know are actually having supposedly secret affairs, you'd be shocked.'

Mia remembered something. He'd revealed so much, she did not think one more question would hurt. 'Last night I was walking one of the waiting staff home to her accommodation after everyone had left after dinner, and we went past Lisa's tent just as she was opening her door and walking out onto her stoep. She told me she was just getting some fresh air and I reminded her of the rule about not walking anywhere after dark. Was she . . . ?'

'You're very perceptive, Mia. Yes, Lisa and I have slept together a few times. Last night, probably just after you and your workmate had gone, I went to her tent. I'm very sorry we broke the rules. Anyway, the other thing that happened last night was that we agreed to end the physical side of our relationship. Or, rather, I broke it off.'

'Why? She's beautiful and she seems so smart, so driven, so committed.'

'She is all of those things. However, Lisa's made it clear she does not want an ongoing relationship with me, or any other man in the near future. She wants to pursue a political career of her own and doesn't want to be seen as the woman who slept her way into parliament, or to be the wife of a party leader. Like you say, she's driven, but not by love.'

She looked into his eyes and saw a mix of longing and sadness there. Mia was bowled over by all that he'd told her. It was as if he needed to tell all of this to someone who would be politically neutral, non-judgemental. She had an incredible urge to give him a hug, but fortunately there was a solid firewall between the driver's compartment of the Land Rover and the seats behind her.

'Thank you, Mia.'

'What for?'

'For listening.'

Mia nodded. 'People think my job is all about looking, scanning the bush or the desert, looking for wild animals or their tracks on the ground, but it's also about listening. You can tell when a predator is nearby from the alarm calls various birds and animals make, and the roar of a lion; a leopard's grunting can also tell you who else is around. I'm like the bartender of the bush – part of my job is to listen.'

Tony raised an eyebrow. 'While people pour their hearts out to you?'

'Not always, but sometimes. The bush has a way of stripping the layers off people, of bringing them back to basics and what's important.'

He nodded and looked around them. 'Yes, with all this openness there's nowhere to hide.'

'Exactly. Would you like a cup of coffee or tea? We can take our drinks break wherever you like.'

'That would be lovely,' he said.

'We should leave this little family alone.' Mia started the engine and drove off, leaving the ostriches. Along the way she spotted some hartebeest, so they stopped and looked for a while, then she headed along a road that led up a steep incline. At the top of the hill were the remains of a small stone building.

She parked and they got out.

'What is this place?' Tony held a hand up to his brow to shield his eyes from the glare and looked out over the expansive view.

'It's an old farmhouse from around the end of the First World War. There's a few of these in the nearby national park, the Kgalagadi Transfrontier Park, as well. Early in the war the South African army was given the job, by Britain, of taking South West Africa from the Germans. The advancing soldiers dug wells along the way – there's one here – and after the war these little outposts were given to returning soldiers so they could set up farms. Imagine living out here.'

'It's so desolate,' Tony said. 'So lonely.'

'Yes,' Mia agreed, 'but I like it.'

He spun to look at her. 'I love it.'

She laughed. 'Really? Out here in the middle of nowhere?'

'It's my dream, sometimes. Like I said, I know I'll have a political shelf life, whatever happens at the next election, and when that part of my life is over, what I really want is to live somewhere totally wild, away from politics, big business, malls, people.'

'Wow,' she found herself saying yet again. It was a time of surprises. 'I feel the same way. It's why I always ask guests to "imagine living out here". Most of them say they couldn't handle it.'

'With the right person, this would be paradise.'

Mia had often thought the same. She'd just never found the right person. She went to the rear of the Land Rover, dropped the tailgate under the last row of seats and hauled out a cooler box.

'Let me help you,' Tony said.

'I'm fine, thanks. Though I've usually got a tracker to help . . .' She tailed off, realising she'd just been thinking of Luiz. 'Sorry.'

'Not a problem,' Tony said. 'I haven't forgotten Luiz, and the reason I'm here, but I'd be lying if I said this was anything other than bliss.'

He took one side of the box and they set it on the ground while Mia flipped up a folding table built into the Land Rover's front bumper bar. She locked the table in place and produced a white linen tablecloth and insulated flasks and cups from the cooler box. She also took out some jars.

'We've got rusks, cookies and some mini quiches which are still warm, wrapped in foil. Coffee?'

'I'd love a cup,' Tony said.

Mia poured hot water into a plunger and made Tony and herself a cup each. 'Milk?'

'Yes, but no sugar,' he said.

'I do have Amarula if you'd prefer,' she said.

He laughed. 'At this time of day?'

'You'd be surprised,' Mia said. 'I've also got champagne in the other cooler box and some guests even want a brandy and Coke at this time of day.'

'True nature lovers, I'm sure,' he said dryly. She laughed.

'Actually . . . maybe I will have a little splash of Amarula. What the hell; there's no paparazzi hiding behind a rock anywhere here.'

'Coming right up.' Mia unscrewed the cap on a miniature bottle and poured the cream liqueur, distilled from the fruit of the marula tree, into Tony's cup before handing it to him.

He took a sip. 'Mmm, delightfully decadent. Will you join me?'

Mia shook her head. 'Not while I'm on duty.'

'Understood. Maybe I can buy you a glass of wine at dinner tonight?'

She smiled. 'You know all local drinks on your bill are included in your rate.'

'I know, but I also saw that there's a premium wine list. I'd just like to let you know how much I appreciate you being my guide.'

'You don't need to do something like that for me, Tony. But thank you.' Mia felt a little flutter. If he was trying to make a move on her, then he was doing a good job. She sipped her coffee and told herself to keep her wits about her. 'Any requests for the rest of the game drive?'

'Honestly, I'm just enjoying being out here.'

They each had a rusk and a quiche and finished their coffee. Tony helped Mia pack the cooler box into the Land Rover and they took a quick look around the abandoned farmhouse. It was tiny – one room with a hearth and the remains of a chimney.

'Cosy,' he said.

Mia was acutely aware of his presence when they were inside the little ruined house. He took care, she could see, not to stand too close to her, but she could smell his aftershave.

Tony looked around the four walls, then at her. 'Bliss,' he said again.

She smiled, but couldn't think of anything to say in reply. Tony gestured to the doorway opening. 'Shall we?'

'Yes, of course.'

They went back to the Land Rover. 'Mia?'

'Yes?' she said as she got in behind the wheel.

'Would it be OK if I sat next to you, in the passenger seat, rather than in the game-viewing seats behind? It seems a little odd, since it's just the two of us.'

She moved her birding book and her binoculars off the passenger seat and into the cubby box next to her. She smiled. 'I think I'd like that, Tony.'

17

Adam and Sannie arrived at Dune Lodge mid-morning. Adam had showered and shaved and changed into his smartest casual clothes before leaving Kuruman. He wore a short-sleeved shirt, chinos and Veldskoen shoes.

He thought Sannie looked beautiful in a khaki sleeveless safari dress and tan sandals.

'Welcome, Sannie,' Shirley said, introducing herself as the lodge manager. 'Mia's out on a game drive with one of the guests but will be back just now.'

Adam shook hands with Shirley. 'You're Luiz's niece?'

She nodded. 'I am.'

'I'm so sorry for your loss,' Adam said. 'Your uncle was a great man.'

Shirley looked down. 'Thank you. I'll show you to your suites now, if you like. They were empty last night so we've arranged an early check-in for you. Oh, and Sannie?' Shirley added.

'Yes?'

'I'm terribly sorry that Mia is unable to take some leave days to spend time with you.'

'No problem,' Sannie said. 'We can catch up in between drives and in the evenings, I'm sure.'

As Shirley led them through the lodge's main reception and dining area towards the accommodation units, a man with curly dark hair flecked with grey walked in. He stopped and stared at Adam. He smiled at Shirley, who nodded in reply.

'Evan?' Adam said, after a moment.

'Adam. Sheesh, how long has it been, man?'

They clasped hands. Evan hugged him, but Adam did not return the embrace.

'It's been too long, bru.' Evan stepped back.

Adam nodded, the memories swirling in his mind. While he knew Evan had visited Frank, the three of them had not been together since 1987. Adam studied Evan. They had all aged, but he still looked much the same, though he had put on weight. His casual clothes looked expensive and new, in contrast to Adam's pressed but fraying collar and hems.

'Adam, you're looking good, my boet. Do you like, work out every day?'

He smiled. 'I walk a lot, and run, and my job keeps me in the water a lot.'

'What are you now, an Olympic swimmer? Champion surfer dude?'

'I'm researching sharks and I work in . . . security, part-time. It keeps me fit.'

'Tony googled you,' Evan said, 'and told me you foiled a cash-in-transit heist. Shot a guy?'

Adam shrugged. He was grateful that Evan had glossed over mentioning that Adam's version of 'working in security' was being a car park guard. 'Anyone would have done the same thing.'

Evan held up his hands. 'Not me. I had enough of AKs back in the day.' He turned to Sannie. 'Pardon me; I'm Evan Litis.'

Sannie took his hand. 'Nice to meet you. Sannie van Rensburg. I'm a friend of Mia Greenaway's and I happen to live near Adam, so we travelled together.'

'Well, any friend of Adam's . . . lovely to meet you.'

Sannie smiled at him and Adam realised, again, how that simple gesture changed her in an instant. He had met her as the rather stern-faced police detective, and in a short time he'd learned that she was carrying a burden of sadness and some guilt over the death of her husband. A simple smile freed her, or perhaps gave him a glimpse of the woman she had been at some point in her life. She smiled when she talked about her children. She had seen and been through so much in the police service and her personal life, but she still had hope.

Adam turned to Evan and they made eye contact. Adam wondered if they were both thinking about the exact same moment in time, not long before they'd lost contact and not seen each other again. Until now.

ANGOLA, 1987

ANOTHER MORTAR BOMB EXPLODED NEARBY, and Adam felt the vibration through the ground and up into his chest. Instinctively, he lowered his head. There was the sound of gunfire coming from the direction where the lieutenant, Rassie and the San trackers had headed with the missing airman.

'That's where the others are,' Frank said, reading the sound and direction. 'Litis, Rossouw, get up there, see what's happening, and report back to me.'

Evan left. Adam was picking up on Frank's anger and confusion about what was happening. He felt jumpy.

Adam saw movement through the bush in front of him. 'Frank?' he hissed.

Frank looked to where Adam was pointing, raised his R1 and fired. 'FAPLA!'

Adam looked down the sights of his machine gun. He saw three soldiers in camouflage and squeezed the trigger. He used his left hand to pull the butt of the gun hard into his shoulder and brace against the recoil. Spent brass casings and metal links clinked into a pile beside him. The man Adam had shot at was still running. Adam took a deep breath, aimed off and squeezed again. The Angolan pitched forward. the smell of cordite and gun oil invaded his nostrils.

It was not elation Adam felt, but nor did he have time to feel pity or excitement. A primeval force surged inside him on a mini wave of adrenaline. It was the same, he thought, as surfing – that feeling when the inescapable energy of the water lifted him, then his guts falling as he slid down the front of the blue wall.

Frank fired again, but it was clear the Angolans were many, and closing on them. He fired twice and an advancing soldier fell. 'Fall back!' Frank yelled, jabbing a thumb over his shoulder.

He wanted them to link up with the others.

Adam realised that they were being surrounded. He saw another target. This guy was wearing Cuban camouflage. Adam fired a long burst, which felled the man, then Adam hauled himself and his gun up and started to run, just as Frank covered him.

Adam covered fifty metres then turned and dropped to the ground, ready to start firing so that Frank, now taking cover behind a tree, could come back past him, then they would repeat the drill. Frank fired again and then his rifle clicked on empty. Adam saw two Cubans emerge from the bush and charge towards Frank, who was busy reaching into a pouch for a fresh magazine.

One of the men was in clear view of Adam, so he pulled the trigger and dropped him. Frank, however, was between Adam and the other man, so Adam couldn't shoot. Frank was slapping the new magazine into his rifle, but the Cuban was almost on top of him. Frank peered around the tree trunk and the enemy soldier barrelled into him, each as surprised as the other.

Frank brought his rifle up, still uncocked, swung it sideways and smashed the butt into the Cuban's face. The man lurched backwards and Frank closed on him.

Adam ran towards them, his LMG pressed against his side, ready to fire. However, Frank had grabbed the Cuban in a bear hug, preventing the other man from using his rifle, and was running him backwards. Adam could not get a bead on the Cuban and shoot him without the risk of hitting Frank.

A FAPLA soldier with an RPD machine gun erupted from the trees and opened fire indiscriminately.

Adam swung and fired from the hip. The other gunner stumbled and fell.

Meanwhile, Frank staggered as the Cuban fought back against him, the pair of them locked in a dance to the death. Adam left his weighty machine gun on the ground. He jumped up, and as he ran at the two men he unclipped a hunting knife from a sheath on his webbing and drew it. When he came to them, he rammed the knife up and under the Cuban's ribs. The man arched his back, letting go of Frank, who fell to the ground and dropped his rifle in the process.

The Cuban was bleeding, but Adam must have missed his vital organs. When Adam lunged again the other man sidestepped him and brought up his AK. Adam stared at the man and the barrel of the weapon pointed at him. He knew he was about to die.

Then the Cuban's eyes opened wide, as did his mouth, in a gesture of surprise. Blood welled over his lips and he fell to the ground. Frank was standing behind the Cuban, his own bloodied combat knife gripped in his hand.

'Thanks, bru,' Frank said. 'You saved my life.'

'But . . .' Adam tried to find the words as he looked at his bloodied hand.

'Forget it. Let's get moving.' Frank was businesslike as he finished cocking his rifle. There was a wild yet controlled look in his eyes.

'I . . . I almost died,' Adam said.

'Ja, but you didn't. Come on. Get your LMG and let's get to the others. We've got to get back to the border,' Frank said, and they moved off as quickly and cautiously as they could. 'There's no way the air force will send a chopper into this shit.'

There was no more gunfire from where the others were.

Adam thought that could be a good thing, or a very bad omen.

Adam smelled smoke. He could hear voices ahead, but was not close enough to tell what language they were speaking.

Frank nodded, indicating he'd also heard them. They slowed down. Frank raised his R1 to his shoulder and aimed forward, indicating to Adam that he would move ahead while Adam covered him.

Adam advanced to a stout tree, knelt and raised the LMG to cover Frank. The sergeant seemed to be able to move as silently as a leopard, his eyes scanning the bush as he rolled the outer sole of each of his boots slowly on the ground, feeling for anything that might give away his position.

Adam's face ran with sweat, which stung his eyes as he concentrated. His heart was pounding. He felt like it might burst from the overdose of adrenaline.

Frank moved through a thick stand of bush; Adam waited a few seconds then got up and ran.

'ADAM?' Evan said.

Sannie looked from one man to the other. It had only been a matter of seconds since they had reunited, but Adam had just stood there staring at Evan, or maybe through him, and seemed to have blanked out momentarily. She had seen that look before in the short time since they had met.

'I said, this sure is a different setting from where we last saw each other, in Angola, hey?' Evan said.

Adam nodded. 'Um, yes, for sure.'

'Tony's out on a game drive, with Mia – Frank's daughter. It'll be lekker to have the old crew back together again, even if it is for a sad occasion.'

'Yes,' Adam said, unconvincingly.

Sannie tried to read the situation. Evan was being positive and outgoing, but Adam seemed to be retreating back into his shell. She wondered what they had been through, these men, along with their dead comrades, Luiz and Frank. Sannie was also interested in meeting the DA's rising star, Tony Ferri.

An attractive woman with red hair walked into the lounge area.

'Morning, Evan,' she said. 'Are you feeling better?'

'Yes, much better, thanks, Lisa. I think it was just a minor bug.' Evan introduced Lisa Ingram, Ferri's campaign manager, to Sannie and Adam.

'You missed the morning game drive, Lisa?' Sannie asked.

'Ja, someone has to work, I'm afraid. But don't get me wrong, I love what I do and Tony's going to make a fantastic leader, not just for the party, but hopefully for the country one day.'

'It must be an incredibly stressful job, for both of you,' Sannie said.

'It is. What do you do for a living, Sannie?'

'I'm a police detective.'

'Oh.'

Sannie smiled. She was used to less-than-enthusiastic responses from people when she told them what she did for a living. People were always happy to see a cop when they had been robbed or assaulted, or were the victim of some other crime, but the rest of the time many were wary, even distrustful, of the police.

'I can't thank you enough for everything you do for our community,' Lisa added. 'I'm in awe of our police service and it's one of our priorities to boost numbers and the budget for our law enforcement.'

Well, well, Sannie thought to herself. Perhaps she had misjudged Lisa. However, in her decades as a police officer Sannie had heard every politician from every political party say pretty much the same thing.

'Actually, I'm thinking of retiring,' Sannie said.

'You are?' Adam sounded surprised.

'I want to enjoy life a little, now that my kids are all grown and the last one will soon leave the nest.'

Lisa looked from Sannie to Adam. 'So, are you two a couple?'

'No,' they both said in unison.

Evan laughed. 'I think that was a pretty clear answer.'

'Yes,' Sannie said. 'Adam and I only just met. We're friends, and I was coming here anyway, and then I learned that Adam wanted to come for Luiz's funeral, so I offered to give him a lift, or, rather, to share the driving.'

'And I'm very grateful,' Adam said.

'I see,' Lisa said, drawing out the second word.

Sannie thought Lisa was suddenly looking at Adam through different eyes. In fact, Sannie was sure she was now scanning him from head to toe. Oddly, she felt a little pang of jealousy. There was a predatory air about the other woman.

Shirley, who had been politely standing by while her various guests introduced themselves, seized on a possible lull in the conversation. 'Perhaps I can show you to your rooms now?'

'Of course,' Sannie said.

'You can all catch up again over lunch,' Shirley continued, 'which is soon. Would you like me to set one big table for all you?'

'You'll all have plenty to talk about,' Sannie said, 'and I'm actually friends with your guide, Mia. I don't know what the protocol is here at Dune Lodge, Shirley, whether your guide usually eats with you, like in some other lodges, or not?'

'We do whatever our guests wish.' Shirley smiled.

'I really want to talk to Mia, as well,' Adam said.

'Do join us, Sannie,' Lisa said. 'And we'll invite Mia, even if she wouldn't normally dine with guests.'

Sannie had hoped for some time alone with Mia, but accepted that her friend would probably be just as keen to talk to the group of veterans as they were to spend time with her. Sannie was not, by nature, a jealous person, so these newly surfacing emotions troubled her.

'Fine,' she said.

'OK, all settled,' Shirley said. 'Sannie, Adam, let me show you to your tents.'

'That would be lovely,' Sannie said.

Porters collected their luggage from Sannie's Fortuner and Shirley led them along a sandy path demarcated by dried tree branches. Hurricane lanterns, converted to electricity, lined the walkway on hooked metal stakes stuck in the sand.

When she saw it, Sannie thought that the only connection her suite had with a 'tent' was the use of tan-coloured canvas for some of the wall panels.

'It's beautiful,' Sannie said to Shirley when the lodge manager led Sannie up some wooden stairs to a timber deck and the suite. At first glance, the room seemed totally open to the elements at the front, then Shirley showed her the stackable glass doors, which tucked neatly out of the way so that guests could feel they were in the desert, but under shade. The roof was waterproof material stretched over a series of poles, giving a Bedouin feel.

Inside was a king-sized bed, a lounge area with comfy sofas and a coffee table made out of an old steamer trunk.

'Fully stocked minibar, indoor bath and shower, and outdoor shower on the side deck,' Shirley said. 'All meals and drinks are included, even though Mia is using some of her bed nights for your stay, and whatever you drink from the minibar will be replaced each day.'

'It's amazing, thank you, Shirley.'

'If there is anything else you need, please just use the walkie-talkie. And, in an extreme emergency, please use the air horn beside your bed. If you need to use the horn at night-time, please turn on your stoep light so we know where to come to.'

Even though Shirley was smiling and being brisk and professional, Sannie saw that she was wringing her hands. 'Shirley, are you OK? I know it must have been very hard, not only losing your uncle, but the way he passed.'

Shirley paused on the deck and looked down at her giveaway hands, which were now still. 'Thank you for asking. I just keep wondering what I could have done, why I didn't see the signs, and . . .' She wiped her eyes.

'I'm sorry. I know the wound is still raw, but it can help to talk. You wanted to say something else?'

'It's terrible, selfish even, but I just want to know why he didn't ask me for help?'

Sannie nodded. 'That can be the hardest thing, for friends and relatives – they always ask themselves those questions. The fact is that if someone is deeply depressed enough to want to end their life then they don't think of the consequences of their actions on others. It's not your fault, Shirley.'

'Thank you. I've tried to tell myself that, but it helps to hear it from someone else.'

'My pleasure.'

Shirley thanked her again and left Sannie to settle in.

Sannie flopped down in the cocoon of an egg chair hanging from a frame on her stoep. She looked out over the red dunes of the desert. It was a long way from the Natal South Coast and her former home in Mpumalanga, on the edge of the Kruger National Park. The only common denominators in her life, she realised with a sigh, were crime and death. Even here on holiday. She went inside again, unpacked her bag and then decided to head back to the main part of the lodge and wait for Mia to return from her game drive. She checked her watch. Judging by the briefing she and Adam had received from Shirley, the morning game drive should have been back already. Lunch was from twelve-thirty, however, which was soon, so Sannie thought that Mia and Tony Ferri would have to be back by then.

Sannie walked down the stairs into the heat of the Kalahari day. The sky was the most perfect azure dome overhead, contrasting starkly with the desert sands on the horizon. Guests were allowed to walk around the lodge during the day, though Shirley had told her this was forbidden at night-time.

As she passed Adam's room he was also coming down his stairs.

'Can I join you?' he asked.

'Sure.'

He had changed into a pair of tailored shorts and sandals.

'I hope you realise you're seeing me in both my outfits today. The one thing about living on the south coast with no money is that no one notices if you spend every day in rugby shorts or swimming trunks and slops.'

She laughed. 'So I've seen, though I've been spending half my spare time in Toti buying beach gear.'

He gestured to the view. 'Plenty of sand, but no surf here.'

'Do you feel out of the water here?' she asked. 'Literally?'

'Yes and no. The desert reminds me of the sea. Wild, empty, almost never-ending. I like both.'

'I certainly feel like we've got away from it all,' she said, then checked herself, realising what she'd just said. 'I'm sorry, I didn't mean to gloss over or make light of the reason why you're here.'

'Don't be sorry. Luiz was a warrior, hardened and fierce, but he loved to laugh and play jokes on the other San. He tied a piece of fishing line around his brother Roberto's ankle one night when Roberto was asleep in the bush and attached a chop bone to the other end. When a hyena grabbed the bait and started tugging you could hear Roberto's scream a kilometre away. I thought Roberto was going to kill him.'

'Quite a character, hey?'

'Very much so. But most of the time he seemed deep in thought. He was hard to read, but a consummate professional. Every platoon and section wanted Luiz as their guide. We loved the San, but him in particular.'

They walked on in silence until they were close to the main part of the lodge. Sannie saw a game viewer that had not been there earlier parked at the entrance. She hoped it was Mia.

Adam stopped. 'What is it?' Sannie asked.

'I suppose Ferri will be back.'

'I'm hoping Mia will be as well. Is there a problem, Adam? What's he like?'

Adam was silent for a few moments and Sannie was torn between her impatience to see her friend and mild annoyance at Adam's moodiness. She started to walk, but stopped and looked back when she realised he wasn't coming. 'What is it?'

'I don't know if I can be in the same room as that man,' Adam said.

Sannie put her hands on her hips. 'Why, Adam?'

'I haven't seen him since 1987, since Angola.'

'Are you going to tell me what happened there, all those years ago?'

He drew a deep breath. 'I don't know if I can.'

ADAM TURNED and headed back to his accommodation. Inside he sat down and picked up the phone. He called housekeeping.

'Howzit, it's Adam Kruger here in tent three. Can you do room service for lunch, please?'

'Of course, sir.'

The operator went through the menu and Adam ordered a club sandwich and a Coke.

'No problem, sir, we'll have your meal brought to you in about fifteen minutes.'

'Thank you. Actually, can I change that Coke to a double brandy and Coke, please?'

'Of course, sir.'

Adam exhaled. He was not afraid of Ferri, but rather of what he might say or do when he saw him. He had known, since the war, that try as he might to avoid it, the day would eventually come when he would have to confront the former officer. He hated that his first reaction had been to turn to some Dutch courage, strong liquor. He tried to supposedly to reach out to him, to see how he was doing, and, probably, to try to make amends for what had happened.

Adam realised he had been running from them, and from Angola, ever since he'd left the army. Frank had wanted to escape the past by drinking it away, but in the end, it had been too much for him. The memories had overtaken him and they had killed him. Adam was sure of it.

An increasing proportion of the voting population of South Africa saw Tony Ferri as the solution to their woes.

Ferri had actively courted the African vote. He had famously lived in his domestic's house in Diepsloot, in Johannesburg, while she and her two children lived in his home for six months, so he could get a true feeling for how the country's majority lived. His experiment, initially treated with disdain or outright hostility by many, had eventually won him millions of hearts and minds around the country.

Was he, Adam wondered as he sat on his stoep, trying to atone for what had happened in Angola?

His meal arrived, and so did Sannie.

'I thought you were catching up with Mia,' Adam said.

She held a hand to her brow, to shade her eyes from the midday sun. 'She couldn't stay after she dropped Tony Ferri off. She had to go to Askham – something about relocating a rescued pangolin and she had to pick up some stuff for the funeral service.'

'Did you have lunch?'

'No, but the waitress in the lodge told me my "friend" was having room service, so I told her I'd join him.'

On cue, a room service porter walked up the pathway and carried a second tray into Adam's room.

'We even ordered the same thing to eat, though there's no brandy in my Coke.'

'You're checking my drinks bill as well?' Adam asked. He was pleased to see her, but he felt a little as though she was pushing herself into his life.

'I could smell it wafting on the breeze. What is that, a triple?'

'Double.'

They thanked the porter, who left.

'Are you going to invite me in, or must I eat my sandwich out here in the desert?' Sannie asked.

He stood and motioned for her to come up the stairs. 'After you.'

Adam went to the table where the food had been laid out and picked up his drink. He took it through the suite to the bathroom and tipped it down the sink.

When he turned back to Sannie, she was open-mouthed. 'I'm sorry, I didn't mean to criticise or be judgemental.'

Adam set the empty glass down. 'Please sit. Let's enjoy the food. I have had a problem with alcohol in the past, which is why I limit myself to one or two beers per day now. Also, it's all I can afford. I wanted a stiff drink just now because of the way I was feeling, and I know that's not a good sign.'

She took her glass, reached over and poured some of her cola into his glass. 'OK. Peace offering. Now, are you going to tell me what's troubling you, about Ferri, and what this is all about?'

His initial thought, when she'd first asked, had been that he wanted to spare her the horrors of what he had been through, but as she herself had said, she had seen the worst of life and humankind in her job as a police officer. So he sat down opposite her and nodded.

'Ferri's hiding something, and whatever it is cost the lives of some good men.'

18

Tony started with a cold gazpacho soup. It was delicious. He savoured the cool, crisp tang and he thought about what it might be like to kiss Mia Greenaway.

'What are you thinking?' Lisa asked him. 'You look like the cat that got the cream.'

He smiled. 'Nothing. It was just great to be out in the wilds for a few hours with no one else around.'

'Hmm . . . No one except a pretty twenty-something safari guide who probably thinks you're the hope of the nation, and drop-dead handsome.'

'How rude of me not to mention Mia.'

Lisa shook her head. 'Just be careful, Tony. You've already bared your soul to her; I don't want to be reading in the Daily Maverick how you've been sexting her selfies.'

'I'd never do something that silly,' he said. 'But yes, she's a lovely young woman and it was good spending time with her. She's a good listener.'

'And I'm not?'

'You're a good teller, Lisa, an excellent adviser. It's why I hired you.'

She lowered her voice. 'I thought it was the way I give head.'

He coughed, almost choking on his soup.

'Honestly,' Lisa picked at her prawn entree, 'do you like her?'

'Where's Evan, by the way?'

Lisa pointed at him with her fork. 'Don't try and change the subject. I saw him when I left my suite; he was on the stoep talking on his phone. Sounded like he was on one of his marathon business calls. Do you like her?'

He put down his spoon and wiped his lips with a linen serviette. 'You said yourself you wanted to keep it causal between you and me, and you don't want to be the next Mevrou Ferri, not even after the election.'

'I did, and I don't. But it's a woman's prerogative to be jealous, especially of those nice legs of hers in those short shorts.'

'She's smart – like you.'

'Nice save,' Lisa said. 'For goodness' sake, Tony, just be bloody careful. We've come too far for you to throw everything away on a schoolgirl.'

'Mia's in her late twenties, Lisa.'

'Whatever. Where's your other old army boet, Adam? I met him. Now he would be worth me leaving you for. He's gorgeous. I thought you two would have been hugging and telling war stories by now. In fact, maybe I could have invited you both back to my room tonight.' She laughed.

Tony didn't. He pushed his plate away and thanked the waitress who took it. When she was gone, he lowered his voice. 'No, on all counts. Adam hates me, but I've been trying to get in touch with him for years.'

'Why, if he hates you? Do you want to kiss and make up? And why exactly does he hate you?'

'I had him and his buddy, Frank Greenaway, charged with cowardice in the face of the enemy over an incident that happened in Angola. I haven't told Mia that, and I don't want her to know. It's bad enough that her father killed himself, but I think his alcoholism might have been related to that shameful day. It's better she remembers him as the troubled hero rather than a mutinous coward.'

'And it won't help your chances of bedding her if you shatter her girlhood illusions.'

'That is not what I meant,' Tony said.

'Right.'

The waitress brought their mains and Lisa ordered white wine.

Tony asked for a Windhoek Lager.

'So what happened to make you charge Adam and Frank?'

Tony started on his ostrich burger. 'We were on a mission to locate a South African aircraft, a light plane with two men on board. We found the wreck; it had been shot down. The pilot was dead, but the passenger was gone. We got into a gunfight.' Tony paused to swallow a mouthful of his burger. 'Then we pulled back and went looking for the missing guy. It was hectic. The Angolans knew we were in the area and started mortaring us. Luiz and Roberto, our San guys, found the tracks of the missing crew member and then we caught up with him. He was wounded, shot in the torso, and Erasmus – our medic – and I gave him first aid.'

Tony took another bite of his food and stared out over the desert. He could hear the dull crump of mortar bombs leaving their tubes and feel the earth-shaking effect of howitzer rounds.

'Tony?'

He chewed slowly, trying to calm himself. 'Our patrol was split in two – partly my fault, for being young and too keen for my own good, and partly because Frank Greenaway was obstinate to the point of being insubordinate. No sooner were we all reunited than Greenaway said we should retreat, back to the border, on foot.'

'I would have thought that was a good idea?' Lisa ventured.

'We were in contact with the enemy, fighting for our lives and Greenaway and Kruger turned tail, leaving the rest of us plugging away at a wave of Cubans and Angolans.'

'Sheesh, Tony. What happened? How did you all get out?'

'We didn't all get out. Roberto Siboa, Luiz's brother, was killed by a direct hit from an artillery shell. Even if we'd had time to try and collect his remains there wouldn't have been enough to fill half a garbage bag. I'd never seen anything quite so shocking, not before nor since. Duarte – that was the air force guy we rescued – died of his wounds. The enemy were so close that I called in our artillery, by radio, on our own position. We were surrounded by the time Greenaway and Kruger had left us. It was hell, Lisa.'

She was staring at him. 'My God.'

'We were clawing at the dirt with our bare hands, Evan and I huddled together next to the trunk of a big tree that had been blown over. Evan kept firing, all through the bombardment.'

'It's a miracle the rest of you survived.'

'We didn't. Rossouw, the radioman, was shot and killed. The Cubans and Angolans eventually pulled back, thanks to the artillery. I filed a report with the sector commander when I got back. Greenaway and Kruger were charged and went before a court martial. Evan didn't directly accuse Frank or Adam of cowardice, but nor did he speak definitively in their defence. I'm sure he was just protecting his friends, but he just kept saying that he couldn't hear what they were saying because he was too busy engaging the enemy.'

'Evan and Adam seemed to get on OK.'

Tony shrugged. 'Evan is the peacemaker of the group. He went out of his way to reach out to Frank and Adam after the war and to tell them he forgave them for what they did. I nominated Evan for an Honoris Crux, one of our highest medals for bravery, but he received a lesser commendation. I think the high command was worried that if there was too much of a spotlight on the action we were involved with, and Rossouw and Roberto's death, news of Adam and Frank's cowardice would also come out.'

'That was good of you, anyway,' Lisa said.

'It was the least I could do. But that's why Evan and I have had this unshakeable bond ever since. I don't like talking publicly about my military service because it won't win me any African votes, but I think you can also now understand why I don't try and talk it up generally.'

Lisa nodded. 'Understood. I'm sorry for prying.'

He held up a hand. 'No need to apologise. It actually does feel good being able to talk about this stuff, and it was the same with Mia, even though I didn't tell her everything about her father.'

'Well, your secrets are safe with me, as I'm sure you know.'

He smiled at her. She was beautiful, and they had enjoyed each other, physically. However, he knew there was a far greater risk of a nosey reporter uncovering his relationship with Lisa, whom he was with most days and nights while campaigning, than if, say, a pretty young safari guide fell into his arms for a night or two. He finished his burger.

'I think I'll go back to my room for a nap.'

'Alone?'

He forced a smile. 'Yes, alone.'

'You sure I can't join you?'

'I'm sure, Lisa. Like I said last night, we need to cool it. Anyway, I've revealed far too much to everyone today – I don't need to strip any more of me off in front of someone else. I just need some quiet time. I need to think about what I'm going to say to Adam. I can't avoid him forever.'

'Take care, Tony. See you for the afternoon game drive?'

'I'll be there.' He got up, thanked the wait staff, then left the dining area for the sandy pathway to his accommodation.

'What do you mean when you say Ferri's actions cost the lives of good men?' Sannie asked Adam as they sat opposite each other in Adam's tent.

'His arrogance and stupidity on the battlefield cost us casualties, but there's something else, more a gut feeling I have,' he said.

She slouched in her chair and threw her hands up in the air. 'I'm a police detective, Adam. We deal in evidence, facts, motives.'

'You're telling me you've never followed a hunch?'

'No, I'm not saying that. Tell me what happened with you and him in Angola.'

'It's a long story.'

Sannie checked her watch. 'Mia's due back at the lodge in two hours' time. You've got 120 minutes.'

'OK.' Adam began to tell Sannie the story of the patrol.

ANGOLA, 1987

ERASMUS, his medical pack bouncing on his back, ran through the bush. Adam saw Frank lower his rifle as soon as he recognised Rassie.

'What the fuck is happening?' Frank said.

Rassie was breathing hard. 'Sheesh, Sarge, Ferri . . . He doesn't know what he's doing. He sent me to get you.'

'Why do I have to go to him? Why hasn't he pulled back?' Rassie shrugged.

'Stay here, Rassie, watch our rear,' Frank said. 'Adam, come.' Adam got up, hefted his machine gun and they moved forward.

They came to the others. Frank looked around, and at the man on the ground. 'And him? The air force guy?'

'Duarte,' Ferri said. 'DOW.'

Died of wounds, Adam thought. Duarte's torso was bandaged, and he was lying on his left side, motionless.

Frank shook his head. 'All right. Adam, Evan, pick up the dead guy.' He turned to the signaller. 'Rossouw, call in the casualty report.'

'Yes, Sarge,' the signaller said.

'Come,' Frank said to Adam and Evan, 'get the body and let's get out of here, back towards the border.'

Adam started to walk to the airman. Evan hovered next to Lieutenant Ferri.

'No,' Ferri said. 'We stay here and I will call the sector commander to send a chopper to come get us.'

'Are you fucking kidding?' Any residual trace of respect disappeared from Frank's voice. 'We're completely surrounded. We go immediately, before we get overrun. As it is, we can't get a chopper in here, so we have to walk – run – for the border, now, at least to a safe place where they can pick us up. Where are the trackers?'

Ferri shrugged. 'I don't know. Gone.'

'Halfway back to the border if they've got any sense,' Frank said. 'What a mess.'

An automatic weapon opened up from their front, shredding the bush above Adam's head. He dived to the ground. Frank, still standing, returned fire.

'Rossouw,' Ferri said, 'call Ondangwa, get us a chopper.'

Frank fired again, then dropped to his knees and started crawling.

'Rossouw, you will not ask Ondangwa to send a chopper to this location; it's too risky and they'll only say no. Let's go. Now. Evan, come on, we need to pull back.'

Adam looked at Evan, who turned his head from Ferri, to Frank, and back again.

'Litis, Rossouw, you stay here with me,' Ferri said. Evan's attention was drawn away by more shots coming at them. He took aim with this R4 and fired on full automatic. 'Greenaway, Kruger, go! Do whatever you want!'

'Why stay? It's a death sentence!' Frank's tone was almost pleading.

Adam didn't know what to do. Like Frank, he simply wanted to ask Ferri why he was choosing to stay in the middle of this shit-fight in the bush. They were outnumbered.

'We're here to fight the enemy, not run,' Ferri said.

Frank shook his head. 'You're bossies, Loot. You said the mission was to find the okes on the plane and we've done that. They're both dead.'

Frank went to Ferri. Adam had been on the border long enough to know that bossies was short for bosbefok. To be bush-fucked was what the military called shell shock in the First World War. Ferri did look crazed at that moment.

'Go!' Ferri screamed at Adam and Frank. Evan's rifle boomed away.

'Evan,' Adam called. If Litis heard Adam, he gave no sign of it.

Adam saw a person moving in the bush to his front, and fired his machine gun.

'Kruger, move!' Frank said. 'This is madness. Rossouw, Litis, with me!'

'Right behind you, Sarge,' Rossouw called. 'I'm not staying here.'

Adam started to fall back towards where they'd left Rassie. He saw Frank rise to a crouch, cover the remaining distance to Ferri and grab the officer by the arm.

Ferri, still beside Duarte's body, turned and pointed his rifle at Frank. 'Go.'

Adam watched, horrified, as Frank stared Ferri down. The officer raised his R4 to his shoulder and sighted down the barrel. Frank shot his left hand out and knocked the weapon aside, then he dropped his R1, drew back his right fist and punched Ferri in the jaw. Ferri staggered and dropped to his knees.

'Leave the dead guy,' Frank said to Adam. 'We're going to be slow enough as it is. I hate to do it, but they'll have to send someone else back for his body. Everyone – move!'

'I couldn't believe it. In the middle of mortar bombs falling, shooting, enemy all around, Frank *klapped* Ferri,' Adam said to Sannie as they sat in his suite.

'Crazy,' Sannie said.

'Ferri was crazy. I think Frank and I were sure that Ferri would just fall in behind us at that point. He looked broken. Evan, meanwhile, was fighting the war, blazing away like John Wayne and paying no attention to Frank. He – Frank – grabbed me and we started to pull back. I made eye contact with Evan and he nodded to me. I was sure he was ready to come with us.'

'What a terrible situation to be in,' Sannie said. 'How did you feel?'

He seemed to ponder her question for a few seconds. 'I've thought about that moment hundreds, thousands of times over the years, always asking myself what I should have done. I distinctly remember

Ferri telling Frank and me to leave, but he later denied saying that. I really did think he'd just follow us, but I feel bad for not making sure.'

'Why would he do that – tell you to go?'

'I keep asking myself that, as well. Even as we were pulling back, Frank realised the others weren't with us and started making a plan to go back for Evan and Ferri once we regrouped with Rassie. We were spread out everywhere. I thought Rossouw was with us as well, but he got separated from us when we were pulling back, and we still didn't know then where the San trackers were.'

'Why didn't Ferri just listen to Frank?' Sannie asked.

'He was mad – bossies – or arrogant, or he was a glory hound. He shouldn't have stayed, but the fact that he then called in fire on his own position to stop the Angolan attack – and that he and Evan survived – made them heroes, and Frank and I were branded as cowards.'

'But you were ordered to retreat, by Frank and by Tony Ferri.'

'Later, there was an inquiry and a court martial. Both Frank and I testified that Ferri ordered us to leave. Putting aside the moral issue of us leaving them behind, even if Ferri was crazy, the loot also testified that he never told us to go, but rather that he wanted us to stay with him and Evan.'

'What did Evan say to that?'

Adam shrugged. 'He said he never heard Ferri give us the order to leave. That's possible – Evan was firing like a madman, so with all those bangs in his ears it's quite plausible that he never heard half of what Frank and Tony were saying to each other. They were angry, both of them, but they were also trying to keep their voices down because of the presence of the enemy.'

'What happened to you and Frank?'

'The court martial found both of us guilty. It was worse for him, because he was my sergeant and I was following his orders. I got a severe reprimand and was sent to another company.'

Sannie thought through all Adam had told her, digesting the

details of the story, and the missing pieces. 'Where was Luiz while all this was happening?'

'I don't know,' Adam said. 'It was like he and Roberto had just melted away somewhere, into the bush. He turned up later, independently of Evan and Ferri. When the bombardment was over Frank, Rassie and I went back to find them. Clearly, Evan and Ferri survived. Roberto and Rossouw were dead.'

'My goodness,' Sannie said, 'it does sound like hell. Did Luiz not testify at your court martial?'

'No. Frank tried to have him called, but we were told he was off in Angola, on another mission at the time.'

Adam closed his eyes. She reached out, on impulse, and put a hand on his, on the table between them. He opened his eyes and looked at her. They said nothing, but he put his other hand on hers.

'Thank you,' he said at last, and they removed their hands.

'What for?'

'For listening, and not judging.'

'I wasn't there. So, you didn't see Ferri again after that?'

'Not since the court martial, no. Except for seeing him on television more recently. Both he and Evan came looking for me, over the years, but I stayed out of their way.'

'Was that why you went to Australia?'

'Partly,' he said. 'Mostly it was my wife, Sarah, wanting to go. I think I was running away, but my heart was always in Africa. I guess I knew that I'd have to face Litis and Ferri again someday. And there was something else –'

'Knock knock,' called a female voice from outside the tent. Adam and Sannie stood and went to the sliding doors.

'Mia!' Sannie strode down the stairs from the timber deck and hugged her friend.

'Hello, Mia,' Adam came down and joined them, extending his hand. 'I'm –'

'Adam. I remember you.' Mia broke from Sannie's embrace and shook his hand.

He smiled. 'You've grown – a lot – since I last saw you. Thank you so much for agreeing to host me here. The lodge is beautiful.'

'It's so sad about Luiz, but I'm also thrilled to meet more people who knew my father. Thank you for coming. Can I steal Sannie away from you?'

Adam spread his arms wide. 'Fine by me. I think I'll take a nap, or maybe read.'

Sannie turned to Adam. 'There was something more you were going to tell me.'

'Later,' he said. 'You two go and catch up and I'll see you for the afternoon game drive.'

Sannie fell into step beside Mia, who led her back to the main communal area of the lodge.

'I'd forgotten how handsome Adam was,' Mia said.

'You think?' Sannie said.

Mia laughed. 'Don't be coy.'

'He is nice,' Sannie admitted. 'But he's troubled, by what happened to him, to all of them, in the army.'

Mia nodded. 'I was out with Tony Ferri all morning. He's really down-to-earth, a good guy. He'll make a brilliant leader for the DA, and a fantastic president if things ever change, one day. He's so . . . empathetic.'

'Uh-huh,' Sannie said neutrally. Her opinion of the charismatic, popular politician had just changed after listening to Adam. As a detective, however, she had to keep an open mind – Adam could have fabricated or distorted some of his memories. She knew full well that if she interviewed six different witnesses to a crime she would get six different stories, though Adam had been quite open about what had happened to him. She wondered if Mia knew her father had been charged with cowardice and disciplined. Sannie decided not to mention it.

'He's also very good-looking and, well, I shouldn't say this, but he's also available.'

'Really?' Sannie looked at Mia over the top of her sunglasses. 'I read online that he's married with two kids.'

Mia lowered her voice. 'His wife's a lesbian. They have an "arrangement". I got the feeling he was interested in me, if you know what I mean.'

'You sound like you're interested in him, Mia.' It also sounded to Sannie like Mr Tony Ferri was being rather indiscreet on this visit to the lodge.

She smiled. 'Maybe. Anyway, I only just met the guy and he's famous. I'm a safari guide. I don't think I'd want to swap life in the bush to be a politician's . . . Whatever. I learned a lot about my dad from him today, as well. Tony said they didn't get on a lot of the time – I knew that my dad was stubborn, but it sounds like he was a whole lot worse when he was in the army. But Tony respected him, for sticking up for his fellow soldiers.'

'I see.' That was definitely a different version of the story from the one Sannie had just heard. She told herself again that she would not get involved in these old soldiers' telling and re-telling of war stories, especially if it meant Mia being hurt. She did, however, feel she had an obligation to protect her younger friend. 'Just be careful of politicians, Mia. I've met a few of them in my time. They always promise things – more police, more money, tougher laws, crackdowns on crime – but they rarely deliver. They'll say what you want to hear.'

'Yes, well, I don't think Tony's like that.' Mia's eyes blazed for a moment. 'Why else would he have told me that he and my father didn't get on? He could have spared me.'

Because, Sannie thought, he knows someone else will probably allude to the troubles between Tony, Adam and Frank. 'I hear you, Mia.'

'I'm sorry, Sannie. I didn't mean to sound so defensive. It's just great to see you again.'

'You as well.'

'Would you like to go out on a quick drive, just the two of us?'

'That would be lovely,' Sannie said.

They went to Mia's Land Rover via the kitchen, where Mia picked up a cooler box containing some drinks and snacks. They drove out of the camp.

'The air here is so clear,' Sannie said. 'It's nice on the coast; the weather is lekker warm and there's always the roar of the sea nearby, but this is . . . peaceful.'

'I come out here a lot to think,' Mia said. 'It was so intense, finding out that Luiz had served with my dad. I tried to engage him in conversation just generally about the war when I first came, but it was difficult. In retrospect I get the feeling that when I told him where my dad had been stationed in the war, his name, and which unit he was in, Luiz clammed up even more.'

'Greenaway is not such a common name,' Sannie said. 'Perhaps he realised who you were, who your dad was, and decided to deliberately keep quiet.'

'But why?' Mia said. 'Just because my father was a stubborn young goat who turned into a stubborn old goat?'

'One thing I picked up from Adam, Mia, is that there's some bad blood between these guys. Adam shied away from even meeting Ferri today at lunch.'

Mia looked surprised. 'What's he afraid of?' she asked.

Adam was superbly fit, had faced down armed hijackers, and was a combat veteran. Sannie did not think he was scared of a fight with Ferri.

'Himself, I think,' Sannie said. 'What he might do.'

19

An air horn sounded.

Adam had been lying on his back on his bed, hoping a a nap would chase away some of the memories. Instantly alert, he stood up and went outside. Even though it was broad daylight, someone had just set off their personal alarm.

The door to Sannie's unit was closed and as Adam strode along the path leading to the tents he saw that the third one he came to was in some disarray. The doors were open and a chair was lying on its side in the entryway. As he climbed the stairs, he saw a man lying on the floor, the horn in his outstretched hand.

'Bliksem.' Tony Ferri got himself up onto his hands and knees on the polished concrete floor of the suite.

Adam paused at the entrance. The covers were half pulled off the bed and a writing desk had also been pushed over. A lamp lay on its side, minus its shade, and shattered glass littered the floor like scattered diamonds.

'Ferri,' Adam said.

Tony Ferri groaned and turn his head to look backwards. 'Adam Kruger.' The politician gingerly touched his fingers to the back of his head and inspected them.

Adam saw the blood starting to stain the other man's collar.

He went to him. 'Let me help you up.'

Adam held out a hand and Ferri grabbed it. 'Funny,' Ferri said, touching the back of his head again. 'My first thought was that it was you who had ambushed me. It wasn't, was it?'

Adam shook his head. 'No. I heard your air horn go off.'

Ferri walked unsteadily to the bed and sat down heavily. 'I was asleep and woke up. I heard a noise and as I got out of bed, someone whacked me on the back of the head with something.' He looked down at the lamp. 'That.'

'Who?' Adam asked.

'I have no idea, I didn't see them,' Ferri said. 'A guy, I guess. I didn't think they'd have thieves out here in the middle of nowhere, but you never know.'

'I could ask you if you know of anyone who wants you hurt, or dead . . .'

Ferri winced as he forced a laugh, still touching his head. 'The list would be long and esteemed, and would include you, I'm guessing. But, no, I don't think political assassinations or rough stuff are in the ANC's battle plan. Probably just a theft gone wrong.'

Adam looked around. 'Did you lose anything?'

Ferri leaned over to check his bedside table. 'No. Wallet's still there, as is my laptop.'

Adam looked down at him. 'I was dreading meeting you.'

Ferri cast his eyes up. 'I can guess why.'

'No. I thought I might hit you.'

Ferri shook his head. 'Someone saved you the trouble.' He straightened up. 'I'm sorry, about what happened back in Angola, Adam. I've been hoping to apologise to you for years, in person. I tried to find you a few times.'

'I heard. You ruined Frank's life.'

'Frank killed himself, Adam. He was a good soldier. He could have bounced back. Half the company hated me for charging him and you with cowardice.'

It was Adam's turn to laugh. 'Half?'

'After Frank had been arrested someone put a grenade in my tent, on my stretcher, with a note on it: This is for Frank Greenaway. The next one won't have a pin in it.'

Adam knew what that meant, if it was true. They had all heard stories of American soldiers killing unpopular officers in the Vietnam War by 'fragging' them with a grenade.

'When I explained to Colonel de Villiers what had happened across the border it was his idea to charge Frank with cowardice. He wanted Frank out of the unit – I think he believed Frank was bossies enough to get a message to one of the men to kill me, for real. He put it to me that it would be the best thing for both of us.'

Adam shook his head in disgust. 'Fucking officers. The men in our company wouldn't have needed Frank to tell them what to do.'

Ferri swallowed. 'I'm sorry you got caught up in our feud, Adam.'

Adam sat down on a steamer trunk coffee table. 'Sheesh, Frank was, like, collateral damage so you and de Villiers could cover up your fuck-up and get rid of one of the most experienced soldiers in the company, and one who really cared about the troepies. You and Evan and the others should have come with us when Frank told you to. There was no way Ondangwa would have sent a chopper into that shit-fight and your stupid heroics got Rossouw and Roberto killed.'

Ferri spread his hands and Adam saw, again, the blood on them.

'Is everyone all right?' Shirley, breathless, appeared at the entryway to the unit.

'Fine,' Tony said.

Shirley surveyed the damage. 'Doesn't look like it. What happened? Oh . . .' She put a hand over her mouth. 'You two weren't fighting, were you?'

Tony shook his head. 'No, it was an intruder.'

Shirley gasped. 'Oh, my word, no!'

It was, Adam guessed, a lodge manager's worst nightmare – to have a criminal come into a place such as this, which was supposedly safe because of its remoteness, and attack and/or rob a paying guest.

'That's terrible, I'm so sorry, Mr Ferri,' Shirley said, the tension evident in her voice. 'Did they take anything? Nothing like this has ever happened at our lodge, I can assure you.'

Tony looked around his suite for Shirley's sake. 'No, not that I can see.'

Shirley pointed at the blood. 'You're hurt. Can I call an ambulance?'

Tony touched the back of his head again and inspected his fingers, which were sticky with blood. 'No, thank you, I'll be fine. It's more my pride that's hurt. I wish I could have got hold of him.'

Shirley unclipped a radio from her belt. 'Meshach, Meshach, this is Shirley,' she said into the walkie-talkie. 'Meshach Shabangu's our head of security,' Shirley said in an aside to Tony and Adam while she waited for the reply. A man came online and Shirley quickly told him what had happened and asked him to come with another man, Ernesto.

'Ernesto is another of our San trackers – younger than my uncle Luiz was, but very good at his job. Hopefully he'll be able to pick up the spoor of whoever did this and he and Meshach will be able to catch him.' 'And you say this hasn't happened before?' Adam said.

'Absolutely not,' Shirley said. 'Mr Ferri, please, what can I do for you?'

'I think maybe just some ice for the swelling, please, Shirley, and maybe a beer to soothe my bruised pride for not being able to stop the guy.'

'I'll organise that right away, and I'll be back in five minutes.'

Shirley left them and Adam picked up their conversation where they'd left off. 'So, de Villiers wanted Frank out of the company?'

Ferri spread his bloodied hands wide. 'You knew what had gone on. You were a witness to the problems between Frank and me. You could have stayed with Evan and me – I was the senior man there, so you know you should have done as I ordered.'

'You were wrong and Frank was right. You told us to leave and you put your life and Evan's at risk needlessly.'

'That wasn't your call to make, Adam.' He took a deep breath, as if to settle or calm himself. 'OK, today, now, I can see that Frank probably was right, but I was a young officer and Frank was doing his best to undermine me. I've thought about that day many times. I think I told you and Evan to stay simply because Frank said the opposite thing. I can admit that, and apologise for it, even if I can't undo the damage my actions caused to Frank and his reputation.'

Adam shook his head. 'You told Frank and me to go,' he said. 'You pointed your rifle at Frank and he hit you. Are you saying none of that happened?'

Ferri rubbed his forehead with his hand, shielding his eyes in the process. 'Some of that day is a blur for me, Adam. Frank was –'

Adam stuck his chin out. 'Frank was a fine soldier and a good man.'

Ferri moved his hand; his face was pleading, pathetic. 'You were there, Adam. You remember how crazy it was; the bullets were flying, those mortar bombs dropping around us. Rossouw was killed in front of my very eyes after you and Frank left. I was covered in Duarte's blood – that poor airman.'

'You should have come with us when Frank said it was time to leave. We came back for you, and you shit on us.' The words were bitter on Adam's tongue, festering as they had done for decades.

Ferri spread his hands wide again. 'I've told you my side of the story.'

'All of it?'

Ferri looked up. 'What do you mean?'

Adam turned and walked out of the suite, before he did something he would truly regret.

MIA AND SANNIE came across a pair of male cheetahs resting in the shade of a thorn tree.

They stayed with the cats for a while, then continued their drive. It felt good to be away from her other life, Sannie thought, even if the circumstances of this trip had become a little weird.

'That's where Luiz . . . Where I found him.' Mia pointed to a large tree.

'Shame, that must have been tough for you,' Sannie said.

She nodded. 'Can I show you something there, something strange?'

Sannie shrugged. 'If you like.'

Mia drove off the game-viewing road onto a track that led towards the tree. 'We stop here often, for sundowners and morning coffee.'

'Nice spot,' Sannie said as Mia pulled up short of the tree.

The women got out and Mia went to a patch of sand from which a stick protruded.

'I placed this stick as a marker,' Mia said. 'I found Luiz just over there, under the tree.' She pointed.

Sannie shielded her eyes from the sun and the glare off the desert. The tree was about twenty metres from where they stood. 'What's the marker for?'

Mia reached into the pocket of her shorts and pulled out a plastic zip-lock bag. 'This.'

Sannie saw the copper bullet casing in the bag. 'From a pistol?'

Mia nodded. 'Nine-millimetre by eighteen, Russian. Same calibre as the pistol Luiz used.'

'What's a casing doing all the way over here?' Sannie asked.

'My question exactly.'

'Walk me through what you found, please,' Sannie said. Her professional curiosity was aroused. A crime scene was like a book, but like any good book, the ending was sometimes shrouded in mystery, or obscured by red herrings.

Mia walked to the big tree. 'He was here. His body had been attacked by vultures. It wasn't a pretty sight, even from a distance.'

'I've seen cases like that.' Sannie recalled the body of a woman that had been feasted upon by hyenas, just outside the Kruger Park, in one of her earlier cases.

'Did you find the casing from the bullet that killed him?'

'The police did. I spoke to the detective in charge of the investigation, a Sergeant Cele, from Askham, after I found the extra casing. He told me they had the casing for the round that had killed Luiz, and that it was a match to the gun he was holding.'

'But this Cele didn't come out again to collect the second casing?'

Mia shook her head. 'He said he was busy, and that it was probably nothing. He also told me I shouldn't have picked it up.'

Sannie frowned. 'But he couldn't be bothered coming out to collect it?'

'I guess not. There's no way a pistol would have ejected a casing from here all the way over to where I found it.'

Sannie looked at the distance and nodded. 'What else did the sergeant say?'

'He was dismissive,' Mia said. 'He said maybe Luiz had taken a shot at an animal or something before he killed himself.'

'Was the pistol licensed to Luiz?'

'No,' Mia said. 'And Shirley said she had no idea that he'd had a gun. I never saw him shoot a weapon. He loved the wild, and wildlife. I asked him once if he went hunting, and he told me that if he did, he would use his bow and arrow rather than a rifle.'

'So, what,' Sannie mused, 'this guy decides he's going to shoot himself, but first he comes out here, to a well-known landmark in the reserve, and takes a few pot shots before he sits down to end his own life?'

'Bizarre, hey?' Mia said.

'Very strange,' Sannie said. 'Was there anything else unusual about the circumstances of Luiz's death, or anything that happened to him or with him recently?'

Mia chewed her lip. 'There was something.'

Sannie looked at Mia. She knew her young friend well enough to know when she was holding something back.

'I found something in Luiz's room, after his death.'

Sannie put her hands on her hips. 'Mia?'

'A pangolin.'

'What?' Sannie blurted out the question. 'Again?'

Mia nodded. 'I know, right? This time, though, there was no reason why Luiz would have been hiding a pangolin.' The suspect in the earlier investigation had at least been crazy about reptiles and exotic animals. 'Luiz wasn't a poacher, Sannie. I'm as sure as I can be.'

Sannie gave Mia a doubtful look. 'Was this the pangolin you had to take to Askham?'

Mia looked sheepish again. 'Yes. I'm sorry I didn't tell you earlier.'

'So am I, but it's OK. Just explain to me why Luiz couldn't have been a poacher.'

'It makes no sense, none of it. Luiz rarely went on leave and wasn't even due for a break for more than a month. There was no point in him keeping a pangolin in his room for weeks, risking it being discovered at any time. I think it was planted there by someone.'

'Do you think he was murdered, Mia?'

The younger woman threw her hands up. 'I don't know. When my father was found dead I thought that it must have been someone else; that someone killed him and tried to make it look like suicide.'

'You wouldn't be the first friend or relative to think that,' Sannie said.

Mia nodded. 'I know, I know, and I came to terms with the fact that he had killed himself, and that he hadn't left me a note, and that it wasn't my fault – all of that, but I guess that still, in the back of my mind, I was always looking for a different answer. I thought that maybe meeting these guys might shed some light on what my dad was going through.'

Sannie thought of what Adam had told her about Tony Ferri. 'And have you learned anything new?'

'Just that Dad had some issues with authority in the army. That was no big surprise. He was never afraid to tell the senior management in the Kruger Park what he thought of the way the place was being run. It didn't do him any favours when it came time for them to decide who was going to lose their job.'

'Maybe you should talk to Adam,' Sannie said.

'I'd like to.'

'It might be a good idea for you to get his version of what happened in Angola.'

Mia nodded. 'I will. Now, what do you think about Luiz?'

Sannie looked around her at the stark, empty desert. A chill went down her spine. 'Some things sound strange.'

Sannie walked to the spot where Mia had found the spent cartridge. She closed her eyes for a moment, trying to imagine the scene, to put herself in the mind of the ageing warrior who had come out here with a gun. She thought of the time when she had, briefly, contemplated ending her own life. She had not been wild with rage, prone to letting off a stray gunshot – rather the opposite. It had been a moment of despair that had also brought with it a kind of clarity, that ending her life would be her best and only option.

'Do you have Sergeant Cele's phone number?'

'Yes,' Mia said. She took out her phone. 'I'll share his contact with you.'

'You've got signal out here?' Sannie took out her own phone and was surprised to see four bars.

'Julianne paid for her own tower.' Mia sent the contact and Sannie's phone beeped.

Sannie dialled the number and when Sergeant Cele answered she introduced herself and told him she was calling about the death of the San tracker.

'What's your interest, Captain? You're a long way from Port Shepstone.'

'Friend of the family,' Sannie said. It was close enough. 'Can you tell me, did the post-mortem show any traces of alcohol or drug use in the victim?'

'No, nothing. He was clean,' Cele said.

'One of the man's co-workers found a spent bullet casing about twenty metres from the body. She says she reported it to you.'

'Yes, I spoke to her. The guy was probably hunting; maybe he took a shot at a springbok or something.'

'With a pistol?'

'Are you suggesting I don't know how to do my job, Captain?'

'I'm suggesting no such thing. Rather, that you might have come and taken a second look at the crime scene.'

There was a pause. 'The whole area was already covered with animal tracks and human footprints. In that sand we wouldn't have found anything – not that there was anything to find. The guy killed himself, Captain, end of story.'

Sannie was annoyed by the detective's cavalier, almost arrogant attitude, but she could also understand it. No policeman would like another officer, in this case a female, snooping around and questioning his work.

'Thanks for your time, Sergeant.' She ended the call.

'That didn't sound very promising,' Mia said.

'It wasn't. Cele could be right – there could be a dozen explanations for the extra gunshot – but Luiz wasn't drunk or stoned, so it's not like he was staggering about like a madman. Did you tell the police about the pangolin?'

Mia shook her head. 'Mia . . . Why not?'

'Shirley and I only discovered it after the police were long gone, when we were going through Luiz's things. The guy was dead and I didn't want to ruin his reputation.'

'You covered up a crime, Mia! Don't you think that if you have suspicions about the way in which Luiz died, him being involved in a criminal enterprise might have had a bearing on that?'

Mia looked abashed. 'Um, yes, I suppose so. Sorry.'

Sannie waved her hand. 'No, I'm sorry for raising my voice to you. You're a good person, Mia, always thinking of other people's feelings. If Luiz was involved with criminals then maybe he was caught up in a deal that went wrong.'

Mia nodded. 'You could be right.'

Sannie had wanted to get away from crime and guns and the seedier side of life by taking her long road trip across South Africa, but it was beginning to feel like she had never left work. She was not upset or angry, just resigned to the fact that it was almost impossible for her to escape the life she had chosen. She would have loved to have been sitting by the lodge pool sipping a cocktail with Mia, but as her mind turned over the information Mia had just supplied, and all that she knew about the disparate group of war veterans, she felt her investigator's senses start to sing.

'Maybe I should talk to Shirley.'

'That would be great, Sannie, but I don't want to ruin your holiday.'

'I'm sure I'll still have time for some fun.'

'Especially staying in a room next to Adam.'

Sannie laughed. 'We're just friends.'

Mia checked her watch. 'I need to get back to the lodge in time for afternoon tea and the next game drive. Are you going to come with us?'

'I'll see,' Sannie said. 'I was just thinking about some pool time. Also, I'm not sure I want to witness World War Three when the guys all get on a vehicle together.'

'I'm sure it won't be that bad,' Mia said.

Sannie was not so sure. As if to prove her misgivings right, when they arrived back at the lodge reception it was to raised voices.

'Why the hell can't you guarantee the safety of your guests at such a remote place?'

Sannie saw that the woman speaking was Lisa Ingram, Tony Ferri's campaign manager. Lisa banged her hand down on the large communal dining table as she addressed Shirley, who looked like she was doing her best to stay calm in the face of an onslaught.

Mia leaned close to Sannie and whispered: 'I wonder what's happened?'

Sannie was content to keep well out of things and just head to her suite, but Mia announced herself. 'Shirley, Lisa, can I help with something?'

Sannie hovered near the entry and heard from an angry Lisa how Tony Ferri had been assaulted in his tent. Sannie watched and listened. In her experience, this type of attack in a luxury lodge was almost unheard of. Following on from the unusual suicide death of a tracker, who was now implicated in poaching, Sannie thought that it was most certainly not business as usual at Dune Lodge.

20

Adam missed his sharks. At least he knew where he stood with a prehistoric marine predator.

Luiz's funeral was the following day. As he sat in his suite he debated whether or not to go on the afternoon game drive with Ferri and Evan.

'Knock knock,' Sannie called.

Adam went out onto his stoep and leaned on the timber railing. 'How was your drive?'

'Interesting. Did you hear what happened to Tony Ferri?' she asked.

'I was first on the scene.'

'Really? Can I come in?'

'Sure.' He stepped aside as she walked up the stairs. He loved the smell of her.

'I won't stay long.'

'It's fine,' he said.

'I thought I might go to the pool.'

'You're not going on the afternoon drive?' he asked.

She shook her head. 'I've been out already, had some nice time alone with Mia. What about you?'

'I'm in two minds.'

'About confronting Ferri?'

'I sort of did that just now,' Adam said.

She sat down in the same chair she'd been in before she'd gone on her drive. Adam already thought of it as hers.

'Can I get you something from the minibar?'

'Water would be great.'

He took two bottles from the refrigerator and poured the water into glasses with ice from the silver bucket on the bar.

'Delicious,' Sannie said as she sipped hers. 'So what happened to Ferri?'

'Some guy snuck into his tent and attacked him from behind – hit him over the head. I saw the blood, and I think he was out cold for maybe a few seconds. He managed to grab his air horn and press it. I came running.'

'Did you get a look at the attacker?'

Adam shook his head. 'No, he was gone by the time I got there. Ferri said it didn't look like the guy had taken anything.'

'No description?' Sannie asked. She sipped more water. A drop of condensation hit her cleavage, between the open collar buttons of her khaki bush shirt. She wiped her chest, then looked up to see Adam watching her.

He glanced away, cleared his throat and looked back at her. 'Do you think it's a coincidence?'

'After you were attacked just a couple of days ago, in a similar manner?'

He nodded.

Sannie took out her phone. 'Excuse me. I'm just going to call my contact at Scottburgh detectives.'

He waited as she dialled and spoke to an officer. 'So, an ironclad alibi?' she said. 'And just one bullet? Interesting. Thanks.' She ended the call.

'It wasn't Renshaw who attacked me?'

Sannie shook her head. 'Your fisherman friend was at a conference in Durban which was verified by several eyewitnesses, including the professor who was the guest speaker. The prof said Renshaw was in one of the bars at the Suncoast Casino from nine pm, after dinner, until two in the morning, holding court. It seems the casino's CCTV will back up the claim – Renshaw even got into a fight with a guy and it's all on file, according to the Suncoast security people. Would he send someone else to hurt you?'

Adam shook his head. 'I suppose it's possible, but he's got an ego for Africa. I think he'd rather do his own dirty work. What were you saying about "one bullet"?'

'Yes, very interesting,' Sannie said. 'The investigating officer said that the gun we retrieved from the scene, the one I found lying next to you, had just one round in the magazine.'

'That's odd,' Adam said. 'It had to have a capacity of what, twelve or fifteen rounds?'

'Fifteen, I think. So yes, who would go to a gunfight with just one round, and why?'

Adam thought about that. It was careless enough of the intruder who had broken into his home in Pennington to drop a gun, which presumably was his backup weapon. So why, if that was the case, would the man go to commit a crime with a backup weapon with only one bullet in reserve? 'It comes back to what we were speculating about earlier,' he said.

Sannie nodded. 'It was a set-up – the intruder was going to kill you and make it look like you suicided.'

The phone rang in Adam's suite. He got up and answered it. 'One minute,' he said. He held his hand over the mouthpiece. 'It's Mia,' he said to Sannie. 'Reminding me that the afternoon game drive is due to leave soon. She wants to know if I'm going.'

Sannie smiled politely. 'I think that's up to you, Adam.'

'Of course,' he said. He felt his cheeks burn. 'I was thinking – when you talked about chilling by the pool. Would you like some company?'

She smiled again. 'I think that would be lovely.'

She was kind, giving him an out, even though he knew he didn't need her permission. He'd heard Ferri and been less than impressed with the former officer's justification of his actions. The thought of making small talk with the politician for three hours in the back of a Land Rover galled him. 'Hi, Mia. I think I'll sit this one out.'

'Me as well,' Sannie called.

Adam passed on the message then hung up.

'Mia just said she hopes we enjoy our afternoon together. What's all that about?' he asked.

Sannie laughed. 'She's assuming. Adam, I think Mia has a bit of a crush on Tony Ferri.'

'So that's what you were talking about.' He took his seat again, next to her, looking out over the beautiful view of nothing. 'Boys?'

'Ha. Don't flatter yourself. I think Ferri was mounting a charm offensive, and he obviously made no mention of you or her father being subjected to a court martial. As far as Mia knows, Frank and Ferri just had a few healthy disagreements.'

'Bastard,' Adam said. 'Now he'll probably play the sympathy card of being jumped by an intruder who he had to fight off. Typical politicians' bullshit.'

Sannie reached out and put a hand on his. 'Hey. Don't let him get to you.'

He looked in her eyes. She really seemed to care.

She finished her water. 'I need to go get changed. Shall we meet at the pool in fifteen minutes? We can talk about guns and bullets there.'

'Fine by me.'

She stood. 'It's a date.'

He liked the sound of those words. He watched her walk down the stairs from the stoep and along the path to her tent. She was captivating, but his mind returned to Angola.

ANGOLA, 1987

. . .

219

ADAM WAS RUNNING towards the border on pure adrenaline. The machine gun's sling was rubbing his shoulder raw, cutting into the flesh. His legs ached and his breathing was ragged.

'Fok!' Frank stopped and looked behind them. 'The others – I thought at least Rossouw and Evan would come with us. Where are they?'

Adam looked around. 'Shit, I thought Rossouw was right behind me.'

Mortars were still falling, back where they had just been. There was a screech overhead then the louder, deeper sound of a big explosion.

'What was that?' Adam asked, breathless. 'Heavy artillery,' Frank said. 'Ours.'

Another howitzer round screamed through the air and the ground shook as this time the shell exploded just fifty metres from them.

'Get down!' Frank dived into the sand and Adam did the same. 'Someone's ranging in the artillery.'

A salvo of four rounds came in next, further away, back towards where the others were.

'It's Ferri,' Frank yelled over the noise. 'He's calling in fire on his own position, either deliberately because he's about to be overrun, or because he's more of an idiot than I thought.'

Adam lay in the lee of a fallen tree. He could feel the thump of each explosion deep in his chest. This was terrifying enough; he could not imagine the horror of being closer to the detonations than he already was.

A dozen rounds later the bombardment stopped. Frank raised his head and listened. 'Let's go. We have to go back for the stupid bastard.'

Adam's ears rang as he stood. He and Frank retraced their steps. The air was rank with the chemical stench of explosives. Here and there the veld was on fire, the ground smoking and small trees burning from shell impacts. Smoke stung his eyes.

Adam saw a man stand and stagger along a few paces, a rifle hanging loosely by his side.

'Evan!'

Evan appeared not to hear him. Adam went to him and put his hand on the man's shoulder. When Evan spun around, he was raising his rifle, his eyes wide. Adam knocked Evan's weapon aside. 'It's me.'

Evan blinked. Blood ran from his ears, Adam noticed, and his face was smudged with dirt.

'It's me!' Adam said louder. Evan shook his head, and Adam wondered if he had lost his hearing.

'Fok, I thought we were going to die, like, a hundred times,' Evan said, loudly. 'My ears are ringing. It's like I've been listening to Rodriguez on full blast with my head too close to the speaker.'

Adam put a finger to his lips, to let Evan know he was shouting. 'We were sure we'd find you dead, bru.' Adam looked around. Rossouw lay on his back, a bullet hole in his forehead. A rush of anger at Frik's death was the only thing that stopped him throwing up. Ferri, dazed, was on his knees, summoning the energy to stand.

Frank was striding towards Ferri. 'Where are the others? Roberto? Luiz?'

Evan wiped his mouth. 'Frik didn't stand a chance. Roberto took a direct hit from a shell. One minute he was there, with us, and next second, there was nothing left of him.'

'Hectic,' Adam said.

Luiz emerged from the smoke, holding his R1 loose in his right hand.

'Luiz, I'm so sorry,' Adam said to the tracker. 'Where is Roberto's body?'

'*Ele está morto.* Dead.' Luiz shook his head.

'Fok,' Adam said. Luiz seemed not to have understood the question. Clearly, there was nothing left for them to return home to Roberto's family. He went to Ferri.

Frank was already with the officer, holding out a hand to help him to his feet, but Ferri brushed it away and used his rifle to steady himself and stand.

'Why didn't you follow us?' Frank asked him.

Ferri glared back at him. 'I told you to stay. You disobeyed an order.'

'You told us to go.' Frank stabbed a finger at the lieutenant. 'And you got Rossouw and Roberto killed, all over an air force guy who was already dead. For fuck's sake, why didn't you listen to me?'

Adam looked at the ground and saw that the body of Duarte, the crewman, seemed to have been further mutilated by a blast from a mortar bomb, or shrapnel from a South African artillery shell. His left side was a bloodied mess and his left hand was completely missing.

'I was in command,' spittle flecked Ferri's mouth, 'I am in command.'

Adam looked to Evan who, out of sight of the other two men, just shrugged.

Frank ignored Ferri. 'Kruger, Litis – you carry Rossouw's body. Lieutenant Ferri, you and I will take the air force guy. We're not leaving them behind. Litis?'

'Yes, Sergeant,' Evan said.

'Where's Roberto?'

'There's . . . There is nothing left of him, Sergeant. Luiz showed me . . . Roberto was hit by an artillery shell. One of ours.'

'Shit,' Frank said.

'What about Luiz?' Ferri interrupted. 'Can't he help carry the bodies?'

'He needs to scout ahead of us, make sure there's no FAPLA trying to encircle us.' Frank fixed Ferri with a cold stare. 'You're responsible for these men's deaths, Lieutenant, for not pulling back when I told you to, and then for calling an artillery barrage too close to your own position, which killed one of our trackers. Now, listen to me, all of you.' Frank looked around at all their faces. 'We're going to walk, about five klicks back towards the border. Rassie!' The medic came through the bush to Frank. 'You'll relieve the men carrying the dead guys as we move and everyone will switch out and take a turn carrying the radio. In the meantime, Rassie, call Ondangs and request a hot extraction.'

'Yes, Sergeant,' Rassie said.

Ferri stood there, clearly livid. Adam could see that no matter what anyone said, Frank was in charge, and only he would get them out. Frank took a map from his uniform trouser pocket, consulted it, and read out a grid reference for the extraction point they were going to head to. Rassie relayed the pickup point to the operations room at Ondangwa.

'Listen up, okes,' Frank said, grim-faced, 'we're not out of the shit yet. So let's move and stay together this time. Anyone wants to disagree or not carry his share of the weight, I'll fokken kill him myself. Understood?'

All of them nodded, except Ferri, who just looked at the ground.

ADAM SHOOK his head to try to clear away the memory of Rossouw's blood and gore on his hands and uniform and the torturous march through the baking Angolan sand veld. He went to his bag, took out his swimming trunks and put them on, along with a T-shirt and base-ball cap. Then he walked to the swimming pool.

Sannie van Rensburg was there, lying on a sun bed in a black one-piece bathing suit, and she looked sensational. A waiter stood attentively by her side.

'Adam, howzit? I'm just ordering a drink. Something with an umbrella in it. What will you have?'

'Castle Lite, please,' Adam said to the waiter.

'Coming right up, sir, ma'am.' He left them.

Sannie was rubbing sunscreen on her legs. She looked up as Adam came to her. 'Could you please do my back?'

'Sure.' He took the bottle and sprayed sunscreen into his palm, then knelt next to her. Sannie's skin was pale and smooth. He rubbed the cream into her.

'You're good. You could be a masseur.'

He laughed. 'Just a keen amateur.'

'I was about to say I've missed that – back rubs – but every time I think of something like that I think of my husband.'

'Sorry.' He removed his hands.

'No, don't stop, Adam. It's not your fault. It's just my stuff, and I need to work out how to deal with it.'

He finished rubbing the cream into her skin and Sannie rolled over. 'You look lost in thought.'

He took off his T-shirt and lay back on the sun bed. 'I was thinking about Angola again.'

'I guess all of this is bringing back so many memories for you. There was something you were going to tell me, about what happened in the war, just before Mia showed up to collect me.'

He nodded. 'Frank had a theory . . .'

'About?'

'There was so much about that fire force mission that didn't add up. Frank thought that Ferri knew more about the mission than he let on to us, and that Ferri had been told to keep information from the rest of us soldiers.'

'What do you think?'

'It's possible.'

'Tell me the rest of the story,' Sannie said. 'Maybe it will help you to talk through the events, and maybe I can help you find a pattern or something like that.'

Adam took a deep breath, nodded, and told Sannie about how Ferri had ignored Frank's decision for them to pull back, and how Adam and Frank had returned to find Rossouw, Roberto and Duarte dead.

'To play devil's advocate,' Sannie said, 'Ferri was the officer, the senior man, right?'

'He was,' Adam said, 'although any decent officer would have taken notice of an experienced sergeant. Also, there seemed no good reason for Ferri to stay behind. Duarte had already died of his wounds, but we could have all got away. It was like he wanted to stay and take on the Angolan army almost singlehanded. Either that, or he was still trying to do something or find something the rest of us didn't know about.'

'What could that have been?' Sannie asked.

'We had no idea at the time, but when I saw Frank later in life, not long before he killed himself, he had come up with a theory. Diamonds.'

'Diamonds?'

Adam nodded. The waiter came with their drinks so he held off saying more until the man had left. Sannie sipped an elaborate cocktail; his beer was cold and crisp.

'There were all sorts of stories coming out of Angola, back then and in the years since, of the SADF being responsible for poaching, and officers smuggling out elephant ivory and rhino horn. I never saw any of our guys do anything like that, but it was common knowledge that Jonas Savimbi was supporting his fight against the government through the illegal wildlife trade. There was also a lot of talk about diamonds.'

Sannie looked over the rim of her glass. 'Did Frank have any proof?'

'He tracked down Tomás Duarte's family. Tomás was the missing airman from the aircraft crash that we were looking for. We'd been told, by Ferri, that we were looking for the crew from a downed Bosbok aircraft. Frank pointed out that the Bosbok only had a pilot, but it was clear Ferri had been briefed that there was someone else on board. We were never told what this second guy was doing on the aircraft. Anyway, Frank found his family, who had never got over his death. His parents pointed Frank towards Tomás's girlfriend at the time. She had married when Frank met her, but she agreed to talk to him. She told him that Tomás had been doing some secret stuff that he was not allowed to talk about. He was in air force intelligence and would sometimes return home to South Africa from Angola and have to report to some general in Pretoria. He would then get a couple of days' leave, which he would spend with his girlfriend, and then have to report for duty again. She said he was a courier of some kind, but he could never tell her what he was doing. She thought he was maybe transporting top secret documents or something.'

'Or diamonds,' Sannie said.

Adam nodded. 'Frank also tracked down a guy from Tomás's unit. The oke said that he, personally, had met Savimbi, and had shipped diamonds back to South Africa himself. The guy told Frank that he was issued with a briefcase which was cuffed to his wrist, like in some old spy movie. When we first came across Duarte in the bush Frank swore he was carrying a bag – I remember Frank making some joke about the fact the guy was carrying "luggage" in a war zone – though there was never any sign of it again.'

'Money – greed – is a motive for many crimes,' Sannie said.

'Frank had this wild theory that Ferri stole the diamonds.'

'You said that the patrol got separated, that Rossouw, Evan, Ferri and the San trackers stayed behind, while you, Frank and the medic, Erasmus, started to withdraw. Is that right?'

Adam nodded. 'Yes. And the two San guys, Luiz and Roberto, were doing their own thing, probably realising that all us white guys were going to get them killed. As it happened, Roberto was killed, by a stray South African artillery shell, when Ferri called in the barrage. Rossouw was shot by an Angolan soldier and died instantly, apparently.'

'We need to find out what Evan saw,' Sannie said. 'Did you ask him at the time?'

'No,' Adam said. 'There was no time. We pulled back and the chopper came and collected us. We were all nearly dead with exhaustion. Back at Ondangwa we were separated. Colonel de Villiers, the sector commander, was waiting for us, with some military police. We were all strip-searched, but none of us was told what they were looking for. This was another reason why Frank later thought this was all about missing diamonds – the colonel was obviously looking for something of value. Frank even tracked down a soldier who worked in the mortuary at Ondangwa – he told him de Villiers wanted to see the bodies of the dead guys. The next thing we knew,

Frank and I were arrested and put in the cells, charged with cowardice in the face of the enemy.'

'But wasn't it just a case of the patrol being separated?' Sannie said.

'That's what I thought, and what I said at my trial. It was typical "fog of war" stuff, and it wasn't helped by the fact that the two senior people in the stick, Frank and Tony Ferri, could not agree on anything. Frank didn't do himself any favours at the court martial hearing – he even said that he wanted to kill Ferri, who he blamed for the deaths of our guys.'

'I see,' Sannie said.

'Ja. The army wanted the whole episode swept under the carpet. Like I told you, I was given a severe reprimand and sent to a different company, but Frank was sent to Greefswald, a base on the border with Botswana, near where Mapungubwe National Park is today.'

Sannie looked puzzled. 'I never heard of an army base up there.'

'It was a secret. Greefswald was a terrible place, where the SADF used to send drug users and homosexuals to try to "correct" their behaviour.' Adam made air quotes with his fingers. 'Frank's kit was inspected again after he was charged over the patrol and the military police found some dagga in his footlocker. Frank swore he never used the stuff, but it earned him a second charge and a non-negotiable excuse for the army to send him to that hellhole. While he was locked up there, he wasn't even able to put together an appeal against the cowardice charge. They would torture the guys there with hard labour, brutal physical training and drill. It broke a lot of men, but Frank survived. He went back to the border – to Angola – but I never saw him again in uniform.'

'I can see why Frank had an axe to grind with Ferri and why he would have been scarred by what he went through,' Sannie said. 'What happened to Evan?'

'He got a medal, for staying with Ferri and holding some bullshit non-existent line against the Angolans, and when Ferri went back to 44 Parachute Brigade headquarters he took Evan with him. Evan never went back into combat again. He sat out the rest of his service as a clerk.'

'I see.'

'Frank played private detective, before his death, checking up on Evan and Ferri without them knowing,' Adam continued. 'Ferri sat the bar exam after the army and became a fully-fledged lawyer. He ended up with his own practice at quite a young age and a fancy house in the Cape, at Clifton.'

'Property is expensive there,' Sannie said.

'Yes, it is. Ferri didn't come from money, though. Frank found out that Ferri's father was an Italian prisoner of war at Zonderwater, near Pretoria, captured by our guys in the western desert during the Second World War. Like a lot of Italians the father decided to move back to South Africa after the war. He ended up running a restaurant in Cullinan, but the family was never rich. Ferri married a fellow law student, but she wasn't from old money either.'

'Interesting,' Sannie said. 'Maybe he just worked hard. And lawyers make good money.'

'Sure,' Adam said. Silence hung between them for a few seconds.

'What about Luiz?' Sannie asked.

'He was with Ferri, Rossouw and Evan, so he most likely saw whatever it was that did happen in the bush that day.'

Sannie thought about that. 'Yes, but he didn't end up as a successful lawyer and politician, or a rich businessman. And he wasn't killed in action. He was a tracker living in staff accommodation at a game lodge, who maybe resorted to poaching to supplement his income.'

'Poaching?' Adam looked genuinely shocked. Sannie told him about her conversation with Mia, and the pangolin the young woman had found in his room.

'Incredible,' Adam said. 'But I didn't know Luiz that well – no one did.'

'And now, with Tony Ferri about to go for one of the top jobs in politics, maybe Luiz thought he could blackmail him by revealing some long-forgotten secret that Tony wanted to keep buried in the past? Like, maybe, stealing a bag full of diamonds?'

'Blackmail can also be a powerful motive,' Sannie said. 'Do you think Ferri did steal the diamonds, if there were any?'

Adam shrugged. 'Ferri wasn't carrying any luggage – we all had our hands full with the dead – but he could have stashed them in his uniform or gear somewhere.'

'Wasn't he searched, like you and the others, when you all got back to base?'

'I don't know,' Adam said. 'Officers look after each other. The orders for our mission came direct from the sector commander, Colonel de Villiers, who took Ferri aside for a private talk before we left. We guessed that the colonel would have been under orders to keep something like the UNITA diamond trade a secret. Frank thought that maybe the two officers cooked up some story for their superiors that the diamonds were missing in action, and that Ferri had the diamonds and he and de Villiers shared them between themselves.'

'That's a hell of a conspiracy,' Sannie said.

Adam shrugged again. 'Frank could never get any real proof. He told me he tried to reach out to de Villiers but the colonel never replied to him. In any case, it wasn't likely that de Villiers would incriminate himself.' Adam was quiet for a moment, then went on, 'What do you think about the attack on Ferri, in his room?'

Sannie sipped her cocktail. 'We all know crime is a problem in South Africa, but this is the first I've ever heard of someone being assaulted in a luxury lodge like this one. That just doesn't happen.'

Adam nodded. 'Maybe it was politically motivated – someone looking for some documents he might have had, or something on his computer?'

'The DA's blueprint on how to lose elections?'

Adam laughed. Sannie pondered the attack. Maybe it had just been an opportunistic thief – perhaps a staff member – and Ferri had disturbed them. It was still unlikely, she thought. Julianne Clyde-Smith ran a tight ship at her lodges and Sannie knew that she put a lot of effort into acquiring the best staff, at every level. She paid well and that engendered loyalty.

Adam stood. Sannie admired his well-defined abs and the muscles in his back as he turned around. He dived into the pool. On impulse she stood up, too.

'How's the water?' she asked as Adam surfaced.

'Bracing. Not as warm as the Indian Ocean.'

She gave a mock shiver.

'Come on in,' he said.

The water looked clear and inviting. Adam ran a hand through his short hair, sending droplets flying. She dived in.

'Brrr. More like freezing,' she said when she came up for air. She swam a lap to try and warm up. Adam caught up with her, matching her stroke as she turned and did another lap. 'You look at home in the water.'

He smiled. 'It's my natural element. I don't think I could live in the desert, or even the bush.'

'I love the beach,' she said. 'As a kid I always used to look forward to our annual holiday. We used to go to Margate.'

Adam laughed. 'Oh, we loved having all you tourists come down to visit every holiday.'

'I bet you did.' She splashed him.

'Haha.' He swam up to her but stopped short of her.

He was so handsome and, their conversation notwithstanding, Sannie almost felt like she really was on a holiday, with a beautiful stranger in a pool. She trod water, looking at him.

'You're shivering,'

'Just paddling, trying to stay warm,' she said.

'You could get out of the water.'

She shook her head. 'I don't want to.'

Adam came to her and Sannie's heart started beating faster. He was tall enough to be able to walk on the bottom of the pool and keep his head above water, whereas she, in the deep end, was just a few centimetres too short.

He spread his arms, under the water.

Sannie locked eyes with him and paddled towards him. She felt like she was approaching the edge of a cliff. When their bodies met, she felt the warmth of him, and imagined she could feel the beat of his heart. He put his arms around her.

Sannie clung to his neck, and they kissed. Adam placed a hand in the small of her back and drew her to him, so their hearts were close. The warmth of his mouth banished the cold and she felt weightless. She had tumbled over the precipice and he had caught her.

'Wow,' she said, when they broke for air.

He laughed. 'You sound like a little girl.'

He held on to her and she did not want to let go. 'I'm shivering, for real.'

'I've got you.' Adam held her tight and they kissed again. He moved slowly backwards, into the shallows, until she could stand.

He led her by the hand, out of the pool.

'What now?' Sannie asked, her heart still pounding. She busied herself snatching up a towel and drying herself. She picked up the brightly patterned kikoi she had brought with her and tied it around her waist. Adam stood on the other side of her sun bed, opposite her, as he dried himself and shrugged on his T-shirt.

'I have an idea.' He smiled.

She had felt him; the cold water had done nothing to hide his desire and she felt the need in her once more. It had been so long.

'We can take it slow, if you like,' he said.

She stepped up onto the sun bed, then, as he took an involuntary half-step backwards, she half fell into his arms as she got off the bed.

'No,' she whispered in his ear, 'fast is good.'

Adam took her hand again and led her down the pathway from the pool back to the trail that led to his tent. He paused to look either way, as if someone might be watching them, or waiting for them. She willed him to move on, faster, before common sense intervened and she changed her mind.

Adam sensed the urgency and broke into a half-jog. She laughed, a nervous titter, and kept up with him.

He took the stairs up to his stoep two at a time, then paused and turned at the top, waiting for her.

'You're sure?'

She shook her head. 'No. But I'm coming in.'

Adam opened the sliding door to the suite and Sannie came up the stairs and inside. She melded into his arms once more. They kissed again. She pressed herself against him and undid the loose knot she had tied in her wrap. It fell to the floor. With only the sheer material of her bathing suit between them she felt him again, hard against her. She wanted him, so badly.

Adam picked her up and waltzed her to the bed, then lay her down. She felt light in his strong arms. He straddled her, supporting himself with his arms, and looked down at her. 'You're beautiful.'

She blushed. 'So are you.'

He touched her through the fabric, gently tracing the outline of her as he kissed her. Her body was afire, almost too sensitive to bear the pressure of his fingertips. Sannie hooked an arm around his neck and drew him down, closer. She wanted to feel all of him, on all of her.

Adam kissed his way down her chest and sealed his mouth around a nipple, erect yet still encased in her one-piece. The friction made her gasp. He peeled the shoulder straps down, reverently yet eagerly unwrapping her. He smiled and his eyes glowed. Sannie arched her back as he slid the bathing costume down and off. She couldn't remember the last time she had felt so open, so vulnerable, yet so certain.

He kissed her.

She ran her fingers through his hair, savouring the feeling and closing her eyes. Impatient, Sannie drew his face back to hers and their lips met again.

'I want you,' he said.

'Me as well.'

His fingers replaced his tongue and she felt herself well up from inside.

How, Sannie wondered, had this happened so quickly? The troubled stranger was gone, replaced by a man who seemed to know every centimetre of her and what to do with her. As she looked into his eyes she felt she should feel guilty, but then he kissed her again and she grabbed him.

Adam opened her, more, then completed her.

She ran a hand over his hard butt, urging him, drawing him in. Sannie started to cry, and felt silly, until he kissed her tears away without a word. She was grateful for his silence. In time, she felt a change in her, and rolled him onto his back. He reached up, his hands covering her breasts as she brushed a strand of blonde hair from her eyes and looked down at him. It was her turn to drink him in, and she revelled in the sight.

He was so perfect, physically, from his hard, spartan lifestyle, yet his eyes were those of a man searching for hope, or redemption, or whatever it was he needed to make him whole again.

Adam opened his mouth to speak, but Sannie put a finger on his lips. He kissed it as she rode him, using the rhythm of their bodies to work away the grief and the uncertainty and the horror she had seen in her life.

This was what she needed, perhaps even who she needed. Someone to care for and someone to hold her. It didn't matter that he was flawed – they all were. What mattered was that she could feel again.

The afternoon light slanted in, bathing their bodies in liquid gold and the glint of reflection directed her eyes to the mirror on the wall. She saw herself, on him, whole once more.

21

Mia lowered her head and said a quiet prayer for Luiz, and her father, and all those veterans who had given their lives, either in battle or since the war.

It had been Tony's idea for them to observe a minute's silence during sundowners at the big tree.

When Mia looked up, she saw that Tony was looking at her. He smiled. He had perfect, even white teeth, which she imagined was a prerequisite for a political aspirant these days.

Tony raised his can of Windhoek Lager. 'To Luiz, and all our comrades.'

'To Luiz,' the others said.

Lisa had joined them on this game drive, as had Shirley, at Tony's suggestion. Evan raised his brandy and Coke and clinked with Tony. 'He was a good man.'

Tony looked to Mia again. 'They all were. I'd like to say a few words, if no one minds.'

'Go right ahead,' Shirley said. 'I'm sure Luiz would have appreciated it, especially from someone he served with and who is, well, so important.'

'Thank you, Shirley. It was my honour to serve with your uncle.'

Tony drew a breath, closed his eyes for a second, then opened them. 'Luiz was born into a country in conflict, and he died in exile from his homeland of Angola, but he was not alone. He and his San comrades found a home in the old South African Defence Force, and in South Africa itself. As those of us who were there know, the San warriors and their families occupied a special place in our hearts.'

He looked around the small group, briefly making eye contact with each of them. Mia could have been imagining it, but it felt like his gaze lingered on her a second longer than the others. 'I am a politician, and I must always choose my words carefully, but I hope I am among friends here today, and that I will not be judged unfavourably if I speak my heart. While we, as South Africans, helped men like Luiz, we also failed them. The fact that a military veteran sees no other option in his life other than to end it is a sign, to me, that someone, somewhere, could have done more.' He held up a hand. 'I am not talking about his direct family, as they are the ones who men such as Luiz seek to spare from their suffering and grief, by keeping it hidden. It is we, their fellow veterans who know what Luiz went through, and what he was probably still going through. It should have been us who he turned to or, better yet, one of us who called him up and asked how he was, and if there was anything we could do.'

Tony raised a hand again and pinched the bridge of his nose, then continued. 'I have visited Platfontein and met with the San people there; I have travelled to Angola with veterans' groups on several occasions to extend the hand of peace and assistance to the veterans and civilian victims of our war there. I have tried to be a good friend to my fellow soldiers' – he looked to Evan, who gave a small nod – 'but I have also failed in my duty of care, to others.'

Tony turned to Mia and paused. 'As we remember Luiz, today, Mia, I especially want to tell you how sorry I am that your father passed in similar circumstances, and was not able, for whatever reason, to reach out to one or more of his former comrades for help. I also apologise for failing him, as his one-time commander, for not making more of an effort to reconcile our differences and to support him when he needed it most.

'Friends,' he spread his hands wide to encompass all of them, 'true leadership is like true friendship; it must be a two-way street, with people talking to each other, not just in good times but in bad, and showing a way forward, together. So, in the Lord's name, I ask for forgiveness for those of us who have not been there for our brothers and sisters, and for eternal light for those who have found no end to their darkness here on earth.'

Mia felt the tears well up inside her and wiped her eyes. Evan sniffed and Mia could see that Shirley, too, was crying.

'Thank you, Mr Ferri,' Shirley said. 'That was beautiful.'

He went to Shirley, held out his arms, and when she nodded he enfolded her in an embrace. Ferri shook hands with Evan and clapped him on the shoulder, then came to Mia.

As he held her, the dam burst inside her and Mia cried into the politician's shirt. 'Thank you,' she sniffed. 'I'm sure my father would forgive whatever there was between you two, Tony.'

'I can only pray,' he said softly into her ear. He gave her a squeeze and she hugged him back.

Mia straightened and wiped her eyes again. She had a duty to care for these people while they were out in the desert, and needed to keep her wits about her.

'More drinks, or snacks anyone?' Mia asked.

'Sure, may I have a beer, please?' Evan said.

Mia put on a smile. 'Coming right up.'

She missed Luiz; at sundowners he would be helping her with drinks and maybe taking a guest or two aside to show them some interesting tracks. He had been quiet, almost withdrawn around her, but he had an easy way about him when he was in the company of guests, despite his limited English. He was adept at making people laugh.

'What's on your mind?' Tony said as he helped himself to another beer from the cooler box.

'I was just thinking about how funny Luiz could be. He loved to laugh. It just makes it so hard to reconcile what little I knew of him with the way he died, and his past troubles.'

'We old soldiers become experts at hiding our true feelings. That is, until we meet someone who penetrates our armour.' He smiled at her.

Mia blushed.

'Is it possible to arrange private dinners at the lodge, away from everyone else?' Tony asked.

'Of course,' she said, pleased to be on safe ground again. 'We can have a table set up at your suite, on your stoep if you like, and one of the wait staff will bring your food to you. You can dine alone if you want a break.'

'I want you to have dinner with me,' he said.

She looked into his eyes and was fairly sure that was not all he had in mind.

'You have dinner with your guests some nights, don't you?'

Mia nodded. 'Er . . . Yes.'

'So if you had a single guest it would not be unusual to dine with him, or her?'

'Technically, you're right, but it would usually be in the main area of the lodge, where everyone else eats.'

'I like you, Mia, and I want to get to know you better.'

Mia glanced over at Lisa, who was, as Mia had half suspected, watching them. Perhaps she just liked to watch over her boss all the time, but Lisa was attractive and Mia wondered if there might still be something between her and Tony.

'I want to tell you more about your father, Mia,' he pressed.

'Really?' That sparked her interest. Maybe she was misreading him and his intentions.

The next morning was going to be Luiz's funeral in the nearby town of Askham, followed by a service at the lodge for all staff. Mia had mixed emotions. She liked this handsome politician but wondered if anything could come of a relationship with a high-profile man with an incredibly complicated personal life.

Mia took a deep breath. 'Let me run it past Shirley, as we're technically not supposed to socialise with guests in their rooms.'

He grinned. 'Thank you. It would make me very happy, if Shirley agrees.'

'We aim to please at Dune Lodge,' she said.

'Mia?' Lisa walked over to them. 'May I please have another gin and tonic?'

'Of course,' Mia said, feeling relieved. For a moment she had thought Lisa was going to butt in and tell her to stop monopolising Tony.

Mia went to the front of the Land Rover. As she reached for the blue bottle of gin on the fold-out table fixed to the bull bar, the bottle exploded.

Mia snatched back her hand and spun around. Lisa dropped her empty glass and screamed. There was a clang and a hole appeared in the passenger door of the game viewer. Mia realised that someone was shooting at them. 'Get down!'

Tony jumped up onto the Land Rover's running board and reached over the seats for Mia's rifle, which was in a green canvas zippered bag on the dashboard.

'Tony, get down!' Mia went to reach for him, but another bullet slammed into the vehicle just centimetres in front of her, forcing her to duck.

Tony leapt down, pulling the rifle from the bag as he backed into Mia. 'You get down.'

Another shot rang out. Mia registered that the rounds were coming from a high-powered rifle, some distance away. Perhaps the shooter was using a silencer, she thought, as she could not clearly hear the report of each gunshot, just the sound of their impact.

Tony placed a hand on her, urging her to drop to the ground. 'Take cover. I've got this,' he said.

Tony was on one knee, his body shielding her from the direction of fire. Evan had hustled Shirley and Lisa to the far side of the Land Rover. Tony worked the bolt of Mia's rifle as he scanned the dunes.

'Got you.' He raised the rifle to his shoulder and squeezed the trigger. The big .375 boomed and kicked back into his shoulder.

Tony chambered another round with practised ease.

'Tony! Give me my rifle.'

Another round punctured the skin of the Land Rover, less than a metre from Ferri. He ignored Mia's command, took aim and fired again.

'I think I might have hit him,' Tony said. 'Get everyone into the vehicle, Mia, now.'

Mia scanned the dune line, where Tony had been aiming. She saw nothing. She got up and went to the other side of the Land Rover, where the others were crouching. 'OK, everyone get on board, and stay low, between the seats, on the floor.'

Evan helped Shirley and Lisa up into the vehicle. The two women lay on the floor, with Evan hunched low on a seat above them.

Mia climbed into the driver's seat and started the engine. 'Tony, get in!'

He looked over his shoulder at her. His eyes were wide and bright. 'No, you go. Get over the next hill, I'll cover you. Wait for me there.'

'Tony, no!'

Tony strode away from them, in the direction the gunfire had been coming from, his eyes scanning the dunes. He had Mia's rifle up in his shoulder.

'Crazy, brave bastard,' Mia said. She turned to check all the others were safe and under cover, and noticed Lisa was now standing up and had her phone in her hand. 'What are you doing?'

'Videoing him. This is priceless,' Lisa said.

Mia shook her head, rammed the truck into gear, and accelerated away. Glasses, bottles and the sundowner snacks flew from the still-raised table on the front of the vehicle. She drove down the game-viewing road and over the hill Tony had indicated. When she was on the other side she stopped and took out her radio.

'Dune Lodge, Dune Lodge, this is Mia, we've got an emergency here at the big tree sundowner spot. Call the police. Shots fired – someone was shooting at us, over.'

'Copy that, Mia,' said Meshach, their head of security. 'I'm sending the APU now, copy?'

'Affirmative,' Mia said. The guys in the APU, the Dune Lodge anti-poaching unit, were heavily armed and experienced and they would get here much quicker than the local police.

Mia turned to her guests again. 'Stay here. I'm going back for Tony.'

The two women climbed down out of the Land Rover. 'I'm coming with you, Mia,' Evan said.

Mia shook her head. 'Thanks, but no. You stay here with the others, please, Evan.' She took a handheld radio out of the cubby box between the front seats and handed it to him. 'Stay in touch, and you can contact Meshach at the lodge on channel six.'

He took the radio and, reluctantly, got out. 'OK.'

Mia took off again, driving back the way she had come, accelerating hard and changing gears fast. When she arrived at the big tree, she saw that Tony had continued to advance towards the gunman. She swung the steering wheel to the left and drove into the sand. Pausing to put the Land Rover into low range, she gunned the engine and ploughed up the gentle slope of the dune towards Tony.

He looked back at the sound of her engine and she drove up to him.

'He's gone, I think,' said Tony.

'Get in,' Mia said. As much as she admired his heroism, he had taken her rifle and gone off like a lone wolf.

'Yes, ma'am.' He laughed and climbed into the front passenger seat.

'I'm glad someone's enjoying this.'

She drove on, slowly climbing as the gradient steepened. When they got to the top of the dune Mia stopped and they both got out. 'I heard an engine, like a motorcycle or maybe a quad bike, just as you were leaving,' Tony said.

Mia put a hand up to her eyes and scanned the horizon. She could see an indentation in the sand where someone had been lying, and blurry tracks led over the next dune. Mia saw the glint of sunlight on metal. They both walked to the place where the shooter had been lying and Mia crouched down to examine several empty cartridge cases.

'A .300 by the look of it,' she said. Tony nodded. 'Poacher?'

Mia shrugged. 'We have a small population of desert black rhino here on the reserve, but they're intensively monitored. We don't have a problem with poaching here because we have a very well-resourced anti-poaching unit that tracks our animals constantly, and we benefit from being far away from towns and main roads. This calibre's too small for rhino.'

'I wonder what he was doing here,' Tony said.

Mia looked at him. 'Who's after you, Tony, and why? First the guy in your suite, and now this.'

He shrugged. 'A conspiracy theorist could come up with a hundred possibilities. Maybe the government sees me as too much of a threat; hell, it could even be someone in my own party who's jealous – this sort of thing has happened in the ANC, with municipal coun-cillors and candidates bumping each other off. It might even be a jealous husband for all I know.'

'This is no time for jokes, Tony.'

He smiled. 'Sorry.'

'*Sjoe*,' Mia exhaled. 'You're not taking this very seriously. A sniper just tried to shoot up a game-drive vehicle full of tourists.'

'It's serious, Mia, but . . .'

'What?'

'For a moment, there, with the sound of the bullets in the air, the weight of the rifle in my hand, it was almost like being back there, being in my twenties again.'

'Angola?'

He nodded. 'People can say what they want about the war and why we were fighting it, and whether we won or lost, but I have never felt so alive in my life. It all came flooding back, just then.'

She frowned. 'Give me my rifle back, please.'

He handed it to her and she checked that the safety was on. Mia scanned the ground and set off, following the tracks in the sand.

Tony kept pace with her. 'I think maybe someone is out to get me, Mia. Rather, they could be paying someone to kill me.'

'A hit man?'

'Again, it's not unheard of in our country, right?'

'Who wants you dead, Tony, apart from the long list you've already hinted at?'

He increased his stride to catch up to her.

'I think it's someone here, at your lodge, right now, Mia.'

She stopped and looked at him. 'Who?'

'Adam Kruger.'

22

The sun was low when Sannie woke, alone, in Adam's bed. She checked her watch. She had been more exhausted than she thought – the long trip and their lovemaking had meant she'd slept for two hours.

'Adam?' Sannie called out as she sat up, then saw the piece of notepaper on his pillow.

Gone for a run in the gym and a swim. Need to think. Back by 17h00, the note said.

He had drawn a heart at the end of the sentence. Sannie frowned. She thought about going back to her own room rather than hanging around waiting for him, but five o'clock was in twenty minutes' time. He didn't strike her as a one-night-stand kind of guy, and if he was, he'd be facing a long bus ride home to Pennington. She decided to wait for him.

Sannie went to the bathroom and turned on the tap in the spa. She still felt miffed that Adam had snuck out on her, but the little heart at the end of his note also convinced her to relax and wait. She took a sparkling water from the minibar, added some foaming bath salts to the bathwater and slid in.

Just before five she heard footsteps on the stairs outside the suite.

'Sannie?'

'In the bath.'

Adam walked in and smiled. He was wearing rugby shorts and a sweat-stained T-shirt, which he pulled over his head. 'I skipped the swim.'

He unlaced his shoes, which she saw were dusty, and brushed sand from his calves before taking off his shorts. 'I thought you were on a treadmill, in the gym.'

'I was, for a while,' he stepped into the tub, 'but one of the staff showed me a perimeter track around the lodge that they use for exercise; I was able to do a few laps, which was better than being inside. It helped me think.'

She stiffened in the water. 'Is this where you say "let's just be friends"?'

He shook his head as he sat down, then reached out and brushed wet hair from her eyes. 'Not at all, but what now?'

She relaxed a little, then shrugged. 'We're both free, single and well over twenty-one. How about we play it by ear?'

He smiled, but she thought it looked forced. 'Sannie, I . . . I have nothing.'

She reached over now and put a finger to his lips. 'You're studying and carrying out valuable research. I have some money, and I still have my job. I'm not sure how long I'll stay in the police, or even if I'll retire to Pennington or find another job. But for now, let's just see where this goes – whatever this is. You don't need to support me, Adam.'

He nodded, but looked pensive. She wondered if it was his ego. 'Thank you,' he said, then leaned over and kissed her. 'You're beautiful. Turn around.'

Sannie shifted in the tub so that her back was to him. He put an arm around her and drew her closer, so she was lying against his chest. His right hand moved into the water and caressed her inner thigh. She shifted her leg and he found the right spot, and Sannie rested her head back on his shoulder and closed her eyes. She let her body respond to his touch.

Adam kissed her cheek as she began to shake. He held her tight against his muscled body until she relaxed against him.

Sannie looked at him and smiled. 'I feel like a teenager again.'

'I would have loved to have known you at seventeen, before . . . well, before the army and all that shit.'

'Yes, and before I saw what I did in the police.' She reached over to a side table and took up a face cloth and soap. Lathering the cloth, she took one of his arms and began washing him. 'Do you think it's possible to recapture innocence?'

'I know that it's impossible to run away from your past, but maybe we can start over.'

She nodded. 'I like that idea.'

He sighed. 'If I'd wanted to run away, I wouldn't have come here. I wanted to kill Tony Ferri.'

The sun was setting outside, the sky patterned with red clouds that looked like shell bursts. Sannie placed the arm she had been cleaning back in the water and started on his other. 'You probably shouldn't say that to a detective, just after the man you're talking about was assaulted in his suite and you were first on the scene.'

'He wouldn't be alive if I was serious.'

She craned her neck. 'You were?'

'At one point in my life, maybe. After Frank died; but no, not really serious.'

'Phew.'

'You believe me?'

'I have to. We made love and I'm lying in a bathtub with you.' He ran his fingers down over her left breast as she continued to soap him.

'Frank was angrier than me. I wanted to leave the past behind – he couldn't. I felt guilty after he died, that I hadn't shared his passion for revenge, that I hadn't helped him with his digging.'

'Frank wasn't the police, and nor were you. If he had concerns that one or more of the others in your patrol had committed a crime, then he should have gone to the police.'

'And would they have investigated something that happened in the apartheid-era army in a different country twenty years earlier?'

She stopped her washing and shrugged against him. 'I don't know. The problem with SAPS is that you have to report a crime to your nearest police station and hope that it gets to the right people. You can't just go shopping for a detective who you think might want to open an historic case like this.'

'What about you?' he asked.

'The Hawks at Port Shepstone are hardly likely to approve my travel budget. If Ferri reports the assault on him, in his suite, it'll be investigated by the detectives at Askham. From what Mia told me they weren't interested in digging too deep into Luiz's death. Given that Ferri is a high-profile politician they would have to take his case seriously, but as I understand it, he didn't want Shirley to report it to the police.'

'I've been thinking about Frank's death, Sannie.'

'Go on.'

'He was so fired up, about investigating Ferri and finding out the truth; I always had trouble understanding why he would give it all up and kill himself. I think he might have been murdered. Can you check something for me?'

'I don't know, Adam, what is it?'

'Can you ask some questions about Frank's death?'

Sannie frowned. 'Maybe. The truth is, I'm curious as well. And Mia is a friend – which is a good reason and a bad reason for me to open up someone else's closed case. I can make a couple of calls. I wasn't in the Lowveld when Frank killed himself, but I know some detectives from Hazyview and Nelspruit who would have been around at the time.'

'I'd really appreciate that,' Adam said.

Sannie reached for him, under the water. 'How much would you appreciate it?'

She swivelled her head again and saw that he was grinning.

．　．　．

AFTER THEY HAD MADE love again, Sannie and Adam dressed for dinner.

As they walked along the path to the main area of the lodge, two vehicles arrived – Mia's game viewer with Ferri, Evan, Shirley and Lisa on board, and a bakkie with four heavily armed anti-poaching rangers close behind.

'They're back early,' Sannie said. 'Mia said they'd only return around six-thirty or seven pm, after an hour's night driving.'

'And what's with the armed escort?' Adam asked.

Mia gave her guests the option of going back to their rooms to freshen up or heading straight to the bar. They all opted for the latter. 'Stay close, Meshach,' Mia said to a tall man in uniform. She came to Sannie.

'Something wrong?' Sannie asked.

Mia explained that Meshach was the head of security and antipoaching, and told Sannie and Adam how she and the guests had been shot at by an unknown gunman using a rifle with a silencer at about four o'clock, at the sundowner spot where Luiz had taken his life.

'A guy being assaulted in his tent and now this,' Adam weighed in. 'I take it that this doesn't usually happen at Dune Lodge.'

'If someone gets stung by a scorpion it's a major event,' Mia said.

'Is someone trying to assassinate Ferri?' Sannie wondered out loud. She glanced at Adam and drew a sharp breath.

'I don't know,' Mia said, 'and neither does Mr Ferri. What I do know is that he went off like Chuck Norris. He took my rifle and went chasing whoever was shooting at us.'

Sannie nodded to Meshach, who seemed to be briefing his men. 'Did they follow up?'

Mia nodded. 'I could see tracks where the shooter left on foot, then when Meshach investigated further, he could see that whoever it was had had a quad bike parked over the dune from the firing position. I didn't have time to follow the tracks; I had to take the other guests to safety first.'

'Do you use quad bikes here at the lodge?' Sannie asked.

'Yes,' Mia said. 'Meshach and his guys use them, but Meshach told me he checked and ours were all accounted for. None were being used.'

'Where's your nearest neighbour?' Adam asked.

'There's another lodge about ten kilometres west of us, and to the north is the Kgalagadi Transfrontier Park. The guy on the quad headed east. The main road is about seven kilometres that way; I'm guessing he had another vehicle stashed there. For us to get there we would have had to drive out of our reserve first and it would have taken us over an hour to get to the point where he might have been heading. I could have maybe taken the Land Rover overland, or sent Meshach, but we decided we needed to get the guests back to safety first.'

'Probably a good call,' Sannie said. 'The guy on the quad bike would have outrun you anyway.'

'That's what I thought.' Mia looked to the bar area, where her guests were all standing. 'I don't know if trouble follows all politicians like this.'

'So,' Sannie tried to sound casual, 'if the shooter had another getaway vehicle ready on the main road, seven kilometres from the big tree, then that must be, what, about fifteen kilometres from the lodge, as the crow flies?'

Mia shook her head. 'No, that would be if you drove, but in a straight line it's maybe only about ten.'

A fit man could run that in well under an hour. 'What about the local police?' Sannie asked.

'Meshach called them from his cell phone on the way back to the lodge. They'll send detectives out tomorrow. They said there was nothing they could do tonight.'

Sannie shook her head but said nothing. 'Could it be poachers?'

'Not here,' Mia said.

Mia's phone dinged. She took it out and looked at it. 'Oh my gosh.'

'What is it?' Sannie asked.

'It's another guide friend of mine, Margaux. She says I'm a meme on Instagram and wants to know if I'm OK.' Mia handed her phone to Sannie.

'A meme?' Adam said.

'A short funny video,' Sannie said as she pressed play. 'Except this one's not so funny,' Mia said.

Sannie looked at the screen. She saw Mia, crouched by her Land Rover. A gunshot sounded in the background.

'Tony, get in!' Mia said in the video.

Adam leaned in to watch and they both saw the camera pan to Tony Ferri's face.

'No, you go. Get over the next hill, I'll cover you. Wait for me there,' Ferri said, brandishing a hunting rifle.

'Tony, no!' Mia's voice said.

Ferri headed towards a dune, and now had the rifle up to his shoulder, ready for action.

'Crazy, brave bastard,' Mia said in the recording.

The video had been edited already, turning it into a meme. Mia's voice carried on, over and over again, superimposed over a hero shot of Ferri swinging the rifle, looking for a target.

'Crazy, brave bastard; crazy, brave bastard; crazy, brave bastard; crazy, brave bastard.'

'This is going to go viral,' Sannie said.

'Just what every politician dreams of,' Adam said.

'Well he was brave,' Mia said. 'Sannie?'

Sannie handed her phone back to Mia. 'Yes?'

'Can I, um, have a word with you, in private?'

Sannie looked to Adam. 'I'm fine,' Adam said. 'I'll go say hi to the others. It's probably about time I spoke to Ferri properly.'

'See you just now,' Sannie said. She was rattled. She needed to talk again to the man she had just had sex with, and ask him more about where he had been during the afternoon when he said he was exercising, but it would have to wait.

Mia led her away, to the lodge library. Without preamble, she said, 'Sannie, Tony thinks that Adam might be out to get him, that he might want to hurt him.'

Sannie swallowed. 'Really?'

'Yes.'

'Do you happen to know where he was this afternoon?' Mia asked.

Sannie felt her cheeks colour. 'Yes. He was here at the lodge, in his suite, and later, doing some exercise, for a while.'

'You saw him?'

'Yes.'

'In his suite?'

Sannie sighed. 'Mia . . . Adam and I . . . We spent some time together this afternoon.'

Mia's eyes widened. 'You?'

'We spent the afternoon together.'

'The whole afternoon?'

'Mia . . .' Sannie felt her heart rate increase and knew she was still blushing.

Mia held her hands up. 'OK. None of my business. So he couldn't have been out in the desert by himself.'

'Well . . .'

'Wow. OK. I mean, I'm happy for you, if you're happy.'

'It's early days,' Sannie said. The truth was she had not even had five minutes on her own to think about the implications of what had gone on between her and Adam. The lovemaking had been fantastic and she felt better for it, but now Mia's questioning was forcing her to press pause and think. Adam had been out of her sight for two hours. 'I certainly enjoyed his . . . company.'

'You're blushing!'

'Stop it.'

Mia gave a little laugh then put a hand on Sannie's forearm. 'I'm happy for you. But when Tony said Adam might want to harm him, well, it got me thinking. I don't know Adam, but he seems moody, withdrawn.'

Sannie looked through the adjoining doors to the bar area. Adam had gone up to Tony Ferri and was shaking his hand. Ferri waved to the barman.

'He is, but that doesn't make him a candidate for a crazed gunman.' Or did it?

'He was the first on the scene at Tony's tent after he was assaulted, and just before Shirley showed up,' said Mia.

'You think Adam might have been responsible for hitting Ferri, then pretended to come to his rescue when he saw Shirley?' Sannie asked.

'Maybe.'

'Unless Adam was trying to kill Tony and made a bad job of it, it hardly makes sense. If Adam wanted to pick a fight with Ferri, to get his revenge, then I think he would be man enough to call him out, face to face.'

'Why do you say "revenge"?' Mia asked.

Sannie exhaled. 'I'm worried Tony Ferri may not have been completely honest with you, Mia, about his time in the army and Angola with Adam and your father.'

'I told you that he admitted that he and my dad had their differences,' Mia said.

Sannie knew she had to tell Mia what Adam had told her, even if it caused her friend distress. Mia should at least confront Ferri over Adam's story. 'Mia, it sounds like it was more than just differences of opinion.'

Mia's phone rang and she looked at the screen. 'Sannie, I'm sorry, it's the boss. Julianne. I need to take this.'

'OK. Let's talk soon, though.'

MIA NODDED to Sannie then answered the call as she walked away.

'Shirley phoned,' Julianne Clyde-Smith said in place of a greeting. 'What the absolute fuck, Mia?'

Mia took a deep breath. 'Julianne, I don't know what to say. Someone just opened fire on us when we were at the big tree sundowner spot.'

'I can see. It's all over bloody Facebook and Instagram. We are trending for the wrong bloody reason, Mia. Reservations is already taking calls from people who are cancelling their stays at Dune Lodge.' Julianne paused, then went on, 'Shirley told me no one was hurt.'

'Yes, all the guests are fine.'

'Thank fuck.'

Her British accent always made swear words sound particularly bad, Mia thought, but she could understand her employer's anger. 'I'm sorry.'

'It's not your fault, Mia. I thought Tony Ferri wanted this visit to go under the radar – now it seems his people are broadcasting him on social media. Mr Ferri going full Rambo has not hurt his public image, it seems. The video already has thousands of views and there are new memes by the minute. Shirley told me he was assaulted in his suite as well.'

'Yes,' Mia said.

'Do you think someone's trying to assassinate him on my game reserve?'

'If they were, they weren't a very good shot,' Mia said. 'The gunman fired maybe half a dozen rounds at us. He shot up the game viewer pretty good, but didn't hit Ferri.'

'Do you think the person was aiming at Ferri?'

Mia thought for a moment. 'Yes. A couple of shots came close to me, but I was next to Tony at the time.'

'Tony? Are you two on first name terms already?'

'He's nice,' Mia said.

'And he's married, Mia. I don't need a high-profile guest going Rambo and coming down with khaki fever.'

Mia felt like telling her boss that her personal life was none of her business, but she knew Julianne was right.

'What are you and Shirley doing to ensure Ferri's safety?' Julianne continued.

'Meshach's posting his anti-poaching guys all around the lodge. The police said they'll only come out to investigate in the morning.'

'The way Ferri's trending online, I'm sure that will change. You'll probably have police crawling all over the place before dawn, and get ready for a media storm coming your way tomorrow. I'll have my PR people prepare a media release. No one talks to the media without talking to me first. Understood?'

'Yes, Julianne.'

'All right,' she said. 'Take care.' Julianne rang off.

Returning to the bar area, Mia saw Sannie and Adam sitting at a corner table by themselves and started towards them.

'Mia, come have a drink with me and the other survivors.' Tony blocked her way and held out a glass of champagne to her.

'Um, I don't think I should drink alcohol tonight. I've just been on the phone to my boss. She wants us all focused on security.'

'Could I please have a sparkling water?' Tony called to the barman. 'Come, join us, please.'

'OK.' Mia gave Sannie a smile and a shrug and followed Tony to the long wooden bar. Evan and Lisa were there, drinking wine, and Shirley nursed what looked like a glass of orange juice.

'Did Julianne call?' Shirley asked Mia.

'She did,' Mia said. 'She's told us to get ready for a media invasion.'

'I'd be surprised if they didn't show up.' Tony passed the sparkling water from the barman to Mia. 'I'm sorry for bringing all this down on you. I really wanted this to be a quiet visit, but it's turned out to be anything but.'

'It's not your fault, Mr Ferri,' Shirley said.

'Please, it's Tony,' he said. 'Especially after what we all went through today.'

'I just can't believe it,' Shirley said. 'Here, of all places.'

'I know,' Mia said.

Tony gently touched Mia on the elbow, and she felt a little thrill. 'Can I steal you away from the party for a minute?' he said quietly.

'Sure.'

He led her to the opposite corner of the room from where Adam and Sannie were, but Mia sensed them watching her.

Tony motioned for her to sit in an upholstered leather armchair. She set her drink down on a carved wooden coffee table. Tony sat in a chair next to her, his knee almost close enough to touch hers. He leaned in a little.

'I'm sorry about this afternoon, about taking your rifle and going off like that.'

'I'm sure I don't have to tell a former army officer about firearms safety and protocols.'

'I know.' He set his drink down next to hers. 'It's just that in that moment, with the adrenaline coursing through me and the threat of enemy fire, my instincts took over.'

'Did your instincts tell you to advance across open terrain, in the face of hostile fire?'

He laughed. 'Well said. I think I was a little crazy, Mia, but I felt a duty to put myself out there, to give you time to get away.'

'It was heroic of you.'

He slumped back in his chair. 'No, it was stupid. But war's like that. Sometimes you don't think, you just act.'

'Who wants to hurt you, Tony, or even kill you?'

He shook his head. 'I don't know. Believe me, I've been racking my brain, and so has Lisa. She has all sorts of theories. I think we can discount simple theft, though.'

'You mentioned Adam.'

'I may have been hasty. We shook hands just now at the bar, for the first time since the late eighties, but I can still sense the hostility in him.'

'He has an ironclad alibi for this afternoon. He was with Sannie.'

Ferri raised his eyebrows, but Mia was not drawn to comment on his obvious innuendo. That was not his business, nor hers, except that Mia felt Adam had been undermining Tony in front of Sannie; Mia sensed that was what Sannie wanted to talk to her about.

'Adam's told Sannie that you had more than just a disagreement with my father and with Adam.'

Tony brought his hands together, as if in prayer. 'We were in an engagement, in Angola, and I made a decision – not necessarily the right one – for us to hold our ground. Evan and Luiz stayed with me, and your father and Adam left us, in the face of enemy fire.'

Mia put a hand over her mouth. 'No.'

Tony reached out and put his hand on her knee. 'No, Mia, it's not as bad as it sounds. Frank was most likely right, and I was wrong, but the army did not see it that way. Our sector commander, Colonel de Villiers, forced me to charge Frank and Adam with disobeying a lawful command. They were court-martialled and disciplined.'

'Oh, no.' Mia felt light-headed. She'd only ever thought of her father as a hero – troubled, yes, but not someone guilty of a military crime. 'Disciplined?'

Tony nodded solemnly. 'Your father was sent to a little-known base on the Botswana border. It was a place where soldiers could have certain problems and attitudes . . . corrected. It would have been rough on him. Both he and Adam returned to duty, however, with different units, and I heard that Frank distinguished himself in one of the last combat actions of the war.'

'My goodness.' Mia tried to absorb the new information, aware that Tony still had his hand on her knee. 'So, my father was sent to some kind of punishment unit?'

'You could call it that.' He looked into her eyes. 'I had to tell you, Mia, before you hear it from someone else. I respected Frank as a soldier, but we had a system, and there were protocols and decisions that were out of my power. I tried to reach out to Frank, several times, to offer him an apology. I can't help but think that what happened to him was somehow related to his bad experiences in the army.'

Mia felt tears well in her eyes.

Tony removed his hand, but shifted his armchair closer and put an arm around her. She leaned her head against his shoulder. 'He was a good man, and it was a *kak* time, Mia,' Tony whispered. 'Can you forgive me?'

Mia lifted her head and looked into his eyes again. A tear was rolling down his cheek and he did nothing to hide it. Seeing him cry just made her weep more. She took his hands in hers.

'I am so, so sorry,' he said, carrying on. 'What this war did to us . . .'

Mia sniffed and wiped her eyes, trying to regain control of her emotions. She could tell the others were looking at them. And the lodge chef was hovering, waiting for them to be seated for dinner.

'I want to know more, Tony,' she said. 'All of it, about him and you.'

Tony took a breath. 'It's true Frank and I did not always get on, but it became serious. I was young and I let my ego and my insecurity get in the way of my decision-making. I'd hate to think that our experiences stayed with him, that in some way I was responsible for the state of his mental health. Did your father ever speak about the last mission we went on? We were sent to find the crew of a downed South African aircraft. It was a crazy time.'

'He did mention a big battle a couple of times,' Mia said, 'and a couple of guys who were killed by mortar and artillery fire. But, no, I don't recall him ever talking specifically about an aircraft. Tell me more, please.'

'Have dinner with me, in my suite,' he said, squeezing her hands. 'We can talk properly there.'

Mia hesitated, then looked into his eyes. She was head guide and a stickler for rules and protocol; she prided herself on leading by example. However, she was desperate to know every single thing she could about her father. And Tony was so bloody handsome.

'OK.'

23

The police arrived as the lodge guests and staff were gathering in the main area, prior to dinner.

Sannie and Adam were seated together already, at a private table in the dining area. The detective in charge, who introduced himself to the dining room as Sergeant Thabo Cele, focused on the bar area, where Mia, Evan, Lisa and Tony Ferri were all sitting.

Cele's partner, a woman, started taking statements, beginning with Ferri.

Sannie excused herself from Adam, got up, and went to the detective. His shirt strained over his belly and Sannie smelled beer on his breath when she introduced herself. 'We spoke, on the phone.'

'Ah yes. Are you here on holiday, Captain?' Cele asked.

'I am. I'm friends with Mia Greenaway.' Sannie nodded to Mia.

'Yes, we have spoken.'

'I'm curious. Just explain to me, please, why you didn't think it worth collecting the casing Mia found and seeing if it was a match to the gun used in the suicide?'

The sergeant frowned. 'I don't know what your budget is like in KZN, Captain, but do you have money to make a two-hundred-kilometre round trip to pick up a casing and have it tested, when the coroner has already closed the docket on a suicide?'

Sannie knew she had to play this carefully. She had just insulted him by implying he had not done his job thoroughly. 'I hear you, Thabo, if I may call you that. I'm Sannie – I'm not working and don't want to reopen anyone's case. It's just that some strange stuff has been going on around here.'

He lowered his voice. 'Politicians. I get a call to drop everything to come out here especially because a white man has been shot at.'

Sannie nodded, as if in sympathy.

Cele put his hand to his mouth and belched softly. 'I did tell your young friend, Ms Greenaway, that I would collect the casing when I can. I'm happy to take it now if she still has it.'

'She does.'

'Then good,' he said. 'I must get back to my interviews. Were you at the scene of the shooting?'

Sannie shook her head. 'No. I was in camp.'

'What do you make of it?' he asked. 'Professionally speaking.'

'I spoke to Mia, who was there. Several shots were fired from A rifle. She said the shooter was using a silencer. That speaks to a certain level of expertise, maybe money.'

Cele stroked his chin. 'So it would seem.'

'Yet every shot missed. No one was hit.'

'Someone aiming to miss?' Cele asked.

'Could be,' Sannie said.

'Why? To scare the political candidate? I'm told he was also assaulted in his suite, or tent, or whatever people call the accommodation in this place.'

'Yes,' Sannie said. 'Maybe these incidents were designed to unsettle him, or maybe the opposite – to make him look like a victim, or, rather, a brave hero.'

'Hmmm.' The sergeant looked around the room. 'I think this case is political, whichever way you look at it. I don't like it.'

The female detective beckoned to Cele.

'Excuse me, Captain. It was good talking to you, but I am needed.'

'Of course,' Sannie said.

Adam was looking to her, but she remembered something she had wanted to do, before she fell into bed with her handsome stranger. She held up a finger, and mouthed: 'One minute'.

Sannie left the dining area and walked out into the chill of the desert night. The sky was awash with stars. It was beautiful. She took her phone out of her bra, where she sometimes kept it, and dialled a number.

'Sannie, howzit? Long time.' Captain Henk de Beer addressed her in Afrikaans, their common language. 'Are you enjoying life on the beach?'

Sannie realised her number would have come up on Henk's screen. He was a detective with the Hawks in Nelspruit. 'Hi, Henk. I'm actually visiting Mia Greenaway in the desert, near the Kgalagadi. Long story.'

'Ah, it's lekker there. I want to take my off-road caravan there in July. Say hi to Mia from me.' Sannie had hoped Henk would remember Mia from the last case they had worked together in the Sabi Sand Game Reserve. 'Are you well?'

'I am. Henk, you worked at Hazyview for a while, didn't you?'

'Ja, I was there for five years; I finished ten years ago now.'

'I don't suppose you remember when Frank Greenaway, Mia's father, suicided? He was a former ranger in Kruger, out of work when he died. He lived alone with Mia.'

'Actually, ja, I do,' he answered straight away. 'I'd met Mia's dad a couple of times through a ranger friend I played golf with at Skukuza. Nice guy, but liked the bottle a bit too much, if you know what I mean. Not that that was uncommon among guys like him.'

'Guys like him?'

'My boet told me Frank had lots of bad memories from the army and the war days. It happens, you know. Shame.'

'Yes. Henk, I know this is a long shot, but can I ask you, do you remember anything strange about that case, anything that might have made you doubt it was a suicide?'

Henk paused now. 'Sannie, I'm not sure. Now that you ask . . .

Well, I don't know. I've still got all my notebooks; can I check for you? Do you have the date?'

'I can get it. I'll SMS you. Baie dankie, Henk.'

Sannie rang off, and in the quiet, heard footsteps behind her.

She turned to see Mia.

'Oh, hi. How's it going? Have you spoken to the police?'

'I'm next. I understand Afrikaans – I just heard you asking about my father, and his death. What's going on, Sannie?'

Sannie frowned. She hadn't realised Mia was listening in on her conversation. 'I spoke to Sergeant Cele again about the extra shell casing you found, near where Luiz was. I think that's strange and warrants some forensic investigation. I just checked with Captain Henk de Beer, from Nelspruit –'

'I remember Henk.'

'Yes, well, he remembers your father's case. I've asked him to go over his notes, to see if there was anything odd, anything that maybe didn't fit.'

'Do you think someone murdered my father and made it look like suicide?'

'It's far too early to even suggest something like that, but there might be a pattern here. You really should talk to Adam, Mia. I can see that Tony Ferri is getting closer to you. You should hear Adam's side of their story, from Angola.'

Mia jutted her chin out. 'Your Adam could be the cause of all the trouble here. If he didn't shoot at us, maybe he paid someone to do it.'

Sannie was taken aback. 'He's not my Adam. I'm just telling you, as a friend, not to believe everything you hear, especially from a politician.'

The female detective emerged from the dining area. 'Miss Greenaway? I am ready for you now.'

Mia flashed Sannie an annoyed look, then went inside.

Adam walked past Mia as he came out. 'She doesn't look happy.'

'You need to talk to her, Adam. Tony Ferri keeps feeding her more of his version of events from Angola. I think she's falling for him.'

'Mia won't like my version.'

Sannie nodded. 'I know, but she needs to hear the truth about what happened to her father, and to you.'

'Come back to my suite?' Adam said.

She gave a little laugh. 'What are you, Superman?'

He smiled. 'I meant to sleep. I just want to hold you.'

Sannie reached out a hand and touched him on the arm. 'I think I need to make amends with Mia, and tell her I'm just looking out for her, as a friend. She must have been shaken up by what happened this afternoon. I might see you later, OK?'

'Sure,' he said. 'I understand.' He smiled, turned and headed towards his room.

Sannie went back into the lodge. Mia was seated in the corner, where she had earlier been with Tony Ferri, though now she was being interviewed by the female detective. Sergeant Cele was talking to Lisa Ingram, and Ferri himself, ever the politician, had moved off and was chatting to three of the kitchen staff, who were laughing at something he had just said. Evan Litis was sitting alone at the bar. Sannie went to him.

'Hi.'

'Hello again,' he said. 'Sannie, right?'

'Yes. Mind if I take a seat?'

Evan gestured to the stool next to him. The barman asked Sannie if she wanted a drink and she ordered a glass of sauvignon blanc.

'Pretty crazy afternoon,' Evan said as he sipped his wine.

'So I hear,' Sannie said. The barman poured her wine for her. 'Thank you.'

'Do you think it might have been a poacher shooting at us?' he asked.

'I don't know,' she said. 'I worked in the Kruger Park for many years and while the rangers there had plenty of armed contacts with poachers, we never once had an incident of poachers shooting at tourists. It was the opposite – they usually went out of their way to avoid being seen by civilian visitors to the park. Also, Mia says that poaching with firearms is rare here.'

Evan looked into his beer. 'I see.'

'Was it you who recorded the video of Tony, Evan?'

He shook his head. 'It was Lisa, his campaign manager. I didn't realise how quickly it would go viral, and how far it would spread.'

Sannie wondered what planet Evan was from, but said nothing about that. 'It's certainly very strange.'

'Are you and Adam good friends?' he asked, looking at her.

'We only met recently. We live near each other, in KZN, on the coast. I heard about what was happening with Luiz – it was a coincidence that I was coming here for a holiday, so I offered Adam a lift.'

'I see.'

'You and Tony are close?'

Evan nodded. 'Although he was an officer and I was a *troep*, a lowly rifleman, we went through a lot together in the war, and we reconnected after the army. We've been friends a long time now. It's amazing how time flies.'

'Sure is,' she said. 'Adam told me some things about your time together in Angola, one patrol you were on. I think you received a medal for it.'

He looked into her eyes now. 'What did he say to you?'

Sannie thought his tone was defensive rather than aggressive, but the conversation had clearly ratcheted up a notch from small talk. 'That Tony Ferri wrongly charged him and Frank Greenaway with cowardice. I don't think Ferri's told Mia about her father being court-martialled.'

'I don't know what Tony's told her.' He sipped his beer and glanced away.

'You're protective of Tony.'

He turned to look back at her. 'Like I said, we're friends. He's come a long way in life, and he's so close to greatness.'

An interesting way to describe the trajectory of a political career, Sannie thought. Evan's eyes had lit up for an instant. Now he was back to brooding into his beer. 'Are you OK, Evan?'

He kept staring at the amber fluid. 'Tony got off on this afternoon; the sound of gunfire, the bullets hitting the truck – it excited him. I had a different reaction.'

She said nothing, waiting for him to continue.

'Mia told me to help the other two, Shirley and Lisa, into the truck. It was all I could do not to rush in first and hide on the floor of the vehicle, crying. It was terrifying.'

Sannie nodded. 'The gunfire brought things back to you?'

'Yes. In Angola, Tony and I nearly died – probably should have. If you've been talking to Adam then I guess you know some of it. Tony ordered us to hold a position; there were Angolans and Cubans everywhere, and then the mortars and artillery started. Tony called our own guns in on us. It was a gutsy move – we were virtually surrounded and about to be overrun, but as Parabats surrendering was not in our nature. We found cover where we could and, miraculously, he, Luiz and I survived and the enemy retreated. It sounds brave, or crazy now, but at the time it was like hell. I remember crying and praying.'

'As you continued firing your weapon,' Sannie said.

He stared at her. 'I was half out of my mind with the noise, the concussion, the ground shaking around me. I didn't know what I was doing, or what was going on. I remember very little of that day.'

As he picked up his dewy glass again, it slipped in his fingers and he nearly dropped it. Sannie could see that his hand was shaking.

'It must have been awful.'

'It was, and confusing. I just did what I was told to do, which was to stay put. I had no idea who to listen to, but Tony was the officer.'

'Frank and Adam came back for you two.'

'Yes.' He slumped on his bar stool. 'The army didn't want to know – or didn't want the public to know – about soldiers arguing with officers, or lieutenants making bad decisions. It was easier to break us up, to divide us, by court-martialling Adam and Frank and sending them to different units when Frank did his time. The whole thing was swept under the carpet, but we've all had to live with it every day since, in our different ways. For Frank and Luiz, it was obviously just too much.'

'Tell me about Luiz,' Sannie said. 'I'm curious. Where was he after

Frank and Tony had their argument, and when the stick got separated?'

'To tell you the truth, I don't know. Luiz was like a ghost. He moved so silently through the bush; he and his brother Roberto used to sneak up and surprise each other – not a good thing to do when people are carrying loaded rifles. I went to look for them, when the shelling stopped, and . . .'

Sannie stayed silent. She could only imagine what it would be like to see someone killed by a direct hit from an artillery shell.

'I think I thought that it was Luiz who had been killed in the barrage, but when my ears stopped ringing and I was wiping away the blood from a nosebleed, he appeared beside me. Who knows, maybe he was just taking cover a few metres away from Tony and me?'

'And the airman you set out to rescue . . . ?'

'Duarte. He died of his wounds and then his body took most of the blow from a mortar bomb. We were, that is, I was . . .' Evan gave her a pleading look, almost as if he was asking if he had to continue. Sannie held her nerve and stayed silent again. 'I was,' Evan gulped, 'using his body for cover.'

Sannie closed her eyes for a moment, trying to shut out the horror. She opened them again and looked at Evan. 'Was Duarte carrying something, Evan?'

He looked away again, signalling to the barman for another. 'If he was, it was probably blown to smithereens by the bomb that landed next to him. I can't remember. I know that when we all carried the bodies out – that is, Duarte and Rossouw, our radioman – there was no extra gear or bags.'

'Could Duarte have been a courier, maybe transporting something valuable?' she said. 'Adam said that none of you were ever told specifically what or who it was that you were looking for, just that they were "crew" of a downed aircraft.'

Evan shrugged. 'Who knows. In the army they only told us what they thought we needed to know, and for *troepies* like Adam and me, that was fokol. Excuse my language.'

'No problem. Did you ever get to discuss this stuff with Frank Greenaway?'

'I tracked Frank down, to the Lowveld, and spoke to him once. He had some crazy theory that Duarte was carrying diamonds, from Jonas Savimbi, and that someone had stolen them. It was ludicrous.'

Was it? Sannie wondered.

'Like, how would we smuggle diamonds out of Angola?' Evan continued. 'I do remember that after we got back to base, we were all searched, but no one was told what the people were looking for. I asked Tony later, specifically, if he knew anything about diamonds, or whatever, and he told me that he had just been told to retrieve a brief-case that one of the air crew was carrying.'

'And did he?'

Evan closed his eyes and seemed to think for a few moments. 'No. He said he didn't, that it was lost during the mortar and artillery bombardment. Tony and Erasmus, the medic, gave Duarte first aid, but we couldn't save him. Then his body was hit by mortar fire – it tore off his lower left arm and part of his body. Then Rossouw was killed – he was shot – and Roberto . . .'

'I'm sorry,' Sannie said.

Evan opened his eyes and looked into hers. 'Can you imagine what it's like to see someone vanish before your very eyes?'

Sannie shuddered. 'Again, my apologies.'

'That's what happened to Roberto. There was nothing of him to take home . . . to his family. As for Rossouw, I was covered in . . . his blood.' Evan took a long sip of beer and swallowed it down. 'Adam and I carried his body.'

Sannie felt bad, but she had to ask. There was still something about all of this that did not add up and could not be ascribed to the horrors of war or PTSD. Evan looked away from her again.

'What about Adam?' she asked.

'What about him? He was charged with disobeying an order, and with cowardice. Adam said that Frank ordered him, and me, to with-draw, even though Tony said we should stay and defend ourselves against the enemy. I never heard that – I was too busy shooting. Frank and Adam bugged out and when I realised it was just me and Tony left, in the bush, I couldn't very well leave him. I think Tony was a little bossies himself, high on the action. He was firing like crazy and then he called in the artillery fire on our position. It was the scariest moment of my life.'

Sannie nodded. The 'fog of battle' clearly was a thing, but she could not shake the feeling that there was more to the story.

'And Luiz?' she asked. 'Did he reappear when the others returned?'

Evan looked up at the canvas roof over the bar. 'Maybe just before. I can't really remember. It was like he might have been somewhere else nearby. I do remember thinking that I was glad he was there. My ears were ringing and I was thoroughly disorientated after the South African artillery shells started landing – you can't imagine the noise. The landscape was pure devastation – trees shattered and uprooted. I couldn't have found my way back to the rest of the stick, so I was pleased Luiz was there; I knew he could guide us.'

'I see,' Sannie said. 'Did you and Adam talk, after the battle?'

'No. They kept us apart – Adam, Frank and me. I guess it was deliberate, since Colonel de Villiers had decided to charge Frank and Adam with desertion, or whatever. Tony has told me since that he didn't want any charges laid.'

'Yes, he told Mia that, as well.'

'He's a good man, Sannie.'

He was a politician. That did not mean he was, by definition, a bad person, but it meant that he would be acutely aware of his image, and his past. Everyone had a past – Sannie herself had once disobeyed her superiors, crossing the border into Mozambique on an unauthorised investigation. It was how she'd met her second husband, and she had nearly lost her job over that rash decision. 'He seems like it.'

'This country needs him.'

Sannie sipped her wine. South Africa needed many things, but most of all it needed a leader who was honest. Was that Tony Ferri? She was not sure.

'Adam's hurt, and I don't blame him,' Evan said. 'It's hard for me to let the past go, and to live in the moment – we all have to try to do that, and it's not always easy. It's no secret that I'm heavily involved in Tony's campaign, and the party, and I think it would be a bad thing for the country if Adam was to . . . say stuff. Or try anything.'

'What are you suggesting?' Sannie asked.

Evan shrugged. 'Nothing. It's just that, I know he has an axe to grind with Tony, and I worry that Adam might be a little unstable. I'd understand if he was, but I wouldn't want to see him do anything rash.'

'Of course not, but that's a matter for him.'

Evan leaned back on his bar stool, as if appraising her. 'You two seem to be good friends.'

'We haven't known each other long.' Her guard was up.

'Can you help me, to heal some old wounds? It might be good for everyone, and we have a funeral to attend tomorrow.'

'I don't know. What are you suggesting?'

'Adam was barely able to acknowledge Tony just now, when they both met at the bar. If I can get Tony to agree to formally apologise to Adam, for what happened in Angola, do you think you could ask Adam to at least give him the time and place to do so? I'm sure Tony will. He wants to bury the past.'

I bet he does. Exactly how keen was he, though? If a formal apology did not work, was he ruthlessly ambitious enough to have a person killed? Had Tony Ferri been behind the deaths of Frank and Luiz, and, if so, what had they had on him?

Sannie now looked at Evan. He could make eye contact and appear earnest and honest sometimes, but at other times his eyes wandered, or he tugged an earlobe; she had seen these signs in lying criminals in the past. Was Evan so enmeshed in Ferri's campaign, so tied to his political coat-tails, that he would kill to protect his candidate's reputation?

Sannie looked around the room, where others were either talking to one of the police detectives or waiting their turn.

Lisa Ingram saw Sannie looking at her and locked eyes with her.

She stared over the rim of her wineglass, and Sannie looked away. What about her? She was the pretty campaign manager, and Sannie wondered if Ferri had slept with her. From what Mia had said, and what Sannie had observed, Ferri had a roving eye and, allegedly, permission to flirt, or more. Lisa would want to protect Ferri's reputation at least as much as Evan did, if not more. Sannie had known, and arrested, women who had killed. Anything was possible in South Africa, and hit men were cheap.

'This Colonel de Villiers . . .' Sannie said.

'Yes?' Evan set down his beer.

'Do you still have contact with him?'

'He passed away. I did talk to him about ten or eleven years ago. Jaco – Colonel de Villiers – had moved to Australia.'

'Why did you contact him?'

'You're very direct, Captain.'

'Comes with my job.'

Evan frowned. 'When Tony was getting ready to make his first serious run at the leadership, we – his closest supporters and advisers – wanted to clear the decks, to make sure there would be no nasty surprises waiting for us. I tracked down de Villiers through Facebook.'

'I see. What did he have to say about Tony?'

'He was glowing.' Evan finished his beer and nodded to the barman that he wanted another. He waited for his beer to come, and for the barman to move out of earshot again. 'He said Tony was a fine young officer. We talked about the business of Frank and Adam being court-martialled. De Villiers was unapologetic. He saw Frank as a troublemaker and thought of Adam as nothing more than collateral damage.'

Sannie controlled her anger and waited for Evan to finish, after he drank some more of his beer.

'De Villiers said he wished Tony well for his campaign. He more or less confirmed that it was all his idea to charge Adam and Frank. He'd basically wanted rid of Frank. I later tried telling Frank that, but he didn't want to listen. He took his grudge against Tony to his grave.'

Sannie digested what Evan had just said, again wondering if someone had hastened Frank Greenaway to an early death.

'Was your visit to Frank part of this "clearing the decks" exercise?'

Evan seemed to bristle at that, but he had more or less implicated himself already. 'Frank was a comrade, a fellow veteran who was doing it tough. I reached out to him because I heard he was having troubles.'

'And you wanted to know if he would upset Ferri's eventual run at the leadership.'

Evan said nothing for a moment, then sighed. 'I'd be lying if I said otherwise. I spoke to Frank. That was when he told me his theory about Tony smuggling diamonds out of Angola. Frank had been talking to some of Duarte's fellow airmen and they told him that was what he sometimes carried out of Angola. Frank had no proof, though, that Tony was actually involved. I was with Tony. He was too busy calling in the artillery strike and saving our arses to steal any diamonds.'

Sannie said nothing; it was the same thing that Adam had found out from Frank, about Duarte being a possible diamond courier. She wanted Evan to keep talking.

'So,' said Evan, 'I told Frank that was the first I'd heard of that and that neither Tony nor I had made a fortune from stolen diamonds. To be brutally honest, Captain, my family was wealthy and I had no need to get involved in a diamond heist. Tony had his sights set on becoming a lawyer after his military service; a criminal record would have sunk that. He sat the bar exam after the army, did well, and set up a successful practice. He made a good living before getting into politics.'

'But you said Frank didn't believe you?'

Evan spread his hands wide. 'I don't know. I think he didn't want to forgive Ferri, and that his conspiracy theory was more attractive to him. I told him that if he ever went to the press with it, no one would believe him, and that he had no proof to link either me or Tony to any missing diamonds.'

Sannie knew there were ways to check the truth of what Evan had just told her – financial records, a little digging into both his and Ferri's backgrounds – but this was not an investigation and no one had alleged a crime had been committed – yet.

'I'll tell you who worries me, Captain, though I bear him no ill will.'

'Who?' she asked.'Your friend, Adam Kruger. I think he wants Tony dead.'

Sannie said nothing. But she couldn't ignore the fact that Adam had left her alone in the afternoon for a couple of hours and returned with sand and dust on his shoes and legs, as if he had been out in the desert.

24

'Lisa, can I have a moment of your time?' Sannie set her glass of wine down on the side table next to where Lisa was sitting.

'I was hoping to get another drink, after my grilling,' Lisa said, her eyes cast towards the bar.

The female police detective had just finished interviewing Mia and had moved on to speak to Evan.

'I saw your video online.'

'I think we're up to nearly a million likes,' Lisa said.

Sannie tried to read her. Was she surprised? Proud? Perhaps both.

'It must have been quite scary, having someone shoot at you,' Sannie said.

Lisa took a sip of wine and nodded. 'Yes. Terrifying, actually.'

'Yet . . .' Sannie let the word hang there a second, 'from the angle it looks like you're standing up in the back of the game viewer, to get a better view. Mia has to tell you to get down.'

Lisa looked away, as if trying to remember something. 'It was a crazy moment. I'm not sure I knew, or remember, what I was doing at the time.'

Sannie smiled. 'I'm sure it was crazy. But most people's inclination when they hear gunfire is to take cover. You were remarkably calm.'

Lisa now looked into Sannie's eyes. 'I know you're a detective, Sannie, but are you interviewing me – questioning me – as part of some sort of investigation?'

Sannie held up her hands. 'Not at all. I'm more curious, that's all.'

Lisa narrowed her eyes. 'Are you saying I did something wrong, or that Tony did something wrong?'

Sannie shrugged. 'All I know, like a million or so other people, is what I saw on the video. I think Tony taking Mia's rifle and charging up a sand dune at whomever was shooting at you all put Mia in a difficult situation. It's not appropriate to take someone else's firearm, and Mia was responsible for protecting you all. Tony forced her to split up the group.'

'Well, as you no doubt heard, he's a crazy, brave bastard.'

He was at least one of those things, Sannie thought. 'Does he have many enemies, Lisa?'

Lisa laughed out loud. 'He's a politician running for leadership. I'd say a sizeable proportion of South Africa wouldn't have shed a single tear if he'd been shot and killed.'

'And now?' Sannie said.

'What do you mean, Detective? Are you suggesting that me taking a video of Tony charging after some poacher might improve Tony's popularity?'

'From what I've learned, it seems unlikely there would have been an armed poacher in that part of the reserve.'

Lisa looked away again. 'All I know is that someone shot at us and Tony tried to save us.'

'What about the assault on Tony in his tent? Any ideas?' Sannie asked.

Lisa returned her gaze to Sannie. 'I think this place, for all its luxury, needs to take a long, hard look at its security.'

'I'm sure Julianne Clyde-Smith will be doing that. I know that she takes security at her lodges very seriously,' Sannie said.

Lisa picked up her wineglass and stood. 'If you'll excuse me, I think it's going to be time for dinner soon.'

'Of course,' Sannie said.

Sannie sat for a moment after Lisa had gone, thinking about what the other woman had said and how she had said it. Political candidates often tried to talk up threats to their personal safety during elections; everybody wanted to look like the underdog these days, to encourage more people to vote for them. Tony Ferri was campaigning on law and order and the environment, so to have him taking on an armed assailant – the campaign team could brand the criminal as a poacher or whatever they wanted – would emphasise his tough stance with graphic video imagery.

It was one thing for a candidate to throw a brick through their own campaign office window and claim they were the victim of a hate campaign, but another thing altogether to have someone fire several rounds from a rifle into a game-viewing vehicle. If the attack on Mia's game drive was a stunt, then it had been an incredibly foolhardy and risky one.

Sannie took out her phone and went to Instagram. There was a message from Ilana asking if she was safe. *I just saw the video of Tony Ferri at Dune Lodge. Isn't that where you are?* Ilana had written.

I'm fine, Sannie typed in reply. *Nowhere near me.*

Ferri is amazing, Ilana typed back as Sannie watched. *And hot. Shame he's married, or else you should let him buy you a drink!* Ilana followed up with emojis of love hearts, kisses and a winking smiley face. Sannie shook her head.

'What are you smiling at?'

Sannie looked up from her phone to see Mia standing in front of her. Mia was smiling too, though it looked forced. Their last exchange had been tense.

'My daughter. She just made a joke,' Sannie said. 'Can I ask you a question about Dune Lodge?'

'Sure,' Mia said. She appeared to relax.

'Who is Shirley's superior here at the lodge? Who does she report to?'

'No one. She's the big boss – she runs the place. Just because she's under forty and a woman of colour doesn't mean she can't run a lodge.'

Sannie tried to ignore the barb in Mia's response, though clearly they had some bridge-building to do. 'Of course not; it's just that in my experience the general manager is not usually the front-of-house person.'

'Sorry, I didn't mean to insinuate you were a racist or anything like that, Sannie.'

'It's fine. But Julianne Clyde-Smith doesn't greet all her guests in person.'

'No. Shirley is very hands-on. She's actually a shareholder in the lodge as well as the GM. She's a real success story in the industry and Dune has a fantastic reputation for luxury and service. Her father bought the land here back in the early nineties and after he passed away Shirley expanded and improved the lodge her father had built, pretty much from the time she graduated with a business degree from UCT.'

'I see. When did Julianne buy the lodge?'

'She hasn't – well, not yet. Julianne's company has a commercial contract to market Dune Lodge and handle reservations as part of her group of lodges, but she also wants to buy it outright. It's a bit hush-hush, but I believe her offer has been accepted and just needs to be signed. I'd wanted to work with some San trackers and learn from them for a long time, and Julianne wanted me to come here and assess the quality of guiding and the guest experience, in case any changes were needed when the sale goes through. The deal is that Shirley will stay on as GM for at least a year, to oversee any changes.'

'And what was your opinion of the lodge and its staff?' Sannie asked.

'Hundred per cent,' Mia said without hesitation. 'There's nothing I could do to improve the standards of guiding and tracking, and guests are treated like royalty here. Like you say, it's probably unusual for a GM or owner to be handing out cold towels and welcome drinks to guests, but it's part of what makes this place so good – and expensive. Shirley's attention to detail is faultless.'

'And security?'

Mia cast her eyes around the dining area, where the two local detectives were wrapping up their interviews, and outside to where two of Meshach's men stood guard, armed with rifles. 'This is crazy, Sannie. Nothing like this has ever happened here before, according to Shirley. To have a guest assaulted in a suite and then a game drive shot up by a sniper is, well . . . It's just nuts.'

'Tell me,' Sannie said, 'did Meshach and his men or any of your trackers look for spoor around Ferri's tent after the assault? Surely they'd have the skills to at least get an idea of where the intruder went.'

Mia rubbed her chin. 'Good point. I need to follow up on that with Shirley.'

Meshach walked along the pathway, stopped to chat briefly with one of his men and then headed towards the next.

'Look at them; they're all armed to the teeth, even Meshach,' Mia said.

The head of security had a rifle slung over his shoulder, Sannie noticed, and his men carried LM5s, the semi-automatic version of the South African army's R5 assault rifle.

'So, you wouldn't say Shirley has skimped on security?'

Mia shook her head. 'Absolutely not. To tell you the truth, when Julianne was asking me about the staffing structure here a few weeks ago, I told her that if anything, I thought the security here was overkill. We've never lost a rhino here to poachers, so there's no serious armed poaching, and we're to hell and gone from Askham so it's not even like we get any burglaries, yet Shirley is very proud of Meshach and his team. The security guys themselves have ATVs, four-by-fours, night vision, a dog team – you name it.'

'Like you said, overkill?'

Mia shrugged. 'Better to be safe than sorry. It just makes it even more ridiculous that these two incidents happened.'

Sannie nodded. 'Would you like to have dinner, just the two of us,

Mia? I feel like we've hardly seen each other, and today must have been very difficult for you. Also, we're friends. I don't want us to argue.'

Mia's shoulders sagged. 'I know, and I hear you, Sannie, but –'

'Well, hello there, ladies.' Tony Ferri moved through the dining area and came to Mia's side. 'I'm sorry to steal Mia away from you . . .'

'Sannie,' she said.

'Yes, sorry, Sannie. Captain van Rensburg, right?'

'Yes, correct,' Sannie said.

'I'm sorry, Sannie, but I need to steal my ranger away from you. Duty calls. I need her to escort me through the dark to my suite.'

'I thought that was the job of lodge security?' Sannie said. She glanced at Mia and saw her friend's cheeks colour.

'Well, it's also a custom here for rangers to have dinner with their guests and Mia has agreed to have dinner with me in my suite this evening, haven't you, Mia?'

Mia looked from Tony to Sannie. 'Um, well, Shirley says it's OK given the trying time we've all had today.'

Ferri was smiling, his campaign-poster teeth as white as a shark's.

'Enjoy your meal,' Sannie mumbled. Her reservations about Ferri aside, Sannie had travelled across South Africa to see her friend and now she was being fobbed off in favour of a politician. She felt a fool, now, for suggesting that she and Mia have dinner together.

'I'm sure we will.' Ferri placed his hand in the small of Mia's back. 'I've just told Shirley that we're ready for dinner, Mia.'

Mia looked to Sannie and gave a little frown. Sannie gritted her teeth.

Wait staff were hovering at the edge of the dining area and a chef in white uniform and hat was looking on anxiously from the display kitchen. Shirley started moving from person to person and stopped to talk with the two police detectives, who were putting away their notebooks. Next, Shirley came to Sannie. 'Are you ready for dinner, Sannie?'

'Sure,' she said, trying to contain her annoyance. 'Can I maybe have a talk to you, after dinner?'

Shirley looked at her watch. 'Um . . . We're terribly behind schedule for this evening and I have a mass of paperwork to catch up on. Is it urgent?'

'Tomorrow would be fine,' Sannie said.

'There's also the funeral tomorrow morning.'

'Of course,' Sannie said.

'Will you be attending?'

'I hadn't thought about it.'

'Mia will be at the service, but you're welcome to go on a game drive with Isaac, one of our other rangers.'

'No, I think I'll go to the funeral. My friend, Adam Kruger, will need a lift in any case.'

'Very well,' Shirley said. 'Perhaps we can have a word after the service, but I've already spoken to the local detectives.'

'I didn't say that I wanted to talk to you about what happened here; that's an ongoing investigation.'

'Oh, yes, right. Is it something to do with the lodge? Is everything fine with your room, Sannie?'

'My room is fine.' Sannie could see how flustered Shirley had become. Her eyes darted around the room, to the police and the guests, anywhere but Sannie herself. She was nervous, maybe worried or hiding something.

'Let's talk tomorrow,' Sannie said.

'Fine.' Shirley moved off and called everyone to dinner at a long, communal table. Sannie went to Adam, who had chosen a chair at the far end of the table, away from Evan and Lisa, who sat next to each other and had their heads together, talking.

Sannie sat next to Adam. 'How did it go with the detectives?'

'Fine,' Adam said. 'I told them I was in camp all afternoon, while Ferri was busy shooting at alleged poachers or assassins. I said you were my alibi.'

'Oh.'

He grinned. 'Don't worry; I said we were both reading by the swimming pool. I hope it's OK to lie in that context.'

'But that's not true, Adam, and no, it's not OK.'

He recoiled a little from her and Sannie could tell she was not controlling her emotions well. There was no escaping what she had to say next. 'You went out for a run, and you were out of my sight for maybe two hours while I was sleeping.'

His eyes widened. He lowered his voice. 'What? You think I slipped out to try and kill Tony Ferri?'

'You told me yourself you wanted him dead.'

'That was in the past.' He spread his hands wide. 'Please. I told you, I ran on a track around the camp. I can find the oke who showed me where to run, and he saw me pass him from where he was working, every time I did a lap.'

Sannie exhaled. 'I'm sorry, Adam. But please don't lie to the police. You need to tell Cele you went for a run.'

'OK. I will. What do you make of it all – the gunfight on the game drive, and Ferri being attacked in his tent?'

'He wouldn't be the first political candidate to stage a publicity stunt to make him look like a victim – and a hero – but having someone shoot up a game-viewing vehicle full of civilians is a high-risk piece of theatre.' Sannie was glad Adam had changed the subject; for Adam to have been involved in the attack on Ferri he would have needed to source a rifle from somewhere and, apparently, a quad bike. That would have taken a good deal of pre-planning and required one or more accomplices. He had seemed genuinely shocked, and he did not come across like a liar, but he had not told the truth to the investigating officer and this was a loose thread that needed to be tied.

'Yes,' Adam said, 'but the stakes are very high.'

Sannie thought about the video. She lowered her voice. 'And Lisa was very cool under fire, filming the whole thing. Also, I can't help but think that if there was someone armed with a silenced high-powered rifle and they wanted to kill Tony Ferri that they were either a very bad shot, or they were aiming to miss.'

'We'll wait and see what tomorrow's newspapers report,'

Adam said. 'While you were talking to Lisa and Mia, Ferri was on the phone to News24.'

'I wouldn't be surprised if the TV crews show up here tomorrow.'

'Will you come to the funeral with me?'

'Shirley just asked me the same thing. I came here to visit Mia and now, well . . . I . . .'

He reached out and put his hand on hers, on the table. Sannie looked to the others, who didn't seem to notice, and she found that she didn't care.

'I'll be there if you'd like me to be there,' she continued.

'I would. I want to kiss you now, but I won't.'

Sannie gently removed her hand from the table. 'Thank you. I feel the same way.'

Waiters brought out an entree of prawn cocktail and Shirley came to them and put a hand on the back of the chair next to Sannie. 'Do you mind?' Shirley asked.

'Not at all,' Sannie said.

'Phew.' Shirley sat down. 'At least dinner's now under way. I've set a table for the two police officers in the library. I think the guests have been questioned enough tonight.'

Sannie took a bite of her starter. It was delicious. 'I'm sure they'll appreciate a meal like this.'

'I didn't mean to seem rude, before, Sannie,' Shirley said. 'Perhaps we can talk now, over dinner.'

'OK, fine with me,' Sannie said. A waiter asked if she wanted still or sparkling water. Sannie chose still and took a sip. She would lay off the wine until after dinner, and after she had spoken to Shirley.

'What can I help you with?'

'I was interested in you.'

Shirley raised her eyebrows as she paused, a prawn on her fork. 'Me? Whatever for?'

'Mia told me you're a part owner of the lodge.'

'That's right. I often get mistaken for an employee, but I'm fine with that. I want guests to be able to tell me anything, and I like to surprise them by having any problems fixed immediately. I've been very fortunate in life, thanks to my parents.'

'So, Luiz was your uncle, is that right?'

'Yes, my mother, Maria, was Luiz's sister, or, rather, half-sister. They had different fathers – my mother was half Portuguese.'

'And they had another brother, Roberto?'

Shirley set down her knife and fork. 'You're very well informed.'

Adam, who had been listening in, leaned forward so he could make eye contact with Shirley. 'Sorry, that's my doing,' he said. 'I told Sannie that we had served with both Luiz and Roberto during the war.'

'Yes, poor Roberto,' Shirley said, 'though I wasn't born when he died.'

Sannie noticed that Adam sat back in his chair, probably lost in thoughts of the war again.

'And your mother? Did she stay in Angola?'

'No,' Shirley said. 'She moved to South West – Namibia – with Luiz and Roberto when they joined the South African army. A Catholic priest left Angola around the same time, an Irishman named Father Hennessy. He – this is a bit embarrassing – he fell in love with my mother and left the priesthood. They married and he, my father, Christopher, took Maria to South Africa when the Bush War ended. Christopher's family had money and he was able to buy a farm – this place. Early on he could see that the desert was a better environment for wildlife than it was for cattle. Being married to my mother, he was also close to the San people and did a lot for the former soldiers who were settled at Platfontein. Even though he failed as a priest he had a kind heart.'

'It sounds like it,' Sannie said.

'The San people who live in this part of South Africa are the Khomani. We're different people from them linguistically, but they accepted us and I've done as much as I can to offer jobs on the reserve to local San people, as well as those from my family's clan.'

'And what will you do, once you've sold the lodge to Julianne Clyde-Smith?'

'My, you're very well informed. I think I'll have a holiday. My mom died young, in childbirth, with her second child, and the baby, a little boy, also didn't survive. My father ran this place, first as a hunting farm to earn some money and, later, for purely photographic safaris like it is today. When I went to varsity to study ecology and business it was always my plan to run Dune Lodge. My father passed away five years ago and ever since then I've been running this place on my own.'

'Sounds like you deserve a break,' Sannie said. 'And the other owners of the lodge?'

'We did a major refurbishment of the lodge about ten years ago – partly my idea, fresh out of varsity, as I wanted to lift us into the same league as the top-end luxury safari lodges, like the ones Julianne runs. We needed a major capital investment so my father and I decided to sell a share to a company involved in the food import-export business. They're very much a silent partner.'

'Well, the lodge looks lovely,' Sannie said, 'and the service is impeccable.'

'Thank you. We try to please.'

Adam leaned forward again. 'Do you have much of a problem with poaching here, Shirley?'

'I think every reserve or national park has a poaching problem on some scale. Meshach and his guys patrol the reserve and the fence line continuously. On a few occasions they've come across people catching pangolin – they tend to get stuck or electrocuted burrowing under our fence – but that's about it.'

'You're lucky,' Adam said.

'I prefer the word "vigilant",' Shirley replied.

'Point taken,' Adam said.

'Is the pangolin business big here?' Sannie asked.

'We don't lose many here, and WESSA, the Wildlife and Environment Society of South Africa, sponsors a couple of pangolin experts in Askham to rescue and rehabilitate any trafficked animals that get seized. The local police are pretty attuned to the trade, but the Kalahari region has plenty of pangolins, so it's rich pickings for poachers. The pangolins that do go missing are quickly moved out of this part of the country.'

'Is it worth the effort?' Adam asked.

Shirley nodded. 'If a pangolin can be shipped out of South Africa and makes it to a market such as Vietnam still alive, it can be worth hundreds of thousands of rand.'

'Sheesh,' Adam said.

'Shirley . . .' Sannie paused. 'Did Luiz ever talk to you about the action that he, Evan Litis, Tony Ferri and Adam were involved in during the war? It was the one in which your other uncle, Roberto, was killed.'

Shirley was silent a moment. 'No. Luiz was a man of few words. He was a very private person.'

'Has Evan been here before?' Adam asked.

'Yes.' Shirley thanked a waiter who cleared away their starters. 'Wine?'

'Sparkling water for me, please,' Sannie said.

'Same, thank you,' Adam said. When Shirley didn't continue, he prompted her again. 'Evan?'

Sannie looked down the other end of the table. She thought she saw Evan cock his head slightly, as if he might have heard his name spoken.

'Mr Litis has visited Dune Lodge a couple of times, yes. He's a supporter of the Platfontein San and has travelled to Kimberley on many occasions. He's organised fundraising among veterans' organisations to improve facilities in the San communities, and I believe he's contributed a good deal of his own money. They built a school and a community centre, funded teaching positions and started a program to bring young San people to lodges such as ours to learn tracking and, hopefully, find work. We've employed two more trackers from Platfontein, and Luiz acted as their mentor as part of the program.'

'Very commendable,' Sannie said.

'The San saved many South African soldiers' lives during the war, so it's good to see the veterans acknowledging that,' Shirley said. 'My people had a hard time after the ANC came to power, and even though Mandela granted us the land near Platfontein, it's really only in the bush, or here in the desert, where San can truly live their traditional life.'

'And do they?' Adam asked.

'Whenever they can, yes,' Shirley said. 'The San trackers and other staff are allowed to go on hunts a couple of times a year, to practise their traditional hunting skills. I'm hoping Julianne will continue this practice. Guests will sometimes pay to go along.'

'That would be fascinating,' Adam said.

Sannie was not sure she would have the stamina to accompany San hunters for several days as they tracked a gemsbok. 'What do they hunt with? A bow and arrow?'

'Yes.'

Two waiters brought their main courses, springbok fillet stuffed with apricots, a large bottle of sparkling water for Adam and Sannie, and a glass of white wine for Shirley.

'Your food here is superb,' said Sannie after her first mouthful.

'We're happy with the standards we have achieved but we're always striving to do better,' Shirley said.

'Even though you're selling the lodge?' Adam asked.

Shirley finished chewing and took a sip of wine. 'Dune Lodge is my family's legacy and I hope it goes on to provide a place where San can find work and the skills that will help them in their lives. As well as conserving wildlife, the lodge is about preserving my people's heritage. I hope that good work continues long after I'm gone.'

'Where will you go?' Sannie asked.

'Portugal. Many of us Platfontein San have direct links to that country, through the colonial heritage, and I've got Portuguese blood.'

'It's also an easy place for South Africans to emigrate and get a European passport, so I've heard,' Sannie said.

Shirley drank some more wine. 'Is that so? I'm not the sort of person who would emigrate, but I'd like to visit Portugal on a holiday. I'm African, directly descended from the first nations people of this continent. I don't think I'd be happy living in Europe or anywhere else long term. What I'd really like to do is visit Angola some time, to see if it might be possible to start up a tourism venture there, with the long-term aim of preserving or reintroducing San culture into that country.'

'That might be difficult,' Adam said, 'as I understand your people were persecuted by the other peoples of Angola as a result of the war there during the Portuguese days.'

'That's true,' Shirley said. 'But times change. You've no doubt seen how Tony Ferri led a tour of South African military veterans to Angola and literally embraced former enemies and set up programs to help disabled former soldiers there.'

Sannie looked to Adam and from the way he rolled his eyes so that only she could see, she could tell he wasn't convinced by Ferri's sincerity.

'What do you think of Mr Ferri, of his chances?' Sannie asked, turning back to Shirley.

'We all know that despite its many failings and the stench of corruption, the ANC is still firmly entrenched in this country, but I think change is in the air. Mr Ferri's got a way of bringing people, old enemies, together.'

Adam, Sannie noticed, chewed his springbok in silence. 'Did your uncle Luiz own a gun?' Sannie asked Shirley.

Shirley dabbed her lips with a linen serviette. 'That's the sort of question I already answered, and the answer I gave Detective Cele when he first visited was the truth: I had no idea Luiz had a pistol and, if it wasn't his, I had no clue where he might have got one. However, this is South Africa, and I'm sure I don't have to tell you how many illegal firearms are out there.'

'Sure,' Sannie said.

'And before you ask me, no, he did not seem distressed or upset before he took his own life, but who knows the wounds old soldiers carry, the pain that eats away at them from the inside.'

Sannie shot a quick glance to her left again and saw that Adam's eyes were now downcast. She looked back at Shirley.

'After Mia first spotted Luiz's body I was the next person to come to the scene. I identified him.'

'So I heard,' Sannie said. 'I'm so sorry you had to see such a thing.'

'This place,' Shirley set down her knife and gestured out through the open side of the dining area, 'it's so empty, so remote. There was no one else in the reserve that day. Meshach and his men tracked around the sundowner tree site; there was no sign of anyone else having come or gone, other than Mia and Luiz. I only found out later, after talking to Mia, that Luiz had not reported for their scheduled game drive. Mia didn't want to keep the guests waiting, so she told them Luiz was unwell, which she assumed was the case, and took the drive by herself.'

'So, it wouldn't have been feasible for Luiz to have gone there with anyone else, someone from outside the lodge?' Sannie asked.

Shirley shook her head. 'I would have known if Luiz was meeting a visitor; we always keep a record of all vehicles entering or leaving the property and, like I said, there was no evidence of anyone else having been there.'

25

Tony Ferri poured the wine.

Mia had noticed the way Sannie had looked at her when she left with Tony, and she felt guilty for not spending enough time with her friend. She looked at Tony. He had convinced her to bend a rule, coming to a guest's tent on her own, by offering her more information about her father.

The lodge staff had set a beautiful table on the stoep of Tony's suite. The silverware and glasses reflected the warm glow of candlelight. Above them, the sky was ablaze with stars. Mia tried to stay dispassionate.

'Just beautiful.' Tony held up his glass.

Mia raised hers as well. When he looked into her eyes it unsettled her, every time. 'Is that a toast?'

'It's the truth.'

She clinked. He was flirting with her. 'You mean, the night, the lodge is beautiful.'

Tony just stared into her eyes. Mia shivered. 'To life,' she said.

Tony gave a little nod. 'To life.' They drank and Tony uncovered the first course. 'This is how life should be. A man and a woman in a beautiful setting, leaving their daily work behind. Mine consumes me.'

'I'm lucky that I can switch off, but only in between dinner being finished and me waking up at four in the morning.' She needed to remember why she was here, which was to learn more about her father.

Tony gave a theatrical grimace. 'I hate early starts, but I also have plenty of them, especially for breakfast TV appearances.'

'I don't even have to try to wake up, it comes naturally. My dad was ...'

'It's OK,' he said, and reached out a hand and put it on hers.

His touch was electric. 'I was going to say that he woke early, no matter how much he'd had to drink the night before. But I don't want to speak badly of him.'

'Did he ever tell you about Greefswald?'

She shook her head. 'No, what's that?'

Tony set down his knife and fork and put his elbows on the table and hands together, as if he were praying. 'The place the army sent him after the court martial. It was said to be terrible. You said you wanted to hear everything.'

'Yes.' Mia clenched her fists.

He drew a breath. 'There was also a drugs charge.'

She sat there, open-mouthed for a moment. 'What?'

Tony spoke of a search, of marijuana being found in her father's footlocker, and the penalty for drug offences in the old South African Defence Force. Hard labour, brutal physical exercise and re-education.

'Today it would have been a slap on the wrist,' Tony said, 'and the damn stuff's legal for personal use. That was the way things were done back then and Greefswald was designed to "fix" people,' he made quote marks with his fingers, 'or break them. Your father did go back to Angola after that, back into combat, but that place could have had a lasting effect on his mind.'

Mia looked down at her food, no longer hungry. 'I see.' She felt the sting of tears in her eyes. 'He never told me about either of the charges. He must have been ashamed. I need a moment, please.'

She pushed back her chair and stood. She walked to the end of the generous stoep and stood there, hands on the railing, looking up at the desert sky. She heard the decking boards creak and felt Tony's presence beside her. She smelled his aftershave; it was lovely. He didn't touch her.

'He would have been so proud of you.'

Mia kept her gaze upward, as if she could see Frank's face in the stars. 'He was. And he hated drugs, maybe as a result of his time at that place. More than once he sat me down and told me how evil they were, and how it would break his heart if he ever lost me to drugs. The irony was that if he hadn't killed himself then his smoking and drinking probably would have killed him before his time.'

'I'm so sorry.'

She turned to him and saw that the politician's white-toothed facade was gone. His face was contorted in sadness. 'It's not your fault, Tony.'

'Mia.'

He opened his arms and she wasn't sure if it was a gesture of despair or an invitation. All Mia knew right then was that she needed to be held, and to feel the warmth of another living human being. She went to him. Damn, this was not what she had planned at all.

Tony wrapped his arms around her and held her as she cried. She felt his hand on her hair, soothing her, stroking, and the beat of his heart. She missed her wonderful, flawed father so much. So many times in her life she'd found herself looking up at the stars wishing he was there, or that there was someone she could turn to.

'You're such a good girl, Mia.'

The words were condescending, and she should have bridled at them, but right then, in this moment, they completed the warmth of her embrace with Tony. She looked up from Tony's chest at his face. He was so much older than her, but he was handsome, and smart and powerful. Mia closed her eyes.

'Hey!'

Mia couldn't see past Tony's broad chest, but there was the sound of someone running up the pathway then the clomp of feet on the wooden stairs leading to the stoep. Tony was wrenched backwards out of her arms. Mia saw Adam Kruger, who looked furious.

'You bastard!'

'No, wait –' Tony held up a hand, but Adam drew back his fist and landed a hammer blow on Tony's chin, sending him sprawling backwards on the deck at Mia's feet.

'What the hell?' Mia jumped back. She saw someone else coming up the pathway. 'Sannie!'

'Bliksem, Adam, what are you doing?' Sannie called.

Ferri sat up and rubbed his jaw. Adam stood over him, fists up and ready like a boxer waiting for round two.

Sannie ran up the stairs. 'Adam, come away.' Adam ignored her and looked to Mia.

'Who do you think you are?' Mia said to him.

'Whatever this guy's telling you is most likely a lie,' Adam said.

'What?' Mia felt her anger burn inside her. 'That my father was court-martialled? That he was sent to some punishment camp? That it might have broken him? I've learned more from Tony than any of my father's so-called friends ever told me.'

'He,' Adam pointed down at the politician, 'was the cause of all that. Him and the colonel, and all the other bloody officers covered up for each other.'

'But it was over a minor drug bust,' Mia said. Tony had said nothing about other officers, or cover-ups.

Ferri started to stand, and held a hand up in surrender. 'It's OK, Mia. Part of what Adam's saying is true.'

'I'm sorry, Mr Ferri,' Sannie said.

'You don't have to be,' Ferri said. He looked Adam in the eye. 'Adam, if I could change the past, go back and do things differently, believe me, man, I would.'

Mia looked at Adam. She was still angry with him and she went to Ferri, standing by his side, in case Adam took another shot at him.

The other man looked conflicted. His fists were half raised now, his jaw set. She saw the anger, maybe hatred, in his eyes.

'I don't need you to protect me, Adam,' Mia said. 'Or if I did, it was long ago. I don't need to be shielded from the truth about who my father was or what he did.'

'He was a good man, Mia.' Adam lowered his hands at last. 'Adam, let's go,' Sannie said.

Adam ignored Sannie. 'What happened to the diamonds, Ferri?'

Ferri moved his lower jaw from side to side. 'What diamonds?'

Adam squared his shoulders again. 'Don't play dumb with me or I'll klap you again.'

'Adam!' Sannie moved between the two men.

'Diamonds?' Mia said, surprised and confused.

Adam shot a glance at Sannie. 'Let's hear it from him.'

'All right.' Ferri held up both hands now, in case Adam wanted to hit him again. 'I was told by Colonel de Villiers, the sector commander, that there was an airman on board the downed aircraft we went to find who was carrying important cargo in a briefcase chained to his wrist. When I was at headquarters, I would see flights scheduled in and out of Angola to pick up items from Jonas Savimbi's people. There were whispers that it was diamonds or rhino horn, or ivory, so I assumed that if it was a briefcase then it was probably diamonds.'

'Why didn't you tell Frank and the rest of us?' Adam said.

'I didn't know for sure. I asked de Villiers: "Is this valuable cargo?", and he just told me that it was high priority and that I must not tell any of you what I was looking for.'

'So what happened to the briefcase Duarte was carrying?' Adam asked.

Ferri shook his head. 'You saw him, after the mortars and the artillery had finished. His left arm was blown off. I had to carry him, for God's sake.' Ferri looked to Mia. 'Frank made me do that. I was shell-shocked and I knew, deep down, that I'd done the wrong thing by making Evan and Rossouw and the San guys stay behind when Frank wanted to pull back. Those few minutes of me trying to be a hero cost two good men their lives, Mia.'

Mia felt the tears well in her eyes. Sannie stood there in silence. 'I was stunned, probably concussed from the shelling, but I looked around for the briefcase. I saw it, half under the stump of a tree that had been uprooted. It had been shredded to scraps of leather. Duarte's body took most of the hit from a mortar bomb after he'd already died. I remember seeing some papers, fragments, scorched and smouldering. If there were diamonds in that bag, they were blown to kingdom come. Duarte's . . . his hand was still . . .' Ferri choked on the words.

Mia put an arm around him. She looked up into his face and saw that the tears streaming down his cheeks were real as his body heaved with sobbing.

Ferri sniffed and ran a finger under his nose then stared back at Adam. 'His arm had been severed. You saw the body.'

Adam, Mia saw, was also back then in that terrible moment. His nostrils flared as he breathed deeply. His eyes looked past Tony now, into the distance, back in time. The way he had punched Tony had been sudden, shocking. She wondered at the violence these men were capable of.

But Tony needed her now.

'Mr Kruger,' Mia said formally, as she might address a new guest rather than a man who had perhaps congratulated Frank and her mother on Mia's birth, 'I think you should leave this suite now.'

'ADAM!' Sannie strode after him as he walked down the pathway, past his suite, and then on past the swimming pool. 'Where the hell are you going?'

He didn't look back. 'Away from all this kak.'

'You can't keep running, Adam. And if you do, you'll end up in the desert.'

He stopped at the edge of the cone of light cast by the last of Dune Lodge's lanterns, and Sannie went to him. She was angry, at him and at herself.

Adam stared up at the night sky.

'I hated the war after what happened on that mission, with Ferri.'

'You mean you liked it before that?' she asked.

'No. Yes. I don't know. It's hard to put it into words. Sure, some people were conscientious objectors, opposed to the war for religious or political reasons, but for most of the rest of us it was something different – exciting, even. Through our training, especially in the 'Bats, we just wanted to get into action. It was different, after.'

'I see,' she said.

He looked to her. 'Ferri's lying like a politician.'

'What do you mean by that?'

'He's telling us – Mia – part of the truth, but not all of it. He gives just enough information to appear to be coming clean, but he's holding back. I know it. Something else went on there, in Angola, in the time Frank and Erasmus and me were away from him. Do you believe that bullshit about Duarte's briefcase full of diamonds being blown up?'

Sannie thought about it. Ferri's story about how the diamonds were blown away by a mortar bomb sounded convenient. 'But you were all searched when you got back to base. Evan said the same thing.'

He ran a hand through his short hair. 'I know. I keep trying to put the pieces together, but it's like there's one missing. If the diamonds really were lost, then what was the point of charging Frank and me, of splitting up the stick and sending us all to different units?'

'I don't know, Adam, but what you did just then, hitting Tony Ferri, was not right.'

Adam glared at her. 'You saw how he was holding your friend Mia. Was that right? How do you feel about that?'

Sannie gritted her teeth. She hated to admit it, but she'd been as mad as Adam was when she saw Mia in the politician's arms. If Mia had a fault, it was that she fell for the wrong men. Her last boyfriend, Graham, had been a handsome young safari guide, but he was a bad boy.

When Sannie didn't reply, Adam continued, 'And do you believe that piece of Hollywood on social media of Ferri charging up a sand dune with Mia's rifle, firing at nobody?'

'It does seem strange. And, no, for the record, I'm not happy about how Ferri seems to be making a move on Mia, but she's an adult and you just assaulted a high-profile politician. You didn't even hit him in self-defence, Adam. If he lays charges against you I'll be a witness and I'll have to testify against you. You've put me in a terrible position.'

His mood changed. 'I'm so sorry.'

Sannie sighed. 'Is this the way you react to stress? If you're the sort of man who starts throwing punches every time you're upset, then . . .'

'Sannie . . . Please.'

She did an about-face and wrapped her arms around herself; the night air was already chilly. Sannie started walking back to her suite.

After a while her phone beeped. Sannie took it out of her bra and checked whatsapp. It was a message from Adam. It read: My daughter, Jolene, and my ex-wife, Sarah. He listed their phone numbers. Call them and ask them what sort of a man I am.

Sannie put her phone away and kept walking. She was not going to waste her time on some brute. If she wanted a man who solved all his problems with his fists then there was no shortage of those still serving in the police.

As she walked along the lantern-lit path, though, her mind turned over the conversations she'd had so far. Instinctively she had begun questioning the people at the lodge as though she was conducting some kind of amateur investigation. This was not her case and this was not her business, but she found herself wanting to know whose version of the truth about what happened in Angola was the real one, and if there was more that was unsaid or unknown.

Evan was hiding something – his body language when she'd questioned him was a giveaway. Sannie remembered the look that had passed between Evan and Shirley, the lodge manager, when Sannie and Adam had first arrived. It was clear they knew each other, but wouldn't they have at least said 'hello' in her presence? If Tony Ferri had stolen some diamonds in Angola, would Evan have known about it? Maybe his subsequent posting to a cushy headquarters job was payment for his silence.

And what of the shadowy Colonel de Villiers, who seemed to have had a personal interest in the paratroopers' mission right from the start?

'Sannie,' Adam said behind her.

She was still annoyed with him, but she could also still feel him and what they had done that afternoon.

'Sannie, I'm –'

'Tell me about de Villiers,' she said as he fell into step with her.

'Frank tracked him down through the South African Military Veterans of Australia Facebook page,' Adam said, sounding relieved that she had not rounded on him again. 'He emigrated to Australia in the nineties, not long after the change of government. He set up a shop in some suburb in Perth selling Ouma rusks and biltong to homesick South Africans. If he was a diamond-smuggling mastermind, then he must have blown all his money in the casinos, or on some bad investments. De Villiers was dying of cancer when Frank found him.'

'Evan told me that already. He said that de Villiers didn't want to talk to Frank, so he was unable to prove or disprove his theory about Ferri smuggling the diamonds out of Angola. And Evan claims Ferri was too busy being a hero in Angola to steal anything.'

'When did Evan say that happened?'

'He said ten or eleven years ago, when Ferri was first getting serious about making a move on the DA's top job. He's obviously been running a long-term campaign. It was when Frank told Evan his diamond theory.'

'OK,' said Adam, thinking. 'Probably around the same time Frank told me, after he'd been talking to Duarte's old comrades. I visited early in the year, around March or April. The bush in the Kruger Park, near where he lived, was lovely and green. Frank died that September, around six months later.'

'Evan also mentioned Frank talking to people who knew Duarte.'

'But then I heard from Frank again, shortly before he died. I didn't speak to him, but I got an SMS telling me that he'd found "the colonel" again and was going to talk to him. Whether or not Frank did make contact with de Villiers, and what they discussed, I don't know. But Frank was dead not long after I got that message – maybe two or three days later.'

Sannie filed this new information away in her mind, then shifted her attention back to the events in Angola. 'So if Roberto, the other San tracker, and Rossouw, the Parabat with the radio, were both killed in action, then the only person other than Evan who might have seen what was actually going on at that time in Angola, when you and Frank were separated from the others, was Luiz,' Sannie said.

'And now he's dead.'

'Yes, but why now, after all these years?' Sannie wondered out loud. 'And we're assuming that Luiz didn't really kill himself for some other reason.'

Adam walked in silence beside her.

Sannie's phone rang and she took it out. 'Henk, howzit,' she said, after seeing his name on the screen.

'Fine, and you?' Captain Henk de Beer said. 'I hope I'm not calling too late.'

'No, not at all. Did you find something?'

'Ja, I checked my notebook and found what I'd written at the time. There was something strange, Sannie.'

'Yes?' She resisted the urge to tell him to just spit it out.

'Mia, Frank's daughter, and his friend – my boet who I played golf with – said Frank Greenaway never owned a gun. He always said that his rifle, which he was issued with by the Kruger Park, was a tool, and he didn't want to shoot for fun. Also, he was very at home with the local Shangaan people near where he and Mia lived, just outside of Hazyview, and he used to say he never feared for his safety. We all know that it's easy to buy a gun and it seemed that Frank had done that, just to kill himself.'

'What sort of weapon was it, Henk?'

'A Makarov. And the other unusual thing was that there was only one round in the pistol, the one he used to kill himself with, I mean. The weapon was empty when we retrieved it.'

'Maybe he didn't want Mia finding it and hurting herself with a loaded weapon,' Sannie said.

'Ja, Sannie, that's what I thought at the time. The blood test done on the victim also showed Frank had a low red blood cell count, like he was suffering from malaria or something similar.'

Sannie thought about the information Henk had provided. 'Do your notes say where Mia was at the time?'

'She was at a school camp, in the bush, and not due back home until after Frank died. It was the domestic who found Frank, not Mia, though she was called home from the camp, of course, and I interviewed her the day after.'

That meant Frank could not have been worried about Mia hurting herself with a loaded firearm. Surely Frank would have known that his daughter wouldn't find him. Had Frank been worried that the woman who cooked and cleaned for them might shoot herself accidentally? 'Anything else, Henk?'

'I'm not sure. I'll take some pictures of my notes with my phone and whatsapp them to you. It was all pretty standard stuff.' There was the sound of pages being flicked. 'Not much else, Sannie. Let me see . . . oh yes. You know Greg Mahoney?'

'Who in Hazyview doesn't know Greg?' Sannie said. With his luxuriant mop of curly hair and signature red bandana around his neck, the experienced safari guide was a local institution, as was his feisty English wife, Tracey.

'Greg was another friend of Frank. He was there at the house when we came to investigate. I asked him the usual questions – what Frank's mood was like, was he depressed and what-what-what.'

'And?'

'Let me see . . . I wrote here: Mr Mahoney said the deceased had been angry the last time Mahoney saw him, in September, a week before he died. The deceased had entered into a public argument with a politician who was visiting Hazyview. The altercation took place outside the Checkers supermarket. Ja, I remember this time,

Sannie. Greg was running for the DA. He never got elected, but I remember that visit by the politician.'

'Who was it, Henk? Who was the man who Frank had an argument with?'

'That oke who thinks he's going to be the next president. Tony Ferri.'

'I'M SO sorry about that, Tony,' Mia said. They had gone back into his suite, but neither of them felt like finishing their half-eaten main courses. Tony had topped up their wineglasses and they sat side by side in lounge chairs looking out at the darkness.

'It's not your fault. Besides,' he gingerly fingered his jaw, 'I've probably had that coming for more than thirty-five years. When I say it like that, it makes me feel ancient.'

'You're not.' Mia had felt a whirlwind of emotions in the very short time since she'd met Tony. She didn't even think of him as old, even though he was about the same age as her late father. Clearly, Tony and Frank had not got on, and Adam was still angry over what had happened in Angola, yet Tony seemed to be doing as much as he could to clear the air and atone for the past. 'You're very handsome.'

He smiled and held up his glass. 'And you're beautiful.'

Mia felt her cheeks burn, at his compliment as well as the fact that she had blurted hers out. She remembered the feel of his arms around her, but she needed to know more before she let herself tumble over the edge of an emotional precipice. 'Is there anything else you want to tell me about my father, or the war?'

He looked at the floor. 'Only that I wish I'd been a better leader, back then on that patrol, and that I'd had the chance to truly make amends with Frank and seek his forgiveness.'

She nodded. 'He was so troubled. Maybe there was nothing anyone could say to him to make him feel better. I certainly tried.'

Tony reached out and took her hand. 'I'm sure you did.'

'Thank you.'

The wine had made her feel mellow, especially after such a hectic day, and she took another long sip, seeking refuge and courage from the alcohol. His eyes were so damned beautiful in the candlelight.

'There's nothing more I can tell you, Mia, about your father, or about me to make you like me, or to take away the pain of your loss. I'm a public figure, and the world I live in is incredibly stressful and, yes, it can seem artificial, even dishonest at times. At the end of the day I'm just a man, though, a human being with feelings and wants and needs like everyone. I'm far from perfect, Mia.'

'None of us is, Tony.'

'Out here, though,' he gestured to the open sliding doors, 'in the desert, or the bush, it's as close to perfection as a person can find. I want to end up here, Mia, but I've got work to do in the meantime.'

'I understand.'

'You know my crazy personal situation, with my wife, with Lisa.'

'Yes.'

He stared into her eyes. 'I want you in my life, Mia.' Her heart felt like it stopped. Then Tony kissed her.

26

'You can come in, but just to talk,' Sannie said as she and Adam stopped at the foot of the stairs to her suite.

'OK, I'll take that,' Adam said.

'Good.' She walked up to the stoep, opened the sliding doors, and Adam followed her in. Her phone beeped several times.

'Was that your friend the detective? Henk?' Adam asked. He stood in the suite and Sannie motioned for him to sit in one of the armchairs.

'Yes.' They both sat. 'And?'

'If this was an investigation, I wouldn't be passing information on to you, especially in light of the way you behaved just now.'

'I'm not a child, Sannie, and this isn't an investigation – at least I didn't think it was. This is one friend helping another, isn't it?' Friend? Was that what they were? 'Yes, I suppose so.' Sannie took out her phone, opened whatsapp and checked her messages. Henk, as promised, had sent her some photos from the pages of his notebook. She read them quickly.

'What is it?'

'Patience,' she said. 'OK, Henk's notes show that there was evidence that Frank did kill himself. He noted there was a star-shaped wound on the right side of Frank's head, at the temple, which is consistent with a gun being placed against the skin, and the crime scene people found gunshot residue on Frank's right hand. Henk says there was no sign of forced entry to the house, nor defensive wounds on the body or other signs of a struggle. A post-mortem also found that Frank was suffering from hemolytic anaemia, which is where the body's red blood cells collapse. Henk has written: This condition is thought to be linked to either sickle cell anaemia or malaria. The deceased's daughter, Mia Greenaway, reported her father had suffered malaria several times.'

'All right,' Adam said. 'What else?'

Sannie relayed her conversation with Henk about the Russian pistol having contained just one bullet, and the report that Frank had argued with Tony Ferri, in public, in Hazyview, not long before his suicide.

'Ferri,' was all Adam said.

'That does not mean you can go and punch him again.'

Adam gave a small smile. 'I've learned my lesson.'

'Good.'

'But that's an amazing coincidence about the type of pistol, and the single bullet – it's common to Frank and Luiz's deaths, and the attack on me.'

'Yes,' Sannie said. She was never one for coincidences, but it was exactly that which had brought her and Adam together, and to this place in the desert. As far as holidays went, this was not what she'd had in mind, but she found herself unable to walk away from this wartime mystery – or Adam Kruger.

'At least you're still talking to me,' Adam said.

'For the time being. What is the link in all of this?'

'Tony Ferri,' Adam said.

'You're too quick to say that,' Sannie cautioned. 'You must think this through, Adam, logically and without emotion, like a detective. And you must be wary of trying to make facts or evidence fit your theory.'

'All right. How?' he asked.

'To commit a crime, a person needs motive, means and opportunity. Who had motive for wanting Frank dead, and why?'

'I hate to sound like a broken record, but that would be Tony Ferri. Frank knew the truth behind Ferri's nice-guy public persona.'

'Frank was carrying a grudge and from what you say, with good reason. But why, all of a sudden, would Ferri see a need to kill Frank?'

'Maybe Frank confronted Ferri with something in Hazyview, something he threatened to go public with? The diamonds, maybe?'

'Frank had already flagged the diamond theory with you and Evan six months earlier. Why wait so long to confront Ferri about it? Also, it seemed he didn't have any proof.'

'But Frank had a public fight with Tony Ferri, then died a few days later.'

Sannie thought about what Evan had told her, and her discussions with Henk and Adam, about the period before Frank died. 'You told me that Frank made contact with Colonel de Villiers again, just before his death.'

'Yes. Frank wasn't big on social media, but I remember he told me that someone had found de Villiers for him via Facebook, through a veterans' organisation in Australia.'

Sannie nodded. 'Evan told me that he had been in touch with Colonel de Villiers around part of what he called "clearing the decks" in preparation for Tony Ferri's first tilt at the leadership. He told me that de Villiers gave Ferri a glowing reference.'

Adam snorted. 'Like I say, officers looking after officers.'

'Is that a private Facebook group, for the South African veterans in Australia?'

'It is,' Adam said, 'but I'm a member.'

'Can you check something for me?' Sannie asked. 'Sure, what?'

'I don't know what. Well, not exactly.'

Adam took his phone out and Sannie waited while he opened the social media app. 'Got it; I'm viewing the group,' he said.

'Maybe search Frank Greenaway's name?'

Adam nodded and his fingers tapped the screen. 'I've got a message about Frank's death. It reads: *Devastated to learn of the passing of Sergeant Frank Greenaway, 1 Parachute Battalion. Sadly, it seems Frank took his own life, in South Africa. He had recently been in touch with our members here in Australia.*

'Can you scroll back, please, before that, in September?'

Adam alternately swiped the screen and read posts. Sannie thought while she waited, then took out her phone and composed an SMS to Henk de Beer.

Henk, can you please do me a criminal record check on the following people: Evan Litis, Luiz Siboa, Frank Greenaway, Anthony/Antonio Ferri. I will find Ferri's DOB online and will dig to find birthdays for the others. Thanks. S.

'Found something,' Adam said.

'One minute, please.' Sannie added another name to the list, then looked up. 'I'm all yours.' She blushed when she realised what she had just said.

Adam seemed to have missed the significance of her remark. 'There's a post by Jaco de Villiers: Seeking urgent contact with Sergeant Frank Greenaway, believed to be living in Hazyview, SA. The colonel had ignored Frank when he first tried to contact him.'

'When was that post?'

'Eighth of September. There are a couple of comments from guys who know Frank and they offer to give him Frank's number in a private message.' Adam passed her his phone.

'Urgent,' Sannie said. 'Maybe de Villiers had something he wanted to get off his chest. Evan told me de Villiers was full of praise for Ferri and that the colonel had only ever thought of Frank as a troublemaker.'

Adam went back to scrolling and reading. 'Here's another entry – a death notice for de Villiers. I hated that man for a long time, but I wouldn't wish cancer on anyone. He passed just a few days after his message trying to find Frank. It says he'd been in hospital, in palliative care, for a month.'

Sannie nodded. 'He was on his deathbed, Adam.'

They both sat there for a few moments, processing the chain of events, as recorded forever on the internet.

'De Villiers wanted to tell Frank something, and it was sure as hell not what a good oke Tony Ferri was,' Adam said at last.

Sannie had to agree. 'And twenty-four hours after that exchange online, Frank was embroiled in a public fight in a supermarket in Hazyview with Tony Ferri.'

Sannie's phone beeped. She looked at the screen and saw a message from Henk, and read it quickly. 'That's my police contact. He says he just found another entry in his notebook about Frank Greenaway that backed Greg Mahoney's claim. Frank was arrested by the local police in Hazyview and charged with making a public disturbance, at the Checkers supermarket, the day he faced off with Tony Ferri.'

'There would have been police on hand for a political visit,' Adam said. 'Sounds like Frank got arrested and muzzled before anyone could hear what he had to say to Ferri.'

'And a couple of days later, Frank kills himself,' Sannie said. 'Shit.'

'What is it?' Adam said.

'Mia's still with Tony Ferri, and you, Adam Kruger, probably just drove him straight into her arms by punching him.'

'I'll kill him.'

Sannie glared at Adam. 'You will not.'

He held up his hands. 'Just joking. But what are we going to do about Mia?'

Sannie pointed her right index finger at him, like a gun. 'You stay here, or we're through.'

Adam drew a deep breath, stilled himself, and nodded. 'Be careful.'

MIA LET Tony walk her deeper into his suite, then, at his urging, sat down at the foot of his bed with him. He continued to kiss her, one hand in the small of her back, the fingers of the other caressing her hair, at first, then moving down over her shoulder. It had all happened so fast – too quickly. If anything, Adam's barging in on them had made her feel sympathy for Tony.

He hadn't fought back and had acknowledged his wrongdoing in the past, and that just made her want to hold him again, and for him to put his arms around her.

Now, all thoughts of sympathy or right or wrong were being banished by the signals from her own body. It had been five months since she'd broken up with Graham and there had been no one since him. Unlike Graham, who had been handsome but immature, Tony was older, wiser, and yet still had a great body.

His touch told her he knew what he was doing. He brushed the fabric of her green bush shirt with the backs of his fingers and she felt her nipple respond to him. Her breath came faster as she tasted his tongue. He was a great kisser.

Tony started unbuttoning her shirt and Mia did nothing to stop him. She wanted to feel his skin on hers, his touch, and she felt the heat rising from deep inside her.

'God, I want you,' he whispered as his lips broke from hers.

'Yes,' she said, then found his mouth again.

Tony's hand was inside her bra now and his fingertips were electric on her skin. She bit her lower lip as he touched her breast. 'Tony . . .'

'It's OK, Mia. This feels so right.' His lips were next to her ear. She felt a hand on her knee, fingers running up the inside of her thigh as he parted her legs. Next he was expertly undoing her belt and the buttons on her shorts, and pulling down the zip.

Mia leaned back a little, arching to help him as his hand slid into her pants.

They kissed, deeply, as he continued his exploration.

IT WAS AGAINST CAMP RULES, but Sannie went out of the suite and onto the sandy path alone, making for Ferri's suite.

Her anger at Adam was abating, partly because the more she thought about Tony Ferri taking advantage of Mia – and that's what it seemed was happening – the more she channelled her annoyance into the politician. But she needed a clear head and walking outside in the chill of the desert night, even if there was some element of risk, helped her.

Sannie took out her phone again. She searched for Cele and found the local detective sergeant's number. She called.

'Captain, how are you? I'm still busy driving back to Askham.'

'Sorry to bother you,' she said. 'I just had one more question for you, about Luiz Siboa?'

'You know I can't discuss the details of a case with an outsider.'

'I know, but we also wear the same uniform. I just want to know, did you see a toxicology report, or blood tests from Mr Siboa's post-mortem?'

'Of course.'

'And? Was there anything unusual?'

'No drugs or alcohol, if that's what you mean.'

'No,' Sannie said. 'Anything about an illness maybe?'

'Well, yes, now that you mention it, the ME said Siboa had some sort of blood disorder, anaemia something.'

'Hemolytic anaemia?'

'Yes, that's it. Maybe from malaria or some other disease. He was not a well man, not that it would be of much consolation to his family. Why do you ask?'

'Just curious. Thank you.' Sannie ended the call, then opened the web browser on her phone.

MIA WAS on her back and a rising wave of pleasure was threatening to break within her.

'What if someone comes?' she said, catching her breath.

'Relax,' Tony said. 'No one is going to come, except you.'

The corny joke broke the moment just enough to make her pause. She could go either way, surrendering completely to his touch and what would follow, or she could call a halt. Something she had seen or said tugged at the corner of her mind. She kissed him, then moved her face a little way from his, so she could see his eyes.

'You're not worried about someone trying to hurt you, maybe break into your tent again?'

He laughed and shook his head. 'Not at all. I mean . . . There are security guys everywhere, right? All of them are carrying rifles.'

'Yes.'

'Mia . . .' He knew exactly where to touch her and her body wanted to move against his.

SANNIE STOOD outside Tony Ferri's luxury suite and drew a deep breath. As she raised her right foot to take the first wooden step to the stoep, the sliding doors above her were flung open.

'Mia!' Tony Ferri called from inside.

Mia appeared, buckling the belt on her shorts and hastily tucking in her shirt as she came down the stairs. She stopped short when she saw her friend. 'Sannie?'

'I'm . . . sorry, I was –'

'Forget it,' Mia said. 'I think I may have just avoided doing something stupid.'

'What?'

'I'll tell you later. You shouldn't be out at night, Sannie.'

'I know, but I needed to see you.'

'Then come with me,' Mia said.

'All right.' Sannie was aware of Ferri standing in the open doorway, then ducking quickly inside when he saw that Mia was not alone. 'Where are we going?'

'To the strongroom.'

Sannie quickened her pace to keep up with Mia, who was striding back towards the main dining and lounge building. Instead of going in through the front, however, she took a path signposted Staff only, to the rear. Inside, they went past Shirley's office into a more solid area at the back of the building. Unlike the steel and canvas structure that gave guests the illusion of being in a luxurious tent, this wing was constructed of bricks and mortar. Mia led Sannie to a heavy steel door and took her keys out of her pocket. As head guide, Mia was obviously entrusted with a key to the strongroom.

'What's going on, Mia?' Sannie asked.

'Something Tony Ferri just said about men carrying rifles got me thinking.'

Inside, Sannie smelled the familiar odour of gun oil even before Mia switched on the light. On a rack lining the wall were about twenty weapons. There were LM5 semi-automatic rifles for the anti-poaching unit, a couple of older 7.62-millimetre R1 rifles, and an assortment of heavier-calibre hunting rifles. Sannie noticed most were Czech-made Brnos. One, however, stood out as different. Mia took the rifle out of the rack.

'This is a .300 Winchester, fitted with telescopic sights and a suppressor.'

'What do you need the suppressor for?' Sannie asked.

'Occasionally we shoot a springbok or an oryx for staff rations. We don't want the guests in the lodge or on game drives to hear gunfire.' Mia worked the bolt, opening the breech, then raised the rifle up to her nose and sniffed. Next, she stuck her little finger down into the barrel. 'This thing's been fired, very recently, and not cleaned as it should have been after shooting.'

Sannie knew what Mia was thinking, but said nothing. Mia closed the breech, fired the action and replaced the rifle in the rack. Next, she went to a ledger sitting on a table at the end of the line of weapons and opened the book. She ran a finger down the list of names.

'Meshach?' Sannie guessed.

Mia looked up from the book. 'Yes. How did you know?'

'I only just remembered, when you picked up this rifle, that when we were watching Meshach inspecting his anti-poaching rangers, he was carrying a different rifle from his men, and you said something like, "Even Meshach's armed".'

Mia nodded. 'Yes. He's management. Usually, if he's armed, it's only with a pistol. Fuck.'

'What do you want to do, Mia?' Sannie asked.

'Let's go see him.'

Sannie just nodded. Mia turned out the light, locked up, and led the way to the path that took them to the staff quarters.

Sannie heard music playing softly on a radio and a few lights were still on in the row of small accommodation units. Mia stopped outside a larger dwelling, brick with a sloping green tin roof. She knocked on the door. 'Meshach?'

'Coming,' said a voice from inside. When the door opened, Meshach was in a pair of shorts and a Springbok supporters' T-shirt. He had a can of Carling Black Label lager in his right hand. 'Yes?'

Mia stood with her hands on her hips. 'Meshach, we need to talk.'

He looked her up and down. 'It's late, and I'm off duty.'

'You have a high-profile politician in camp who has been the subject of an attempted assault and was shot at on a game drive,' Sannie said.

'Sorry,' Meshach said to Sannie, 'I didn't catch your name. Are you a guest?'

'I'm Detective Captain Susan van Rensburg, South African Police Service Directorate for Priority Crime Investigation. You know – the Hawks.'

Meshach's mouth dropped open. He started to close the door. 'It's late.'

Mia put her foot in the door. 'We need to ask you some questions.'

Sannie took her police identification wallet out of her pocket, flipped it open and held it up to him.

'I don't have to talk to you,' Meshach said.

'No, technically, you don't,' Sannie said. 'But I can come back with a warrant tomorrow, or you can help yourself now by telling us what's going on at this bloody place.'

'You . . . you know nothing.'

'We'll see,' Sannie said.

The door of the unit next door opened and a staff member looked out. She gathered a red satin dressing-gown closed across her breasts when she saw Sannie and Mia standing outside of Meshach's quarters.

'Come in,' Meshach grumbled.

'Why were you carrying the Winchester rifle tonight?' Mia asked him once they were inside.

'I'm head of security; I can use whichever weapon I want.'

'True,' Mia said, 'but it's night-time and we're supposedly on alert for a gunman. Wouldn't an LM5 or a shotgun make more sense than a hunting rifle with a scope and a silencer?'

'It's a good rifle.' Meshach looked away, seemingly unable to make eye contact.

'The firearms register says you signed it out today, not long before someone shot at my game viewer full of guests.'

He looked at her defiantly. 'So?'

'Why did you sign this rifle out?'

'I went to the shooting range, to do some practice,' he said.

'Rubbish, Meshach,' Mia said. 'You know that we never use the range when there's a game drive out. You knew I was out with Tony Ferri and his people; everyone at the lodge was briefed. Did you try and kill Tony Ferri?'

This time he locked eyes with her. 'No.'

'But you did shoot at him, and at Mia and the others,' Sannie said.

Meshach looked to Sannie, then away. 'No!'

'Mia, I want you to secure the armoury,' Sannie said. 'I'm going to get a warrant to search it and seize a firearm suspected of being used against Tony Ferri, yourself, Evan Litis, Lisa Ingram and Shirley Hennessy. That will be five counts of attempted murder, assuming the bullets we retrieve from the game viewer or the ground at the sundowner spot match the rifle. What do you think, Meshach? Will they be a match?'

He looked from woman to woman. 'You can't prove it was me.'

'We'll test your hands for gunpowder residue. Meshach . . .'

Sannie looked to Mia. 'Shabangu,' Mia said.

'Meshach Shabangu, I am arresting you on suspicion of –'

He held up both of his hands. 'Wait, wait, please. I was not trying to kill anyone. I was just following orders, and the people on that truck, they knew that I was going to be shooting at them.'

'I didn't,' Mia said.

'I'm sorry, Mia. I was very careful where I aimed, and you know that I am the best shot on the reserve.'

Sannie could see that Mia was fuming. 'Yes. But what the fuck . . . ?'

'Meshach,' Sannie held up a hand to him, 'talk to us. Tell us what's going on here.'

He gritted his teeth and set down his can of beer. Gesturing to a couple of cheap plastic chairs, he said, 'Sit, please.' Meshach sat down on the end of his bed and his body seemed to sag. 'I am not going to go to jail because of some politician. Let me explain.'

27

It was after midnight by the time they finished questioning Meshach. Sannie told him to stay in his room and to talk to no one until she had spoken to the local police.

'You won't arrest me, will you?' Meshach said as they left.

'That will be a matter for Mia, if she wants to lay a complaint,' Sannie said.

Mia just glared at Meshach, then turned on her heel and walked out into the night.

'I'm so angry at him,' Mia said as they walked along the pathway back towards the main lodge area, 'but Julianne is going to be furious when she finds out.'

'We need to talk to Shirley,' Sannie said. 'Now.'

'OK.'

'Mia?'

'Yes?'

'Tony Ferri . . .'

Mia sighed as they carried on towards a much larger house, set away from the rest of the staff accommodation. 'Nothing happened, Sannie. Well, not too much. We kissed – fooled around a bit...'

'You don't have to tell me,' Sannie began.

'No, I want to. You're a good friend. I liked Tony; he's handsome and charming, and he was sweeping me off my feet, but something just made me call a halt. He laughed off being assaulted in his tent, saying he wasn't worried about security – and this after we'd all been shot at. That's when I thought about Meshach and remembered him carrying the hunting rifle. I realised then that they were hiding the fact that the attacks were set up.'

Maybe he was hiding something more. Sannie didn't press the point and, anyway, Mia had arrived at what Sannie assumed was Shirley's house and was walking up the concrete pathway to the front door. Mia knocked, waited, then knocked again.

'Coming. Who is it?' Shirley said from inside.

'It's Mia. I need to speak to you, urgently.'

'It's after . . .' Shirley, in blue satin pyjamas, opened the door. 'Oh . . . Sannie. Is everything all right?'

'No,' Mia said, and walked into the house.

'Excuse me?'

'Why did you let Meshach shoot at me, and at my game viewer, Shirley?'

'I . . .'

Shirley seemed lost for words, but Sannie saw the guilt in her reddening cheeks and her facial expression.

'I could have been killed. There could have been a ricochet. One of those other idiots on the vehicle could have been hit. I can't believe they talked you into such a ridiculous PR stunt, Shirley!'

Shirley looked at them both and then hung her head. 'I . . . they offered to pay for all the repairs. They needed this, to help Tony Ferri's campaign, Mia. It was all Lisa's idea.'

Sannie and Mia exchanged a glance.

'She's ruthless, that woman,' Shirley said. 'She won't take no for an answer.'

Mia shook her head. 'Tony Ferri's polling numbers are sky-high for a white male politician in this country. Why on earth was it so important for them to get a vision of him charging around the desert like Rambo?'

Shirley shrugged. 'I couldn't say no to them. You don't know what they're like.'

Sannie thought about her conversation with Lisa. The woman was cold – ruthless was a good word. If Lisa was calculating enough to put lives at risk by staging a mock shootout, what else was she capable of? Could she have arranged to have Frank Greenaway murdered after he possibly uncovered something embarrassing about Tony Ferri?

'What are we going to do?' Shirley said, filling the void. 'The media is coming to interview Tony Ferri tomorrow. You won't say anything about the lodge's role in all this, will you?'

Sannie ignored Shirley's plea. 'Who else was involved in the planning for this?'

'I only dealt with Lisa, but she said the others knew – Evan and Tony. She's the one calling the shots.'

'And because Lisa asked – or demanded, or whatever – you said yes and ordered your head of anti-poaching to shoot up one of your Land Rovers. Does Julianne Clyde-Smith know about this?'

'No.' Shirley looked horrified. 'Please, no. Don't tell her, not just yet. I need to explain it to her.'

'Shit.' Mia turned and made for the door. 'I'm done with this place.'

'Don't say anything to Lisa for now,' Sannie said to Shirley.

'Are you kidding? I'm terrified of that woman. I don't want to talk to her.'

Sannie nodded, then followed Mia outside. 'Mia!'

'I'm going to strangle that bloody political flunky.' Mia strode on.

'No, Mia,' Sannie cautioned. 'Not yet. We still need more information.' Sannie caught up with her. 'There's more to this than just a political publicity stunt. I need your help, and somewhere to work, with internet and a computer.'

Mia stopped and took a deep breath. 'All right. Let's go to Shirley's office. Screw her.'

'Let's get Adam first,' Sannie said. 'Safety in numbers, and who knows what other plots are being hatched around here.'

True to his word to her, Adam was waiting in Sannie's suite. They collected him, and Sannie filled him in on Meshach's confession as they headed to Shirley's office.

'Mia,' Adam said as they walked briskly down the path, 'despite what we know now about the set-up, I'm sorry for hitting Tony.' Mia waved her hand in the air. 'Forget it. I'm sorry for getting angry at you. You were trying to save me from a liar and a cheat who's got a staff of crazy people.'

'He probably hit himself over the head just before he sounded the air horn alarm,' Adam said. 'I expect that incident will be in the news tomorrow as well.'

Mia led the way and Sannie and Adam followed. It felt good to have Adam by her side – not that she thought she needed protection. In fact, it was the opposite. She realised that she felt better knowing he was with her so that he would be safe from Lisa, or Tony, or whomever.

Mia took them through the communal lounge area to the offices at the back. She opened the door to Shirley's office and turned on a light, then showed them the adjacent room, which contained a round boardroom table. 'This is where we hold our staff meetings. There's a hot desk computer in there with internet access and I can log into Shirley's computer using my password.'

Mia got behind Shirley's desk and logged in.

'Mia, do you know how to do a CIPC search?' Sannie asked. 'It's the Companies and Intellectual Properties Commission.'

'No, but I'm sure I can work it out. What's it for?'

'I want to find out who else owns Dune Lodge. Shirley told me that she's a shareholder, but she has a silent partner, a food company.'

'Oh, I know who that is,' Mia said.

'Really?'

'Yes, a company called Sea Star South Africa.' Adam snapped his fingers. 'Hey, I've heard of them.'

'How so?' Sannie asked.

'They own fishing operations along the east coast. They were in the news recently, but I can't recall exactly what it was about.'

Sannie gestured to the meeting room computer. 'Check them out online, Adam. Find out what you can about them. Also, see if you can see from the press reports where Tony Ferri and his campaign manager would have been on the night you were attacked.'

'OK.'

Sannie turned to Mia. 'Do you know who runs Sea Star?'

Mia shook her head. 'No, but I know we get bookings in their name sometimes – execs and their friends coming up here for free-bies mostly. I don't pay that much attention to who's who as we try to treat all guests equally.'

'Check the CIPC website and search for Sea Star SA. You should be able to get a list of company directors.'

'Will do,' Mia said. She started tapping on Shirley's keyboard. While Adam and Mia were working, Sannie used her phone to open the South African National Parks website. She figured they would soon need a secure base, away from the intrigues of Dune Lodge, so she made a booking for three people in the Kgalagadi Transfrontier Park.

When she was done, Sannie took out her phone and called her new boss, Gita Kapahi. She grimaced as she glanced at the time on her watch.

'Sannie . . . Are you all right?' said Gita, who had clearly been asleep.

'I'm very sorry to call you so late, but you know that case of the guy who was assaulted in his home, in Pennington?'

'Kruger? The one from the shootout at Scottburgh Mall?'

'Yes. I've got a good idea who organised that attack, and the same person is possibly responsible for an historic murder at Hazyview, in Mpumalanga.'

'Sannie, that's all very interesting, but an assault in Pennington can wait until you get back, and you can refer the other case to the local Hawks, most probably in Nelspruit.'

'They know already. I called my contact Henk de Beer in Nelspruit.'

'Sannie, I hate to labour the point, but do you really think this was worth waking me up for at two in the mor—'

'Tony Ferri, the DA politician, is involved.'

There was a pause on the other end of the line. Gita was ambitious and wanted to make a name for herself. Rightly, she was destined for greater things in the SAPS, and Sannie knew that she saw the media as a means to boost her profile and accelerate her progress through the ranks. 'All right, you have my full attention.'

Sannie filled Gita in on what they knew so far, and what was educated guesswork. A shadow fell across the desk and she looked up to see Adam standing over her. He slid a handwritten note in front of her.

'Gita, I've just found out that Tony Ferri and, most likely, his campaign manager Lisa Ingram were in Port Shepstone the night Adam Kruger was assaulted. We believe the gun that the intruder left at the scene was going to be used to fake Kruger's suicide.'

'Port Shepstone!'

Gita couldn't hide her elation. Possibly the highest-profile case of her career to date had just landed in her lap.

'I've got enough to arrest Lisa Ingram tomorrow morning – I mean, later this morning, in a few hours – if Mia Greenaway, the safari guide who was shot at, makes a statement.'

'Hmm.'

Sannie could tell what was going through her boss's mind. 'Hold off, Sannie,' Gita went on. 'By all means get the statement from Mia, so we have a backup charge of attempted murder, but tell Ingram I want to interview her as soon as possible.'

'OK.' Another detective might have resented a superior officer muscling in on their case, but Sannie knew what she was doing. She did not want publicity, glory or politics in her life. Part of her felt bad; like millions of people in South Africa she had thought Tony Ferri might make a good leader, if he beat the odds and managed to oust the ANC government one day. 'Of course, this is all just theory and hearsay so far, though I have a statement from the lodge owner, Shirley Hennessy.'

'It's enough,' Gita said quickly. 'What will you do now, Sannie?'

She had already thought about that, and was aware that Adam and Mia were listening in. 'If it's OK with you, I'd like to liaise some more with Henk de Beer in Nelspruit, to reopen the case of Frank Greenaway's death, and we also need to get the case of another death, Luiz Siboa, reopened here in the Northern Cape. These people are crazy, boss, so I think the best thing might be for Adam Kruger, Mia and me to get out of this lodge and away from these people for a few days.'

'Yes. I agree, Sannie. But leave your phone on. Where will you go?'

'I think we should go into the Kgalagadi for a couple of days. I've booked us into Nossob rest camp. It'll just be us there. We'll be close enough to the outside world if you need me to do anything, and out of harm's way.'

'Good plan.'

'Thanks,' Sannie said. 'There's one more piece of this puzzle missing, Gita, but I'm counting on a call from Henk in the next few hours to confirm a hunch I've got.'

'Can you tell me about it?'

'It's too soon. Like I say, just a hunch.'

'All right. Take care, Sannie.'

She could hear the disappointment in her commanding officer's voice, but Sannie wanted to keep at least one surprise up her sleeve. 'Will do.' She ended the call.

'Are you two happy to leave later today?' Sannie asked Mia and Adam.

'I never want to see this place again,' Mia said.

'After I've said my goodbyes to Luiz, I'm happy to go anywhere,' Adam said. 'But as much as I want to close this chapter on my life, I can't let it go until the person responsible for Frank's death is in prison.'

Sannie looked to Mia, who nodded. 'In prison, or –' Mia cocked her head. 'Did you hear that? Outside the office?'

. . .

SHIRLEY HENNESSY WAS TERRIFIED as she melted away into the shadows. She had shifted her feet to avoid a scorpion, just in time, and Mia had heard her.

It wasn't the arachnid that had scared her – it was the fear of death, and of losing her lodge and her livelihood.

She hid behind a parked Land Rover as she saw light spill from her office and Mia standing in the open doorway. Mia took out her torch and shone it, but Shirley ducked out of sight. Quickly, she took out her phone and typed an SMS.

Kruger, Mia and the cop are all going to the Kgalagadi after the service, to Nossob.

A minute later, Shirley's phone, set to silent, vibrated as a message came through in reply.

I will find them.

28

Sannie, Mia and Adam worked through the night until dawn, when they went their separate ways to shower and change in their own rooms. They agreed to meet back in the lodge dining area at seven am, which was the pre-arranged time for everyone to have breakfast before leaving for the funeral. When Sannie walked into the dining room with Adam at ten minutes to the hour she was surprised to see Detective Sergeant Thabo Cele sitting at a table with Lisa Ingram. 'What's going on here?' Sannie said.

Lisa looked up at her. 'Sorry to steal your thunder, Captain. I contacted Detective Cele and he rushed out this morning.'

Mia arrived and walked over to Sannie.

Cele rubbed his red eyes. 'Yes. A docket has been opened and I am taking this woman's statement.'

'This morning, Tony accepted my resignation as his campaign manager,' Lisa said to Sannie.

'They're going pro-active,' Mia whispered, 'trying to whitewash what happened on the game viewer. Bloody Meshach must have talked.'

'It was a PR exercise that went wrong,' Lisa said, then turned to Mia. 'I regret that no one informed you what was going on.'

'This is bullshit,' Mia said. Sannie felt the same.

'Please, if you will excuse us,' Cele said. 'I am working here.'

'You need to charge this woman with attempted murder, of me,' Mia said.

'From what I understand, this seems to be a case of people not talking to each other, and, of course, the highly inappropriate use of a firearm,' Cele said.

Tony, Evan and Shirley walked into the dining area. 'Coffee or tea, anyone?' Shirley said. 'I'll be serving you all from the kitchen this morning. I wanted to keep it intimate.'

'Sit down, please, Shirley. All of you, as well,' Sannie said to the others. To Mia and Adam, she said, softly: 'You two cover each of the doors.'

'Will do,' Adam said. Mia nodded and they each moved to an exit point.

The others all took seats around the long dining table. From his post by one of the doors, Adam was facing Ferri and glared at him.

'Thabo, you can take notes,' Sannie said, 'but I have to warn you that the DPCI Port Shepstone and Nelspruit are now involved in an ongoing investigation concerning certain individuals here.'

'But . . .' Thabo began, then thought better of it and lapsed into silence.

Sannie took her notebook out of her handbag and started reading, ignoring him. 'This morning the Hawks have issued a BOLO – a "be on the lookout" – for Roberto Siboa, aged sixty-six years, and a red Nissan Navara bakkie registered in his name.'

Adam turned to Sannie. 'What?'

She gave him a small smile. 'I only just got this information, from Henk, but I think you'll find it interesting.'

Evan, Sannie saw, was looking down at the table, his hands clasped in front of him. He was difficult to read just now. Guilty?

'What? How?' Tony Ferri was wide-eyed. For a politician, he was a terrible liar.

'Who is this Roberto Siboa?' Detective Cele asked.

Now it was Sannie's turn to be taken aback, though she tried to cover it. 'Oh, maybe you don't remember, Sergeant. You arrested him, twice, for possession of pangolins, and once for assault, in Askham.'

'Oh . . . I . . . well, I can't be expected to remember every case.' He studied his notebook.

You can wait, Sannie said to herself. 'Roberto Siboa is, unless someone would like to contradict me, the brother of Luiz Siboa and the man Mr Ferri, Mr Litis and Adam here served with in Angola in the late 1980s.' She studied their faces.

'I'm sorry I didn't tell you our family secret, Captain,' Shirley said, breaking the silence. 'Unlike Luiz, my uncle Roberto is not a nice man.'

'Seems not,' Sannie said. 'His record also includes assault charges and convictions in Platfontein and Cape Town.' Sannie was not ready to say this publicly, but Henk had said the charges dealt with by the local police at Askham had all been dropped due to lack of evidence. She had thought that was fishy enough, without Cele being so quick to claim he didn't remember the serial offender. She had already emailed Gita, mentioning the ineptitude, or possible corrupt behaviour, of the local detective. 'For one of those assault offences, which we will be looking into in more detail as to victim, motive and so on, Roberto spent a year in Pollsmoor Prison. I doubt that experience reformed him.'

Sannie surveyed the table again. 'Would anyone like to tell me how it is that Roberto Siboa is, apparently, alive and well and, for a man of his age, still very active in crime circles, when he was supposedly killed in Angola in 1987 by a direct hit from a South African artillery round?' Sannie looked to Shirley, who in turn shot a glance at Evan.

'Evan?' Sannie pressed.

He stared back at her. 'If this is now an official police investigation then I need to call my lawyer, as should anyone here who now considers themselves under interrogation.'

'This is no interrogation, Mr Litis; I'm merely conducting inquiries at the moment. However, the Port Shepstone office of the Directorate for Priority Crime Investigation – whom you would all know better as the Hawks – will soon be in touch with some or all of you, depending on how or if you answer my questions now. It's time to start talking, people.'

'Port Shepstone?' Lisa said, sitting straighter in her chair. 'Why? We're nowhere near there.'

'No,' Sannie said, 'but you and Mr Ferri were in Port Shepstone at a political rally on the night that someone assaulted and possibly attempted to murder Adam Kruger in his home in Pennington, about forty-five minutes' drive away.'

'What?' Tony said.

'That's preposterous,' Lisa said.

Sannie produced a beatific smile. 'What is preposterous?'

'That ...' Lisa seemed to lose her new-found confidence. 'That we ... I ... might ...'

'Might what? That you or Mr Ferri might attempt to murder Mr Kruger, or arrange someone to do that for you?'

Ferri thumped the table with his hand. 'Insane.'

Shirley, who had been fiddling with the rings on her left hand, gave a start at the loud bang. She glanced at Evan again, then looked to Sannie. 'I want to say something about my uncle.'

'Shirley, you don't have to say a thing without representation,' Evan said.

Sannie saw the way she looked at him. Interesting. 'What is it, Shirley?'

'Like I said, it's our family secret. My uncle, Roberto, he did survive the war. I'm not exactly sure what he did, but he ended up back in Schmidtsdrift, and then Platfontein, and no one seemed too worried by the fact that he had supposedly died, or that he had deserted, or left the army or whatever. Uncle Luiz said that sometimes San men just left when they had decided they'd had enough of fighting.'

Shirley paused as if collecting her thoughts, or maybe deciding whether to continue or not. Sannie noticed how the lodge manager once again briefly made eye contact with Evan, but then she looked back to Sannie and continued.

'Unlike most of the San veterans, Roberto had money,' Shirley said. 'When I was a little girl I remember him with a car with a booming radio, and always a pretty girl, sometimes two, on his arm. For a while, I thought he was like a TV star, but my mother, his sister, told me to be careful around him, and not to be alone with him. Later, I learned why. When I was older my father told me that he and my mother had gone into business with Roberto, and that between them they had bought some of the land here, on what is now Dune Lodge. My parents expanded the property, but Uncle Roberto was a part owner of the original farm my folks bought. Later, my father bought him out, when Roberto needed his money back.'

Sannie was making notes as Shirley spoke, and writing down questions. 'Carry on, please, Shirley.'

'Uncle Roberto would hunt on the farm and, later, the lodge property. It was something my father agreed to, even encouraged initially. My dad told me that it seemed to him the only time Roberto was truly happy, at peace, was when he went into the desert and lived and hunted for days on end just as he had when he was a young man, before the war in Angola. Roberto was troubled, and I learned he could be violent. I also learned from an early age that if anyone "official", such as the police or military, ever asked about Roberto's service in the Border War, or his alleged death, no one was to say anything, or there would be serious consequences. Uncle Luiz used to go hunting with him, but he later gave up when he became a fully fledged guide at Dune Lodge. Luiz said he had killed enough in his life. Roberto . . .'

Sannie let the sentence hang there a moment, but she was concerned Shirley might clam up again.

'You said Roberto had money after the war. Do you think that might have been from conflict diamonds, taken when he was in Angola?'

Shirley looked at her and blinked a few times, then looked to Evan. 'I . . . I can't say for sure.'

Damn. Sannie addressed Tony Ferri. 'Mr Ferri. Did you know that

Roberto Siboa survived the war, and did he steal the diamonds you and your patrol were sent by Colonel de Villiers to recover?'

Ferri looked down at his hands, and continued to do so as he spoke. 'You cannot imagine the madness of war, or artillery fire.'

Sannie felt her heart harden. 'My husband was killed in a rocket attack in Iraq while working as a bodyguard. Try me.'

Ferri looked up. 'I'm sorry for your loss.'

She tried to stop herself from sneering. 'Please answer my question.'

'Tony,' Lisa interjected. 'Not without a lawyer. In fact, screw this. I'm done with this kangaroo court.' She stood.

'Sit down, Ms Ingram,' Sannie said, ice in her voice. 'If Sergeant Cele hasn't charged you with anything I'll arrest you right here and now for the attempted murder of Mia Greenaway.'

'Works for me,' Mia said.

Sannie nodded to her, grateful for the support, but she now needed Mia to keep emotions out of this. 'Mr Ferri?'

'When I say "you cannot imagine", Captain,' Ferri said quietly, 'I mean that perhaps your frame of reference is limited to good men – and I assume your husband was such a man – and the way they react under fire. Things do not always go according to plan, and never as they do in a war movie.' He shifted his eyes to Mia. 'Men disagree, they fight with each other, even those on the same side. Some men act bravely, others run. Some are just terrified.'

'Tony . . .' Lisa was almost pleading.

Ferri held up a hand to her and continued. 'To tell you the truth I have blanked out – or buried, or retold myself – so much of that day over and over that I can barely remember what happened, save for the deafening explosions and the blood on my uniform – other men's blood. I remember Evan acting as a hero, and I put him up for our country's highest medal. For reasons I don't want to go into, that award was denied and he got a lesser award, but it was earned. Did a bag, a briefcase containing diamonds go missing that day? Yes. It did. I can tell you, categorically, that I did not see Roberto leave the battlefield with that briefcase or even see a single solitary diamond. Nor have I seen Roberto Siboa since that day in 1987.'

Sannie nodded. It wasn't surprising, given the place he had reached in a back-stabbing game such as politics, that he was a master of committing sins of omission. 'But you assumed, or were told by someone else, that Roberto Siboa lived and took the diamonds to South West Africa, or some other destination?'

Ferri engaged her, as he probably had hundreds of tough television interviewers. 'As I just said, I can tell you, categorically, that I did not see Roberto leave the battlefield with that briefcase or even see a solitary diamond. Nor have I seen Roberto Siboa since that day.'

Sannie was in equal parts impressed and chilled. He had repeated those last couple of lines virtually verbatim. He had been preparing for this day, maybe for thirty-five years. 'Mr Ferri –'

He interrupted: 'I don't think I have anything more to say today. I'll be happy, of course, to answer any formal questions if and when any proper investigation is opened.'

He could wait, as well. Sannie turned to Shirley again. 'Shirley, just a question for my benefit, my personal understanding. You told me earlier your uncle hunted in the traditional ways of the San people?'

'Yes,' Shirley said, quickly, perhaps relieved, 'with bows and arrows.'

Sannie nodded and flipped back some pages in her notebook. 'I believe they're actually only very small weapons, not what we might think of when people go bow hunting with those huge bows and long arrows, right?'

'Yes, that's correct. The San coat their arrows with a poison made from the larvae of the *Diamphidia nigroornata* beetle. The toxins weaken the prey so that the San hunters can catch the animal and finish it off.'

'Exactly,' Sannie said, 'and as I learned last night the poison works by rupturing the prey's blood cells, which leads to paralysis. The poison has also been used by San for committing murder. Blood samples taken from both Frank Greenaway and Luiz Siboa showed evidence of cell damage. It was put down to either a blood disease or malaria. I believe that both men, who were experienced military veterans and not easy to subdue, were poisoned first, somehow, and while incapacitated they were shot in the head by a killer who held a firearm in each victim's hand, pressed to the side of his head. This gave the appearance of suicide.'

'I can't believe it,' Tony said. 'Roberto?'

Sannie studied the politician for a moment. How much did he know? Who gave the orders for both Frank and Luiz to be killed, in the same way? No one else spoke, so Sannie addressed Shirley. 'I'm sorry to inform you that your uncle Luiz's burial cannot proceed today.'

'No!'

'I apologise.' To Sergeant Cele she said: 'If you don't organise the order to send the body for a second, more detailed postmortem, Sergeant, then I will.'

'Please, Captain,' Shirley said.

'I'm sorry. Your uncle needs to be professionally examined to confirm the circumstances of his death.'

Shirley bit her lip. Sannie watched her closely, but then had to turn her attention back to the others. 'It is my belief,' she continued, 'that shortly before his death by apparent suicide – maybe murder – Frank Greenaway was contacted by retired Colonel Jaco de Villiers, who had moved to Australia. A Facebook post shows that de Villiers urgently wanted to contact Frank. We can consider this unusual, because de Villiers was responsible for Frank being sent to the Greefswald SADF punishment facility on what appear to be trumped-up charges of cowardice and drug use. De Villiers died of cancer just days after speaking to Frank, so this has the hallmarks of a deathbed confession. We know that de Villiers was contacted by you around that time, Evan, as part of a deck-clearing exercise.'

'Um, yes, that's right,' Evan said.

Sannie flicked back a few pages in her notebook. 'You told me, Evan, that de Villiers was "glowing" in his assessment of Mr Ferri, and that he was unrepentant about Frank having been a trouble-maker who got what he deserved. Is that right?'

Evan jutted out his chin. 'Yes. More or less. That was the gist of it.'

'And you said that Frank told you he believed you and/or Tony Ferri took the diamonds out of Angola.'

'Yes, well, we now know that was not the case, and as I told Frank, clearly neither Tony nor I carried any diamonds back to South West Africa, or SA. Like him and Adam, we were all searched. Even the bodies of the dead guys were searched,' Evan said.

Sannie nodded. 'So I believe. And for the record, I do not think Tony stole the diamonds, or that you couriered them out of Angola, Evan.'

'Then are we done here?' Tony placed his palms on the table, hopefully.

'No, not quite, Mr Ferri.'

'What now then?' Ferri asked.

'I don't think Frank made allegations of diamond theft against you, Mr Ferri. I think it was something different.'

Ferri made two fists on the table.

'Let's call a lawyer, Tony,' Lisa said.

He looked sideways at her. '*I* am a lawyer. None of you ever seem to remember that.'

'Claims of diamond smuggling from a long-ago war would be very hard, if not impossible, to prove,' Sannie said. 'And although you've had a successful career in the law, Mr Ferri, I detect no obvious signs of you living a life of opulence.'

'I don't, but thank you,' Tony said.

'The only thing more damaging for a politician than a criminal conviction,' Sannie said, casting her eyes over all of them, 'is some-thing that damages his or her character and, as a result, their standing in the community, and chances of being elected.'

Ferri stared at her, though his trembling lower lip betrayed his true emotion.

'I personally find it hard to believe that Jaco de Villiers would urgently contact Frank Greenaway just to tell Frank, once more, that de Villiers believed he was a troublemaker and a coward. From what I know of him, Frank seemed like an obstinate man, but one with the interests of his soldiers at heart. And I have heard of no evidence of cowardice.'

'I . . .' Ferri began. Sannie waited.

'Tony,' Lisa hissed.

Silence hung around them, and the quiet was as intimidating, perhaps as terrifying, as the thunderous destruction of an artillery barrage.

Sannie knew she could lose them all in a heartbeat. Ferri was, as he had pointed out, a lawyer, and Evan had already threatened to call his. Sannie knew that her case, her theories, were nowhere near watertight, and it would be difficult for Gita and the best detectives in the country to prove any of this without a confession from at least one of these people.

She was not a gambler, not ever. But Sannie's life had changed with Tom's passing. In her beloved country, South Africa, too often the rich, the powerful and the politically connected got away with terrible crimes, sometimes through plain old-fashioned bribery. They had reached a stalemate, and this meeting would end, now, and she would go back to KwaZulu-Natal and spend what years she chose to remain in the SAPS visiting murder and robbery scenes and comforting the crying loved ones of victims of crime.

Like so many she had wanted Tony Ferri to be the one to deliver a new future for South Africa, but the country was already heading towards momentous change once more. It would be worse to let a weak man, perhaps another criminal, take the reins from the current administration. The DA needed clean air, and the right man or woman to bring about that change.

'Tony,' she said, deliberately using his given name, 'I think there is something you want to tell me, to get off your chest.'

He bit his lower lip, seemingly to still it, and glanced at Lisa, who shook her head. Evan hung his head.

So, this was it. Sannie drew a breath. 'Whatever Frank knew about you, Tony, was so damaging that it would have destroyed your first run at the DA leadership even before it began. For a man, an army officer, a Parabat, what could be worse than committing a crime? Something so terrible that it would be worth killing a man to stop the news coming out?'

Sannie looked at Adam. He had remained impassive, but she could see he was fighting to keep his emotions in check. Mia's face was pale.

'Somehow, for some reason I don't know yet, that information was about to be made public again, on the eve of you being confirmed as leader of your party and, hopefully, taking the DA to victory at the next election. Maybe Luiz Siboa was threatening to drop the same bombshell, though I have no idea why he waited so long. And, whatever it was that you were so scared of the voting public of South Africa finding out, Tony, your campaign team here thought that some video of you charging up a sand dune firing Mia's rifle at an imaginary assailant would counter it.'

'I've admitted that was a bad call,' Tony said.

Sannie waited for him to say more, but another stern look from Lisa silenced the would-be leader. Sannie had one card left to play and if it backfired, it would probably cost her her job. Gita would be furious at her if she ruined this case before it even got off the ground.

'Tony,' Sannie said, her voice soft, 'did you also fake the attack on yourself in your tent?'

Ferri put his elbows on the table and his head in his hands. He nodded.

Sannie cleared her throat. 'Tony Ferri, I am arresting you for conspiracy to murder Frank Greenaway and –'

Lisa stood. 'No! Stop.'

'Sit down, Lisa,' Sannie said. 'Is there something you want to say?'

Lisa slowly returned to her seat. 'Tony had nothing at all to do with Frank's death, in any way, nor Luiz's, and he was not involved in any assault on Adam Kruger.'

'You're his campaign manager, Lisa, why should I believe you?'

'Because I sent Roberto Siboa to . . . counsel Greenaway and Luiz.'

'Counsel?' Sannie would have laughed if the crimes had not been so heinous.

'Lisa . . .' Tony sounded shocked. 'Why on earth would you send a man like Roberto? He was a ruthless killer. I came across him and Luiz in the bush after Hennie was shot, with the two of them standing near a dead Angolan who'd been shot in the head. At first I thought Luiz had done it, but from what I later learned about the two brothers, I think it would have been Roberto who executed an unarmed man.'

'You don't need to say anything, Tony,' Lisa said.

'So why did you send Roberto to "counsel" Frank and Luiz?' Sannie asked.

Lisa glared at her.

'Unless you can tell me more, Lisa,' Sannie said, 'you'll give me no choice but to charge Tony, and I will arrest you for conspiracy to murder. You are both free, of course, to engage legal representation after you've been arrested.'

Lisa drew a deep breath. 'Leave Tony out of this. Frank contacted our campaign team after he spoke to Colonel de Villiers. De Villiers told Frank certain things in a phone call, which Frank taped, on a cassette recorder, with de Villiers' permission.'

'What did de Villiers say?' Sannie said.

'I am not prepared to go into that in public,' Lisa said.

'You'll be questioned about it in due course,' Sannie said.

Lisa nodded. 'I'm sure.'

'So,' Sannie said, playing along for now, 'what were your instructions to Roberto?'

'I gave him money, Captain, a sum of 200,000 rand from campaign funds to buy the tape from Frank, and any photos Frank had of him and Tony, and the others from Angola. I handed the same amount to him all these years later to bribe his brother, Luiz, to say nothing publicly about what happened on that patrol in Angola, now that we're so close to Tony's leadership being confirmed.'

'And what happened to the money?'

'Roberto returned from visiting Frank Greenaway with the news that Frank had killed himself – at least that's what he told me. Roberto returned the money and I paid him a bonus for his honesty. He also gave me a photo album of pictures from Greenaway's war days, which I destroyed. I shouldn't have done that.'

'You are so fucking right, you shouldn't have,' Mia hissed.

'Where is Roberto Siboa now?' Sannie asked.

Lisa shrugged. 'I have no idea. I expect he will contact me at some point, unless he has run off with the money this time and disappeared. Perhaps finding his brother dead was too much for him.'

'You lying bitch!' Mia strode from the exit she had been guarding towards Lisa. Adam moved from his position and intercepted her, grabbing her around the waist, just before Mia landed a blow on Lisa.

'Let me go!' Mia tried to remove Adam's arm, but he held her tight.

'Mia, please.' Sannie saw the pain on her friend's face as she went limp in Adam's embrace.

'Fighting's the wrong way, Mia,' Adam said. 'I made the same mistake. Let Sannie find the truth, and justice.' Adam gently ushered Mia back to her doorway and returned to his in case anyone had any ideas about running.

'How did you meet Roberto Siboa?' Sannie asked Lisa.

'I met him at Platfontein. Evan and Tony were visiting some of the old San veterans from the war. They both did a lot of good work in the community. Evan made a point of introducing me to Roberto, away from Tony. I think we both knew that it wouldn't do for Roberto to be photographed with Tony.'

'And Evan?' Sannie noted that Evan had said nothing during these revelations. 'How did you introduce Roberto to Lisa, and why did you do so?'

Evan shrugged his shoulders. 'I said Roberto was a tough guy, a good fighter.'

'In case Mr Ferri's campaign ever needed the services of what? A standover man? An assassin?'

'No comment,' Evan said.

'Were you aware, Evan, that Lisa had ordered Roberto to allegedly purchase a cassette tape from Frank Greenaway?'

'No, I was not. I was not even aware Roberto had visited Frank.'

'Do you wish to correct what you told me, of the substance of your conversation with Jaco de Villiers, as to Tony's character?' Sannie asked.

'No comment, Captain.'

Sannie switched her gaze back to Lisa.

'Evan's telling the truth,' Lisa said. 'He didn't know I'd sent Roberto to pay the money to Frank, or to Luiz. Evan might be Tony's friend, but his view about the . . . New information . . . Was that if it cost Tony his political career, then so be it.'

Sannie quickly scanned their faces. Tony looked surprised, maybe hurt, but Evan seemed to be more the calculating, successful businessman who only backed winners, rather than the kindly peacemaker he'd first presented himself to be. 'And the attack on Adam Kruger?'

'I sent no one to talk to Adam Kruger,' Lisa said.

'Nor did I,' Evan said. He looked Adam in the eye. 'If you want to know what Colonel de Villiers told me and Frank, what he knew, then I'll tell you, though I'll deny it if I'm ever asked publicly.'

'Why would you tell us now?' asked Mia. 'To save your own skin?'

'To convince you,' Evan tossed his head towards Sannie, 'and her, that this isn't about bloody diamonds, and not worth killing for.'

Adam glanced at Sannie, who nodded. 'Talk,' Adam said.

Evan put his palms on the table in front of him, as if to steady himself. 'When Sergeant Frank Greenaway made the call that we should all leave with him and Adam, to link up with Lance Corporal Erasmus, the medic, things got crazy. Tony pointed a gun at Frank and ordered him to leave, and Frank punched Tony in the face . . .'

ANGOLA, 1987

. . .

332

'OK, Loot,' Evan yelled, 'pick up your rifle and let's go.'

The ground shook as a mortar bomb detonated about thirty metres from them. Evan, still on one knee but ready to get up and run, glimpsed movement through the bush and let off two rounds.

Ferri left his rifle next to the unmoving body of the airman, Duarte, and crawled over to Evan. 'You have to help me.'

Evan looked at Ferri and saw that tears had carved clear streaks down his cheeks, through the dust, blood and camouflage cream. Rossouw, who had been taking cover behind a tree, stood and jogged to them. 'Wat de fok are you two doing? You heard the Sergeant, let's _'

The radioman's head snapped backwards and he fell. An Angolan's bullet had punched a hole through his forehead, killing him instantly.

Ferri scuttled like a crab, on all fours, back to Duarte, and rolled him over. Evan strode to the officer, incensed at Rossouw's death and intent on dragging the lieutenant with him. He grabbed his collar, but Ferri spun on his knees. Evan saw the combat knife in his hand and then the blood on the dead airman's left wrist.

'What are you doing, man?' Evan said.

Ferri blinked at him. 'Diamonds, I have to get the diamonds. It's our mission. I wasn't supposed to tell anyone, but . . .'

Ferri started sobbing and the knife fell from his grasp. The Angolans had stopped firing their rifles now that there was no return fire. Evan scanned the bush. Maybe they thought the South Africans were all dead; if that was the case they would be coming for them soon.

Evan raised his R4 to his shoulder, flicked the selector to automatic, and emptied his magazine into the bush, in a sweeping arc. He heard a yelp somewhere and a few shots were fired in return. As Evan removed the empty magazine and fitted a fresh one, the mortars started firing again. The Angolans would not be rushing them right away. He returned his attention to Ferri and the dead man.

'Hell.' He could see now that Ferri had been trying to cut Duarte's hand off, but had given up. There was a pool of vomit next to the briefcase chained to the airman.

A mortar bomb landed close by, showering Evan with dirt and stones. Ferri rolled onto his side and into the foetal position, his hands over his ears. 'No, no, no!'

The officer was howling and crying. Evan saw movement through the leaves and raised his rifle. Just before he fired, he saw that the face staring at them was Luiz, the tracker. Luiz's eyes were drawn to the pathetic figure writhing on the ground.

Evan pointed with his rifle to the tree line, urging Luiz to give covering fire. The San warrior needed no convincing. He took aim and fired.

Evan set down his weapon and picked up Ferri's knife.

SANNIE SHUDDERED at the thought of what Evan had done.

Adam shook his head, clearly disgusted. 'You cut the dead guy's hand off?'

Evan looked at the dining table. 'I'm not proud of it, Adam, but I thought, fuck, we'd lost good men already over this stupid briefcase, we may as well finish Tony's mission, even though he never thought to tell us what it was.'

Sannie glanced at Tony Ferri. He still couldn't raise his face to look at any of them. 'And the diamonds?'

Evan looked to her. 'The Angolan mortar fire became more accurate, and as their barrage crept closer, I grabbed Tony and dragged him behind a fallen tree. I left the briefcase next to Duarte and I took the radio off Rossouw's body. Then a mortar bomb landed next to Duarte and shredded him and the briefcase. I was beyond caring about diamonds or the mission by that point. I thought we were going to die. I could see Angolan soldiers advancing on us, behind where the mortars were landing. I knew we only had minutes at best. It was me who called in our artillery – not Tony – and pretty soon the shells started landing.'

'You told me Roberto was killed by a direct hit from one of our shells,' Adam said.

'Ja, I thought that at the time, boet, but later I realised it must have been an Angolan soldier who got hit – they were that close to us by then and it was confusing.'

'I'm not your fucking boet.'

Evan nodded. 'Roberto turned up out of the blue later at headquarters when I was there. I was surprised. Colonel de Villiers offered me a deal when we all got back to Ondangwa. I had my suspicions about the colonel, like maybe he had some side hustle going on with diamonds. De Villiers was desperate, for whatever reason, to cover up what happened to us in Angola. He offered me a cushy job at HQ if I promised to keep my mouth shut and to say nothing about Roberto – I don't know what those two had going on. He said if news got out about a near-mutiny in Angola then the shit would hit the fan, big time. He claimed it was all about PR, and opposition to the war at home and what-what-what.'

'You could have been a real Parabat and ignored him, and told the court martial what really happened before they sent Frank to that hellhole. You're a coward, Evan, looking after your own skin and landing yourself a jam stealer's job at headquarters, rather than sticking up for your brothers.'

Evan tried to hold Adam's eye, but broke first and cast his gaze downwards. 'I'd had enough of the war after that day, Adam.'

'Is there anything else you want to say, Evan?' Sannie said, then, after a pause, continued, 'How did Frank find out about Mr Ferri's . . . behaviour that day?'

Evan shrugged, then looked up at her. 'All I can think of is that near the end of his life, de Villiers might have wanted to apologise to Frank, and that he probably told Frank what really happened. It was nothing about diamonds, but everything about Tony's reputation, about him having a breakdown under fire. I'll wait for my lawyer now, if you don't mind.'

Sannie turned her attention to Lisa again. 'I will ask you, once more, did you send anyone to "counsel" Adam Kruger at his home, when you and Mr Ferri were in Port Shepstone?'

Lisa glared back. 'No. And I want my lawyer now, too.'

Sannie closed her notebook and stood. 'I think we're done here, for now. Either myself or Colonel Gita Kapahi from the Hawks will be in touch with you all again soon. Sergeant Cele, I'll leave you to do the paperwork to organise a second post-mortem for Luiz Siboa.'

'I –' Detective Cele began.

'"Yes, Captain" are the words you're looking for, Sergeant.'

Cele looked to Evan and then Lisa, as if their plans had all changed, then back to Sannie. 'Yes, Captain.'

Shirley looked distressed, almost like she was about to burst into tears.

'Adam, Mia, I don't think there's much point us staying here at Dune Lodge any longer than is necessary,' Sannie said. She needed to get these two out of this dining area before one of them tried to kill someone.

Tony and Lisa both stood and Tony touched his campaign manager on the arm. 'Lisa, why did you send Roberto to, um, talk to Frank and Luiz?'

She shook his hand from her. 'Because I fucking loved you.'

29

Sannie drove her Fortuner with Mia sitting in the passenger seat next to her. Adam was in the back, looking at his phone, as they headed towards the Kgalagadi Transfrontier Park.

The landscape was more red dunes with fringes of yellow-green grass, and here and there they passed modest farm buildings, mud-brick houses with tin roofs, rusting cars in yards.

'I'll be pleased to never see that place again,' Mia said, 'but I won't rest until someone's behind bars for the death of my father.'

Sannie braked as a donkey ambled out into the middle of the road, seemingly oblivious to the car hurtling towards it at 120 kilometres per hour. 'We've only just begun, Mia. We need to get some solid proof of what Roberto was told to do and by whom. All Lisa's done at this stage is put Roberto at the scene of your father's death. I'm sorry, but we're probably going to have to get a court order to exhume his remains.'

Mia exhaled. 'I figured that might be the case. It's horrible to think about, but I'll sign or do whatever it takes.'

Adam looked up. 'Mia?'

'Yes?'

'Do you know if the booking for Evan, Ferri and Lisa at Dune Lodge was made under one of their names, or a company name?'

Mia shook her head. 'No. I often check NightsBridge, the booking software, to see who's coming to the lodge next, but with everything going on after Luiz's death I didn't have time. Is it important?'

'I think so,' Adam said.

'I'll call Audrey Uren, Julianne's assistant. She can access the system.'

Sannie listened in as Mia made the call and spoke to Audrey.

'Thanks, Aud,' Mia said, then rang off. 'It was a Sea Star booking. A comp. Maybe Sea Star's a supporter of Tony and the DA?'

'Why do you ask, Adam?' Sannie said.

He had his head down again, looking at his phone. 'I'm just checking some stuff online about Sea Star.'

'What about their company structure, their management?' Sannie asked.

'Already been through all the names,' Adam said. 'No one familiar. Sea Star is just one of a number of companies in the African Star group. I'm searching that now.'

'Sannie, I want to apologise for how I acted over the last couple of days,' Mia said.

Sannie swerved to miss a goat. 'No need.'

'There is a need. I'm sorry. I allowed myself to be swept off my feet by Tony Ferri. It's no wonder so many politicians get caught having affairs – silly people like me fall for their fake charm and bullshit.'

'If it's any consolation,' Sannie said, 'my daughter SMSed me before I arrived telling me that she thought Tony Ferri was hot.'

'He sucked me in. That coward. Thank you, as well, Adam.'

'I shouldn't have hit him, but he had it coming.'

Sannie's phone rang and she answered it, on hands-free. 'Captain van Rensburg, hello.'

'Captain, it's Sergeant Thomas Lebope from SAPS Twee Rivieren, in the Kgalagadi Transfrontier Park. How are you?'

'Fine, and you, Sergeant? I'm actually heading your way now.'

'Very good. Captain, I have your name as the contact for a BOLO for a Roberto Siboa.'

'Yes, that's correct.' Adam had looked up from his phone and Mia was leaning closer to her, as if not wanting to miss a word.

'I was coming back to the park from a meeting in Upington this morning and I came across a Red Nissan Navara abandoned on the side of the road, about twenty kilometres from Twee Rivieren.' Sergeant Lebope read out the car's registration number.

Sannie was doing her best to sound calm, but her heart was pounding. 'That's Siboa's vehicle.'

'Yes, I only realised once I got to work and read your BOLO. Captain, when I searched the vehicle, which was unlocked, it was most unusual. A man's shirt, trousers and shoes were found in the car, along with a wallet with the ID card and driver's licence of one Roberto Siboa, the man in question.'

'I see. Thank you, Sergeant.' She checked her sat nav device. 'I'm now thirty-two kilometres from Twee Rivieren. Can you meet me at that bakkie as soon as possible, with as many officers as you can spare? This is a Hawks matter.'

'I understand. It is just myself and one other officer here on duty and at least one of us must stay. But I will come myself.'

'Please do, and please call for backup from Askham or wherever the next nearest station is. Siboa is a dangerous man, and he will be armed.' She rang off.

'What's he doing there?' Mia asked.

'Is he making a run for it? Disappearing into the desert?' Adam said. 'Has one of the others tipped him off already that we're looking for him?'

'That could be the case, but why this road, why now?' Sannie said. A more sinister thought crossed her mind. 'Perhaps he was tipped off – not that we're after him, but where we were going to be, and when, on our way to the park.'

'You think he's waiting for us?' Mia said. 'An ambush?'

Sannie glanced at each of them, then returned her eyes to the road. 'What do we want to do? I don't want to put either of you in danger.'

'I want to see Roberto,' Adam said. 'I'm not going to run from him.'

'Same. I've got my rifle.' Mia had quickly crammed as many of her belongings and clothes as she could into a backpack before she left, and told Shirley she would send for the rest of her things. She had also gone to the armoury strongroom and signed out her rifle and fifty rounds of ammunition she had bought for herself.

'And I've got my Z88 in my wheelie bag,' said Sannie.

'What about me?' Adam asked.

'Reach under my seat, Adam.'

He did as asked and pulled out her personal backup weapon, a .38 Smith & Wesson revolver. Adam put it on the seat next to him and went back to his phone.

'Shit,' Adam said.

'What is it?' Sannie looked over his shoulder.

'You'll never guess who the chairman of Africa Star holdings, the parent company of Sea Star South Africa, is.'

'Who?' Sannie said.

'Evan Litis. I've got a News24 story here about Sea Star purchasing a number of family-owned fishing companies around South Africa. I remember now where I've seen that name before – Sea Star now owns Renshaw's boats, the guy who tried to feed me to the sharks. The online news story has a quote from Evan promising to clean up Sea Star's governance after one of his subsidiary fishing companies was busted for shark finning.'

'I was saving Evan for later,' Sannie said. 'Henk de Beer did a criminal record check on Evan for me, which I got him to pass to my boss, Gita. Evan has a pretty impressive history of offences, starting with assault charges as a teenager and moving on to abalone trafficking, and, later, tax evasion. We were going to look into him further.'

'He's a poacher,' Adam said. 'He told me he'd been looking for me and I think Renshaw told him who I was when I started making waves for his shark-finning operations. Sannie, I think it was Evan who came for me in my home that night.'

'But he's based in Cape Town. What makes you say that?' Adam read from his phone. 'Mr Litis was speaking after delivering the keynote address to the Sustainable Commercial Fishing conference at Durban's Suncoast Casino on –'

'The night you were attacked?' Sannie pre-empted.

'Exactly.'

'Sheesh,' Sannie said.

'Let's stop and let me get my rifle out of its case, Sannie. Just in case Roberto's waiting for us somewhere,' put in Mia.

In most other countries of the world that would have been a ridiculous suggestion, but Sannie thought it a good idea. She put on her left indicator and checked in her rear-view mirror.

A double-cab Ford Ranger bakkie was accelerating fast behind her and indicated to overtake her as Sannie started to slow. As the other vehicle came alongside her Sannie noticed the tinted side windows start to come down. Her first thought was that some aggressive male was going to abuse her for slowing down on the main road.

Then she saw the rifle barrel. 'Gun!'

ADAM HEARD Sannie's shout and looked right. He saw the weapon and picked up the revolver next to him, then fired a shot, left-handed, through his closed window. The glass shattered just as a dozen shots punched through the skin of Sannie's Fortuner.

Sannie floored the accelerator and wrenched her steering wheel hard to the right. The Fortuner slammed into the Ranger, whose driver veered hard to the right and onto the dirt shoulder. The driver probably wasn't expecting that, and overcorrected as Sannie shot ahead.

Adam punched the shattered window on his side, but couldn't make a bigger hole in it. Instead he opened the door, hung out of the Fortuner and took aim. He fired a second shot and saw the bullet go through the Ford's windscreen.

'Heads down!' Adam saw an LM5 assault rifle protrude from the passenger side of the pursuing vehicle and more bullets thunked into the Toyota's body. The rear windscreen broke and Adam felt a bullet whoosh past his head. 'You both OK?'

'Not hit, but I'm losing power,' Sannie said. 'Shit.'

Mia had Sannie's phone and was dialling someone, hopefully the police.

Adam felt the Fortuner slow and, through the open door, saw the Ford begin to close on them. Sannie tried weaving from side to side, which made them a more difficult target, but Adam couldn't get his gun hand steady enough to try another shot with his precious few remaining rounds.

The Ford roared up next to them and Adam would have fired again, but six more rounds came slamming into the bodywork and past him.

Sannie hauled on the steering wheel, once more turning towards rather than away from the other bakkie. The driver of the Ford held his nerve this time and the next fusillade took out Sannie's right front tyre.

Sannie fought with the wheel as steam hissed from a punctured radiator. The Ford Ranger rammed them this time and Sannie was forced off the road. Adam slammed his door shut as the Fortuner hit soft sand and rolled.

Fortunately they were all wearing seatbelts. They came to rest upside down and Adam released his belt and opened his door. He came out of the vehicle with Sannie's revolver in his hand. As the Ranger pulled up and the doors flew open, Adam advanced. His bold charge caught the attackers off-guard and the second shot from the six-round chamber caught the man with the LM5 rifle in the chest, which knocked him backwards. As the man fell, Adam looked into his face and saw it was Meshach, the head of anti-poaching and security at Dune Lodge. So he was Evan's man, as well.

Another uniformed man, perhaps also surprised that Adam was coming to them rather than running away, thought better of opening his door. Adam saw the pistol in the man's hand and fired through the rear passenger-side window, hitting the man in the head.

Adam crouched and as he bobbed his head up and saw who the driver was, two bullets came his way.

'Evan! Come out. It's over.'

'Fuck you, Adam,' Evan yelled from inside.

The engine was still running. Evan put the car in reverse, stood on the accelerator and swung the steering wheel hard to the right at the same time. The nose of the Ford came around too fast for Adam to jump out of the way and the blow knocked him over. Adam rolled onto his belly, feeling numb down his left side, and took aim at the windscreen.

Evan stopped, changed gear and revved the bakkie's engine. The Ranger raced towards Adam. He knew he had just two shots left. He took aim and fired, once.

The Ranger slewed to the left and passed close enough to Adam for the left front tyre to run over the loose flapping tail of his shirt. Evan careened off the road, through the sand, and collided with a tree.

Adam rolled over. Pain was shooting through his body now. Something was broken, because he couldn't stand. There was blood in his eyes.

'Adam!'

It was Sannie's voice. He twisted his head – more pain. Mia was leaning into the open back of the upturned Fortuner, and Adam remembered something about a rifle and Sannie's pistol being in her bag.

'Run!' Adam yelled to the two women. 'Leave me!'

He needed them to get away from Evan, to get help, to get away from Roberto, wherever he was. Adam was not afraid of Evan, and not scared of dying.

Evan opened the door of the Ford Ranger and staggered out and towards him. Like Meshach, he'd been hit, but unlike the head of security, Evan was alive, and walking, and grinning.

'You think you can threaten me?' He advanced on Adam, who

held the pistol up. Evan was a long way off, and he knew it. Did he know that Adam only had one round left?

Adam took aim, but his hand was shaking. He squeezed the trigger. The bullet missed.

'Close.' Evan laughed loudly as he walked towards Adam. 'But no cigar, bru.'

Evan came to him and crouched down next to him, even as Adam saw Mia pull the hunting rifle from its case. Evan moved behind Adam and lifted him up into a sitting position and then sat behind him.

'Get your fucking hands off me,' Adam spat. He found that he couldn't force Evan away. He had lost the use of his left arm and when he looked down at his left leg he saw it was at a crazy angle from where the bakkie had hit and broken it.

'This way, ladies, guns down, please,' Evan called to Sannie and Mia. 'Unlike your hero here, I've got plenty of ammo. Oh, and there's one of the finest killers I ever met in my life, in wartime and peace, watching you, right now, from the trees somewhere.'

Mia and Sannie both looked around them.

'Gun down, Mia!' Evan pressed his pistol hard into the side of Adam's head.

'Shoot . . . him.' Adam was finding it hard to talk.

Evan might have guessed that Mia would not have left her rifle loaded in its zippered case. He raised his pistol and fired a shot at her. 'Drop it.'

Mia dived to the ground.

'Did you . . . did you order Roberto to kill Frank?' Adam asked. He wanted to distract Evan, and maybe give Mia and Sannie a chance.

Evan shook his head. 'No, China. That was Lisa. She makes Roberto look like a pussy cat. But you got in my way, old son. Roberto and I had a nice sideline selling pangolins and your pal Renshaw was doing a roaring trade in shark fin until you got in the way, "Sharky". Renshaw had told me about some maverick academic who was causing us grief, but it wasn't until you foiled the robbery at the mall and your name was splashed all over the news that I realised it was you. Killing you would have solved two problems, for me, and for Ferri.'

'What . . . what about Ferri?'

Evan smiled. 'Him? Nothing but a coward, but unlike what I told you all this morning, I do care about his political career. With what I've got on Tony, it'll be a river of gold for me when he gets into power and the DA has to start handing out tenders. Sorry, Adam. This is the way it has to be.'

Evan stood and pointed the pistol down at Adam, taking aim between his eyes.

'No!' Sannie yelled.

'Goodbye, Adam,' Evan said. His finger took up the slack on the trigger. Adam hoped Sannie lived. She was lovely.

Adam heard a pfft sound just as the arrow pierced Evan's throat. Evan dropped the pistol as a jet of arterial blood shot from the wound. He tried desperately to staunch the flow with his hands, then collapsed to his knees.

Adam was aware of Sannie and Mia running towards another man, bare-chested, barefoot and carrying a small bow.

'Luiz!' Mia yelled.

30

It was time for the killing to stop.

Luiz breathed deep as he ran, his chest swelling with each inhalation like a proud young man's once more. Even as he remembered the battles past, the enemies vanquished and the brothers lost, he knew that this was, at last, the end.

Adam was on the ground, hurt but alive. His eyes were wide, like he had just seen a ghost. Luiz grinned, but his senses, dulled neither by age nor the confines of peace, were still sharp.

This was like the war, again. The good, and the bad.

Angola, 1987

Luiz sighted down the barrel of his R1, saw an Angolan advancing through the smoke of a freshly detonated mortar bomb, and pulled the trigger. The man dropped.

Sergeant Greenaway, the man who should have led this mission, and Adam, the gentle giant with the machine gun, had just left, after

Greenaway had fought with the crazy officer, Ferri. Luiz was ready to go as well, but then Rossouw was shot, in the head, in front of him.

And then, there was peace, a lull in the battle. The whites had stopped firing and the Angolans might have thought they had defeated them, with their bullets and mortars. Roberto, a few metres to his right, looked to him, and nodded towards where the officer was kneeling next to the dead airman.

Luiz closed up on his brother and together they crept through the bush and watched the strange goings-on. The young lieutenant, Ferri, looked like he was possessed by some malevolent spirit. He cried like a child and dropped a bloodied knife to the ground.

Evan, of a similar age but with eyes as cold as Luiz's brother's, slapped his superior in the face. Luiz was surprised by that. Ferri fell to the ground and crawled away from the airman, and from Evan. The lieutenant curled into a ball, like an unborn creature still in the womb, and hugged and rocked himself.

No stranger to blood, Luiz still winced as he watched Evan slash and saw his way through the dead South African's hand. Roberto got up and broke from the cover of the bush. Evan spun and held up the knife, but relaxed when he saw it was Roberto. Luiz stayed in hiding, and also watched out for the Angolans, who would be circling, closing in on them now like hunting dogs. Evan held up the brown leather bag. 'You know what's in here?'

'*Sim, diamantes,*' Roberto said.

'Ja, diamonds. For the colonel, right?'

Roberto nodded. Luiz and his brother had worked for the colonel before, sometimes meeting UNITA soldiers on foot, inside Angola, taking packages back to Ondangwa for de Villiers. The colonel paid them; Roberto asked no questions. Luiz was disdainful of the missions, for he guessed they were the work of thieves. He was a warrior, and stealing was beneath him. Not so his brother. They were of the same blood, but different, though Luiz would never betray his sibling.

Evan hesitated, thinking; 'making a plan', the South Africans called it. 'Take these, on foot. Get out of here, back to Ondangwa. You understand?'

Roberto nodded as Evan handed over the briefcase. 'You get word to me, once you get back – if we bloody get back – through your brother.'

Luiz revealed himself. Roberto looked at him, then ran, to the south, with the bag.

Evan reached into one of his webbing pouches and took out a grenade. He pulled the pin and Luiz half raised his R1, thinking for an instant Evan might be about to kill him. Instead, Evan bent and dropped the grenade, just a couple of metres from Duarte's mutilated body. Evan leapt over the airman, came to Luiz and grabbed him by the arm. The two of them ran to where Ferri was cowering and threw themselves down behind the fallen tree.

The grenade erupted with a whump and this was a cue for the Angolans to restart their mini offensive. There was the crump of mortar bombs leaving their tubes and the rattle of AK-47 fire. Luiz could see, now, that Evan was covering up the fact he had stolen the bag by planting the grenade next to the dead man.

Evan rose and, at a crouch, went to Rossouw, who had been shot, and hauled the radio from his body and back to them. Evan spoke into the handset: 'This is Romeo-Mike-Zero-Nine, request urgent fire mission, over.'

While Evan waited for the South Africans to reply and organise artillery fire, he looked to Luiz.

'Go, Luiz. Get out of range, take cover, hide. We need you alive to get us out of here, if we survive.'

Luiz was no coward, unlike the sobbing officer on the ground next to them. 'I must stay, do my duty.'

'No. But when you see them – Adam, the sergeant, the others – you tell them your brother is dead, right, by the artillery?'

Luiz shook his head. 'He is alive. I am not a criminal.'

Evan held up a hand as Ondangwa replied and he relayed the coordinates of where they were. He spoke rapidly into the handset, and moments later the first shell landed. The earth shook.

Evan was wide-eyed and yelled over the noise of the next salvo. It was close enough for the dirt and rocks to rain down on them. 'You do as I fucking say, Luiz.'

'I must –'

'You have a sister, yes?' Evan said.

'Yes.'

'I will have her killed if you tell the others the truth of what just happened.'

Luiz blinked. He knew evil when he saw it. It confronted him most days, when he looked into the eyes of his own brother. He stood, turned, and ran off into the bush, away from the rain of death screeching through the air.

LUIZ FORCED the memories of the past from his mind. Evan was bleeding from the neck, but he was still alive. Luiz ran towards Adam and Evan.

Luiz knew his arrow had flown true, but Evan would be harder to kill than a snake. From the corner of his eye, Luiz saw Evan's hand move from his terrible wound.

Even as he was dying, that one, like Roberto, was still evil. Evan scrabbled for his dropped pistol; Adam was trying to stand, but his body failed him. Luiz, still running, reached over his shoulder for another poison-tipped arrow from the quiver on his back.

Evan brought up his weapon and pulled the trigger, but Luiz leapt, with the agility and power of a springbok, to cover the final short distance between them. The pistol boomed and the bullet sailed close enough to Luiz's chest to burn the skin, but when he landed it was with the arrow gripped in his right hand, the point facing downwards.

As Luiz hit the ground, he drove the sharpened tip into Evan's heart.

EPILOGUE
TWO MONTHS LATER

'*E*ast Coast Radio news on the hour. In breaking news, embattled *Democratic Alliance leadership hopeful Tony Ferri has announced he will be quitting politics for the good of his party and for personal reasons. This comes just a day after Ferri's campaign manager was charged with an historical charge of conspiracy to commit murder.*'

Sannie switched off the radio in her new Fortuner, got out and went around to the passenger-side door. Mia, in KwaZulu-Natal on holiday, climbed out of the back and together the two women helped Adam ease out of his seat. Sannie walked beside him and Mia followed, protectively, as he made his way on crutches up the stairs to his house. He had been discharged from hospital but would need ongoing rehabilitation for several months. His doctor, however, was certain he would be back to his normal routine of running, swimming and surfing in a few months.

Sannie opened the door.

'Wow,' he said. 'I know you said you'd got a builder in to finish some things, but this is amazing.'

'Wait until you see the kitchen,' Mia said. 'Shall I put the kettle on, Sannie?'

'Please,' Sannie said. Mia squeezed past them and went on ahead.

The house was, now, at least liveable, mainly due to the fact that Sannie had moved in while Adam was in hospital, and she could not continue to live as Adam had been doing. She had paid for a builder to finish off Adam's study, the main bedroom and one of the guest-rooms. The old kitchen was gone and the new cabinets and bench-tops were in, as was a smart new chequerboard tile floor.

Adam followed her down the hallway, nodding his approval as he went.

'I hope you like the kitchen floor,' she said, worried about his reply.

'I love it.' He smiled at her. 'Thank you.'

Mia was leaning against the kitchen counter just looking at Sannie and Adam. Sannie felt herself blush.

'Hello!' a woman called from the front door.

'Stay here, sit down at the breakfast bar,' Sannie said to Adam. 'I'll get it.'

'Hi, am I too early?' Gita Kapahi said.

'Come in, Gita. We just got home.'

Gita followed Sannie through to the kitchen. 'Hello again, Mia. Adam, how are you doing?'

'Better each day, thanks,' he said. He had been interviewed by Gita in hospital.

'You heard the news about Ferri?' Gita said.

'Just now, on the car radio,' Sannie said.

Gita nodded. 'I can't help but feel a little disappointed. This has been a big case for me – for us, I mean – but like a lot of people, I really thought Ferri was the real deal.'

'We all did,' Mia said as she poured water into their cups. 'Trust me and my appalling taste in men. Coffee, Gita?'

'Just water, please, Mia.'

'How confident are you of the charges against Lisa Ingram?' Mia asked Gita.

Sannie passed Adam his coffee and sipped hers. Although Adam hadn't noticed yet, she had put in a lithium-ion battery and six solar panels on the roof to get them through load shedding; she hoped he wouldn't freak at her spending so much money.

Gita gave a small shrug. 'She's got an expensive legal team, but Luiz Siboa and Shirley Hennessy have agreed to testify in court, in exchange for reduced charges for what they got up to.'

'I've been wanting to talk to Luiz,' Adam said.

'I can understand. His story is pretty incredible,' Gita said. 'Evan Litis would have gone to prison for a long time if Luiz hadn't killed him, and Tony Ferri won't come out of the court case looking good, based on Luiz's accounts of him in Angola and everything that's happened since.'

Adam shook his head. 'And Frank found out the truth about Tony Ferri.'

'Yes,' Gita said, 'from Colonel de Villiers. While Jonas Savimbi was partly financing his war in Angola with conflict diamonds, de Villiers was involved in a purely criminal enterprise. Duarte, the airman who was carrying the diamonds, and others like him, thought they were part of an official operation, but de Villiers had a side channel to a senior UNITA officer with access to his own source of diamonds. This was all about cash – that's why de Villiers went to such lengths, such as having Mia's father sent to Greefswald and all the soldiers in the stick split up, to stop people from asking questions and talking. Luiz and Roberto sometimes acted as couriers, though Luiz maintained he never approved, nor took any money. I believe him – his brother was clearly a career criminal in the making, whereas Luiz spent his life in honest work after the war, even if he did turn a blind eye to Roberto's crimes. And Evan, of course, emerged as a major player in the smuggling.'

'He was a criminal all along?' Adam said.

'Yes, and it was Sannie who first uncovered that,' Gita said. 'Henk de Beer found a list of convictions for Evan and other members of his family. Evan saw an opportunity and took it. He was ruthless.'

Sannie remembered Luiz telling the three of them – her, Mia and Adam – what had really happened in Angola while they waited for the police and an ambulance to come after Evan's death.

'Terrible,' Sannie said, and she had seen some awful things in her life.

'So when Ferri went back to headquarters he took Evan with him, and Evan continued running the diamond smuggling operation with de Villiers?' Adam said.

'Exactly.' Gita thanked Mia for her water and took a sip. 'Even though he was listed as killed in action, Roberto found a job with Evan and de Villiers on the quiet, moving diamonds during the rest of the war from Namibia into South Africa, and acting as an enforcer for Evan once peace came. I'm satisfied that while Luiz knew about some – not all – of Roberto's activities, he wasn't involved, even though he didn't report his brother to the police, which is understandable.'

'What happened between de Villiers and Evan?' Adam asked Gita.

'I did some digging and spoke to de Villiers' daughter in Australia. She didn't know anything about her father's business dealings during the war, but she did remember her father being very angry with Evan over an investment deal. De Villiers made some bad business decisions over the years, but Evan offered him a get-rich-quick deal, investing in one of his takeovers of a fishing company. The daughter said that de Villiers hadn't realised how much the deal was stacked in Evan's favour, and there were no dividends for the colonel, just more requests for capital funding as the operation's fleet supposedly needed overhauling. De Villiers had to pull out and was bitter towards Evan. He also saw no need to protect Tony Ferri's secret any longer.'

Sannie thought about this as she sipped her coffee. She had suffered a cracked collarbone in the car crash after Evan opened fire on them and had been on leave while most of the investigations had been carried out, so she was as keen as Adam to find out all the details.

'So why was Roberto suddenly ordered by Lisa to pay off Luiz?' Mia asked Gita.

'Shirley Hennessy filled us in on that one, in exchange for her deal,' Gita said. 'When Roberto learned that Shirley and Evan were selling Dune Lodge to Julianne Clyde-Smith, for a huge amount of money, Roberto demanded a share of the profit. Shirley's father had bought Roberto out decades ago and allowed him free access on the property to hunt, but Roberto now claimed he'd been short-changed. He tried to bully his niece, but Luiz argued with him, taking Shirley's side. In a menacing outburst, Roberto said he could make Luiz disappear in the same way he had killed Frank Greenaway, under orders from Tony Ferri's campaign manager. Luiz was shocked by this, as was Shirley, who quizzed Evan about it. Evan denied that Ferri's people would have ordered Frank's killing, but both Shirley and Luiz were unsettled. Luiz said he confronted Roberto again, accusing him of lying about killing Frank: how, Luiz asked, could a criminal like Roberto overcome a warrior like Frank and fake his suicide? Roberto boasted that he had drugged Frank by setting a simple booby trap – a number of sharpened stakes placed in the grass on Frank's front lawn, covered in poison from the Diamphidia beetle larvae. He waited and watched until Frank, who often went barefoot, stood on a stake and poisoned himself. Once Frank was suffering from the poison, Roberto was able to confront him and kill him, making it look like he'd taken his own life.'

Adam shook his head. Mia bit her bottom lip and a tear ran down her cheek. Sannie went to her and put an arm around her.

Gita paused, then continued: 'Luiz might have been able to keep silent about Roberto's other crimes – he also knew Roberto was poaching pangolins and selling them to Evan as a sideline – but he could not overlook his brother's claim that he had murdered a former comrade. Luiz called Tony Ferri's campaign office and was put through to Lisa.'

'Shit,' Adam said.

Gita nodded. 'Exactly. Lisa, who was unaware of the family feud going on between Roberto, Luiz and Shirley, sent Roberto to allegedly buy Luiz's silence. Roberto went to Dune Lodge and arranged to meet Shirley at the big tree, where the game drives stopped for sundowners and morning coffee. Shirley said Roberto threatened her, saying that unless she gave him a cut of the lodge sale and Luiz stopped asking questions about Frank's death, then Roberto would kill Luiz, whom Shirley was very fond of. Both Shirley and Luiz say, specifically, that Roberto told them he had orders from his "boss" – who we now know was Lisa – to kill Luiz if he refused to stay silent. They argued and Roberto became violent, punching and throwing Shirley to the ground. He drew a gun and said that he would make it look like she had killed herself. He put the gun to her head and at that point, Luiz, who had been hiding in the dunes nearby, shot a poisoned arrow into Roberto. Roberto fired a shot at Luiz, but missed.'

Mia wiped her eyes. 'The second bullet casing I found at the scene.'

'Exactly,' Gita said.

'Wow, just like how Evan died,' Mia said.

'Almost,' Gita said. 'Luiz overpowered Roberto, but Shirley says that Roberto, though wounded, pulled a knife, grabbed Luiz and stabbed him in the side. Luiz put the pistol to Roberto's head and killed him.'

'So, Shirley and Luiz arranged Roberto's body to look like a suicide and left him for the vultures to find,' Sannie said.

'Yes. Their plan nearly fell through when Mia found the body before Shirley could get back to the lodge to make her own report, but the vultures had already attacked the body, making it hard to identify from a distance. Fortunately, Mia had guests so she couldn't go closer to check the remains. From a distance, she thought it was Luiz, as the two brothers looked very much alike.'

'And I had no idea of Roberto's existence at that time,' Mia said.

'Yes, and Shirley, as the next of kin,' Gita made air quotes with her fingers, '"identified" the body as Luiz.'

Adam shook his head. 'Shirley or Luiz could have gone to the police with what they knew about Frank's death.'

'Agreed,' Gita said, 'but in her defence Shirley was, I believe, very much cowed and under the influence of Evan, who assured her Roberto was lying. Not only was Evan the secret shareholder in Dune

Lodge, Shirley revealed they had been having an ongoing affair for a number of years. Shirley was part in love, part scared of Evan, and from a financial perspective she wanted the sale of Dune Lodge to go through, supposedly so she could break things off with Evan and start again. Shirley also helped you two, by letting Luiz know where and when you were heading to the Kgalagadi. She was communicating with him via SMS to Roberto's phone, and so was Evan, who sent him a similar message, thinking he was communicating with an alive Roberto, and telling him where the ambush would take place. Thanks to that ruse, Luiz was able to be there for you – just.'

'Just,' Sannie repeated. 'I could see how worried Shirley was when I told everyone at the breakfast meeting that we were going to conduct another more detailed autopsy on the body. I was pretty sure she was hiding something then. And the pangolin?'

'Shirley wasn't sure,' Gita said, 'except for the fact that she was sure Luiz was not involved. They think that Roberto had no intention of letting Luiz take the hush money from Lisa, whatever happened. Roberto wanted Luiz gone so that he could make Shirley do as he told her and as proof of this, he stashed a pangolin in Luiz's room so that it would be found after he had killed his brother, and paint him as a guilty poacher.'

'I pray that Lisa is convicted,' Mia said.

'I hear you, Mia, and I do feel for you, trust me, but that's up to the courts.' Gita finished her water and set down her glass. 'Now, if you'll excuse me, I need to get back to work. I just wanted to check that you two were, um, what's the word, settled? Sannie, it looks like you've made yourself quite at home here.'

Sannie shrugged. 'I needed to move out of my brother and sister-in-law's flat and Adam needed someone to take care of his house while he was in hospital.'

'What Sannie means,' Adam said, 'is that I had no medical aid or money to cover my busted leg and arm, and she's paying the bills by way of a loan until I sell this place and make some money. Free board for as long as she needs it is part of the deal.'

'That's why I've had two bedrooms renovated already,' Sannie added quickly.

'And why I'm leaving this afternoon,' Mia said.

Gita smiled. 'Sannie, judging by the amount of time I've seen you spending at the hospital, it looks like you and Adam have become very good friends out of all this sorrow.'

Sannie and Adam looked into each other's eyes. Gita cleared her throat. 'I'll be on my way, then.'

'I'll follow you out,' Mia said. 'I feel like one last long walk on the beach before I have to start driving back to Mpumalanga.'

Mia gave Sannie and Adam a little wave just as she closed the door behind her.

They kept staring at each other, saying nothing, for a few long seconds. Sannie's heart was beating faster, but for the first time in a long time she felt like she was home. Hopefully Adam felt the same way.

He reached out his hand to her and she took it. Adam drew her to him and she put her arms around his neck.

'War's over,' he whispered, and they kissed.

ACKNOWLEDGMENTS

It seems the longer I spend living and travelling in Africa, the more I learn about threats to the natural environment and the illegal trade in wildlife.

The statistics about shark finning are horrifying, but as mentioned in this book, South Africa has banned the practice and was one of the first countries to institute protection of great white sharks. I'd like to thank David Booth, Professor of Marine Ecology at the University of Technology, Sydney, for helping me with my research into sharks and the marine environment, and for planting the seed of this book in my mind.

A number of veterans of South Africa's Border War in Namibia (formerly South West Africa) and Angola helped with the research for this story and read the manuscript. Two of them happened to be practising or retired doctors, so they also helped with the medical aspects as well. I'd like to express my deep thanks to Fritz Rabe, Kevin McDonald, Richard Tustin and Ronnie Borrageiro. Thank you, especially, to the person who told me about his exploits, couriering diamonds out of Angola during the war – you know who you are, and that you were the inspiration for this part of the book.

Thanks, also, to my team of diligent but unpaid editors: my wife, Nicola; my mother, Kathy; my mother-in-law, Sheila; and my expert in all things Afrikaans and Africa, Annelien Oberholzer.

I referred to a number of online sources for information while researching the role of the San people during the conflicts in Angola, and the subsequent relocation of soldiers and their families to Platfontein in South Africa. I hope that I have been able to do justice to their culture, their place in history, and their story in some small measure.

As with all matters relating to research, if I've made an error or inadvertently caused offence, then the fault is mine and I apologise in advance!

A number of good people paid good money to be good and bad guys and girls in this book. If you ended up as a baddy (and there are plenty of villains in this book), please don't be upset, because in my eyes you are true heroes for supporting the causes listed below.

Thank you to the following people and the charities they donated to in order to become characters in this story: Chris Hennessy (Guide Dogs, on behalf of his late mother, Shirley Hennessy); Evan Litis (Painted Dog Conservation Inc.); Tony Ferri (Wildlife and Environment Society of South Africa); and Geoff Hoddy (Painted Dog Conservation Inc., on behalf of Lisa Ingram).

Thank you, as always, to my wonderful work families at Pan Macmillan Australia and South Africa, for getting the first edition of this book into print. In particular, thanks to Alex Lloyd, Andrea Nattrass, Danielle Walker and Brianne Collins.

Last, but certainly not least, if you've made it this far then thank you. You're the most important person in the whole business of writing and publishing books.

www.tonypark.net

IF YOU ENJOYED THIS BOOK...

Sannie van Rensburg has appeared in several of Tony Park's other books. If you enjoyed 'Vendetta', you can check out her earlier adventures:

Silent Predator
 The Hunter
 The Cull
 Blood Trail
 Details at www.tonypark.net